FACES IN TIME

ALSO BY LEWIS ALEMAN

COLD STREAK

FACES IN TIME

LEWIS ALEMAN

MEGALODON ENTERTAINMENT, LLC.

Published by Megalodon Entertainment, LLC. (USA)
www.MegalodonEntertainment.com

First Printing: December 2009

Visit **LEWIS ALEMAN** and the world of FACES IN TIME on the web at:
www.LewisAleman.com

Printed in the United States of America.

ISBN: 978-0-9800605-5-3
ISBN-10: 0-9800605-5-9

FACES IN TIME is a work of fiction; all of its characters are inventions of the author. Any resemblance to the living or the dead is entirely coincidental.

BULK INQUERIES:
Quantity discounts are available on bulk orders of this novel for educational, fund-raising, promotional, and special sales purposes. For details, please contact www.MegalodonEntertainment.com

"REALITY IS MERELY AN ILLUSION,
ALBEIT A VERY PERSISTENT ONE."

ALBERT EINSTEIN

"THERE ARE GROUNDS FOR
CAUTIOUS OPTIMISM THAT WE MAY
NOW BE NEAR THE END OF THE
SEARCH FOR THE ULTIMATE LAWS OF
NATURE."

STEPHEN HAWKING

"What is apparent
is not always certain,
and what is possible
is not always apparent."

Chester B. Fuze

CHAPTER 1

L ines of surgery run along the back of her jawline, close to her ears, and to the top of her forehead. A billion dollar face is a common phrase. But, how many of us actually get to find out? To the exact penny? Rhonda Romero found out today. Her façade fetched more than ten times her accumulated debt, and to the world's astonishment, she took the offer.

Chester has watched the whole thing unfold since the media were leaked the information. Sensationalism has exploded out of all media outlets, interviewing everyone from Rhonda's former costars to childhood friends and expert plastic surgeons. The same pictures are recycled every half an hour with minor updates, eclipsing all other news of national and world significance.

The television is a flickering tormentor, basting him in a painful glow like a live bird in an oven. It slides over him, slowly burning up all of the fluid of life left inside.

He has remained in shock, having trouble believing that this would be happening to her. For nearly his whole life, he had known that Rhonda and he were supposed to be together. Somehow with her face gone now, the dream has floated away from him.

When he was in college, he imagined they would meet when he moved out to L.A. He'd be a famous television writer, and they'd be at the same party. He would know what to say that none of the others could imagine. He would know the one thing that would make her cling to him as if all of her future happiness were within his mind.

But, time passed.

Then he imagined he'd meet her in his thirties. By that time, she'd be bound to be divorced, and he could make her believe that she could love again. He'd be the only one with the right words.

The next decade crashed quickly, just like most of his experiments had, taking his credibility along with them. That's when the solution presented itself. That's when his hope was rekindled. That's when people stopped calling him eccentric, and that's when they began to look sad whenever mentioning his name.

Her life has been documented on his walls. Pictures and articles have formed a homogenous collage tinted with loneliness. Even in his worst mental trials, he could recall her birthday, her most embarrassing moment, her first acting job, and where she met her first husband.

Surprisingly, Chester never tried to contact her; he never wanted to be one of those crazy fans that only made her shake her head and want to hire more security. He wanted his opportunity to be untainted without a pathetic, fanatic past. The only letter he ever sent her was an anonymous one following the death of her son. He wrote the kindest words he could envision, but he didn't want to attach his name to them. Not until she knew him for real. Not until she met him the right way.

So, he waited.

Dreams turned to the vision of spending their middle aged and retired years together. He knew her everyday activities; he knew they would get along well. His work could be ignored if it were for her. And, her company would be enough to entertain him. It would be a victory over the last two decades of his life. A triumph over every harsh word that had been thrust upon him.

But, all of the dreams of being with her in the future have crumbled away with today's unusual surgery.

Now, he knows he has to complete his project. The one that placed him in a straight jacket for several years of his life. The one that estranged his own mother from him. He let it go for himself. Now, he'll pick it back up for her. God help us all.

CHAPTER 2

C hester knew how to beat the paradox all along. The never-ending war of the physicists debating over defying the laws of conservation of matter, the arguments of the philosophers worrying about losing continuity, and the theologians' warnings of treading on God's domain; he knew he was the one to prove them wrong.

He knew it long ago, since the first truly lonely day, and he knows it still.

The only paradox that he cannot overcome is that, if he succeeds completely, no one will ever know he has done it. His name will never be in history books. His work will never be studied by those to come. But, right now he doesn't care about posterity or proving to the harsh world that he is indeed genius.

Like his hero, Nikola Tesla, his key work will be hidden from the masses and repeated by none. Perhaps it's best that no one can duplicate his hazardous feat. But polar to his role model, he chooses to sacrifice his work for love.

The last few days have been a flicker of things that he has never wanted to see. Dreams being defiled rips at a person's fragile inner fabric, but it also frees that person to act boldly and unfettered by the fear of having something to lose.

The media has gorged itself until bloated on the story of a downtrodden starlet whose life has become so grim as to sell her own face to sustain herself. The same images of the ordeal have been regurgitated and reconsumed in a vicious cycle. One would blame the networks, but if the ratings didn't support the inordinate coverage, they would move on to another story.

The first picture of the actress, with the highest bidder's face attached where her famous countenance used to reside, was treated with the importance of the moon landing or a worldwide armistice. It almost made him laugh in the middle of his preparations when it was announced that the picture was a forgery. The security at the French hospital had made several dozen arrests of members of the press trying to catch her in their lenses. Thankfully, no one breached her room as she recovered.

The first legitimate images came from the official press conference of Chrétien DeVeaux, the winning bidder of Rhonda's famous face. It happened merely three days after the surgery and against the surgeon's recommendations.

Mrs. DeVeaux still didn't have control of her newly-purchased face. She did none of the talking, but just stood there modeling the famous visage she had bought, trying to keep her mouth closed and free of drooling while her spokesperson fielded the barrage of questions. The drool proved to be unstoppable but was restricted to a skinny, shiny stream down the left corner of her lips.

Sometimes that which one wants to see least is the hardest from which to look away. It was a meek moment thrust into audacious light when Rhonda Romero, the fallen star and facial donor, exited the hospital two days later. The clicking, the flashing, the calamity of it all: it was both a sad intrusion and a powerfully obscure perversity.

The only one guiding Rhonda on her way out was her mother, who loudly instructed to the gaggle of sensationalists that her daughter could not speak due to the surgery. It did nothing to stop the questions directed specifically to Rhonda. The mother had to repeatedly push away microphones that were dangerously close to her daughter's newly swapped face.

Harvey Price, her only agent over her whole career, one whom she had not heard from in over ten years and who rarely returned her calls for much of the two years before that, tried with mixed success to get the reporters' attention.

Harvey persistently stayed close to the scene as soon as he heard of the unbelievable transaction involving his old client on the news. He pleaded with both her and her mother to set up a big press conference whenever they would listen to him. He was certain she could at least turn this thing into landing a few movie roles. He stated that they needed to cash in on the public's renewed fascination with her—now that she'd sold her face, she needed to sell herself too while there were still buyers.

At this, Rhonda's eyes clenched tightly, an old woman's voice raised in protest, and a button was slammed down for the nurse. Morphine slightly helped half of her pain.

As she writhed in the bed and the agent was retreating to the hallway without a trace of regret on his expensively-manicured brow, her thoughts wondered what life may have been like if either her or her mother were better at running off dirtbags.

But, then again, Rhonda knew that if her mother had that strength, she would never have been born.

Her exit from the hospital was earlier today, capping the end of Chester's tolerance for watching the story being commented upon by well-spoken, polished vultures who gleefully raped that which was sacred to him.

The transplant was deemed a success by the morbidly curious eyes of the world. Few cried out in protest of breaking a natural boundary, but the voices of those that did protest were not granted much airtime, being in the group that is typically ignored and ridiculed by those who make decisions.

But, his eyes cry with the persistence of a cracked dam. Seeing the face he has cherished for decades from afar attached to a foreign landscape of bones and artificial cheek implants, it is as if someone has made a ghastly marionette out of his love's corpse, and the world snickers as it dangles and bounces in its grotesque dance.

It is the end for him. He doesn't want her now, and she has been all that he has desired.

One might deem him shallow—a worshiper of her body only. But, that is not it. He would still love her if she had met any manner of horrible accident. Disfigured, he would love her still. Brain damaged, he would love. But, this is self-mutilation. It is the highest form of prostitution, and it touches the part of her that he has always deemed to be untouchable. She has willfully sold that which represents herself and that which she could offer to him. He could've loved a reconstructed face if she were injured, even a transplanted one, but he can't imagine kissing another woman's face that Rhonda was paid to take in exchange for her own.

Even if he could grow to love her new face, this self-inflicted tragedy has to have taken its toll on her, scarring the part of her that could make her love again. He owes it to her to save her from it all, not just to help her deal with it.

If his hope of being with her now is thwarted beyond repair, why does he continue to toil? He reasons that, if he can't have her in the present, he'll look to the past.

Refusing to stop until he has either broken an unnatural boundary or his mind, he toils.

CHAPTER 3

E uphoria explodes through his body as he is immersed in a full-color version of his favorite yellowed memory. And, this memory tingles over him like an electric breeze or a mild poison.

One discriminates one's company shrewdly in youth, lightly in adulthood, and with broad abandon in age. In youth, one expects the most interesting and perfectly uniform friends. By old age, one brightens just at the sight of another born within the same decade who might remember the same song, movie, or event—one who might hold some knowledge on how to defeat their ticking nemesis or, in the least, help one better enjoy life's slow, automated ride.

The joy and contentment of the latter expand inside him, threatening to burst his very being. It's the next dimension past the perfect dream. It's a meta-awareness: a pinching yourself and verifying that all the wonderfully unbelievable things around you are real.

Scaling an emotional peak not often reached by man, he is aware that he's found his way back into the most crucial period of his life. He stands in the field of his youth, twenty years before he left his room, two decades before his love's face was pilfered. But this time, he has brought a lifetime of knowledge and piercing regret to do things differently.

The fields of dimension in his mind morph, shifted in red and blue, as only the imagination, an artificial computerized generation, or a blast through time can, into a field of green grass and two thick oak trees with a stagnant, tadpole-filled, rainwater pond between them.

The only sound in his ears is a faint metallic jingling.

A chain-link fence encloses the field from the sidewalk and the street, its diamond-shaped holes dividing the surrounding world into tiny tiles. He remembers as a child running past the fence and watching the world distort and move through the chain-link holes, as if he were warping the scales of reality along with those of his vision, while the buildings, houses, and surroundings slid from one fence tile to the next and smeared with the speed of his sprint. Perhaps we could all still manipulate our surroundings if we never grew taller than the fence that makes us question what is real. Regardless, most of his time here was directed toward different activities.

The field is one of the few places on earth where he has felt peace. Being such a meager spot, he is unsure if he's proud or humbled by it. His joy in it is immense, pure, and nothing material, but it's just a grassy lot to most—just a place waiting to have something built on it. And, eventually something is built on it: a large housing complex that covers the entire field all the way to the canal that runs behind it. He had liked it better when it was nothing but an open plot for children's games, just as it is now. A building should be a fulfillment of a childhood dream, not something that replaces one.

The field was also the first place where he found a use for his storytelling except as an escape. For most of his life, his tales were a personal substitute for the living he wished he could do, and later on they would become his living. But, in the schoolyard it made him popular with the female third-graders, which was an astounding development for him.

With a small cypress tree behind him and the fence just behind the tree, the girls would sit around him in a semi-circle, little uniformed skirts draped on the ground around them mimicking the shape of flowers. They would listen to him tell his stories with the reverence of a crowd peering through time to watch Michelangelo paint *The Last Judgment*.

He learned quickly that if he put the girls' names in the story, their little cheeks would blush and their smiles would reflect more light in the grassy field. They would act out roles in his tales, following a hand-written script or ad-libbing a situation that he would make up as they went along.

Usually he was the only boy, forcing him to perform every male role, but he didn't mind at all having the chance to interact with so many of the girls. Occasionally a boy would come and sit near them, and Chester would be sure to include him in the story, pairing him with a girl that he knew the boy had a crush on.

Sometimes the boys would ask him to play their game, which was an amalgamation of football and soccer mostly, with flurries of pro wrestling and bare-knuckled boxing. The only rule was that the goals were the opposing ends of the field and a team scored a point by touching the soccer ball against the chain link fence. This could be done by kicking the ball into the fence or by holding it in one's hands and tapping it into the fence. Either method could be done repeatedly, and the team would continue to score points until their opponent got the ball back from them in any number of ways, most involving tackling, shoving, or punching.

It has long been a wonder in his life how the teachers never paid any attention to their spirited game, despite the class's accumulated injuries of two head wounds that required stitches, a broken forearm, countless busted knees and elbows, several bloody noses, and a sprained ankle.

However, he was always thrilled to play, although it usually only occurred when the boys had uneven teams. He didn't decline an opportunity to play a game instead of imagining doing so, but the offers did not come until that year. The year before he would often be alone beneath the giant oaks, watching the tadpoles and creating stories of what their society might be like, so he was happy to tell his stories and play rough sports the following year.

He could've lived his whole life in the third grade; the years to follow weren't as kind.

The thrill of youth and open possibilities energizes him like a soul opiate. He thinks of shimmering red hair lit by emerald-green eyes. The sound of her voice is the breeze in his paradise, his reason for demanding a second chance at his life. He knows she won't be ready for him for a few days, but her image won't leave his mind until then.

Despite the ecstasy of arriving in his field of youth, he knows he can't linger. He has to test out exactly what he is allowed to accomplish in this reality. Is he trapped as an observer, forced to watch himself waste away his life a second time, unable to change a single thing?

Torturous.

If this theory is true, it would preserve a constant reality by keeping him from changing the future. It would prevent the possibility of a time paradox, such as going back in time and killing one's parents before one was born. It would force Chester to relive his disappointments again, and while it would maintain a consistent and secure future, it would turn the joy he currently feels into a living hell.

His life was sad enough the first time around. The thought of having to watch it all happen again terrifies him like a prisoner of war who has been recaptured and knows what agonies await him. Reliving it all without any hope of good things since he already knows how his story will end, the fear of it freezes.

Then he remembers her face.

Returning to him in a rush is all of the energy and thrill of having made it back to the field where he has long wanted to be. Adrenaline rushes alongside of the fear, and he is pulsing to act. He knows he must get some answers, and unlike anything he has encountered in his former experiences, he feels the power to seek them relentlessly.

The air in his nostrils hasn't felt or smelled this way since the third grade. It smells like springtime, and it gives him hope. But, he knows from his first go-round that hope alone will leave one unfulfilled. Belief plus the will to act is the strength of faith. He is flooded with both.

Shaking his head, he turns from the field to the blacktop parking lot between it and the first school building. A shining object is illuminated majestically on the sea of asphalt. But as most of us are, his eyes are not prepared to look something majestic head-on, especially not without warning. Since it is the lone object in the parking lot, he assumes it is the late afternoon, possibly even the weekend. He squints his eyes and makes out a familiar shape in the luminescence.

It's beautiful, and it scares the hell out of him.

A car. One he did not own in this year to which he has travelled back. It looks to be his 1969 Chevelle Super Sport that he bought from an original owner when he was twenty-seven, some five years later than the time in which he's returned.

It's Fathom Blue Metallic with a black top and stripes; the car itself, much less one with the exact color scheme, is not likely to pop up randomly. It must be his car.

When he was wrapped in a white jacket in a padded room, his mother sold the car to a college student who came all the way down from Colorado to purchase it. When Chester was released, he tracked the new owner down to buy it back, but at that point it was rusted from salted snow roads, and the interior was destroyed from the new owner placing his skis inside the car.

It was one of the few times that Chester nearly lost his temper with a stranger. Usually, he was meek when he was angry, but this violation almost turned him to harsh words.

The worst part of it was the young man, by then having graduated and working as a financial analyst, demanded that he receive ten thousand dollars for the car, despite its physical damage and that it was twice what he had paid Chester's mother for it.

Chester opened his mouth to protest or at least to negotiate, but instead he took out his checkbook from his pocket along with the pen that he had brought with him.

In front of him now, the blue automotive icon shines in its factory condition. As he approaches, he can see the original interior. When he restored the car following the ski incident, he had taken every effort to obtain the factory materials, but he couldn't find an exact match for the interior. His car came with the deluxe upholstery, and the reproduction market only offered the standard cloth in various colors, many of which were a shade off the original, leaving him to settle for second best.

Now his smile cracks as he scans over the original, long-lost, unworn deluxe seat covers that welcomed his lonely limbs far more often than any woman he knew. If not for a tiny scratch on the rear quarter panel and some dents in the bumper, it would be perfect, nearly just as it was before his mind broke.

He reaches in his pocket and feels the electronic wonder that he has brought with him. It was in the pocket of his slacks before he left and should certainly still be there now, but he is relieved to confirm it. Since the car is here without explanation and shouldn't be, he worried the electronic device would not be with him even though it should be.

Losing the device would be the most dangerous thing he could imagine.

The keys are on the ground in front of the driver's door. It is his old key ring, complete with the script Chevelle logo key fob. Picking it up and holding it in front of his face with one hand, he pushes the back of his other hand through their shiny, dangling parts—a familiar jagged touch.

Pushing the key into the door, he hears that metallic click that disappeared from vehicles somewhere in the nineties. He pulls the key out carefully to not scratch the paint. Pushing in the button on the door handle, the heavy door comes unlatched.

He slides onto the seat, and the smell, the wonderful smell of the vintage interior fills his nostrils. It's a comfort in the flames of his anxiety.

The car shouldn't be here, yet now he sits in it. Burning and racing, his mind tries to think of what else he might find here that simply should not be, things beyond science and reason. Most specifically, he worries that something will keep him from reaching her. If the car is here, and it shouldn't be; then, maybe Rhonda should be here and isn't, or at least maybe she won't be where he thought he'd find her. And even if she is, maybe he won't be allowed to interact with her, which wouldn't be any different than the first time around.

He glances down at the passenger seat. A familiar sight sits atop the cushion: his dark purple shirt. Having never been one comfortable with fashion, this shirt was one of the few in which he felt easeful. He never liked himself in red, too flashy; he was never comfortable with eyes being drawn to him. Something about the hue of the purple made him feel stylish and at home at the same time.

A psychologist might wonder if it was the color of his baby blanket or of a shirt his mother used to wear, but it is simply a shirt that he did not feel silly wearing. And, that made it a rare find.

The only odd thing about it now is that it was thrown away years ago, by then faded and worn, after staining it while laboring over the device—the one that eventually shot him back in time. Until it finally worked earlier today, all that machine brought him was to the brink of insanity, which is something that he questions even now as he looks over the fabric beside him.

He'd much rather be wearing the purple garment than the plain, white button-up shirt that he is wearing now and has been since he left the sad room of his former present to return to this field of his youth.

He can't quite explain the purple shirt's reappearance. Logically the shirt could be in his closest in his modest student's apartment that he had at this time, but he can't reconcile it being in the car, or even the car being here for that matter. Besides knowing something is horribly askew, he has no theory at the moment that could make sense of the unexplained objects.

But, there are other matters that are far more pressing than the car and clothing curiosity. Like his age. Scanning over his body, he is still indeed an adult, but his right hand is different. The pinky finger that he had broken on his first attempt to return to his past is still crooked, but its scar has faded much more since traveling through time. He marvels at the scar that has half disappeared.

He hasn't been so stunned since he received the positive response to his first spec script in his early twenties. It was a shot in the dark sending an unsolicited script to a successful television producer as a lark, an assumed failure, but he was offered a staff job on his favorite show as a result.

Fear courses through him. Just like the shirt, this physical change in his finger is beyond his reasoning and possibly beyond logic altogether, but some would argue that love, guilt, and even the placebo effect make no practical scientific sense either. To be within the realm of those three things, which lie outside of rationalization, leaves him in a state of panic.

All he has been prepared to do is to use his science to protect himself on this journey and to use his heart and soul to choose his actions. The shirt that shouldn't be here, the car that shouldn't be here, and his inexplicably healed finger—these irregularities knock out the plan that he was counting on as his support.

He had expected calculated results without any anachronisms questioning his theories. Falling randomly through time is not what he had planned, and his right hand with the faded scar starts to shake.

Through the side window, his eyes' focus begins to slip on the field, making it lose its definition and look like a spotted watercolor version of his childhood yard.

As his hands slide over the wheel that is faintly slick

from its last protectant treatment, he glances over his finger's faded scar again. His mind flies ahead, and he leans to look at himself in the rearview mirror. His face appears to be so much younger that it is startling despite its familiarity, looking like he's in his early twenties. There is nothing to account for the wrinkles and drooping facial muscles that have flown off his countenance. There is no reason for him to have become younger.

A traveler ages at the same rate relative to himself regardless of the speed at which he travels—a time traveler ages during his own travels according to every second he has experienced, not according to what people outside of his craft have experienced. So, he should still be minutes older than when he left. None of this adds up to him looking younger, and he wonders where he has thrust himself if science can't explain what is happening to him.

The engine fires and so does his resolve. He brushes the thoughts aside as he races off to rip a hole in the future.

CHAPTER 4

H is fist crashes through the glass, shattering the pane completely. As the shards fall to the ground at his feet, his tense fingers slide over the poor-quality paper, trying to grasp it out of its receptacle. The entire gesture is quite unnecessary as he has more than enough change in his pocket to pay for the newspaper, but an urgency and an audacity that he is quite unused to have taken over his nervous demeanor.

His eyes scour over the top of the newsprint like a ghost searching for its reflection to prove it's real.

He finds the date.

He has gone back to the exact day that he had envisioned. This offers a shallow flooding of relief, but it still doesn't explain the car, his clothes, his half vanished scar, or his body that looks about twenty years younger.

The other pressing matter is that he still needs to find out if he can change anything or if he is merely an observer. He has to find something upon which he'll be able to test this theory. For that, he'll need a situation that he clearly knows a specific historical outcome but one in which he is capable of changing single-handedly.

He pats his pockets frenetically, still clutching the paper in his right hand. The device is still there, and he knows he needs to get to a place where he can use it.

His mind lingers on the horror of not being able to alter anything—the thought of reliving New Year's Eve after New Year's Eve with no one to kiss, no one to hold, with no one to dream of what could happen over the next four seasons. And on the occasions when he did have a date, he was almost sadder because he knew she wasn't the one for him, and he knew there were no future dreams to be made with her.

The throaty rumbling of his car calls to him in a perfectly-timed hum. Its vibrations course through him and bring him to attention.

He glances at the clear shards around his shoes and suddenly realizes that he did indeed shatter glass with his fist. And on top of that, it's glass that belongs to someone else. He can't afford to spend his first day back in time in jail; after all, he has an audience with destiny in two days. If he's late, things will go horribly awry, and he has to test out his abilities before then.

He runs to his car, slams the door harder than he ever has, and accelerates quickly down the side street.

The street itself has been of no consequence to him, and he has paid it no attention until now as he looks around in his mirrors to see if anyone has spotted him. The newspaper receptacle is on the side of a small gas station at the end of a strip mall that also contains one storefront with a faded FOR RENT sign and a fried chicken restaurant with half of its lights burned out, leaving the body of the chicken illuminated and its head missing somewhere in the darkness.

The strip mall is just around the corner from the schoolyard. During his childhood, the gas station convenience store was a popular hangout for the students after school getting an ICEE, some candy, or a comic book. The larger street that it faces is Planeline Highway, and the side street that he barrels down now remains nameless to him, but the houses are very familiar.

Even through his panic to test his surroundings, he notices how nice the houses look before leaky gutters will leave rust-colored stains on the sides of the homes and before time will tear at the wood trim on the windows and doors. He knows that within ten years time the aging Planeline will turn into a crime-ridden area where only the gas station will remain open in the strip mall, but after 6 p.m. customers will have to make their transactions through a tray at the bottom of a bullet-proof pane of glass.

Had he a moment to spare, he'd enjoy returning to the neighborhood before its ruin.

It occurs to him that he was able to shatter the glass. It didn't prove to be unbreakable to his hands; he changed something in this reality. He wonders if it will cause any alterations to the old reality that he knew in his past life, the history that he's experienced.

Will those jagged shards of glass pop someone's tire, causing an accident and killing someone who was supposed to be alive in the old reality? Maybe some kid would've broken the glass pane later that evening anyway, leaving things just about as they originally were. Maybe some drunk in a pickup truck would've backed his bumper through the glass pane on his way to fill his ice chest from the ice machine to the left of the newspaper dispenser.

Possibly, that glass would've been broken regardless of his actions, and that's the only reason why he was allowed to smash it. He hopes not, as that would suggest events can't be changed and reality is constant. The one original reality that he's known includes his love marrying an abusive egotist that she will meet at a party in two days. That reality includes his previous miserable life of lonely hours and regret. Weighing in heavier than those on his mind is the sad life that costs Rhonda her face. He doesn't want to think about being helpless to alter any of those events, especially the last one. He has a shot at bringing this old dream back to life, and he wants to cling only to logic that will allow him to do so.

He has to get somewhere where no one will see him, and he'll find a way to test out the above.

He reminds himself to slow down that he is far enough away from the gas station and that he should not draw notice to himself speeding in a thundering attention-attracting car down a quiet street painted in dusk. Reluctantly, his foot pulls back on the pedal, and the old familiar houses become less blurry. All the while, his heart races, and his finger with the faded scar twitches against the steering wheel.

Normally he is much too cautious and calculated to speed in a residential area, but the drive to test out his limits in this time he's shot himself into is too strong for his personality to hold back.

The golden twilight that was present at the school field is fading into evening. The last hue of the sun hangs over the tops of the houses, lighting a candle on suburbia.

Despite his later life in Hollywood as a writer, he's never felt more at home than in these neighborhoods of one car garages, basketball goals in driveways, and modest, self-maintained gardens of periwinkles and inkas. There is an honesty and a sheer lack of pretension that allows you to operate without wondering what someone else's angle might be or looking over your shoulder to see what's coming at you. A pile of unchained bikes on a front lawn of a friend's house is more comforting than a policeman on the corner.

Without consciously deciding where to go, he turns corners in a familiar pattern that he has not followed in years. The sky above is swollen with indecision. Dark clouds loom, threatening an evening downpour, but they have not overtaken the lingering hue of the bowing sun, unsure if they'll give birth to a crisp breezy evening or a sullen tempest.

The engine hums as smoothly and powerfully as a white tiger moving through a Siberian terrain. It's almost enough to comfort him. The feel of the slender rectangle in his pocket as it rests on his left thigh is a reminder of what he needs to do. Things are not quite as planned, and he longs to glance at the device, but he's not far enough away from the eyes of others to take it out yet.

The cockpit of the car is poorly lit. It's one of the crucibles of car restoration to add modern lighting or to leave the expensive car, an accomplishment of time, dedication, worn flesh, frustration, and tears, with illumination as poor a smudged flashlight that is low on batteries. The faint light is a mockery of the quality of the rest of the vehicle, a masterpiece in an unfinished splintery frame. Some opt to add underdash or underseat lighting, and some balk at the idea of tampering with a classic, meshing it with technology of a later time and violating its factory condition.

His interior seems dim to him like the failing glow of a dying fire, but it also makes it hard for anyone to see him. And right now, a little inconspicuousness is just what he wants. The car is sure to stand out, but its driver is harder to see.

He had thought about upgrading the outdated, original stereo. He shopped around and even bought one especially made to fit his car without any gaudy installation panels to fill the extra space, but he could never bring himself to remove the original stereo. He felt like he had listened to it for so long that it was a part of him.

The device in his pocket is capable of broadcasting music to the old stereo via FM signal, but he's still not ready to risk taking it out of his pocket to operate it. It would be odd to hear modern digital music coming out of the ancient, feeble speakers. He hopes that his mad dash through time ends up being more than having his mature mind spout out the same futile lines through his young body. Like his device, he hopes he can spout a new line into the past.

Turning off the paved road, his slowly-turning tires eradicate the loose pieces of dirt, a sound that clearly signifies one has gone off the road most traveled. The road is a faintly worn path through an unkempt field, which becomes a parking lot at crowded school events, an arena for students to fight after school, and a refuge for a despondent loner to regain composure on a terrible day.

His headlights reveal a lone tree off to the right. He has always imagined its branches drooped due to absorbing the sorrow of decades of dejected teens.

He is certainly no stranger to the tree, although his last visit there was the best one. It was his prom night at Riverview High School, and he was there with three girls. None of them had dates, and they all knew each other from running the school newspaper. So, they decided to all go together. They managed to secure their own table, and he danced one slow song with each of the girls. At the end, they all danced one fast song together.

All three had a crush on him; after all, he had been nicer to them than any boy they'd ever known. However, their affection for him was completely a secret to him. His meager confidence was such to dismiss a flip of the hair or a squeeze of his arm as a harmless act of kindness, never bold enough to discern a flirt.

After the prom, they sat under the tree with a few battery-powered lanterns and a stereo. One of the girls brought a bottle of schnapps, but no one wanted to drink any. There was a tension of a date-type situation with the romance snuffed out. Being lonely with others was certainly better than any of his other trips to the tree, but it was still lacking. Still pining for something that he knew was out there. Aching for her.

As he shifts the car into park, he rushes to grasp the device.

The smooth plastic is cool on his fingers as he slides it out of his pocket. He raises it to his chest level and marvels at its illuminated screen. In the darkness of the unknown variables of his trip, one glowing object has performed exactly as planned.

The glowing suddenly reminds him of energy, and he panics.

He pats his left pants pocket, and finds nothing. Frantically he slides his hand into his right pocket and pulls out a tangle of wires with a bulb dangling from it. He smiles. The car charger was in his pocket, just as it was when he left his old life.

Relief rushes through him as if it were the glow of the device warming his chest.

His finger pushes a series of buttons with the facility of one writing one's signature, making the screen flash and dance at his commands. To an outsider the device might appear to be a part of his hand, and it might as well be with so much of his time, energy, and hopes inside it. Its casing came from a manufacturer, but all of its innards have been replaced or modified by him.

Through all of its advancements, it now displays an archaic picture of black and white, and it is exactly what he wants to see. He compares it to the pilfered newspaper on his vacant passenger seat, and they are an exact match. He has indeed gone back to the specific date in which he intended. Now, he has to determine if it will do him any good.

He makes the device flip forward to tomorrow's paper. Tomorrow has suddenly become a relative term. The front page is of little use, containing only national news of the upcoming presidential election.

He makes the device turn pages to the local Riverview section. There is a picture of a woman wearing a ridiculous hat handing a teacher a present. The caption below it reads, "Mildred Sinclair, chairwoman of St. Christopher's PTA, hands 20-year service award to drama club director Edna Hoover."

"That's it!" he shouts aloud to the car.

With his free left hand, he smacks the steering wheel. He looks at the time on his device and the darkness of the sky, deciphering if the digital numbers are in synch with the world he's gone back to.

"Gonna be close!" he exclaims as he slams the car into gear, tosses the device atop the t-shirt and paper where his copilot would sit, and turns the Chevelle around rapidly. Sending dirt floating up in the air into a gritty haze around the tree and spattering specks on his rear fender, his glowing taillights are a bouncing blur.

He pulls his car into St. Christopher's parking lot, the third school of the evening. It is the only one of the three that he did not attend. He has, however, been to St. Christopher before to see its plays.

For the first time in his life, he parks his car in a handicapped space. Despite his current urgency, he has to convince himself that it's alright because the play must be nearly over and it's not likely anyone will show up to use the spot.

He walks along the side of the gym breathing in the childhood smell of the exhaust of industrial air condition units. The warm, synthetic breeze reminds him of awkward days waiting in the long lunch line that would extend outside of his own school's cafeteria. That uneasiness reminds him of why he's here, and he quickens his step.

He had been in this gymnasium in his youth for several different plays. It is a standard rectangular school gym with a deep stage that is cut into one of the long walls, making a performance on it look like the audience is watching a video screen mounted flush against a wall.

The stage itself is spacious and professional enough with curtains, lighting, and proper sound equipment, but two basketball goals are raised above the stage, which can draw the audience's attention away from the play.

Despite the folding chairs for the audience, the bouncy acoustics, and the painted markings of the basketball court on the floor, St. Christopher plays have been the envy of every school in the area, leaving many to wonder how the school gets so many students who can sing year after year.

Without much thought, he finds his way inside, pays for a ticket, and nods his head as he is told there are only a few minutes left of the play.

He opens the door, which allows a slant of light to fall

upon the darkened audience. Immediately, he sees that hat. It sits on the seat closest to the doors in the first row. The woman next to the ostentatious headpiece appears to be the woman from the newspaper photo. The door shuts behind him quickly pulling the light back out with it.

By the splashy level of the children's overdone singing, he knows this must be the finale of a play that he has never seen.

He steps close to the front row. All eyes are firmly lined up to the stage with the intensity of believing their momentary undivided attention will produce a successful life for their children as opposed to years of sound parenting. The thunderous applause does seem to hold some power over reality as it echoes and bounces in the gym. He is to the far left of anyone's view.

The stage lights grow brighter as the children strain to hold the climactic final note. Following the cues of the vocal intensity, the increased illumination on the performers as they turn to face the crowd; the audience of family, faculty, and neighbors rises to its feet with more robust applause. They are all consumed with the stage.

The hat remains sitting on the chair next to its socialite owner.

He can feel the heat sizzle in his fingers as he reaches for it. He takes a quick scan over the audience to his right. He may as well be invisible.

His fingers grasp the brim and smoothly pull it off the chair, and as he turns away from the newly empty seat and the crowd to walk back toward the doors, he hugs the flamboyant hat tightly to the right side of his chest.

The applause continues to pound out of their proud hands, creating a pulse like a drum roll that arouses both his adrenaline and his nerves.

The room, despite the brightened stage illumination, is dim, devoid of any house lights. His eyes scan the darkened shapes along the wall, and there it is in its dark blue spray-painted majesty between the two sets of double exit doors. It's too perfect; it even has a lid. For the first time in his life, he feels the power of a trashcan.

The ludicrousness of it makes him want to smile, but his frantic neurology only allows a quick twitch at the corners of his mouth. To be able to test his ability to change past events and to get rid of the evidence of his crime so easily grants him an unusual appreciation for the cylinder nearly filled with plastic cups, stale popcorn, and play programs from the night before that are mostly rolled into tight little tubes and crudely constructed airplanes.

The lid fumbles out of his nervous left hand and falls to the gym floor. The hat's rim bounces off the curved walls of the trashcan, wobbling to a stop on top of the refuse.

The lights flip on suddenly, and he jerks his right hand away from the garbage grotto. Bending quickly he grabs the lid.

Approaching footsteps pound on his eardrums, and his heart beats as fast as the overly-generous clapping hands. Two of the hands aren't clapping, and one lands on his left shoulder.

He drops the lid atop the trashcan and turns quickly to see who has grabbed him.

"Are you alright, pal?" asks a tall, slim man in a gray suit that hangs off his wiry frame.

Chester's mouth and tongue commit one false start before saying, "No, no, thought I was gonna vomit. Where's the bathroom in this place anyway?"

The man's head bobs in verification, "Yeah, I thought you'as sick by the way you'er staring so hard in there like you lost your whole life or a ring or something. Sick or you had lost something—I knew it had to be one o' the two."

Chester leans forward and puffs his cheeks out as if regurgitation were imminent.

The man in the suit speaks with more urgency as he points to the left side of the stage, "There's one right over there, pal. Just walk through the hallway beside the stage. Pass the kitchen, and there's a bathroom on the left. Bigger bathrooms are in the lobb—"

Chester lets out an interrupting, "Than— ," and puffs his cheeks again. If only some of the actors on the TV shows that he wrote for would have been so convincing.

The man in the suit takes a step back from Chester's swollen cheeks, and then watches Chester as he makes his way toward the bathroom.

As he steps toward the hallway opening beside the front of the stage, the clapping is finally starting to subside itself. He can hear adolescent feet clomping across the wooden platform; the children must be finishing with their curtain calls. He looks over his shoulder back at the trashcan that he hopes will prove his fate can be changed.

The tall suit has left, must have wanted to beat the traffic.

Chester can see the woman in the front row glance with wide eyes at the seat to her left. She looks under her chair and then stands to look around the floor of the immediate area. Lastly, her gaze rises higher at about hand level, and she scours over the crowd.

Some groups of people make their way to the stage, and others quickly walk toward the front of the gym area that is serving as the lobby and file into two lines, one through each of the double exit doors.

The hatless woman's appearance begins to tear at his chest as it no longer looks on with anger, but it quakes with violation. He suddenly feels horrible for taking it from her. He thought it would be a very harmless method of testing his ability to change the future. If the picture in the paper tomorrow comes out without the hat being in it, he's proved his theory. No one would be physically hurt, nothing of much monetary value would be stolen, and he wouldn't have revealed some type of a secret that would draw attention to himself and be dangerous to others.

There are not many subtle ways to distinctly change the future, be able to prove you've done so, and cause such minute harm; yet, he still feels guilty.

He sees a woman with red hair walking toward the

trashcan from the left line of exiting people. The crimson reminds him of the one he's come back to be with—the one whose future he wants to change for the better. She walks with a drink in a paper cup topped with a plastic lid and a straw. He watches her lift up the garbage can lid on the left side, place her drink underneath, and drop the lid back down. Unknown to her as she walks away, the top of the drink gets caught between the rim of the trashcan and the lid pressing down on it from above. There it rests.

The lid pops off the drink, the watery soda and tiny melting pieces of ice fall to the floor and run in a puddle on the left side of the garbage can. His heart rate rises. *Surely someone will see the mess. Someone will clean the mess. Maybe they'll see the hat.*

He raises his hand to bite his nails, but he keeps it from touching his face, not wanting to fall back into that old habit again. It seems inappropriate to do so on his return to the past. If things are going to be better, they have to be different. Either his inhibiting apprehension will fade away, or in the least he'll have to deal with it differently if he wants a happier life.

Two children run in and out of the streams of people that lead to the two main exit doors of the gym through the lobby and into the parking lot. He wants to reach out; he wants to scream for their parents to stifle them, that they're bound to hurt someone, possibly even someone who is not present in the building. The beaming adult faces are too preoccupied to notice the sticky brown puddle that has spattered onto the floor with its miniscule icebergs melting away into the carbonated sea.

The older brother chases the younger again through the left human stream. Before they can reach the right stream, the youngest one's feet slide from underneath him, his hands go up in the air, and his torso falls toward the sticky, soda-soaked wooden floor. His feet slide into the garbage can sending the lid screeching across the floor into the second stream of people, and the contents of the trashcan spill onto the planks.

Chester knows it before he can even see it. The hat. The

hat is going to make its way back to the old lady.

All of his efforts might be useless.

His fears become hot, making him feel as if the searing walls of hell are forming all around him, filling his nose with the pungency of sulfur. An elbow to the back of his right rib cage interrupts his thoughts.

"Excuse us, just trying to take out the trash," says the cheerful voice of a young parent volunteer.

"Yes, pardon us," adds a deeper voice from around the other side of the trashcan.

Chester flattens himself against the wall, and they sidestep their way past him and into the main area of the gym.

As soon as they move out of his way, he can see the socialite woman bending down daintily in her heels and brushing away at the brim of her hat. He can also see a man yanking his son with damp pants harshly by the arm into the lobby and a woman following close behind shaking her head at his younger brother, whom she pushes ahead of her by the shoulder.

Chester's heart sinks, but his mind snaps to attention, much to his surprise. His brain spins trying to concoct a new plan.

He turns from the main gym room, looking toward the bathroom again. All of the doors are on the left side of the hallway, the wall that is the end of the stage being at his right.

He sees the kitchen area—the first door. No one is in the room, and on the left wall the metal pull-down shutters are closed against the ordering counters, enclosing the room from the lobby. A door is open at the far end of the right wall; it must be a hallway that runs behind the bathroom. Straight ahead, he sees a sink, and one item on it catches his attention.

He steps into the room briskly. Children's giddy voices can be heard echoing down the opened hallway. He realizes that it must lead to the backstage area where children might be changing. He makes it a point to look straight ahead at the sink, despite his urge to make sure no one is watching him from the hallway.

He focuses on a lump of steel wool. His hand fights his mind as it reaches out to steal the pad of shredded metal. It has already been forced once tonight to commit this foreign act when it lifted the hat off the folding chair, leaving it reluctant to do so again. The images come to his mind of the awful news reports that were airing when he left of Rhonda's bizarre surgery. Finally his five-fingered grudging thief grabs hold of the steel wool, and he is quite happy to find that it's dry. The grimy grill and un-emptied deep-fryers can attest to its unused condition. He squeezes it tightly in his fist, and its jagged edges dig into his skin slightly.

He walks out of the room quickly and makes a hard left to the bathroom. The door is opened. He steps inside, flips on the light, shuts the door, and slides its simple lock into position. He tugs on the handle to make sure it's secure.

He fumbles in his pocket and takes out the device. Flipping it over quickly, he slides his thumb roughly over the battery panel. He drops the thin plastic cover to the ground as he hears the sound of heels approaching noisily down the hallway. He hopes it is the two he saw moments ago carrying out the trashcan, but their patter does not stop at the kitchen.

He can hear them talking loudly as they reach the door.

"*My* Stephen was the star of the show. I tell you that boy has such talent. He certainly doesn't get any of it from his father. Now, what is this, is someone in the restroom?"

"Yes, Doris, it looks to be occupied."

Doris raps her fingers on the door harshly, "Anyone in there?"

"Ummm, yes, it'll be just a minute."

"Well, please, try to hurry," commands Doris as she turns her gaze to her counterpart, "Now, Stacey, it is truly commendable that they gave your Tabitha a song to sing this time. It's great that they're getting everyone involved."

Stacey starts, "Well, she certainly did a wonderf-"

His ears block out their conversation as he places the device back in his pocket, holding its battery in his hand. Glancing up at the ceiling, he sees what he's looking for. He sits the battery on the counter beside the sink, and then ripping the steel wool in half, he kneads a piece of it into a skinnier and denser shape. He puts the steel wool on the counter and touches the battery's positive and negative terminals to it. The wool turns red, and the sparks move and spread across its shredded metallic fibers as if it were a virus coursing over it. He leans down and blows on it; the sparks flame up, and he holds his rolled-up play program over it. The flames scorch the program, but he continues to hold it steady and blow over the wool until the paper has its own flame.

The knocking returns to the door, followed by, "Two ladies out here need use of the facilities, sir."

"It'll be a minute, madam," he says without glancing in the direction of the door.

He can hear her voice saying, "I hope it doesn't smell horribly in there. Well, anyway, Stacey, it's great that they're letting your daughter try this year; it's not right to always give the best kids the spotlight, and I always say..."

He grabs the faucet with his free hand, and places his right foot atop the small counter around the sink. With an awkward lunge, he pulls his other foot to the left side of the sink, accidentally smacking the tip of his program against the mirror. Standing straddled over the sink, he reaches up holding the still burning program and waves it directly in front of the smoke detector.

He coughs. The room is getting a little hazy. His mouth hangs open, and his eyes widen as nothing happens.

"Are you smoking in there?"

"No. Now please give me some privacy."

"I'll bet he's smoking in there," Doris says in a whisper that is more of an exasperated version of her regular speech than it is quiet.

Stacey offers, "Maybe it's the popcorn. You know they always burn it at every school function."

The playbill is mostly black, and it begins to fold over the back of his hand. The heat scalds his skin, and after another moment of determination, he drops it to the floor. Quickly, he twists the smoke detector free of its base and unplugs its terminal. He pops out the nine volt battery and puts it to his tongue. It gives off no charge.

Damn it, maybe it's not getting power.

He places the smoke detector on the counter beside his feet and then grabs the dangling wires that are hanging out the base plate in the ceiling. With his other hand, he yanks at the terminal on the end of wires, trying to pull it completely off. He grunts as he struggles.

"Oh, dear," complains from the hallway.

The terminal pops off and drops to the floor.

"What is going on in there?"

Ignoring the question, he looks at the three wires he has just exposed. He takes the bare tip of the red and taps it against the black. Sparks. The detector should have been getting power. Bending down, he picks up the detector off the sink. He wraps the black wire around the far right prong on the detector's plug and then he shoves the red onto the other side. Lastly, he touches the green wire in the middle.

Crouching atop the sink again, he grabs a wad of toilet paper from the roll in the holder attached to the side of the counter. Then he grabs the unused lump of steel wool. Using the battery, he makes it spark again. The toilet paper catches fire quickly, and he stands with it pressed against the grill of the detector.

A faint, annoying hum is all he can hear from the unit.

"There is definitely smoke coming from in there; you need to come out right now—this is unacceptable…"

"Calm down, Doris, he'll be done in a minute. We could just go use the bathrooms up front."

"Use the front bathrooms after those children have been in and out of there? *No, I don't think so.* Don't you smell that smoke, Stacey?"

"Whatever it is, he'll be out in a second. No one's going to burn the building down with themself locked in a bathroom. Don't get so excited."

"Is that the advice that you gave your Tabitha before

she went on tonight? Lord knows she could've used some more energy."

"Now, wait one minute, Doris, I've listened to you brag about your spoiled brat of a son all night, and if you think I'm going to let you be a big old bit—"

The door swings open. Dark smoke comes out of the small room. Female faces crinkle at its presence.

"See, Doris," she says pointing a professionally painted and manicured fingernail less than an inch from his face, "I told you he was smoking. Smoking in a grammar school."

His face is emotionless, and his eyes are watery as he responds, "This is the gym, ma'am, and I was putting out an electrical fire."

"An electrical fire? Did you put it out with water?"

"No, water's a conductor; don't use it on electrical fires. You smother it."

Angrier than before, Doris continues, "That's it; I'm getting the principal and some of the fathers. I don't know what you were up to in that bathroom, but you can't leave it all smoky. I'm going to get…"

"Get anyone you want, lady. It doesn't matter anymore."

He makes his way into the gym with her on his heels, her knees pressed tightly together and screaming loudly for someone to do something about the exiting man and the smoke in the bathroom. He continues to walk into the lobby and out the doors without anyone approaching him.

In his car, his mind circles around the same thoughts, while he struggles to keep his vision focused on the road.

The hat should've been easy enough. What are the odds of a fire alarm not working in a school? Don't they have fire drills every month or so to make sure the system works? Maybe that's just to scare the hell out of the children…I'm trapped...this is it...I can't change anything...steal a hat, a drink squirts on the floor...children knock the garbage can over—what are the odds? Couldn't even use that in one of my TV scripts—would've been called a hack, too unbelievable...and the smoke detector...how? how could all of it not work at all? Was getting power, hooked up to the alarm too...nothing...couldn't get rid of the hat, couldn't clear out the building, couldn't change one lousy photograph in the local section of the paper...trapped...can't change anything...don't want to see all those lonely years again...too much...too much...can't help her, can't even help myself...everything I try to change, universe will set back the way that it was...reality is constant...they were right...can't go back and change anything...there's no hope...

Thirteen minutes later.

Sour burns its way into his esophagus. Until its present return, the familiar discomfort had disappeared from him since embarking on this trip. His stomach is a biological anomaly with diagnoses of ulcers, acid reflux, spastic esophagus, and a hiatal hernia.

Treatment for all four of the ailments has provided at best haphazard relief. His doctors have had their own differing theories on his condition and why his treatment has consistently failed, but they all agree that his personality and stress level are the chief culprits.

Antacids have been his most expensive amenity since junior high, taking them in such quantities as to produce routine kidney stones from their high calcium content. The sharp sting of kidney stones paled in comparison to the perennial burn of a stomach fire fueled by an unsure mind and a discontented soul.

His forehead and back break into a cold sweat, and he's well aware of the petite hell that awaits him.

He rocks slowly on his knees wishing his esophagus and hernia would relax enough to allow him to get the burning, sloshing, gurgling beast out of him. It feels that his nervous uncertainty has formed itself into a gelatinous demon, swelling and pushing against the tender walls of his stomach and shoving a scalding pitchfork into his lower chest. The feeling itself is miserable, but what torments him most about his condition is knowing he won't be allowed relief for hours.

A memory flashes before him: another sour night that should have tasted like hope. He had won his first Emmy during his first season of writing for a television series.

For once he felt like he could behave as the person he'd always wanted to be and not have it be a venture into self-humiliation, but years of stifling himself and self doubt had carved a deep trench of shy habits and familiar inhibitions for him to climb out. Since routine digs a steep ravine from constantly retracing its route, he should have known that any liquid would make the assent slipperier and more difficult. Yet, he drank anyway.

The after-party was a barrage of toasts and beautiful young actresses bringing him drinks and trying to lure him onto the dance floor. Eventually, one persistent actress succeeded. While they danced, other aspiring women continually worked their way in the area. But, she managed to keep the others squeezed out of the space between her and the tipsy scribe, as if she were clinging onto a casting appointment.

Eventually the pulse of the bass and the blur of the lights meshed into a crashing rhythm of burn inside him. He leaned forward suddenly, placing his hands on her waist. She turned her ear toward his lips awaiting words her ambition longed to hear.

He eloquently stated, "I'm going to be sick."

Her face was a mess of emotions before she settled on serious and said, "Okay, my name is Susan, and I'm the one who is taking care of you. Remember; it's very important that you remember me. My name is Susan."

The walk off the dance floor appeared to him as if the

room were a ball rolling through space and he were inside of it as it rotated around him. The next memory was the cool of the tile floor seeping through his thin tuxedo pants into his knees and his forehead resting on the back curve of the toilet seat.

The sound of a female, "Ew!" is all that he remembers hearing besides his own guttural spasms.

The heaving convulsed him mercilessly.

"Honey, just shove your finger down your throat and get it over with."

His hernia and esophagus tensed up tightly, making vomiting nearly impossible, and he grasped his right arm around her left thigh, pulling it against his shoulder. The spasms grew worse, but none of the toxic liquid in him was allowed to escape.

She called loudly for someone to get an ambulance, deciding it would have been a bad career move to have an Emmy-award-winning writer die in a women's bathroom with his arm wrapped around her thigh.

Paramedics arrived quickly, already stationed in the neighborhood to handle any after-party mishaps as quickly and discreetly as possible. All he could see were smears of color and traces of movement.

He asked to a moving object whose colors were familiar to him, "Sandy, Sandy, where are my glasses?"

Her face crumpled up at hearing the wrong name, "They fell in the toilet; they're probably swimming in pee right now."

His eyelids began to shut.

One of the paramedics pushing the cart on the end closest to his head said, "Try to keep your eyes open and stay awake, sir. We're getting you to a hospital."

A faint voice called after, "Remember me; I'm Su…" and faded away as the cart rolled on.

He had no naiveté or illusions about her intentions, but he did try to locate her the next day, unsuccessfully. He didn't have his heart to offer her, but he did have a thank you and an appointment with the show's casting director.

"Susan…," he says out loud, leaning out his car door over the curb of a street whose name he doesn't remember, "Her name was Susan…actress…but she was no Rhonda…No one else is."

He's broken the laws of the universe, shattered the glass of time, only to have its jagged pieces slice into the tender earth and remain standing around him, imprisoning him like the bars of a cage. Each sharp object that steals his freedom holds his own reflection, forcing him to watch that which drove him mad the first time around. He can see her face, and he knows he can't help her. A squeal wheezes out of his mouth, echoing from the canyon of growing darkness that tears through his chest.

CHAPTER 5

S unlight burns orangey-red through the last frame of a
nightmare. Although it fades, he knows its shape well;
he's seen it all night, even before he had fallen asleep.
Emerald green burning in pain beneath a flowing, red breeze
that carries a soft voice calling his name, pleading for him to
help her, to not give up, and his hands, weak and straining,
never being able to reach her.

His eyes open, filled with the unwanted brightness.

Sometime during the night, he had pulled himself into
the backseat, although all he can remember is hanging out the
driver's door and the nonstop clenching and churning of his
discontented stomach.

Now the street comes into focus. He knows where he is
and why no one bothered to see if he was okay or why he was
passed out in the backseat of his car with its front driver's side
tire invading up and onto the sidewalk like a tiger with its paw
hanging out its cage.

He sees an antique shop that is framed between a
clothing store and a retailer specializing entirely in quality

writing utensils. It's Cellar Street, and although he didn't know where he was last night, he couldn't have chosen a better place to sleep off his insurmountable anxiety.

The circular thoughts return to him, and his brow crumbles under their weight. He sits upright on the seat and looks through the windows at his surroundings.

Women in expensive, upscale clothing and younger girls in gothic, funky garb both stroll down the street and in and out of the stores, designer purses alongside flashy colored pantyhose marred with runs, and ornate diamond jewelry reflects the same light as a nose ring.

It is odd that both ends of the social spectrum enjoy shopping in the same quirky, over-priced boutiques, both wanting the feeling of having found something different than what is consumed by the middle class. It's unlikely that they would have much to say to each other; nevertheless, they grab at the same items, counting on the purchases to take them to different and superior places.

The same overpriced lamp might find its way to an apartment or dorm room with black curtains made out of bargain bed sheets and unframed posters tacked to the walls of a bloody Caravaggio or *The Nightmare Before Christmas* just as easily as it could be placed in a room with high ceilings, a glittering chandelier, and crown molding beside a hand-painted Monet water lilies reproduction framed in gold. One could wonder if either woman would still see any magic in the lamp if she knew where else it could be found.

Feeling the urge to get out the back seat and the unpleasant memories and thoughts from the previous night, he exits the car and stretches.

Directly across the street, he can see a bar. The remains of broken bottles line the curb in front of it, their shattered pieces marking the crashing end of its patrons' recent evenings, and the sidewalk near its double doors is stained a different color than the rest of the street.

As he glances around absorbing his surroundings, he thinks that it all is a perfect picture from his memory. Not the specific people, the bar, or the stores, but the style of clothing, the speech of the people, the cars, and the signs on the buildings: they are all as he imagined. He has landed in a crisp photograph of his ideal place in time, and now that he can't change its path, it is one that he knows will leave him hollow.

It's not as gloomy as the night before, but also not as bright as the return to the field of his youth. Something about being in the middle of the extremes feels real, be it a real hell, heaven, or a path betwixt.

Unlike after the failed attempts last night, he feels the urge to investigate his surroundings some more.

After all, the car and his clothing still make no sense. They were indeed part of his life, but not at this place and time. Even if he is doomed to helplessly watch all of the events that ruined his happiness unfold again, there is something else going on in this trip through time, something unexpected, and that will at least provide something to investigate, a distraction from staring at the dismal future that awaits him.

Scientific discovery is no longer of personal interest to him if it can't lead him to her, but discovering the anomalies of time travel is something man has lusted over for eons. For our Chester, it might provide a pillow to clutch instead of the fair, red-maned body he longs to hold and to whisper that she is wonderful and irreplaceable and everyone around her is a terrible person for keeping that from her.

The worst part of this whole mess for him is that it appears he is helpless to save her from her life of heartache, abuse, and misery. In fact, it looks like he won't be able to prevent even one of her ill-fated choices. Images of her lovely façade on the other woman's body and the strange skin attached to her own skull stir up the burn in his stomach.

Part of him can't believe it's so, that she is doomed to that fate. It's not hard for him to grasp that he is incapable of helping her, but it seems that all the universe is a lie if someone that is so special to him, someone whose heart he is convinced is as pure and vulnerable as a child's, is forced to walk along such a painful path.

A small, convertible, baby blue, bubble-shaped sports car pulls up to the curb several stores down the street. A woman with dark sunglasses and a bizarre pink hat that matches her outfit steps out of her vehicle and slams the door with her stretched palm, keeping her fingers from touching it.

She steps around the side of the car, and even from a half block away, Chester can hear an animal yapping from the passenger seat. She wraps its leash around her hand, pulls the dog to her face with a squeeze, and then places it on the ground while hanging onto the end of the leash.

The dog is small enough to be bullied by a large rodent, and at this moment, it lifts its leg at the corner of a dark blue newspaper receptacle. Suddenly the inconsequential scene sparks his attention.

Patting his back pocket, he makes sure that his wallet hasn't fallen out during last night's backseat ordeal. Tapping his other pocket, he assures himself that the device is still there too.

He walks quickly, not knowing if what he's looking for will still be there when he arrives. The dog seems to be finished his business as both he and his owner walk into the store immediately to the side of her parked convertible. The store's façade is still out of his sight.

He digs his wallet out of his pocket and scans over his cards. He saw them briefly last night as he paid for his ticket to the play, but he was too focused on getting to that woman's hat to pay them much mind. His original driver's license from this time, the money dated two decades prior, and his birth certificate all reside in their designated partitions exactly as he had prepared them before embarking on this unnatural journey. He taps his pocket again now that it is missing the wallet. He hears some jingling, which provides a small relief.

Now, he can see the woman and her dog inside a hair salon.

Chester looks at the dark blue machine, and sees there are ample unbought papers inside. He drops in some coins, opens the flap, and yanks a paper onto the top of the machine.

Flipping through its contents, he finds the Riverview section, and he sees the article. The headline is the same, "Drama Director Receives 20-Year Service Award."

But, the picture is different.

The new picture is of the loudmouthed woman from the bathroom hallway handing the same award to Mrs. Edna Hoover. The fancy hat woman is nowhere to be seen. His eyebrows rise as the significance sinks in.

The description beneath the picture is slightly changed, now reading, "Doris Delbeccio of St. Christopher's PTA, hands 20-year service award to drama club director Edna Hoover."

He grabs up the rest of the paper between tight fingers and makes his way back to his car.

It's different. I changed it. Things can be different here! Well, some things can be different that's for sure. At least some things can be changed, maybe even all of them...

He looks at the activity of the people moving along the busy street. Urgency pumps through him, but he knows that the car is unsafe and that he doesn't want to wait a short drive to access the device. He turns around ungracefully, directing his course toward the hair salon again.

The woman from the car reclines in a chair with her head pulled backward and over a black sink made for washing hair. On a hard-looking stylish couch sits the pink hat and her miniature canine beside a fluffy purse that quite resembles the dog.

The dog lets out a few yaps as it watches Chester walk through the door, stepping toward its owner and the stylist testing the temperature of the water with her hand before dampening the customer's hair with it.

The stylist looks up with an annoyed expression, sniffles while crinkling her nose, and tries to hold a smile at him as she asks, "Can I help you?"

"Uhh, yeah, do you have a restroom that I could use?"

The dog owner snorts and snickers quietly without moving her head to watch the scene.

The stylist, whose smile has shifted to a disgusted face, responds, staring at the newspaper in his hand, "Bathrooms are for customers only."

"Okay, I'll get a haircut then."

"All booked up, no openings today," with annoyance clinging to her words.

Knowing he doesn't have much time, his anxiety soars, "Well then, how about I pay you for a haircut anyway, and we'll call it even?"

Her disgusted face breaks a little, "Awright, you're on," pointing to a white door with a light purple frame.

Subtle snorting and laughter find their way to his ears: the kind that should be, but never is, reserved until the subject completely leaves the room.

He shuts the door behind him and turns the lock on the handle. He rattles the handle testing the lock, and it wobbles but refuses to turn. Snickering from the other room follows the handle jiggling.

The bathroom is definitely one decorated and used by women. The light purple toilet seat cover perfectly matches the shade of the soap dispenser, the tissue box cover, the hand towel hanging on the wall near the sink, and the curtain-like material that wraps around the front of the vanity. Framed pictures also speckle the walls, but he has no time or interest to pay them any mind.

Sliding the device out of his pants pocket, his thumb nervously presses on its power button.

Nothing happens.

He tries again. Just a dim reflective screen that shows the fear on his face. It had just worked the night before. It's been a reliable device since he finished it. Panic begins to raise his heartbeat.

Then he remembers his tinkering with the fire alarm. Diving his hand into his pocket, he hopes it is still there, and his fingers slide over its smooth metallic surface. With familiar speed, he pops open the battery compartment and snaps the battery in place.

Sliding his finger over the power button again, the screen illuminates, and so does his spirit.

His machine was designed for speed, but the brief moment that it takes to load its operating system is presently an unbearable wait.

At the sight of the welcome screen, his fingers start dancing along, diving from one folder into another, racing down the path to the image that he needs to see. Finally, it is before him, answering an unsolvable problem to physicists.

The image is the same as the night before, different than the printed paper he dropped atop the sink countertop.

He had theorized that the picture in the device would be the same; he believed it would be, but he had never tested it. No one has ever had any way of testing it before now.

Theorists had nearly universally claimed that if one managed to go back in time that care would be needed to prevent erasing one's own existence. For example, they claimed that going back in time and killing one's father would eliminate one's own birth years later, leading to the disappearance of one in the past time since one would then never exist in the future to journey there in the first place.

It seems to be a logical assumption, but Chester's always known it to be wrong.

A man could buy a stick of dynamite in his youth, keep it for twenty years, and go back in time nineteen years bringing the stick of dynamite along with him. At this point, there would be two sticks of dynamite, the one that exists one year after buying it, and one that he brought back with him from twenty years in the future. Both of the sticks could be placed right next to each other.

If he lights the dynamite stick from the future, it can blow up itself and the stick from the past sitting just beside it. There is nothing to stop both sticks of dynamite from exploding, no mystical force to maintain continuity. According to the theorists, the future stick could not exist without the past stick still existing. For the paradox to hold up, the stick from the future should not be able to blow up the stick from the past because the future stick couldn't exist without the past stick lasting nineteen more years and then surviving a trip to the past to meet itself.

Chester knew that either the universe would have to magically break rules of physics in preventing the dynamite from exploding both itself and its past counterpart, or the paradox is a lie.

A time traveler could go back in time, kill her parents before her own birth, and still exist. She would not spontaneously fade away. If she went back as a witness only, she could watch her past self be born, and then two versions of herself would exist at the same time. If she wanted, she could watch her past self's life unfold year after year. This would add the existence of the time traveler to the mass of the universe at that point in time. There would be two of her when there used to be one.

Just like the dynamite from the future, the time traveler exists independently of her past self. The time traveler's origin lies in a future that has been erased, not a past that is now altered by the time traveler being there. Her existence makes perfect sense relative to herself or anyone else traveling with her. Since she travels alone, her existence makes no logical sense to the rest of the universe unless someone else is genius enough to deduce from when she has come.

Chester loves Doc Brown, but Doc was wrong on this one. A photograph brought back to the past would never change regardless of what happens from that point on. And, neither would the time traveler fade away from changes made from that point on. In the instant that one arrives in a new state of time, one becomes part of that existence and not dependent on the time one came from. Theoretically, as soon as that person enters in the past, by being there, the person has already changed the future that he came from, erasing the future that he knew.

There is no ever coming home again.

Any point in time—the past, the present, or the future—is never any more than the sum total of all events leading up to it. What one is today, what one owns, how one feels, where one lives, and what one has accomplished is all a result of the sum total of the actions surrounding one's life— all of the things that one has ever done and the things that people have done that have affected one. One's sum total at forty years old would obviously be different if one was killed by a neighbor in early childhood, not even being allowed to reach age forty, or conversely if one won the lottery at age twenty.

But, even smaller events change the sum total that makes up our reality at any point in time. Eating, breathing, interacting, walking, talking to people: all of these things change the current environment, which alters the future—they are all new events to be added to the sum total that we consider the present or the future. From the instant the time traveler exists in the past, her existence must be added to the sum total of events making up a new and changed past. The sum total for the future will never be exactly the same because the time traveler's existence has been added to its sum total; the precise future that the time traveler has left will never exist again.

Because of this, one can't exist in the past for even a moment without erasing the exact future from which one came.

If a time traveler goes back in time one year, she could show up at her home and visit herself. If she stays with herself for an entire year, spending every day with her, she'll be back at the same date and time that she left—her original present, her time traveling point of origin, the future that she left. At this point in time, she'll still be there as will her past self that she has been spending time with every day. No magic force is going to make either body disappear when the year has passed. There will still be two of them.

Time travel inherently breaks the law of conservation of mass/matter. Whatever goes back in time has an origin that has been erased from existence. Therefore, there is no paradox to worry about. Independent mass has been added to the universe.

So, a time traveler can never travel back in time and

then return to the future that she left and have it remain the same. The most notable difference will be that the time traveler will find her past self there too, grown up and possibly living a very similar life to what the time traveler was living before she went back in time. And if her past self never decides to go back in time, there is also no magic force that will make the time traveler disappear. Once a time traveler goes back in time, it is a new past, one that has nothing to do with the series of events that are responsible for her existence.

Therefore, how much one changes the *new past* events is irrelevant. If one can exist in the past environment, one is already a being independent of the future one came from. It is enough to make one's head spiral into insanity, like trying to grasp the endless repetition of an image caught between two parallel mirrors. But, Chester has grasped the concept completely, at the expense of a normal life, a battered mind, a few years of institutionalization, and countless lonely hours.

His eyes study the image on the screen, comparing it to the newspaper photo in his hands. It's in the exact position as the original with the same zoom and angle. The background is identical; the only difference is the loudmouth woman from the bathroom is looking directly at the camera smiling broadly, while in the old picture the woman with the hat had looked with a modest expression at the award-winning teacher.

He hasn't changed the actions of the photographer, the existence of the article, or the end result of the teacher receiving the award, but he had changed the hat, which was his goal, and he still exists along with the original picture in the device.

Glancing at the time shown in the bottom right corner, 10:16 a.m., he starts to put the device away, but he feels the need to glance at the screen again before returning it to his pocket, verifying his astounding situation a second time.

He decides to make quick use of his expensive restroom rental before exiting.

The reclining woman is now sitting upright with the stylist patting a towel to her dripping hair. As he scans over a small framed price sheet, he can hear a faint chortle coming from the chair. Slapping a few worn bills on the counter, he scans the room.

"I'm sorry to bother you again, but could you tell me what time it is?"

Not frowning so much since the bills were placed on the counter, the stylist shakes her right hand flinging water off it. Pulling out a small object from her pocket, she glances at it and answers, "10:18."

Quietly, "So the time is still right."

A quiet snicker-snort, a sniort, is followed by, "When is it not?"

Shaking his head as he pushes the door open, he thinks to say, "Yeah, uh, thanks," but nothing comes out of his mouth.

A whisper rises that is hard to hear but is metered to fit someone saying, "What a weirdo!"

He's heard it before.

He thinks of Rhonda and smiles as he imagines changing the scenery around her sad life, mainly placing himself by her side, but in the least keeping her face intact.

Walking down the sidewalk, a smile takes possession of his face for the first time since he arrived in the schoolyard, and he can't find any reason to shoo it away.

He pulls the handle on his driver's door and hops in his car. He realizes he has left the door open all night and while he went into the beauty salon; the keys are still in the ignition. He would never have been that careless with the car until now. As it is not as exigent as the ink that is smearing off the thin paper onto his pressing fingers, he sends the thought out of his head.

He plops the paper on the seat beside him, and fires up the engine. Backing up, his front tire pops off the sidewalk onto the street, and quickly shifting gears he speeds down the narrow lane with cars parked on both sides.

CHAPTER 6

A razor slides over the brim of his head, but his thoughts remain on walking out of the bars to his left. Long strands of hair drop to the floor in quiet smacks. Baring his skin, removing thick masses of hair, a thin crimson streak running from a knick—it all reminds him of dismembering an animal.

He's been incarcerated for four hundred and fifty-eight days, and he holds a separate anger for each one of them. Only one and a quarter years through his twenty-four season sentence, but his mind is set on making this early morning the beginning of his last day.

From the start he's felt that he's been treated unfairly.

His record included aggravated battery, failing to register as a sex offender resulting from an ill-fated relationship with a fourteen-year-old girl, and his latest armed robbery. All three offenses occurred in the first six months following his eighteenth birthday.

He smirkingly admits to all of the crimes, but he feels his sentence is the result of an unfair state law requiring a three time felon to be issued the maximum sentence for his convictions.

He has shouted to everyone around him about the unfairness of receiving a harsher sentence due to past crimes, spouting about backwoods double jeopardy and that sentencing should have nothing to do with one's previous record. Yet, he didn't mind the light sentence he had received for his initial battery charge since it was his first and only offense at the time.

His prison stay has been mostly quiet, having been thought to be involved in several group beatings although no evidence could be brought against him. Guards considered him a ringleader, a boss among a faction of the inmates, but always one degree away from being incriminated.

An unexpected fight last week hospitalized his cellmate, who is aptly named Owl after his robust eyebrows, so he now shaves alone in front of a mirror with a smuggled razor, not the inferior safety razors that are standard issue. His shedding metamorphosis requires a sharper blade.

His face stings with the air tingling over freshly exposed skin. His unkempt beard was part of his persona, hiding his human features behind its fur-like mask. It was as attached to him as his bed is to the floor and the polished stainless steel mirror is to the wall in front of him with its eight tamper-proof screws holding it snugly secure. As his mane is removed from his skull in rows, he feels free of the life he's made in jail and unbound from the narrow rectangular brick cell.

A somber exhale escapes from him as the razor pulls the last strands from his scalp.

He splashes hot water atop his head. Despite the failings of prison life, the water has always arrived hot and fast at the turn of the sink's left handle. Using his polyester bedspread, he wipes away the slain hair remnants from his head.

Taking one more pass with the razor, he cleans up the missed spots. The mirror begins to get hazy making it harder to see the new him, and he turns the hot water down. Throughout his life, excessive heat has often made it hard for him to get a good view of himself.

Tossing the polyester cover atop the bed, his attention returns as it always does to the bars at the open end of his pen. Across the spaces between the bars, walks the man with clothes in his hands.

"Hello, Edmund, glad to see you up this early in the morning and being so industrious at that," whispers the man standing at the locked door in a short-sleeved collared shirt and neatly-pressed, gray, pleated pants.

"I've told you not to call me Edmund; my name is Eddie."

"Well, I don't think you're in much of a position to bargain, Edmund. I could just take your money, make it disappear, and you'd still be here—locked away."

"You wouldn't last a week out there if you crossed me."

"Out there maybe. But, in here," wrapping his fingers around the metal rods, "there are these strong bars keeping all the bad people on the other side."

"Not all of them."

Smiling and looking down at his shined shoes, "Just realize I'm the one who got you this private cell and put that razor blade in your hand."

Shaking his head and struggling to keep his voice at a whisper, "So, you put that crazy idea in Owl's head?"

Nods.

"Poor bastard, nobody's been dumb enough to fight with me since the first week I was in."

"I hear he's healing nicely."

"What'd you promise him?"

"A visit from his wife—a real private one."

Edmund takes his turn in nodding, "That'd do it."

After a moment of digesting the news, Edmund continues, "Was a long two days in solitary. Really appreciate that."

"I'm sure it was a real blast, Edmund, but isn't it worth the reward? The gold at the end of the journey? Besides, the less that it appears you got any special treatment from me, the better it is for the both of us."

"Really, the both of us? Or just you?"

"Hasn't it occurred to you that if they catch me involved in this that they're going to want to nail you even more? To bring the one that got away back and show everyone that everything is back in order again—that no one gets out of here. That the jails are secure—not even corruption can get you out. If people don't think prison is a perfect lockup for all the bad guys, the people start getting restless, lose faith in the system, start thinking of new ways to do things. Nobody in charge will let that happen; none of them want people looking and questioning how things are done. They'll all make sure you get nailed any way they can get at you. Catch you, and it's all back to normal."

Trouble waves over Edmund's face for the first time in any of their conversations.

"Well, you look so different; I'd even have a hard time recognizing you myself if you weren't in your cell."

Edmund stares intently, "Ain't that convenient."

"The new guard is coming on in," looking at his watch, "seven minutes; you better get to getting changed, before he decides to make his rounds."

"Name's Nathan Chapetta—he takes care of his brother's retarded daughter; she just moved in with him. You know that?"

"Of course, I know that—just hired him a few weeks ago, but it's best for *you* not to think about that. You need to think about sticking to the plan, and not about the lives of an unfortunate piece of the plan."

"Uh huh."

"You just be ready before he gets here and stick to what we've said."

"No problem, boss man; this is your show. Just give me the clothes."

A timid hand raises the gray cotton shirt and black baggy pants that were a cash purchase from an out of town discount drug store. As soon as they touch the space between the bars, they are snatched and yanked into the cell with all the savageness of an alpha male tearing off the choicest piece of a fallen prey's flesh before the rest of the pack dives in to get theirs, his knuckles banging on the cold bars in the process.

Turning the clothes over in his hands, Edmund grumbles, "Glad that you shelled out for the good stuff."

"Hey, anything besides that bright orange getup that you're wearing is exquisite stuff, dontchya think?"

"You just get on down that hallway, push the button to release my door, and get out of sight. I'll get these on fast."

"Why is it that an impatient man always thinks he has the right to bark out orders to everyone else? You'd think that the desperate would plead."

Yanking his shoulders out the unbuttoned top of the bright jumpsuit, he says, "Tick tock, Mr. *Deputy* Warden, sir."

"Let me tell you something, dirtball. When Warden McCullough is not here, I am the ex officio captain of the guards; this is my frickin' place, every filthy inch of it, including you; your little bed that's bolted to the wall over there; that filthy, shiny, ice cold toilet; and even the little bits of scraggly hair that you've cut off all over the floor."

"Fine. It's all yours; I want out of here, remember? You're the king of prisonland for all I care, but we need to get moving. Now."

"Well, don't say anything else that might make me want to discuss its meaning with you; it's not the time to be keeping you in line. Stick to the plan."

"I'm a criminal, not a child; I got it."

"Well, you're going to need to get this too," he says holding up a thin laminated card with a dark blue lanyard dangling from it.

Edmund reaches out to grab it, but Rutherford tosses it through bars. Edmund catches it with one hand, driving a corner of its rough plastic into his palm. Glancing at it in his opened hand, the words "Visitor's Pass" glare out at him. The smaller print has the date and the call letters of a local TV station among other words that he is not going to read.

"That should make walking out of here a lot easier."

Turning, taking two steps, and looking back, Rutherford says, "Tell Chapetta I'm sorry it had to be this way. Wrong place, bad time."

Smiling at the prospect, "Sure, I'll send him your regards."

The footsteps grow softer with each echoing step.

Edmund thinks the deputy warden an idiot for not stepping quieter. Rutherford is the prison's steward—it's not unusual for him to wander down the halls inspecting, and any convict who notices him has weak credibility even if he decides to talk. But, it seems simply stupid to do anything to link oneself to a crime scene. Edmund can't make sense of his logic except that maybe there is none. Maybe he's so secure in his job and comfortable in his power that he thinks nothing could condemn him, even being in the vicinity minutes before a jail break.

The reminders to heed the plan were most unnecessary; Edmund's done little but go over the steps in his head since it was agreed upon nearly two weeks ago. During every meal, he has thought of shaving his head and beard and hiding the hairs between the bed cushion and the cover. During every break, he's focused on changing his clothes as quickly as possible. During his work, he's dreamed of the first step into the hallway.

It is a good plan. The electronic doors do malfunction occasionally. In fact, the cells on both sides of Edmund are currently vacant while the prison waits for its budget to grow large enough to repair their faulty doors. Just last year, an incident made the news involving two inmates yelling for the guard when their doors mysteriously popped open. They had no plan, and in Edmund's mind no imagination—the type of prisoners that he thought deserved to rot here. But, the public enjoyed the thought of prisoners not wanting to get into trouble and calling for the guard to lock them back up.

Every time Edmund has heard their story, he has gritted his teeth at the wasted opportunity, the very type of a chance that he's become obsessed with. One year later, their lost getaway makes Edmund's escape seem less a conspiracy and more like an electronic malfunction. No doubt it helped sway Rutherford to believe a plan like this would work without any suspicion of prison staff involvement, especially if it involves the death of a new, inexperienced prison guard.

It's not likely that anyone will be suspicious. Contraband finds its way into prisons in much the same way that the roaches do—any little crack and it'll reshape itself to fit through it and invade. No one will investigate much into a change of street clothes and a razor making their way into a three time felon's cell. In fact, it sounds likely.

Add to it all that today is the day a local news team is coming to film a piece on the prison, a day that the prison will be filled with street-clothed visitors, and it appears flawless. Rutherford isn't a man of morals, but he isn't stupid, having devised a plan that should leave him completely in the clear.

Edmund shoves his head through the neckline of the gray drugstore shirt, completing his street garb, and he immediately stares at the lock. Despite his earlier threats on getting to Rutherford if he didn't uphold his end of their bargain, he's feared a double cross from the first raised eyebrow of their negotiations. An alliance in prison is a sculpture made in the shadows, one never knowing what it will look like when it's brought into the light, or if it will bear any resemblance to the words that formed it or the desired image in one's head.

Surely if Edmund were caught now, face and head shorn too smoothly for the regulation safety razor, standing in street clothes, it wouldn't bode well for the length of his prison sentence. Contraband can add time, especially in the case of the razor which is considered a dangerous weapon, and an attempted escape is a guarantee of more time.

Their discussions began a few months before and were

mulled over and refined until finalized two weeks ago. It all started when Detective Paul Andarus came to the prison to ask some questions about one of Edmund's acquaintances who was a suspect in a homicide investigation. Edmund was offered time off his sentence for cooperation, but he kept his mouth shut. He didn't say whether he knew anything or not. He didn't say a word. Both the detective and Rutherford were sure he knew something, but there wasn't a whole lot else either of them could legally do to make him talk.

The detective seemed almost relieved that Edmund didn't get a reduced sentence, and Rutherford, while irritated on the outside, made a mental note of a man with a colorful record who could keep his mouth shut. That's when the eyebrow first raised; that's when Edmund knew the deputy warden might bend to the right persuasion. The unrecovered money from his armed robbery quickly grabbed the interest of Rutherford, and the engine of avarice revved into redline, kicking out the polluted beginnings of the plan.

The quiet buzz of an electric hum causes the door to pop open. It's excited Edmund every time he's heard it, but never quite like what he feels now. Everything else tells him to run. Tear down the hallway. Escape.

But, malice causes him to smile and be still. Patience has been his adversary as far back as his brain will let him remember, and he grasps it now with two anxious hands as it's the only medicine to satisfy the growling rage rampaging in his chest.

Deputy Warden Rutherford's hand releases the button, and his body turns quickly from it toward the end of the hall. His hand is grasped in an angry, gloved grip. Bewildered, Rutherford looks wildly past the hand that has grabbed him, down the uniformed arm, and up to the face of his aggressor. The clenching hand releases him as roughly as when it just clasped him.

"Chapet—" is all that makes it out of Rutherford's mouth.

Sting burns into his side as 50,000 volts rush through

his body.

The floor seems to reach up and smack the side of his face. Twitching and pulsing flip and flop him on the ground in a quiet excruciation. The only sounds are the flickering and popping of the electricity and a meek, shrill whine that comes from deep within him.

The whine comes in the same rhythm as the pulses of the Taser, much like someone saying a long, drawn out "a-a-a-h" while smacking one's throat at a consistent interval. His whimpering releases memories of the sound his hunting dog once made when bitten by a snake.

Rutherford's vision is jumble, but it's a blur of his newest correctional officer looming over him.

It's supposed to be a five-count. Rutherford has felt this before as all officers are required to experience a five second blast from a regulation Taser. He tries to count in his head without much success. He's certain it's been longer than five seconds, but certainty and neurological discomfort don't mix well.

It's not a physical pain, but a helpless discomfort that leaves him feeling violated and completely defeated. Each pop of the current is a chime reminding him that he is immobile on the floor and incapable of moving any part of him to prevent whatever trauma will come next.

Every muscle is involuntarily listless; every fiber is full of surrender.

His eyes are now on the shiny black shoes of the man lording over him; they come in and out of focus, as fuzzy as the pulse of the Taser. His mind is in a glacially slow panic; the Taser taking its effect there too. The word Taser passes his mind's eye, then each letter spelling it out, and for a reason that he can't connect, Tom Swift also comes to his mind.

The popping stops.

Moving past his eyes, the hand inside a thin glove smashes a piece of duct tape over his mouth. He feels the gloved hands grabbing at his armpits and pulling him off the floor. His shoes drag across the ground, scuffing his polished shine. Shoved forward, his waist hits a laundry cart, his body bends over its rail.

Quickly, he's shoved again, and his body falls headfirst into the cart, his nose smashed and stretched to the right against the bottom seam of the off-white cloth bin inside the metal frame of the cart. The seam roughly presses across his face. His knees rest where they are pressed into and stretching the front side of the cloth cart, while his head is jammed into the bottom rear.

His hands push against the cloth, and he struggles to get a grip to reposition his body so he can lift his head. His hands push into the canvas, stretching it, and his head rises off the bottom. Lurching forward, the cart rolls. Losing all leverage, his hands slip, and his face crashes into the bottom of the cart again.

Rather than trying to hoist himself a second time, his hands move toward his face. Grabbing clumsily at the tape, his fingers struggle to get a hold on an end. Finally, they grab a corner and roughly yank it off.

Just as his lips begin to call out, "Help," the cart stops, and he feels a large, powerful, bare hand come down on the back of his neck. The other ungloved hand grasps his belt and lifts him out of the cart.

Hoisted in the air, panic spills over his face as he recognizes the bits of hair on the floor of the cell he is in.

Looking at Chapetta standing several feet before him, the strong hands send him flying toward the concrete floor. Rutherford's left shoulder hits first with a sickening snapping noise, and the vision of Edmund's towering frame comes into focus just as his boot comes down on his throat.

Pinning the deputy warden to the ground with the standard issue shoe, he looks to Chapetta, "You're a good man; you take care of that little girl."

"Thanks for the chance to do it."

Nods and adds, "You better get outta here."

"You too."

"My offer's still good about the cash," at which

Rutherford begins to squirm but is met with more foot pressure on his throat.

Chapetta shakes his head, "No, just 'cause I pushed him in the trap he put out for me, doesn't mean I'm a scuzzbag like him. You do this fast before I come back to my senses and turn both of us in."

As the young corrections officer turns away pulling the cart behind him, Edmund whispers intently, "Chapetta, one more thing."

Chapetta places his hand on his Taser holster as he looks back into the cell.

"Rutherford wanted me to tell you he's sorry it had to be this way."

Glancing down at his boss that is about to be his boss no more, "Yeah, me too."

Rutherford watches his patsy walk away, the only man who could possibly patrol this wing during the next few hours, taking with him all reasonable hope of leaving the cell alive. The panic swells, and he begins to thrash his body back and forth trying to break free of the foot at his throat.

Without warning, the foot releases his neck. The light shining down on his prostrate body changes suddenly as Edmund lunges straight up into the air. Rutherford rolls onto his side trying to deflect the blow, but Edmund's feet crash into his hip, side, and ribs. His lower torso feels mangled, filling him with the compulsion to wheeze and cough, but he makes little more than a whine.

The inmate grabs the cell keeper by his neck, pulling him off the floor. With two quick steps and a shove with his choking hand, Edmund sends Rutherford's head crashing into the brick wall.

Heat and sting are all that the deputy warden knows.

With a tightening on the throat, he pulls Rutherford off the wall about a foot and quickly slams his head back into the bricks again. Deep red streams run down the wall. Rutherford's eyes roll back, and Edmund lightens the squeeze on his throat as he steps toward him, putting his mouth within an inch of his victim's ear.

"Sorry for the ruse, Mr. Deputy Warden Rutherford, but we needed your prints on the door switch." Air and blood resume their flow, and the deputy warden squirms. Edmund grunts and tightens his grip to maintain his control on the flailing and continues, "Wish we had a nicer way to take you out, but this'll just have to do."

Legs kick at the bed, trying to gain a grip on something in the hopes of pushing off hard enough to break the hold of the powerful arm holding him in place and its hand squeezing the life out of him.

"You see I'm a bad man, but I ain't no one to hurt a child. Our good friend, Mr. Nathan Chapetta, is taking care of his retarded niece," the struggling body moving slower, "I can't have you offing the only person who could take care of her. Foster home ain't no place for a kid like that; been there myself."

While the crimson escapes the back of his head, the blueness begins to overtake the red of his lips, and his tongue hangs out the corner of his mouth. With wide eyes, Rutherford sends a knee flying into the air, on perfect course to crash between Edmund's legs.

Without even glancing downward, Edmund notices the movement in his periphery, and quickly turns and raises his thigh. The knee crashes into his meaty thigh, and his hand loses its grip on the neck holding up the bleeding head.

Rutherford gasps desperately.

Edmund's fist connects hard into Rutherford's chest, knocking the breath that he just sucked in back out of him.

Swinging an uppercut while he gasps again, Rutherford connects with Edmund's mouth. Lower jaw smacks the top one, catching the tip of his tongue in between. Blood seeps onto his lips. Uglier than that is the expression to which Edmund's face contorts as he pummels Rutherford with a fast combination of punches, all pounding his head until he flops back to the floor, resembling a mannequin broken at all of its joints and collapsed in an awkward pose.

Bending down Edmund grabs Rutherford by his throat. The deputy warden's eyes stare at his attacker but are glazed over and devoid of energy. Dragging him by his throat, Edmund hauls him across the tiny room and drapes his neck over the rim of the stainless steel toilet seat. He jams his foot across the back of Rutherford's neck and holds it pinned tightly.

"Have to admit that was more fight than I was expectin' from you."

Edmund spits into the sink. It is bloody, and some of it runs over the edge of the sink with a few drops hitting the floor.

Looking down at the pinned body beneath him, he still sees twitching and a straining to breath.

"Hehe, kinda funny, Rutherford, that you're getting smashed into that same toilet you were running your mouth about earlier. *Your* toilet. It's all yours now."

Rutherford's eyes strain to see. The shiny metal bowl in front of him glistens in the dim light from above, both on the water and the bowl itself. The yellow begins to turn to a flesh-colored orange. On the orange his suffocating thoughts materialize. *Cold metal. Squished throat. Death...Tom A. Swift and his Electric Rifle...It's Taser. Acronym...That's it...* A hint of a smile twitches at his lips which gasp for air that isn't coming. His face turns pale with harsh blue lips, the look of winter, colors of freezing.

Edmund sees the body is no longer moving. He gives one strong kick to the back of his head.

No movement.

He turns around and throws the polyester cover onto the cell floor. With speed he grabs the body and hurls it onto the mattress. Lifting the head he slides the pillow underneath it.

He bends down to pick up the cover and feels his pants slipping at the waist. Looking at the lifeless lump in the bed, he drops the cover and begins unlatching the lump's belt. One fast motion slides the belt out of its loops, ripping one of them and rolling the corpse over. He loops the belt around himself, rolls Rutherford facing the wall again, and tucks the polyester cover around him.

He sees the droplets of blood on the ground and the streaks in the sink and on the wall, but he knows he has to move quickly or his window for escape will close soon.

Wadding up a fistful of toilet paper, he wipes at the walls and the sink frantically. Tossing the paper in the toilet, he repeats the process even faster.

Spinning a knob, cupping water, tossing it into his mouth, swishing it around, and spitting are his final activities in the cell.

As he takes his first step into the walkway, visitor's badge lanyard swaying with his stride, he feels as if something will grab his leg and yank him back inside his little closet-sized dungeon. The door shuts with a clang, and the lump in the bed does not move or breathe.

Looking around, no one is in the hallway of the wing, just as it was planned to be.

Scanning the area, he doesn't see anything of note until his eyes slide over an inmate directly across the hallway from his former cell. He is sitting straight up in the bottom bunk while his cellmate still sleeps. Edmund raises a single finger to his lips, and the prisoner nods his head in agreement. Since he hasn't made a sound yet, Edmund assumes he'll keep his mouth shut.

Anything that would bring Edmund back to the prison would bring a tremendous amount of trouble on the sitting convict. Besides, no prisoners will lament the death of Rutherford. That is as long as none of them had an escape plan with Rutherford too. The only concern is that the man across the hall keeps his mouth shut long enough for Edmund to get a running start; it won't matter if he talks after that. Anyway, after a short while, he wouldn't be telling the police anything they didn't already now, provided that he didn't see Chapetta at Edmund's cell. Edmund just needs about an hour or more to make a clean break.

The hardest thing is to walk slowly. Although he's traversed his current path a thousand times over in his head, he's rarely been down this side of the wing: once when they brought him in the first time, twice when he had to speak with the detective in Rutherford's office, and thrice now.

The other prisoners are still sleeping. The Taser was a quiet torture, and the fight was involved but fast and localized in one cell. You also get used to sleeping heavily in prison. If you woke yourself every time someone was fighting with a cellmate; arguing with a guard; or shouting some lunatic rant about his fate in a desperate voice into the long, absorbing hours of the night; you'd never sleep. The only sound that jolts you awake is the sound of your cell door opening. That's the sound that'll make you leap out of bed in a nervous sweat with both fists clenched, heart thumping, and muscles twitching.

He opens a door on the left side of the hallway. It's a closet with all of its contents pushed tightly against its walls, just as Chapetta had promised him. He quickly steps inside and gently pulls the door closed.

The next forty-five minutes pass slowly with the sounds of the prison coming alive, buzzing like a stirred-up hive. Grumbling, toilets flushing, sinks running, the metered step of Chapetta's two routine walks down the wing: it all sounds familiar yet so different being on the other side of the bars. The noises are identical, but his ears hear them differently in the same way a member of a band hears the clamor of the music differently than those watching in the crowd.

Cracking his knuckles and neck is all that he can do to stay quiet. Sitting down is not an option. If someone unexpected opens that door, he'll have another voice to silence, and he'll have to dispose of the interloper without causing any alarm. Being ready to lunge at a moment is essential to handle any unwanted surprises.

The sound of feet clopping in a herd stops him in the middle of cracking his neck.

He holds his head cocked at a forty-five degree angle; ears feel as if tingling. As the ruckus moves directly in front of his door, he stands in a boxer's stance, his fists making short little circles in the air. His chest heaves with the urge to come out swinging, to hit them before any of them have the chance to find him hiding in a maintenance closet. He clenches his fists tighter. Then, the sound of eighteen soles slapping the ground in a rhythmless chorus grows fainter.

Hand trembling as he reaches for the handle, he hopes it doesn't squeak. Getting out the door unnoticed is the last of two steps that concern him. The other is getting past the guards at the entrance and onto the shuttle bus in the parking lot. His hand turns the handle slowly.

It does not squeak.

Still holding the handle fully turned to the right, he pushes the door open slowly. Although they were silent on the way in, he is still cautious of the hinges. Every time he's heard the closet opened until a few days ago, it's made a loud wail. Chapetta had taken care of the oiling a few days ahead of time to eliminate any chance of sonic metallic scraping. Despite it all, he still holds his breath pushing the door opened wide enough to get his large frame through it.

Glancing down the wing, he sees the gaggle of press at the far end. Still holding the inside handle, he steps into the hallway, guiding his broad shoulders around the edge of the door. He lets go of the handle, and it makes a clack as it returns to its original, unturned position.

With the press at the other end, there isn't much noise in the area of the closet. The clack of the handle echoes as Edmund quickly closes the door and steps away from it.

"Looking for a mop, RE-port-uh boy? I got something for ya to mop in here?"

Laughing and cooing comes from the cells close to the inmate who just called out. None of them care that the euphemism doesn't make much sense. A joke's a joke between three brick walls and one of bars, and a dirty joke needs not make any sense at all, especially if its raunchiness is blatant in tone.

Edmund's face is the color of fury, and he strains to keep his expression from knotting up in his usual scowl. As he clenches and unclenches his fist, he wonders how someone in this prison dares to talk to him that way. Except for the recent Rutherford-influenced mouthing off of Owl, no one has messed with Edmund since his first day of incarceration.

Then it hits him.

They don't recognize him without his beard and long hair. He smiles and starts walking away, although his fists remain clenched.

Calling out from down the hall, "Hey, don't go away mad. I'm sorry. Just come back here, and we'll make you feel right at home, huh, fellas?"

Laughter springs forth again.

Despite his recent revelation, Edmund's anger floods his thoughts, making it hard to even focus on the exit that is just around the corner. His rage screams for beatings on the loudmouth; his fists pulse, aching to answer the call. Hands shaking, he opens his fists, and eight quaking fingers pull back, leaving two extended middle fingers at his sides. He knows he shouldn't raise them, but it makes him feel better that he has at least stuck them out, even though no one else can see them. A secret insolence is something of value to him while pointless and unnoticed to the rest of the world.

Grunting, he forces his fingers to release the gesture as he turns the corner, leaving the cell wing and approaching the security post at the exit. Now that his angry digits have reached their destination, he works on his sneer.

While he's always thought his choleric emotions were justified because it was the outside world's stupidity that heated them up, he has been aware enough to notice that most other people don't have them. To get past the guards without suspicion, he knows he'll have to bury them—the same tempers that have proven to be undead to him, rising to torment him again and again no matter what anyone else has tried to do to put them away.

He struggles to keep a smile on his face as he approaches the guards in the glass office by the exit.

His hands don't want to do anything but make fists, so he shoves them into his pockets. He knows he should be more casual, but he can't trust his hands at the moment. Telling himself that the bigger vengeance is walking out the door, boarding that bus to the penitentiary parking lot, and then running like mad; he fights the urge to pounce unexpectedly on the guards.

Forcing a hard smile, he says in a voice that is much higher than his normal speech, "I'm sorry to bother you officers, but I left my camera in the van, and I really need to go back and get it."

The guard sitting closest to the opened door of the office responds, "Are you sure you're gonna need it? We're going to have to run you through security again when you come back through."

"Yeah, my job depends on it," Edmund responds scanning his eyes over the contents of the security office through the giant glass windows that make up the hallway wall of the office. A television plays scenes of a sitcom that he's never seen, a second officer sits in a chair staring at the show, an opened bag of potato chips sits on a tabletop next to a box of bagels, an unseen coffee maker permeates the air with its brewing aroma, and a grid of monitors flickers visions of hallways that Edmund hopes to never see again.

Glancing up at the dangling visitor's pass draped around Edmund's neck, the guard says, "Alrighty then," pausing while trying to remember if he'd seen someone so large coming in with the group earlier and then pushing the button for the door to open, "but make sure you get it all in one trip. We can't be running the shuttle back and forth all day just for you."

"Thanks," says Edmund. As he walks through the door and into the light of early morning, he can hear the two guards arguing, fading behind him with every step.

"Why did you have to say that to him?" asks the other guard with his words wheezing out of his mouth swiftly and sopping with sibilance.

"Well, it's true."

"Doesn't matter none; you know Rutherford told us to

be on our best behavior with these press people. He's gonna give you hell if he hears you're giving them a hard time."

"Well, let him give it to me then. This is a freakin' prison, not some Hollywood studio. All these press people are weirdoes; that's why they all go out to California, only weirdoes head out to California..."

CHAPTER 7

P ushing his speedometer into triple digits is something he has never done before, but California is a long way away. Cars that are traveling at the speed limit appear to be standing still as he passes them.

Fortunately, other motorists are scarce on the lonely highway that slices a narrow scar across the desert landscape, leaving two dotted, parallel paths separated by a short median, looking like the tracks of a wounded animal trying to drag itself and its partner to safety. Their fleeing blood trail consists of faded white dashes instead of shiny crimson.

Perhaps unrequited love loses its color.

The speed and thrill of being the fastest traveler on the road makes his entire body feel charged. Watching his speedometer, he is glad he resisted the urge to replace the rear gear with a more acceleration-friendly ratio. The stock setup proves better for his highway blast across two thirds of the country.

Being that the interior has reverted itself to its original material and that the car has appeared inexplicably at the field, maybe the ring and pinion gear set would've reverted to its original parts even if he had changed them. To make the matter even murkier, the engine feels as if all of the hot rodding that he did to it is still in place. It certainly feels much more powerful than what its stock engine could muster.

Logic seems to be inconsequential as there is no consistency in what has stayed the same and what has reverted to its past condition. Occurrences that lie outside of scientific explanation are a troublesome prospect, especially to one who has relied on theory to take him away from his normal, safe existence on an uncharted voyage. But, if he doesn't make it in time, it's all for naught anyway.

While his body sizzles in excitement, his mind is a battlefield. He thinks of his love painted and written beneath red bangs and of the immediate trouble that awaits her, which causes his foot to push down harder on the pedal and add a few ticks to the speedometer.

Then he imagines blazing red and blue lights behind him that would threaten to destroy his efforts and dreams.

And what of the device?

If he is apprehended, he'll have to make sure it is completely destroyed, either killing himself in the process or remaining alive but destroying the device, which would render him stranded and unarmed to fight for his happiness in his present time that was all too recently twenty years in his past. He has little hope in either prospect, but he is certain that anything is better than allowing his personal device to be found by anyone else. The implications that it would have on the world could be catastrophic.

How powerful could one become with access to the newspapers of the next twenty years? And, that is only a small part of the information in his device; there are all of his notes, which he dreads the idea of anyone else following his footsteps that jump backward in time and the lonely journey that it takes to gain the means to get there.

It may be a milestone for which man has reached for centuries, but it is an adventure that has a high personal cost.

He knows people would thrill to read about his exploit, desperately wanting to glean his secret over remorselessly ticking time and harness it to go back and fix mistakes that haunt them every day of their lives. The great lengths that would be taken and the deep inner yearning to gain the unwieldy power and reshape their regrets: this desperate need of many he is very aware. After all, it was what had consumed and tortured his mind for more than the last decade of his adult life until he turned down this strangely-ticking corridor. Although he is convinced there was no other way for him, he doesn't want anyone else to believe that for oneself.

The adrenaline courses through his veins now, true, but for so long they were dormant, feeling little except the type of despair that wipes all other feeling away. The current precariousness of so much that is important to him causes his hands to shake.

All of these thoughts have left him with little more direction than a pendulum. He has decided to stay below double the speed limit as that would likely only leave him with a few citations as opposed to an arrest, impoundment, and a vehicle search.

His other resolution is to vigilantly watch the horizon and his rearview mirror for any imperial entanglements, nerves firing erratically the whole way. Despite it all, he is behaving with more certainty and courage than he has ever been able to muster, and that seems to shine as brightly as the sun on the sand.

Once every half an hour or so, he turns on the radio and smiles when he hears happier tunes. Not that he has wonderful memories attached to them, but they all symbolize a period in his life when he was still filled with dreams and the time to bring them about. Inevitably, he'll end up singing along or getting lost in a song that he has forgotten existed, and his speed will slide up too high or he'll realize he hasn't checked the rearview mirror in some time. Then, he'll flip the radio off, only hearing the sounds of the car on the open highway: the rumble of the engine, the clocklike ticking of his keychain slapping on the steering column, and the whir of tires rolling over the concrete. It all gives the feeling of being in a space vessel with numerous activities going on at once. The clock on the radio counts down the hours he has to get to her before she embarks on the path that will ruin her future.

He's been a spectator his whole life—now he races the sun. Countless have tried to beat the celestial body and failed, but for once he thinks he is going to win.

Nighttime in the desert comes on like a ghost blanketing itself over a fire, a void eating the brightness, filling as high, wide, and deep as he can see with a darkness whose density seems all-encompassing until a dim outline of a cactus or a street sign breaks its totality.

The interior light of his car is an electric campfire. The subtly flickering bulbs of the dash lighting appear out of place in the desert, yet more organic than the eerily precise illumination of the device's screen.

A haze of an object darts across the highway ahead of him.

He is unsure if it is a machination of his tired eyes or if it is a coyote. He tells himself it's the latter, because he has no intentions on resting as the first possibility would require.

Hazy creatures, a speedy iconic vehicle, and a device from the future all set against a mysterious and barren landscape: he thinks it could be a setting of an interesting book, but it would be a story like the ones he loves to read, not like the ones that he's written. Most of his writing has been in the form of television shows, all comedies. He was baffled and relieved to find out that so many of the other staff writers were outcasts like himself, a bizarre anomaly that those who dream the best comedies are full of sadness in their hearts.

The miles peel away slowly like scales of shedding skin. Every bit of distance that he travels peels off a bit of what he used to be and years of lost opportunities, leaving him new, free, and raw, but without calluses to protect his touch. The urgency to get to Los Angeles eclipses all other considerations, having decided to not be afraid of failing until he's arrived with enough time to try in the first place.

A trip from LA to L.A. is quite a drive, but considering his giant jaunt across time, this cross-country trek only requires a mere payment of hours and determination. And if all goes well, he should have just enough of both to get there.

The morning rays peek over the points of the mountain range behind him. Large golden fingers reach out toward his car. They flicker at him in the rearview, and he wonders if they're stretching out to stop him or to give him a push on his way. Neither causes him to alter his speed or to keep his eyes from anxiously scanning the area.

CHAPTER 8

T he building's tower slices into the clear blue sky. Looking directly at the edifice, it is in the shape of a backwards L with the fifteen-story tower on the right and the attached three-story wing on the left. Its perfectly lined, giant bricks are reminiscent of those used in an Egyptian pyramid, while its ornate and angular trim around the large front doors and many windows are gothic in the style of early Hollywood. And as if to remind all that it is located in California, towering palm trees are evenly placed in the square garden patches that line the street.

Blue lights reflect on the bricks that look as new as if they were laid yesterday. The illumination casts a feeling of magic on the building, which coincides with the sensation of moving energy in his chest.

The windows on the first floor are tall and rectangular with a rounded top. The lattices of the second floor windows are opened outwardly in a way that makes one expect to see a maiden leaning through them to greet a suitor. Black metal terraces are attached to the bricks in front, spanning the length of three windows each.

He steps onto a red carpet that runs from the door, hugging tightly down three stone steps, across the sidewalk, between two of the strips of palm trees, and all the way to the curb of the street. Before having spent years in Los Angeles, he would've thought it to be too stereotypical to be real, but he's seen similar red material laid out at numerous work-related parties.

Sitting upon a darkly stained wooden easel, a black sign with silver writing declares the event for the evening: *Most Hipness* Start of Season Party.

At the end of the carpet is an elegant black door flanked by two stone lions and a large man in a simple yet formal suit standing at its left side watching Chester as he approaches.

The man extends his arm and asks, "Do you have an invitation, sir?"

Chester pats his pockets although he already knows the answer, "No, I must have left it at home."

With reluctant eyes, the doorman scans over our time violator's clothes, "Hmmm, sorry, sir, but it is invitation only tonight."

"I know; I was invited—I just forgot it at home," he says with certainty, speed, and smoothness that are foreign to him.

"Well, we can see if you're on the list, but I'll have to ask that you take a step back while I'm doing so."

The large man reaches into a pocket in his black coat and pulls out a small object. Pushing a button, he speaks into it, "Craig, can you check the list for a...hang on a second," turning to Chester, "What is your name, sir?"

"Chester Fuze."

"Mr. Chester Fuze," pausing and listening, "Okay, thanks, Craig." With a smile he says to Chester, "Sir, you are indeed on the list. I apologize; we usually keep a printed copy down here too, but we don't have one tonight."

"No problem."

"But if I may inconvenience you one more time, I am supposed to verify you with an ID."

"Oh, sure," Chester says reaching into his back pocket and pulling out his wallet, "Here you are."

Large thumbs enclose both sides of the driver's license. Chester wiggles his lower jaw around his mouth, hoping the doorman doesn't see his nervousness.

The license is perfect; it's his old license from 20 years before he jumped back in time. He never turned in his old licenses at the DMV. He always kept them and claimed that the old one was lost when he went in to renew. He also has several credit cards from the same time in his wallet, but he is afraid to use them just as he is uneasy now about something possibly being suspicious with his license.

"Okay, Mr. Fuze, you just follow the red ropes until you get to the party. It's upstairs. Sorry about the hold up; you'd be surprised how often people try to schmooze into a party here, and you're not exactly..."

The large, well-spoken doorman realizes he's gone just a little too far. His friendly yet stern face now looks upset.

With both hands Chester tugs his shirt away from his chest and offers, "It's the shirt, right?"

The doorman cringes awaiting what will follow.

"It's my lucky purple shirt. I always wear it to parties."

The doorman's smile comes back slowly, "And a nice shade of purple it is, sir."

"Thank you," says Chester as he turns and follows the red rope that sags and rises between one post and the next.

The lobby is a large, spacious room with a high ceiling. The room is outlined with crown molding that is painted with the same fresh coat of white paint as the ceiling. The dark gray walls with gold decorations, wrought iron curtain rods with drapes a slightly darker color than the walls, large mirrors, black leather chairs encircling tall tables: these are the sights in the room to which he pays no attention.

He follows the red rope, his walk a hair away from a jog. Exiting the lobby, he passes rooms on both sides; each a different realm unto itself, a portal into a new environment, like a mixed up library shelf.

Left—leopard-skin couch; narrow room; grayish walls with orange upside-down-seashell-shaped lights; brown bar with an audience of bottles and a long mirror behind it; tall skinny chairs with leopard-print backs; and uncovered windows.

Right—a larger room vibrant in green—too bright to be natural, yet still soothing; tiny tables suitable for dining and U-shaped booths sit underneath large, dangly chandeliers that are equal crystal and transparent green: all of it seems to be sprouting from a gigantic fireplace at the back of the room with a large mixed fruit painting above it.

Another room looks like it fell out of a pre-World War II detective movie; tall half columns along the walls, a check-in desk with a long, skinny antique lamp that remains lit although the room is vacant; everything either black, white, or chrome; tall windows behind the desk bare and rounded at the top—must be the ones he saw while walking to the front door; small, white-clothed tables fill the room, each with a tiny unlit lamp on its center and adjoined by two chairs in tight cloth covers; and walls adorned with framed art deco prints.

Every room has textured walls, be it in the form of illusion in the wallpaper or actual depth in the paint; none of it looks less than palatial.

The red rope ahead of him turns toward a stairway, and his feet follow. As he moves along the staircase which is stained between black and the color of root beer with orange, sponge-painted walls, there is a bronze-framed mirror directly in front of him at the flat area where the stairs make their ninety degree turn. His eyes continue to pass by the lush surroundings without notice; he hungrily looks at the furthest point ahead of him, which is now the top of the stairs.

The sounds of pop music and loud, party conversation fall down the stairwell to his ears.

The dark collection of stairs leads the way to an open room with a slightly lower ceiling than that of the first floor. A sign just like the one downstairs sits in the opening of the room announcing the television show's exclusive party.

Stepping into the room, a long bar stretches from the corner at his right to two thirds of the way to the white brick wall at the far end of the room. The far wall has rectangular windows that stretch from the floor to the ceiling and offer a view of the blue outside lights bathing the gargantuan palm trees.

There's an empty stool at the end of the bar. The seat next to it is also vacant with a half-empty mixed drink, watery and forgotten, on the bar before it.

A part of him as thin as a shadow yearns for the empty stool; the feeling is far less powerful than it was before he punched a hole in time, but it still clings to him, etched into the skin at the back of his neck.

His eyes are on shimmering, flowing crimson breezes across the room, and it will take more than his worst inhibitions to hold him back now.

Surprisingly it is very much like he had imagined it to be, except the music is quieter. The first time around, he had convinced himself to miss the party because it would both give him time to go shopping for more professional clothing and allow him to avoid meeting his coworkers in an environment that would be most uncomfortable for him.

When he found out on his first day of work that Rhonda was there and he missed his chance to meet her, he nearly started weeping in front of the producers and other writers. When they said she left with some jerk who was drinking too much, he just put up a sad, awkward smile as his eyes watered up.

Now, it's odd to be inside an event that he's heard about and imagined in his head for years. Some things are as expected, but other details are different than his mental fabrication.

He makes his way through the room, looking at the thirsty patrons leaning on the bar resembling wolves suckling at their mother's body.

A shoulder bumps into him, "Hey, slick, watch where you're going."

Some of the intruder's double vodka Collins has spattered his purple shirt, but not enough to be very noticeable. The staggering spiller makes his way to the bar, eyeing the half-empty drink whose ice has mostly melted.

Chester's mind races.

Even from the back, Chester knows it's him. He's the one he's seen in many photographs with Rhonda. Chester can almost feel the man's domineering sneer emanating hostility around the side of his face all the way to the back of his head.

He turns his attention away from the lascivious splinter that will soon want to jab his lust into a place meant for more pure things, and Chester stares at the contents of his heart across the room, standing with only her agent and a group of nervous scribes glancing at her timidly every few moments from a table at a safe distance.

Harvey Price talks to her as he looks around the room. His speech involves harsh mouth movements that make her blink at their peaks.

As Chester approaches closer, the agent's words are finally audible to him, "…in this town."

He stops talking and looks at her with an accusing expression.

"Yes, Mr. Price, I understand that it's important to be social."

Her voice tingles the skin around Chester's ears. Were his eyes not focused on her face, he would've realized she is the only actress he's ever heard call her agent by anything other than his or her first name, and knowing her life history, maybe he'd be sad that any respect is being given to Harvey.

Her face beams in Chester's sight in a way that defies biology.

Her eyes catch him approaching. She smiles softly and then diverts her attention. But, he continues to look straight at her, which brings her gaze back to him. A second of awkwardness comes upon her; but a smile gets the better of her, and she watches him from beneath a lowered brow as he steps in front of her.

His voice startles himself as it hits the air, "Miss Romero, I saw your work on *The Arcade Life*. I'm a big fan."

Harvey's face is startled, and Rhonda holds back a blush.

"Well, aren't you sweet? That's very kind of you. Thank you. I wasn't sure if anyone watched that show before it got cancelled."

Harvey throws her a nasty look.

Chester says, "Yeah, I did catch it, and you were the best thing on it."

Her lips purse, but she looks to Harvey before making a response.

"Sir," says Chester extending his hand toward the agent, "I'm Chaz Fuze, a new writer on the show. I'd like to talk with Miss Romero privately. Would that be alright?"

Harvey shakes his hand and smiles broadly, "Absolutely, Chaz. That's what we're here for—err, to socialize and talk shop."

"Thank you," offers Chester as Harvey walks toward a young brunette at the bar who is having a hard time keeping her balance in heels.

"Well, Mr. Fuze, I have to say that you have made my night. I guess I'm supposed to act unaffected, but I've never been very good at these parties."

"That makes two of us."

"I'm sorry I didn't catch that."

"Oh, nothing; I'm just not too fond of these parties either. Writers at their table in the corner, getting drunk and arguing about etymology or some minutia of *Star Trek*."

She laughs.

"And, network executives talking loudly, telling jokes and slapping people on their backs at the punch line. Producers trying to be friendly with staff that they might have yelled at yesterday. Starlets trying to schmooze their way into their next role."

Her smile breaks down.

"Oh, Miss Romero, I didn't mean you. I was talking

more about tipsy over there," as he motions his head in the direction of the brunette who now has her arm around Harvey's waist as both a career and balance support.

Rhonda's smile is half the distance of returning fully.

"You're funny, Mr. Fuze."

"You can call me Chaz. Is it okay to call you Rhonda?"

"Only if I can call you Chester," smiling now.

"Chester, huh? Most people call me Chaz, but, yeah, you can call me Chester if you like." He struggles to keep his excitement from bursting forth and scaring her away.

"It's just," she wrinkles her nose, "different. Different and nice."

He smiles awkwardly, words evaporating in his brain, full of molten emotion at hearing her say his name.

She flings her hand out toward his shoulder, but not touching, which he appreciates more than contact, "O-o-o, I didn't say that well. It's a nice name, and I'm not fond of cutting nice names short."

"That sounds like a great reason to me, and I wasn't offended."

She snickers, "It's a good thing Mr. Price's over there by the bar; he'd've wanted to kill me for being so awkward."

"Oh, I wouldn't worry about him, Rhonda; he's no good for you anyway."

Raising a thin red eyebrow, like the top of a fiery question mark, "Now, what makes you say that?"

Scratching at his neck, "Well, you call him Mr. Price for starters. What does he call you?"

"Rhonda," she pauses, "Well, not all the time. Most of the time I'm 'darlin,' 'sweetheart,' or 'baby.'"

"Does that bother you?"

"No, I don't think it does. He...he doesn't mean anything by it; that's just how agents are. Hollywood's a weird place."

"Well, that's true."

"So, why is he bad for me? Mr. Fuze, you've captured my interest in this one."

"Mmmmm, he's not a nice guy. Working in Hollywood, you hear some things, and he's not a good person."

"Got me work; he got me on my first TV show. Got me in this party tonight."

"Yes, but that's not a reason to be rude to you."

Twisting her lips for a moment, "So, what makes you so convinced that he's bad for me? Didn't you say that you're a new writer?"

"Yeah, I am a new writer, but that's my job: I study people. Good writers study people around them for behaviors. You can't write a believable character without knowing how that character would act in real life."

"I see, and how do you think I would act?"

"You act a lot more polite than Mr. Price. I can already see that much."

"What else do you see, Chester?" she asks with a raise in both corners of her lips.

Pointing inconspicuously with his hand across his midsection, "See Harvey over there? He's picked out the most drunken girl at the bar to have a conversation with. She definitely doesn't work for the show; got to be an actress. And, low and behold; there's his business card. Mr. 'I can make your dreams come true' and an eager and hopeful girl are making a business transaction of sorts. There's nothing friendly about it."

He smiles as he looks back toward her, mildly amused at how fortuitous it was for Harvey to have taken out his business card in the middle of Chester's analysis of the situation. With her eyes growing soft, her face looks like she's been slapped.

"I'm sorry, Rhonda, did I say something wrong? Sometimes I get a little overzealous when I'm trying to be funny. Probably why the show hired me."

Releasing her lip, "That's not how I signed with him. I would…I would never…"

"Oh, oh, of course you wouldn't. Man, I'm an idiot. He would never behave like that with you because you have talent.

This girl is drunk at a party. He has no intention of representing her—he hasn't even seen any of her work. He just wants her to think he will. I mean I wouldn't trust him if I were you. I wouldn't put him past hitting on you, especially as beautiful as you are. I just know you wouldn't go for it."

She sniffles, and turns her face into a smile.

"What? What is it?" he asks.

"You said 'beautiful.' Most boys say 'pretty.'"

"Well, it's true. I hope I didn't make you feel uncomfortable."

"No, it's nice. It's nicer than the shorter version. Just like Chester."

He snickers. He knew she was smart, despite what all the rag grocery store newspapers would purport. He had seen her in interviews, and he felt the depth of the emotion in her movies. No one could be that convincing without understanding the situation of the scene fully: every motivation, the correlation to the other characters, how the person would be feeling. Her job isn't that much different than his.

He also saw her blush when he complimented her. He has always believed she was really shy and not stuck-up, and that others took advantage of her. He knew she wasn't easy, despite what everyone loved to believe.

Brutish movements stir at the bar.

The interloper who sprinkled Chester with his vodka earlier has now spilled the watery drink at the bar that he was sipping, and he asks the bartender loudly, "What're you looking at?"

The people in the immediate area turn their heads away from him at the question, pretending to find their original conversations, their drinks, or their shoes to be more interesting than his spill and shout.

Chester still watches him. He knows the man at the bar all too well, and tonight was the night the man met Rhonda the first time around. The trouble is stirring already, and he's barely spoken to her so far. He has to prevent the sloppy man from getting to her.

His whole trip pends on one conversation, and that does little to calm his nervousness that he so desperately doesn't want her to notice.

The drunk's eyes are on the redheaded bombshell. His brows are raised in appraisal. They dart to Chester, and then furrow with his lips sneering. They return to Rhonda, who looks away quickly.

"So," she asks, "what did you want to talk to me about?"

"Actually, I wanted to ask you out," knowing his time is growing short.

Surprise is followed by a smile, and then it turns to pain as a tray of fried chicken bumps her elbow.

"Excuse me, ma'am," says a woman of similar height, with her hair pulled back into a tight ponytail, wearing a waiter's formal black and white garb, complete with bowtie.

"Are you alright?" asks Chester.

"Yeah, I'll be fine," rubbing her elbow.

The server asks, "Would either of you care for some chicken?"

"Yes, I'd like to try a piece," answers Rhonda.

"Okay, I'll have one too," he says as he watches her daintily grab a leg.

Watching her lips as she takes a bite is something special for him. She's not overly cautious, but her natural grace has always been a point of interest. Without any conscious effort, her movements are mesmerizing. Perhaps that's why acting comes so easily to her.

Placing a hand over her mouth as she chews, "So, just where were you planning on taking me, Mr. Chester Fuze?"

"I don't know. I thought maybe we could go out back behind the dumpster."

She coughs.

He puts his hand up to her shoulder, "Rhonda, I'm sorry. I was just joking. I'm a comedy writer. When I'm nervous, I fall back on jokes."

Her coughing stops, and her face relaxes.

He continues, "Coffee would be nice, maybe a movie, a drink, whatever you feel like. Honestly, I'm sorry. That was a bad joke."

Removing her hand from her mouth, a slick smile takes shape, "So, Chester, what exactly is making you nervous? Do I make you nervous?"

"You always have," the words fly out of his mouth.

Confusion surfaces at her eyes and mouth.

His stomach sinks.

"What do you mean I always have? You just met me. What are you talking about?"

"I...I..."

"Are you one of those—what do you know about me? How could I have made you nervous before?"

The worry on her face hurts him more than the fear that he's ruined his own chance with her.

"I've always been in awe of you."

She stares, lips quivering.

"I told you I'm a big fan of your acting on *The Arcade Life*. Whenever you act, I'm mesmerized. I'm a little star-struck."

Eyes lock. Two yearning, two softening slightly.

"What do you know about me?"

His eyes fall toward his feet.

"Chester?"

He looks up. Her eyes grab hold of his. Their perfect green mesmerizes him.

"What do you know about me? Don't lie to me; tell me what you know."

He sighs, "I know you had a stalker arrested a few months ago. I know that this conversation must be scaring you because of it."

"Well, yes, it is a little scary," she leans forward closer to him, "But, what else do you know? I can tell you know something."

"I know the guy at the bar, the loud one, he's been staring at you. He's drunk, and he's violent, and he's going to hit on you before the night's over. No matter what, please don't go with him."

Feeling his ship is going down, his panic is for her.

She looks to the bar, and sees the man is indeed staring at her hungrily.

"What makes you so sure about him? He is looking at me, but how do you know? How do you know about Harvey? You seem like you could be very nice, but you're creeping me out. And, how do you know about the man I had arrested?"

"The guy at the bar's been staring at you all night. That's no secret. He's been daring anyone to get in his way; he's looking for a fight. He's already bumped into me once. Now that I'm talking to you, I'm sure I'm number one on his target list, and you're at the top of his…"

"Okay, you don't have to say it. What about the other stuff?"

"I buy groceries."

"What?"

"The stalker story was in the grocery tabloids. I read the headlines while I'm in line. Your story was on a day with a new cashier and a lot of price checks."

"Uh huh," she says with confliction.

"Harvey didn't look at you when he talked to you. It was like you were supposed to be watching and listening to his every word, but he couldn't be bothered with granting you his attention in return."

She chuckles awkwardly, "Every man I've ever known has talked to me like that."

"It doesn't have to be that way."

"Maybe."

"I'm not talking to you that way."

"No, you're not. Why aren't you?"

"Because, no one should be talked to that way. And…"

"And?"

"I think you're wonderful."

She smiles and looks to her heels, her expression as unsure as her mind.

"Hey, slick, are you bothering the lady?"

The voice cuts through Chester's eardrums.

He answers, "No, we were ju—"

"Looks to me like you are, slick. Whats about it, red, is he bothering you?"

She only looks up halfway and says, "Yes. Yes, he is."

"Well, you heards it, pal. It's time for yous to get it on outta here."

"I think I'll stay just the sa—"

"This ain'ts no committee, slick. Lady said go; times for you to go before you turns this fancy party into somethin' ugly."

A tender voice rises from Rhonda's lips, "No, I didn't say 'go.' And, he certainly does not have to go anywhere, Mister I-don't-even-know-your-name."

"It's Dane. Dane Fletcher," nodding his head confidently at her, "I host *Weird People Tricks* on the music channel."

"I quit watching that station when they stopped playing music," Rhonda replies.

Dane's face looks like an angered canine, but he strains to hold his temper in check as he knows it's too early to let her see it.

Chester chuckles at her response.

"You think something's funny, faggot? You wanna writes a little story 'bout it?"

"Hey, that's E-nough, Mr. Fletcher."

Dane turns his attention from Chester to Rhonda, as has most of the party at her raised voice.

"Now, Mr. Fuze belongs here. This is his show's party. We are guests. If we're not happy with the party, then we're the ones who need to leave. Not Mr. Fuze. And, I don't appreciate your language either."

His face is still gnarled up. He watches hers and realizes she is not backing down and that he doesn't have a verbal defense. Furthermore, this is no place for a physical persuasion.

"I'm sorry. Sometimes I forget that I'm in L.A., and there's certain words you can't use out here. I's just thought you might need someone to get you outta a bad conversation."

"Well, I do think I want to leave," she says looking between the two men in front of her and toward the bar. Harvey's hand is at the base of the brunette's back, and his lips are nearly touching her ear. He and Tipsy are the only two people at the bar not interested in what is going on between Rhonda and the two men.

Chester has never been a fighter. He's never been an active participant in any of the scuffles he has been in, but he'll fight for her. Dane's voice is biting and causes his heart to jump when he hears it, but he won't run from it.

"Will you bring me home?" she asks.

"Yes, I'll bring you home," offers Chester.

"Mr. Fuze, I wasn't talking to you."

His heart implodes.

"Mr. Fletcher, would you drive me home?"

"Sure, doll, I'll bring ya home," he says oozing machismo.

"Rhonda, please, take a cab…"

"Quiet, loser, she asked me."

She steps between them; Chester's thin fists are clenched.

She says, "Mr. Fletcher, would you wait for me by the door?"

He wants to say something else, but he forces his mouth to release, "Sure, babe, I'll be at the door. Don't take too long though."

He gives Chester one more threatening glance and turns his back as he struts unevenly to the door.

"Rhonda, please…"

"No, Chester, you listen to me. You seem like you might be a nice boy with a crush. I don't want anybody with a crush on me. I'm…I'm complicated. And, it isn't safe for me to be around anyone who knows too much about me. That man that was arrested was sick, Chester. And everyone said he was always a nice, quiet man. Until he was in my bushes with a camera and a knife. I can't have a crush. Even if it's a nice thing. And I can't be like her at the bar either. I can't go on any date with you hoping I'd get a job out of it. I can't be like that, and that's all it could be."

"But…"

"Now, I'm leaving, and don't you follow me."

"But, Rhonda…"

"Don't you follow me, Chaz."

His stomach convulses inward, and his throat expands as his breath no longer wants to be in his body. His head cocks downward. He sees that her dress is a deep blue that he's only viewed in velvet and in dreams. Until this second, he never took his eyes off her face.

CHAPTER 9

L eaves and earth crunch beneath his frantic trample
through the woods. His lungs strain to suck in the air
fast enough while his stomach muscles ache and cramp
with every stride. Legs grow heavier and feel more numb, but
his hate-fueled facial expression and down-pressing brow
refuse to allow his body to give in to capture.

To him, yanking his freedom back from those that have
taken it and getting away with it, not being captured, not being
wrong, are worth even dying while trying.

While Edmund has lifted weights during every trip to
the recreation yard including the week he had a dual bout with
bronchitis and tonsillitis, he's never jogged or run around the
yard's perimeter. He's always deemed it an inappropriate
activity for a leader; a capable leader shouldn't have to run or
rush. A leader's power should be evidenced in his security,
showing he can't be pushed, intimidated, or worried.

Speed is for those who lack the power to act at their
own discretion. Running is a useful ability for a stooge or a
hatchet man, not one with the power to command others and
make one's will a reality with no more cause, planning, or

provocation than a change in one's mood. Now, he doesn't question whether he was wrong; his body aches with it. His wrongness and his anger have always been in direct proportion to each other. And at the moment, both are increasing exponentially.

To the left something scurries through the bushes. Since it is heading in the opposite direction, he assumes it's not a police hound that has caught up to him.

He knows they can release dogs on an escaped convict and that it is the most effective way to run a prisoner down. That thought has been pricking the back of his head constantly, although he hasn't seen a single dog during his run. He saw the flickering of a flashlight coming from behind him a little over an hour ago; he knows the police are moving in on him— closer every minute.

He thought he might have heard barking just before he saw the straining end of the flashlight's beam, but with the pounding of his heart, the loudness of his breath, and the crunching of the ground beneath him, he wasn't sure of it.

Regardless of whether he heard the bark or if his mind was playing tricks on him, there should be loose dogs, and if there were loose dogs, they'd be upon him already. While he's thrilled that he doesn't have vicious canines ripping at his flesh as he struggles to sprint between the trees and the uneven terrain, something about their absence gnaws at him.

Birds shoot out of the branches just ahead of him into the pitch-dark sky. They start out in different directions but regroup to another tree a safer distance away.

His pounding breath and his bombastic heartbeat are the sounds that have taken over his senses, keeping him from paying any mind to how much noise his feet are making as they pummel and displace the foliage, twigs, and earth. The birds' sudden movement is a sure sign to a vigilant officer that the fleeing criminal is in their vicinity. Edmund tries to listen to his own ruckus as he weaves between trees and strains to land his feet steadily on uneven ground.

Significant noise is coming from his standard issue

shoes. So far, his biggest regret in his plan is not having demanded a pair of running shoes from Rutherford.

Disappearing into the wild was his plan from the beginning, believing that any motorized vehicle would likely be detected and caught through an eyewitness, an APB, a roadblock, or a checkpoint.

He had concluded that they'd expect him to escape by the highway, so he saw a hidden getaway route under the seclusion of the oak and cypress trees. He thought it would be slow going with agonizing hunger and fatigue, but he sure didn't envision a chase through the rough with law enforcement close on his trail. He thought he'd be undetected with the officers looking in all the most likely but wrong places. Now sprinting for his life in the dark wild, a lot of good his best planning has done for him.

They must have discovered Rutherford's body faster than Edmund imagined.

If he stops to rest, they'll catch up with him.

The other element he didn't anticipate was the strain on his ankles from the rugged terrain. But then again, he planned on a marathon-plus jog, not a breathless sprint. Two running shoes would certainly be invaluable now.

His feet still clomp harshly. Not only does he not have the time to slow his pace to keep his step quieter, but he doesn't have the energy to halt his feet from slamming to the ground. He barely has the strength to continuously pump them into the air.

While the sound of smashing the untrodden earth is spelling out his doom, trampling the untouched, unspoiled ground gives him a strange pleasure. The snap of his foot breaking a freshly fallen branch, the squish of soft foliage, and the crunch of dead, undisturbed, resting leaves stir up the perverse thrill of a deviant carving his jagged initials into a peaceful pattern of society.

A light swings in front of him, breaking the dark outline of the tree branches and the spaces between them. His ears had detected the intrusive buzzing of the whirling blades above, but his panic for escape did not let him internalize what it meant.

Now he can see the shape of the helicopter passing just ahead of him moving from his right toward his left. It moves slowly, scouring the area for any signs of him, the beam swinging steadily back and forth.

He knows he can't stop or the searchers will grab him from behind, and he can't plow straight ahead or the helicopter will spot him and keep that light on his moving body until someone brings him down. So, he runs at a hard diagonal mostly to his right while still keeping a forward direction, albeit a sideways one, trying to get to the area that the copter has already passed over.

Unfortunately for him, he knows if the copter is moving this slowly this close to the path that he was taking that they already have his position narrowed down and are inching their pincers closer to squeezing him.

Then it hits him. It hits him hard enough to slow his stride to a near stop.

They know where he's going.

The dogs. That's why there are no loose dogs; there are officers ahead of him as well as behind, moving toward him, trapping him in their closing net of trained men behind him, guns, helicopters, and unknown other devices. They won't let the dogs go after him with their own men just ahead of him in the same vicinity in the dark, dense woods. Potential for grabbing the wrong guy is too high. They must be leashed, tracking his scent and leading the mass of men to him.

Fierce snarling erupts somewhere behind him in the lightless wild.

The dark branches all appear to be limbs of the officers lunging out to stop him and send him back to the bars and bricks of his colorless nightmares of the past year and a quarter. His eyes strain to see anything, but his imagination makes out more shapes than his hindered vision. The nothing terrifies him, and he finally understands the lines:

"Darkness there and nothing more.

Deep into that darkness peering,
    long I stood there wondering, fearing,
Doubting, dreaming dreams
    no mortal ever dared to dream before;"

Those lines caused him to fail the first quarter of the eleventh grade, the last that he attended before dropping out and taking his core group of followers with him. Those lines had pushed him to break the windows out of his English teacher's car.

It wasn't over the failure, as he prided himself in his refusal to turn in the work demanded of him, but it was over the argument.

Edmund knew every word that his teacher had spouted about the poem's meaning; he just adamantly disagreed, not believing for a second that darkness could be scarier than something in the darkness. He argued the point for four straight days of class that solid darkness wasn't scary and no person, barring an idiot, would believe it. He didn't stop at a detention, an office referral, and a screaming disciplinarian, so he certainly continued his fight onto his test paper. When his failing grade meant he had lost his argument on the exam, he brought it to the teacher's windshield. He can still see the glass crack and run like a spider web. He broke the windows and the side mirrors too, but the windshield is the one for which he has reserved a special shelf in his memory. All of this flashes in little more than a second, flooding through his mind's pathways that are slick with fear.

Those same poetic lines still antagonize a grumbled response from Edmund, "Damned Poe."

As those two words stain the air around him that he desperately wanted to leave untouched, he pivots back in his original direction and sprints wilder and faster than before.

At least two dogs erupt with a volume that shoots a new wave of adrenaline through his body. Edmund runs as if he were on fire, feeling no more of the soreness or fatigue, filled entirely with burning distress.

"Ahead of us! Just ahead of us! Move, move, move!" screams a powerful and determined voice from the darkness behind Edmund.

Branches scratch and sting his face, arms, and chest as he plows into them, dragging their coarse bark and off-shooting limbs across his skin and thin shirt that offers little to no protection. He hears noises that are coming behind him, but he can't gauge from how far back they are originating.

Every sound to his frazzled mind either belongs to a gargantuan man in a uniform whose fingers are about to slam down on the back of his shoulders or to four paws tearing through the terrain bringing sharp, glistening teeth to his fleshy calves.

The urge to look over his shoulder is tremendous, but he knows it will slow him down. He forces his head straight, trying to see what is coming ahead of him in the dark undergrowth before it threatens to snag his feet. One fall could make his imaginings of what is making the sounds behind him become real and upon his back, and just one of the numerous elements of the undergrowth could send him flying to the ground.

Watching the high branches of the trees ahead of him, he doesn't see what he is looking for. He still has more distance to cover before the branches will thin out, revealing more of the night sky. His hope begins to slip away, and the embers of his enmity expand and fill the space it leaves.

"He's coming right at you guys. Head's up; he's coming right at you!" screams an out-of-breath voice behind him.

A muted and garbled response comes to the voice behind Edmund. Edmund knows they're very close to him if he can hear their communications. Animosity takes more space away from his faith in escape.

Suddenly he can see a twinkling between the high branches that he couldn't a few steps before. A little more sparkling dots emerge between the widening spaces of the ceiling of branches. The fabric of branches grows sparse, and he knows what he was hoping for is just ahead of him. Unfortunately, he is also aware there is a line of officers between him and what he's dying to reach.

Hope doesn't regain any territory inside him yet.

The bushes are rocked violently on both sides of Edmund. He immediately has visions of dogs. It could easily be that a nest of nutria rats has been startled by all of the foreign creatures approaching, and noisy ones at that. They're especially afraid of the dogs. It could be a lucky break if one of the dogs finds the furry rodent to be irresistible and ventures off Edmund's course to chase it.

An unseen voice to Edmund's left and behind him shouts, "Archibald, no! Leave it! Leave it!"

Perhaps it was a nutria or a rabbit that distracted the dog, but since the shouting has stopped, it didn't prove to be a long distraction.

Between the tree branches and through the thicket, he can see a barrel reflecting the moonlight. It is pointed almost straight up and slanted to the left, just peaking over the top of the levee. The officer must be standing sideways on the incline of the opposing side of the levee, looking in the direction of the dog's disturbance.

The ground rises under Edmund's feet, and the tension in his straining calf and thigh muscles is immense, but his pace doesn't slow. He can hear the bushes, leaves, and plants getting thrashed around behind him. He knows something is nearly upon him, and worse, the barrel turns in his direction. Edmund clenches his fists as they pump through the air.

Noises erupt again to his left, and the same voice calls out, "Dammit, Archibald, no! Leave it! Leave it, dammit!"

While remaining pointed at the sky, the barrel turns in the direction of the dog, its handler, and their combined ruckus. The top of the levee grows nearer, and Edmund can see the officer's head just on the other side. Barking intensifies from Archibald, which makes it hard to hear the escalated rustling in the bushes directly behind Edmund.

Reaching the top of the levee, Edmund tightens his calves and lunges at the officer on the other side. The policeman sees the soaring convict just as he lifts off the levee.

A blur of dog that is a large Belgian Malinois jumps off the top of the levee and pierces his sharp, white, shiny teeth into Edmund's calf, immediately twisting and yanking it to the side, trying to make Edmund fall over as the dog has been drilled to do countless times in years of training.

Edmund feels burning and ripping in his lower leg, but he keeps his focus on the target before him. The weight and force of the gnawing animal knock his body crooked as he falls downward at the uniformed man below who turns his barrel toward Edmund. The border of the officer's irises looks electric, horrified, and wild with the reflection of the diving man, the attacking dog, and a dangling leash in their centers.

The canine squirms in its tearing, jerking motion, swinging its body wildly around Edmund's leg. Edmund's left arm swats the barrel hard just before his body plows into the officer, sending the shotgun falling to the ground. The officer grabs the right arm of the human cannonball, and Edmund brings the knee of his free leg into the midsection of the policeman a fraction of a second before they crash into the ground. The officer's head, neck, and shoulders slam into the steep incline first, the dog's rear legs get caught between Edmund's left shin and the ground, and they all slide downward toward the muddy water below.

The slide down is a struggle of both the men trying to free their arms while fighting each other and the force that shoves them to the bottom of the levee.

The jaws of the dog release, and he is dragged another few feet before his legs become untangled from underneath Edmund. Immediately upon being free, the dog struggles to get on his feet and after the prisoner again.

A slew of sounds saturate Edmund's ears, and while none of it is distinct and clear, he is sure all of it is bad for him.

Their slide hits the bottom of the incline at the flat,

mushy land that leads to the river with Edmund still atop the officer, having ridden him down the levee like a sled. Edmund pushes his body off the officer. Once standing, he yanks the officer off the slushy ground.

As soon as Edmund pulls the officer to his feet, he releases one of his arms, bends the other behind his back, and puts him in a headlock. He has little more than squeezed the neck of his victim before the dog latches onto his calf again, this time on the other leg.

"Ahhh!" shoots out Edmund's mouth before he can even think about restraining himself.

He flings his leg back and forth trying to dislodge the seventy-three pound dog and having no luck. Teeth and determination sink into flesh that is three times its own size.

Flexing his bicep into the throat of his captive, he kicks the dog with his other leg, noticing the blood spots that have seeped through his pants.

The dog releases its grip, falls onto its haunches, and leaps right back at the meaty calf.

Holding back the wince that the pain in his leg demands, Edmund looks around the area. He sees officers approaching him from all sides except from the direction of the sibilant river current a few feet behind him.

Guns are drawn and pointed in his direction; trepidation abounds as the writhing dog has not taken the perpetrator down.

Edmund can see nine men approaching, and the sounds coming from over the levee warn that they are just the first of legion to raise their guns at him.

"Stay where you are!" screams Edmund, crouching down trying to hide his body behind the smaller officer.

Steps come slower but continue.

"Damnit, I said, 'Stay where you are!' Your man ain't breathin', and he ain't gonna breathe ever again if you don't stop where the hell you are!"

One of the officers in the front raises his left hand in the air, his right still holding his gun aimed at the bit of Edmund's face that is peaking out from behind the head of their captive associate. They put a moratorium on their pace, but they'd deeply rather bring death to the one that shouts at them from near the water's edge.

"Get this mutt off of me! Now!"

The uniformed man who had raised his hand in the air responds, "You release Henderson first, and we'll call off the dog."

"Henderson is gonna be dead in a few seconds—call off the damned dog now!"

One of the men in the distance calls out in a booming voice, "Kamo! Heel! Kamo! Heel!"

The dog's jaws open, and he instantly runs to the side of his master. Edmund's leg feels as if it will snap if he doesn't get off his feet.

The uniformed man speaks to Edmund again, "Alright, now you let go of Henderson."

Edmund stares over their ranks, carefully moving his face behind the head of the officer before him.

"Let him go, Convict Turley."

"I loosened my grip. He's breathing. That's enough for now."

"Don't be stupid; we've got you trapped. You have to turn yourself in."

"What if I do? How do I know I'm not going to get shot to pieces once I let Henderson here go?"

"You just have to trust us."

Laughing, "No, I don't think so. I'll let your man go as soon as you point your guns at the ground."

"We can't do that."

"If you're not going to shoot me, why not? You know I don't have a weapon. There're sure as hell a lot more of you than me," glancing around he sees more opposition running over the top of the levee, "Hey! You wanna tell these guys to hold the hell up?"

Man shouts, "Stay where you are! Do not move forward."

Edmund hears a squishing sound behind him. Immediately, he lets go of Henderson who drops to his knees and gasps, and turning around quickly, the convict has just enough time to plant his elbow in the face of an officer charging across the three feet between him and the river. As soon as the blow lands, Edmund drops to a crouch and lunges into the stunned officer, driving his shoulder into his midsection, and knocking them both into the water.

Crashing into the river of Twain that has been drowning both the foolish and the unfortunate for untold years, the thought that stays with Edmund's mind is that he didn't even hear the attacker coming, only hearing that one slushy step at the last moment. Anger shoots through him as he thinks that he was set up, made to stand there and jabber like a moron until the guy, who is now in his grasp, crept up along the water's edge and tried to apprehend him from behind.

The officer that he's brought underwater with him strains to swim to the top. Edmund must have knocked the wind out of him, might've made him swallow some water too. Quickly, Edmund climbs around the officer, putting the man between himself and the police on the riverbank.

With a tight bear hug around the midsection, Edmund squeezes the man with all his strength and pulls him backward and further into the river. Hitting deep water, his feet stagger back and forth not touching anything. Kicking with his legs, he pulls both himself and the man wrenched in his arms even deeper in the water.

The current pulls on both their bodies, stirring up only fear in one and both fear and the excitement of success in the other. Releasing one arm, Edmund grabs at the officer's belt until he finds his gun. Yanking the gun free, he kicks the officer in the back, sending him up toward the surface and in the direction of the shore.

As soon as the officer breaks through the water's surface into the night air, gunshots fire in a fury at the area of water just beyond him. To the firing officers on the shore, the water looks like a liquefied version of the blackness of the night sky, providing a remarkable reflection despite its color of a chocolate milk and motor oil mix, stars reflected only slightly less brightly than in the sky itself.

Their bullets blast into the liquid surface, creating an expanding ripple that blurs and warps the image of the reflected sky. The warping is a muddy brown shift similar to that of a red or blue shift that tints one's vision when approaching the speed of light. It all makes the universe seem vulnerable and all that we see uncertain. Although it's not a conscious thought, the police feel helpless as the dark water absorbs their assault; their best attack not able to do any more damage than a disrupted reflection.

Straining to swim both downward and along with the current, pistol grasped in his right hand, Edmund's thoughts grow weak with the sound of bullets firing in the air and breaking with a liquidy blip into the grainy water that pushes him away.

CHAPTER 10

He still feels like there is a hole in his chest. The rim of the imagined hole throbs in his real body. The sickness of it all.

Did she go home with Dane? Did he just bring her home and get her phone number?

Unlikely.

Did he hurt her?

Failure.

Utter failure sours Chester's mind and even the taste in his mouth. He hates himself for not following behind them, making sure that she arrived safely and that Dane did not harm her.

But, he was unwanted.

He would have had to become the stalker that she was afraid of in order to help her. Now that the uncertainty poisons him, he is angry that he didn't follow her anyway.

So what if she would've thought he was a psycho? If she truly needed help, she would not have cared from where it came. Maybe she would have always felt weird about him after that, but she would've been safe.

He's read numerous biographies on her life. They depicted the abuse she endured as a child and later in her married life, but none mentioned any abuse on the night that she met Dane. Maybe it never happened, or maybe it was just never reported.

One thing is for sure though: the night that they met didn't happen this way the first time around. Dane didn't have someone like Chester bringing his anger to a boil—there was no one opposing him for Rhonda's attention. There was no confrontation, nothing to get his temper stirring before meeting her.

He prays that it has not affected Rhonda for the worse.

Once again, he finds himself in the backseat of his car trying to sort his pain through the infiltrating rays of the morning sun. He has keys to his apartment that is vacant. He had rented it a month before he came to work on the show. It's now Sunday morning, and he didn't originally return to L.A. until late Sunday night for work on Monday. He could go and seek refuge there until evening when his counterpart of this time will be arriving, but the idea seems hopeless to him.

He's come all this way, and his own emotion for Rhonda, the fondness that fueled the trip, the one that pushed him to accomplish what no one has done before, has done him in. Honest words made him seem insincere. Passion pulls the impossible within reach, but too much pressure leaves passion's thumbprints, smudging the saintly scene and scaring away the object of affection, reminding the viewer he's only looking through a glass at a dream that he's never reached.

Breaking new ground the night before, Chester beat his social phobias; he overcame his nervousness. He walked right up to her and started the conversation. He made her laugh. She blushed and said he had made her night.

All of these things were beyond his reach during his normal life before the journey back in time. He had never been so forward, never dared to be so daring. So many obstacles were dealt with, and it was all spoiled by the love that made the whole trip possible. There is no sadder soul than one whose embrace has turned to a smother.

Although he's never felt that he truly belonged anywhere, he feels more lost now than anything he's experienced before. The days of the horrible face surgery being broadcast on the television came close. But then, he had the hope of the trip back to relive the life he should have had and to help her avoid the tragedy.

Now that that hope is lost, he feels he is too. The closest he ever felt to belonging anywhere were the few moments in which he conversed with Rhonda the night before. He did what he wanted to do, and it achieved the results he was hoping for, well, at least for a few minutes.

Besides that, the next closest experience was being in the writing room of the TV show, *Most Hipness*, with others who were similar to himself. He wasn't happy with his life or his decisions, but he was at least in a room with others who felt the same way.

He wonders how that first day of work will go now that he made it to the party. His past self is still driving the last leg of the trip to L.A. It will no doubt be a confusing first day tomorrow for his past self, when all the other writers saw him there talking to the stunning redhead that they were too intimidated to approach. And, they certainly all saw the awkward confrontation with Dane and that he took her home.

Chester had stumbled out of the party after less than two minutes of standing there where she left him.

As soon as he saw the head producer, Omar J. Sobelsk, the man who had hired him, walking toward him, Chester made a straight walk to the door. The writers never had much trouble poking fun at each other, so his past self is in for a heck of a confusing meeting on Monday morning.

Despite the uncomfortable first day of work, Chester would almost rather trade places with his old self. At least he'd have something to do; something to occupy. Even an awkward meeting would be a distraction from his failure. He ran the impossible marathon and fell down two yards from the finish. Thinking of anything, even something embarrassing and painful, would be a reprieve from staring at his colorless future.

A short while later.

He stares through a Plexiglas pane at a kitten in a wire mesh cage. The young cat that he watches simply sits at the back of her cage and stares at him. The two kittens in the adjoining cages both stare and whine at him with their paws pressed against the transparent pane. That's why he picked her in the first place.

He bought her after his first day of work in which he learned that he missed Rhonda at the party and that she left with Dane. That won't be until tomorrow, so he came to the mall pet store to visit his feline friend to soothe his female affliction.

The mall itself is gloriously less sophisticated. Stores in which teens can afford to shop, an arcade, black faux-marble floors: it all shines of years gone past—years in which a youth wasn't force-fed the raunchiest bits of adult culture. Were he not so lost, he'd breathe in the scent of an Orange Julius stand and revel in consumerism that was still an enjoyable, personal adventure, not the future experience of checking off social requirements that are grossly overpriced and not much fun.

The Riverview Mall back home was a prime example of the movement. There was a place for everybody then. Even him. The arcade and the video game store were escapes to new worlds in which he could be brave without real life consequences.

The bookstore was another home for him. The long, narrow shop with packed bookshelves reaching to the ten foot ceiling was another of his favorite hangouts. Whether it was reading Garfield, Faulkner, or a biography, there was always something for him to discover there.

In the time that he came from, the chain stores have smothered these bookstores, pulling their locations out of the high-rent malls and even further away from the droves of teens.

The Orange Julius disappeared to make room for a chain-restaurant food court, devoid of the local fried chicken place to which he was partial. The arcade was shut down due to a lack of profit and expensive upkeep.

Even the music store faded away as technology antiqued purchasing music. Something in the experience of being in the store amidst thousands of albums and glancing over the cover artwork lead to building one's own culture. That experience was soon annihilated by complicated strings of 1s and 0s flashing through stale file transfers.

The mall movie theater was another casualty of the two decades he's jumped. The close proximity of the theater being in the mall parking lot created a day of activities for the youth. Spending a day going on adventures in the arcade, discovering new songs in the music store, finding new worlds in the bookstore, and capping it off with a film provided a perfect youth activity, even sufficing for a decent early date.

Despite being pulled away into his own world for most of his life, while still in the future that he left, he did contemplate what scarce options the youth had for honest fun. He did pity them, realizing they were told what not to do, but the choices of what they could do had dwindled away: few to no affordable stores in the mall, no arcade, movie theaters in remote locations that charge four times the cost of admission from two decades before, and no miniature golf.

The saddest part of it all was most of the fun disappeared to turn a larger profit, which usually entailed selling the youth a more adult product. Adults can stay at home and do as they please; they don't need the mall as an escape. The youth have to go find their own way without a means to support an independent lifestyle or their own unsupervised place in which to do it. They seek places like the mall to call their own, so they're herded in, abused, and charged for the experience. Had Chester even dreamed of the confidence to run for public office, he'd start with the idea that the key to repairing a dangerous city is in its protection of its children and providing healthy activities for them.

When adolescents are fed material meant for discerning adults, development fails, and all else with it. His TV show scripts, regardless of whether people found them to be funny (which most did), irreverent, or in bad taste, were all positive in theme. Even when he was tearing down a silly adornment of society in a biting satire, he offered a better alternative.

His characters ultimately sought the right answer.

Being in this environment would have thrilled him five short days ago. Seeing a shopping center in a condition that is more suitable to the young at heart would have had him beaming with joy. Now as he is on one knee in front of a glass window smeared with small finger prints on one side and tiny cat hairs on the other, his chest seems hollow, and its inner walls feel like they're bleeding.

He wants to take the kitten home, call it by its name for the first time, and retreat to get a grasp on his situation. But, his home is not his home. It's the home of his former self, the him of this time, and that person must be already nearing the end of his cross country trek to Los Angeles. And, it's not exactly his cat either. Sure, he could buy it now, but his former self will need the support of an animal friend all the more after the first day of work tomorrow.

The head producer of the show, Omar J. Sobelsk, will likely be annoyed that Chester walked away from him without a word or acknowledgment before he left the party. Omar is a kind man, and he is also a genius in the field of television production and a hero to all of the writers on staff. In fact, his input created nearly all of Chester's favorite shows growing up. But as with many revered men, Omar doesn't appreciate being ignored, especially by someone he's just hired with no experience except a fantastic spec script.

The other writers will also not know what to make of him.

Although he and his past self look nearly identical in age, the past self is one of them, shy in demeanor and very intelligent, but his current self lunged into action in front of a whole group of people to talk to a starlet. He wasn't there long enough to have been drunk, at least not from the party's alcohol, and he left without talking to them and walking away from Omar, their mentor, without a word.

They'll be confused and feel the need to investigate as all intelligent people do, but they are comedy writers. They'll investigate with jokes and satire. It'll be a roast like that of old Hollywood, which will be uncomfortable even if it's an awkward but well-intentioned method of getting to know a new coworker.

He'd feel sorry for his past self if he didn't know he'd end up here as his present self, just as miserable. Thursday doesn't pity Monday when its weather turns out to be just as bad.

He stares at a twitching furry tail, but he thinks about the fabric of time.

Maybe he still can't make any major changes. He wonders if the newspaper picture was so insignificant that even though he was able to alter which person appeared in it, it made no impact on anyone's life in a significant or noticeable way. Maybe that change was allowed because it made no difference in people's life choices. The end result stayed the same no matter which woman was in the pic in the paper. No one died. No one committed a crime or hurt anyone over it. No one quit a job or married someone else.

Had last night been successful, Rhonda would not have gone off with Dane. Had they not started dating on that night, they were not likely to be at another party together. Dane's flash in the pan would quickly fade away, and his behavior would put him on do-not-invite lists very quickly. Had they missed each other last night, they would've probably never seen each other again, much less gotten married. Her tragic life would've been much different. Dane prevented her from taking romantic roles with popular leading men, not to mention the damage he inflicted on her frail self-esteem.

Her adult life was watched by millions, popularly for the first decade and snidely for the second. Had her life gone differently, it would have affected the lexicon of an entire generation. For some, it might have been one less fallen celebrity to make them believe that everyone's life is a wreck and that they needn't bother do anything to fix their own. For others, maybe it would have been one less example of the media and the public joining hands to ridicule someone's demise, to push a star deeper into the dirt than they find themselves currently wading, maybe even hoping to stand upon the famous and fallen skull trying to lift themselves a few more inches out of the filthy mire.

For himself, it might have been far more dramatic. Had she never married, it might have swollen his belief that they should be together to the point of bursting. Or had she married happily, it might have crushed his dreams of being with her altogether, pushing his life onto a completely different course. Were she ever truly happy in love, he would've never dreamed of intruding. He always wanted her to be happy more than anything else, even more than her being with him.

People have pondered the weight, influence, and responsibility of fame for all of civilization and before. But, until this very moment in a pet store, none have considered its hold on time itself.

The tail twitches.

CHAPTER 11

C hester wakes up in his dingy efficiency apartment. It looks much the same as when he rented it two weeks ago. He's added three extra locks to the door and two additional latches to the lone window.

A modest TV, that sits atop an ancient and nonworking console TV, which is bolted to the dresser top, along with new sheets are the only other alterations he's made to the room. Reruns of his favorite shows, nearly all of which haven't even aired in his current time period, consistently flicker on the new screen being fed from the device. Without the television's noise, he'd hear the interstate, which would only remind him that everyone else is racing to a destination and he has nowhere to go.

He has returned to the mall a few times, trying to distract himself with video games that he played years ago. Were she there with him, treading the old territory would have been a fun adventure—rediscovering old entertainments with the person he should've experienced them with the first time around. It would have been reminiscence reshaped into rapture, but it's only been a lonely figure pushing buttons in a dark room.

And sure enough, the kitten was gone when he returned on Tuesday morning. He had no doubt that it would happen as it had before he shot back in time, but it still made him sad. He even thought about going to his past self's apartment, since he still has a key, to visit his tiny friend while his counterpart would be away at work, but worrying that it was too dangerous to have a neighbor possibly notice there were two of him, he couldn't go.

His supply of canned soups, peanut butter crackers, cereal, and frozen dinners are running low along with the cash he's brought with him.

To get money he could use in the past, it had taken him quite a few trips to the bank and making purchases with cash at various places to obtain enough currency that would be dated before his journey. To accommodate any potential flaws in the timing of his trip, he only saved money that was at least five years older than his destination. That way if he arrived a few years earlier than he was aiming for, his money would not be a glaring sign that he was either a time traveler or a sloppy counterfeiter. Had he known that his venture through decades would place him on the exact date that he desired, he would have had a slightly easier time in collecting the older currency.

He had brought enough money to get to her and to maintain himself for a short while after, but he's had to stretch his funds to last this long.

The rent is paid by the week in this establishment, and his landlady doesn't seem to be much of a philanthropist. In fact, he had driven around for a day and a half, sleeping the first night in a motel, searching for an apartment that would prefer cash payments and have no background check. His background would come up clean. He is in fact Chester B. Fuse in name, appearance, fingerprints, and identification, and Chester B. Fuse's background is the boring and spotless type that landlords crave. But, he did not want a record of his name, license number, or any other identifier being on the lease.

Surely, someone would notice the existence of two Chesters, maybe the IRS, maybe Chester's credit report—he wasn't sure, but he didn't want to risk it.

He drove slowly through questionable neighborhoods until he saw her smoking a cigarette outside of her office at the front of her decrepit building. You pay in cash in advance, and that's exactly what he was searching for. And for that type of establishment, it's one of the best, although it is still terribly dismal.

His biggest discomfort is the bed that has to remain in the room. It's old, lumpy, and smells faintly of mildew and decades gone past, but its comfort and scent are not what trouble him. The sanitary issues are his concern. His first purchase for the room was the new sheets and pillowcases.

Had he more money, perhaps he'd buy some pillows, and he has thought about some type of mattress cover to ease his mind. He does spend a significant amount of time lying on it, mostly staring at the TV or the ceiling whose color has turned an unclean shade of brownish yellow.

His choice of dwelling came in handy when he realized his brake tag and license plate stickers were dated twenty years in the future. He scraped them off and quit driving the car until he noticed one of his neighbors who spent a lot of his days in the parking lot taking money from people and handing them a sealed tan envelope. His neighbor's customers occasionally pulled up in cars with no license plates at all and others would show up looking haggard and scared. Most of them seemed desperate.

For a few days, he watched the parking lot transactions through the ugly curtains of his only window. After an awkward conversation, the neighbor agreed that he could get Chester a license plate with valid stickers and a brake tag. The next evening both were delivered, and it took most of Chester's remaining money to pay for them—there was no neighbor discount.

Although it may be unethical, he'll have to go make some money. It's been in the back of his head since before leaving the future, but he's hoped another possibility would present itself. At least he'll be taking the money from people who deserve to lose it, regardless of how sad they may appear.

A few short hours later…

It's Sunday in the early fall, which made it much easier for him to find a venue. What first garnered his attention were the two ,gigantic letters of B and S standing tall on the building's squat roof. Then the high percentage of trucks and sports cars in the large, full parking lot strengthened the likelihood that he had found the right place. It was all settled as soon as he was close enough to read the smaller letters of the sign "Balls & Suds." He couldn't have imagined it much better.

As he opens the door, the rumble of television and loud conversation rolls over his eardrums in myriad sounds of manliness.

The many screens flash quickly from one promo to the next. Despite the style being a bit much for the level of substance, the patrons listen intently whenever a new piece of information is delivered.

The tapping of pool balls can be heard coming from a room to the left, whose only entrance is an open archway at the end of the long rectangular main room he has stepped into.

The serving bar itself is a smaller rectangle centered in the main room and framed in wooden trim. It is surrounded by a fence of loosely connected shoulders, nearly all donning the same two-colored shirts and jerseys, although the duo of colors alternates from being the main color to the trim color, either depicting the team away or at home.

While this isn't an environment that Chester has been inside very often, he knows he'll have to break through that fence of flesh if he has any hope of walking out of here with a pocket full of money. By glancing at the screen closest to him, he sees that he only has eight minutes and forty-three seconds to do so and then find the man that he's looking for, even though Chester doesn't know what he looks like yet.

Football is a sport that he's always enjoyed on the occasions when he's watched it with co-workers. Super Bowl parties have held his interest, and not just for the zany commercials and the plugs for lousy new shows that the network is praying people will watch. He does enjoy the game itself and the excitement of watching it with a group who are all united in rooting for the same team.

He has not enjoyed the few games he's watched with a split and bickering crowd. With the uniform sea of fabric pigment in front of him, he's sure they're a unified group. The device has informed him that the home team is a heavy underdog in today's contest, so the bar patrons are all bonded by a blind hope in the face of certain disappointment.

As he nears the bar, he doesn't see an open space.

Tapping one of the jersey-clad shoulders, he asks, "Excuse me, buddy, but can I get in front of you just to get a beer?"

The apprehension in the stranger's slightly swollen face quickly disintegrates to friendly, "Tell you what: you hold my spot while I hit the bathroom, and your beer's on my tab."

"Sounds like a deal," replies Chester.

The stranger pats him on the shoulder as he passes, and Chester sits down in the newly vacated stool. It's still warm, and for an illogical reason he feels uncomfortable sitting in it.

Despite the stool soaked in body heat, he focuses on his surroundings. Particularly, he's looking for money changing hands. Glancing around the room, he decides the action he's looking for is probably going down in the billiards room to the left. All he can see of it now through the opened archway is that there are several large televisions on the far wall. The angle is still too steep to see much else.

He keeps his glance away from the bartender, not wanting to explain that he's waiting on a guy he doesn't know to return from the bathroom to buy him a drink. He hasn't even found the dangerous part of the adventure yet, and it's already a strange day.

The bartender wears a shirt in the same colors as the rest of the patrons, but hers is tight, tied in the middle of her back, making it a half-shirt and exposing her abdomen. It helps keep her cool in the crowded, body-heat-filled-air, and it also multiplies her tip total for the day. Nothing opens sports fans' wallets easier than seeing a sexy version of their team's colors.

As Chester watches a barback tap the number of empty beer bottles that litter the bar's surface into a garbage can he slides along the employee side of the wooden alcoholic trough, Chester knows this is a heavy-drinking bar.

The potential for trouble is high, but he can't afford to run his plan too conservatively, not if he wants to eat, make rent, and put some space between him and the filth that lies just beneath a thin sheet while he sleeps.

So far, he's not afraid of the bulk of drinkers that surround him. He's never felt at ease in bars. Not being a drinker or an outgoing person, he's felt that he has no business there, but that was before the trip. Now he has to act differently. Even if he ends up at the same sad assisted living facility as when he left, he's vowed to take a different route, even a dangerous one.

This trip may be one of few ventures that he's taken from his motel-grade apartment, but today he'll do more than just watch reruns and spin his mind in introspection that scalds. He begins to wonder why his stomach hasn't responded to his current stress. Typically he'd be burning and nauseous, but he hasn't felt sick since leaving his apartment today. Before his thoughts race too far from the starting line, the hand returns to his shoulder.

"Well, alright, one beer coming up."

"Thanks," responds Chester.

"So, are you a Washington fan?"

"No, I'm a local."

"Good, I'd hate to be buying a beer for the enemy," turning to the bartender who bounces past, "Hey, Tracy, can you get me two more please, darlin'?"

She raises her hand and nods her head as her lips silently repeat the order she's just taken. Some fiddling at the register, a ding that can't be heard over the noise of the televisions, and some scribbling on an order ticket that hangs on a magnetic clip to a square beam that runs from the island to the ceiling behind the register: then she pulls the two beers out of the iced bin and hands them to the stranger before she starts making the shots from the order before.

"Here you go, pal. Thanks for watching my spot," says the stranger with the grateful bladder.

"No problem; thanks for the beer."

After letting a quiet burp out the side of his mouth, he asks, "What's your name anyway?"

"Chester. Uh, most people call me Chaz. What's yours?"

"Lucky. Everybody calls me Lucky. So, Chaz, do you think our boys will pull this one out today?"

"I think they'll at least keep it close enough so Washington won't cover the spread."

"You're a betting man, Chaz?"

"Just getting started with it actually."

Laughs, "Well, it won't take long for you to get hooked—makes games more exciting. Sometimes even more depressing. It comes on like a fever."

"I'm not quite there yet," leaning in quietly, "Is there any action in this place?"

Nodding his head toward the opening of the billiards room, "Yeah, it's big business in there," looking toward their nearest bartender, who is several stools' distance away from him, "I'm pretty sure the owner knows 'bout it, but I keep quiet 'round the bartenders anyway."

Chester nods and puts the bottle to his mouth, pretending to drink as the frothy liquid sloshes to the rim and over his closed lips.

"So, Chaz, are you going to put down some cash on the game? It's startin' in just a few minutes."

"Yeah, I think I might," he says trying to be nonchalant.

"Look, there's this guy Manny in the next room; he's the bookie. My wife should be walking in the door any second with her sister who wanted to be all dolled-up to come here today. I left them 'cause I couldn't wait no longer—like to be here for the pregame and da wife won't know how many I've drank before she gets here."

"Uh-huh."

"Look, she don't like me bettin' no more since I lost our vacation money last year during the playoffs. But I know we're gonna win today. Gotta support the home team and all—gotta believe."

"Yeah."

"So, will you place a fifty for me against the spread?" his fingers fumbling in his worn faux brown leather wallet without looking for a reaction from Chester.

"Alright," responds Chester, and the stranger stuffs some unevenly folded bills in his hand, a random bit of paper falling out of Lucky's wallet to the ground.

"My wife'll be here any second unless her sister decides to change her clothes again," head shakes and eyes roll, "So if she's here when you come back with the stub, don't let her see it, but hand it to me when she's not looking, or better than that wait for them to head to the bathroom—that won't take them very long."

"Alright, what's Manny look like?"

Laughs, "He looks like what you'd expect. He'll be the tallest guy in the room with a pen hanging on his shirt. Can't miss him."

A little disappointed that Lucky didn't offer to bring him to Manny, "Okay, I better get to it."

"Yep," says the man on the stool and adds as Chester is turning away, "and make sure he gives you bettin' stubs."

Chester nods as he takes his first step in weaving through the dense crowd, most of whom seem to be misted with thin pockets of perspiration. The room is warm, but it doesn't seem to be bothering Chester in the same way. He's also not drinking.

As he sidesteps moving bodies, tables, and chairs, the smell of burgers, frying grease, and sizzling chicken fingers infiltrates his nostrils. The combined scent is intoxicating, yet he doesn't feel hungry. In fact, he hasn't truly felt hungry since traveling back to the schoolyard of his youth some two weeks ago. He's eaten periodically because he knew that he should whenever he's realized it has been a long interval since his last meal; it's never occurred out of necessity. Although after eating, he always feels relieved, and his spirits lift a little.

When he has eaten, it hasn't been much, not even for him, so hunger should be a relentless inner predator, but it hasn't been on his trail as if it couldn't follow him to the past. This thought and several others have plagued his mind over the illogical aspects of his tear through time. The only conclusion he's come to is that he doesn't really want to taste anything anymore.

But for now, he doesn't have long to think it over since he can now see the length of the hidden billiards room as he passes through its doorway.

The clacking of the billiard balls is the only sound to rise above the bombastic televisions and the murmur of conversation. Glancing around the room, Chester sees that Lucky's simple description is indeed adequate. Leaning against a small table with two stools, one containing a young brunette with tattoos running down to her elbows like sleeves, daintily drawn skin doilies, is a man who is easily the tallest in the room, and a pen is verily clipped to his sleeveless wife-beater t-shirt.

Chester's heart rate is steady as he dodges pool sharks and guppies who are far more focused on their games and wagers than anyone trying to pass through their bent over bodies and pool sticks in motion like branches in an animate forest of green felt, pools of barley, the frost of powder, trees with four legs and stained wood, blue square acorns used to prepare the tips of the branches, and the wildlife of the competitors.

Manny, leaning on a small table which is pushed into a groove in the wall under his weight, has long, slender arms that are folded across his chest. Other than his height and the pen, his appearance is indistinguishable from the other people in the room.

His behavior is the only other giveaway to his occupation. Everyone else either watches one of the TVs or the pool game in which they are already involved or are waiting to play the winner. Manny watches neither TV nor the tables but stares at the members of the room, routinely glancing at the entrance for any sign of trouble. Sleek, long-limbed, and on alert, he might as well be the panther of their noisy forest.

"Are you Manny?"

Narrowly opened eyes that appear faded and drained of energy look Chester over.

A calm, deep voice responds, "Are you a cop? 'Cause you have to tell me."

Research during Chester's years as a television writer have taught him that Manny's statement is entirely untrue, a common misconception readily believed by those who desperately want its protection yet are too afraid to investigate its validity.

Chester has always been fascinated with people who convince themselves that something is true by repeating it as often as they can, spreading the story to everyone they know, as if an urban legend holds any more truth than the most ridiculous lie told by an idiot.

Chester has been equally baffled at their faith in their own invention and oddly jealous of their blind assurance that they are safe and what they're doing is not illegal, or in the least that they won't get caught. Their belief in their own fabrication actually relaxes them, as evidenced in Manny's complete assuredness.

Unlike them and unable to fool himself into believing some made-up logic, Chester has no illusions that what he is about to do is illegal, if not altogether wrong.

"No, I'm not a cop; I'm Chest—Chaz, and I'm a friend

of Lucky's. I've got bets for both of us."

"I didn't know Lucky's wife let him have friends," silent chuckle from six inches above Chester's head, "I know she won't let him bet no more. Took him this long to figure out to get someone else to do it for him," shakes head, "So whaddayou want: Washington game or a pick sheet for the whole day? We only got a few minutes before I'm locking it down for the day."

"Just Washington. I don't think they'll make the spread. What are the odds?"

"Twelve to ten with a minus seven-point Washington spread."

"What if we make the spread negative seven home team?"

"You're nuts."

"Well then, if I'm nuts, you can take my five hundred bucks on it—but I want two to one odds."

"*Two to one?*" grinning and turning his eyes away from Chester, "No, I don't think so, jack," followed by more awkward chuckling.

"Well, how good are your spread numbers then?"

"Vegas good—they're gold," he snaps with a strong accent on the v in Vegas and the g in gold, folding and flexing his skinny but defined arms as his face turns taut and alive with tense eyes.

"Then it should be nearly impossible for me to win. What are the chances of Vegas being off by fourteen points?"

"Could happen."

"But how often? When was the last time you saw it happen?"

Raising his lanky fingers to his chin, "How much you wanna bet?"

"Five hundred for me, fifty for Lucky."

"Lucky's in on these crazy odds too?"

"Sure, it's his idea."

Manny smiles before he can restrain it, "Awright, I'll make an exception; don't tell nobody—I don't like doing stuff like this."

"So, two to one? Fifteen hundred for me and one hundred fifty for Lucky if Washington loses by seven?"

"Yeah."

"Ok."

Chester hands over the money.

Manny counts it twice, hands it to the young woman behind him, and says, "Awright, we're set."

"Stubs? Lucky said to get stubs."

Manny stares, popping his jaw back and forth making clicking noises, and exhales slowly.

He yanks the pen from his shirt, turns, and starts scribbling on a little white pad. Stops. Tears. Writes a second one. Grabbing them both between giant fingers, he holds them a half an arm's length from Chester's face. Chester takes them and looks them over. The writing is crude; an awkward mix of print and script, but it conveys the terms of the bet accurately.

"Thanks," says Chester without taking his eyes off the stubs.

Manny nods his head and then glances around the room to see if anyone has watched the last transaction closely.

She enters the bar like a blue bird flitting closely over a swine pen. Her cobalt heels step along the grimy floor that was clean three hours ago but now hosts dirt, peeled-off bottle labels, and beer spills.

She follows her sister, a slightly older bird whose feathers are not as bright and whose form is not as rigid, yet she still resembles her flashier sibling in heels.

The heeled one tries not to touch anything as they make their way toward the liquid trough inside the fence of shoulders, pulling her head back to avoid a passerby from accidentally pressing on her shiny hazel hair.

Her fingers occasionally gently tap someone blocking

her path. The reaction is invariable: both male hands move up to his shoulders, one holding a bottle with a thumb and two fingers, and a bawdy smile creeps over his face as her colorful shape walks closely past his lower body. It's a raunchy invitation, a lascivious gesture that is permitted under the excuse of manners with his surrendered yet imagining hands at his shoulders.

She knows enough to know the movement and the appraising thoughts behind it, and despite the mild flattery involved, she knows that no one who behaves in such a way is what she's looking for. Not anymore. She also knows that gesture will never be reserved for just one woman either.

As they near the bar, Lucky smiles but says, "Here comes the fashion parade."

His wife's eyes narrow, and her lips push together tightly as she studies his reaction to her arrival. Her current expression is her standard method of bracing herself for his opening line. It's sheltered her from much, hardening her in the process. But on occasions when he had no intention of mocking her, it's been a false accuser that offends him and brings on the snarky comments from which she was trying to protect herself.

As Lucky touches her elbow with his right hand, she bites her lip and her toes squirm in her worn, old cowboy boots that are mostly covered by her jeans. Her eyes look down, away from her styled hair that hangs slightly in her face. She sees her sister's blue heels not far away. Although she feels trepid about what's going to happen above, she feels sad about the difference in the shoes. Not jealousy, but a hurt that echoes in her empty cavern of confidence.

"Chaz, this is my wife Cindy, and next to her is my sister-in-law, Janet Shrew."

Cindy stops biting her lip and looks up, but her toes are still tense. Lucky leans in and kisses her cheek. Toes relax, and she smiles a blushed smile.

Extending a curved hand and a flash of white teeth that are mostly straight toward Chester, Janet says, "Shrew was my married name; I'm divorced."

"Okay," responds Chester, catching his awkwardness, "nice to meet you."

Cindy says much louder than her sister's speech, "So, where do you boys know each other from?"

Monotone, Lucky explains, "We met in jail when I got arrested for that bar fight at Malcolm's bachelor party."

Both women cringe at that sentence: Cindy at the word jail, and Janet at Malcolm. Lucky returns Cindy's angered stare for about seven seconds.

Chester is relieved that neither of the women are looking at him.

"For God's sakes, Cindy, we just met at the bar. We've been talking during the pregame show."

"Lucky him," she says, not letting on how grateful she feels that his original explanation is not true.

Now, Lucky's stare resembles the bitten-lip look Cindy had when she first approached.

Breaking the exchange, Janet asks, "So, Chaz, what do you do?"

Having planned on keeping to himself for most of this gambling expedition, he did not plan any backstory for himself, which is something he would have certainly done for any character with dialog in one of his scripts. He was always known for overwriting material that could never be used in the show. Sometimes it would be outrageous jokes that would never air but would entertain the other writers in the room.

He feels odd having not put nearly as much thought into the character that he's playing at the moment, for it would be unwise to act as himself, Chester Fuze, who has traveled here from the future or even Chester Fuze of the present, TV writer and moderate social leper.

"I'm a technical writer. Pretty boring stuff."

Her brow crinkles beneath her soft brown hair, "What exactly does a technical writer do?"

"Basically we write instruction manuals, how-to guides, but a lot of it is taking laboratory findings and data and putting it into sentences and terms that other people can understand."

Seeing that she hasn't entirely figured out how his job may be useful, he continues, "We take what the scientists find in the lab, and we phrase it in ways that the people who are paying for the experiments—the CEOs, the shareholders, the owners can understand. Scientists have a hard time explaining their discoveries in simple terms, especially in terms of dollars and cents, which is really all the bigwigs care about anyway."

She nods her head.

"And, the instructions are the same thing. Someone has to take what the engineers or designers say and put it in terms that the average person can understand. It's kind of translating science talk into standard English."

"Oh," she says, her face looking a bit more unburdened.

Lucky says loudly, "See, Cindy, Chaz's a smart guy, and he bet on the game today."

Cindy pulls away from his hand on her elbow and stares at him intensely, "Lucky, did you bet on this game today? Is that why you came here while we were still getting ready?"

Holding both of his hands up, one still clutching a beer, as if he's a defendant on trial swearing on his bottle to tell the truth, "So help me, wife of mine, I have not stepped one foot into that room next door."

"Manny hasn't come out here to get your bet either?"

"Does Manny ever come out of that room? I've never even seen him come out to piss."

She stares at him, her eyes unrelenting.

"No, I haven't seen Manny out here; I have *not* talked to him at all today, and I didn't give Manny any money either."

Her head nods, and the intensity subsides.

"You need to relax, woman," he adds, accenting the last word by following it with a quick swig from his bottle.

"I'll relax when we're on vacation this year. Does that sound like a good idea to you?"

Lucky takes another sip of his drink. The crowd makes a loud noise. He instinctively looks to the television, and the other three follow his movement.

Washington is running the ball past the 25 yard line—a missed tackle; past the 30—breaks through 2 more tackles; the 35—blocks clear his way; the 40—a fast hip movement dodges hands that barely slide over his pivoting waist; the 45—clear sailing; the 50—imposing defenders sprint, driving him toward the out of bounds line; the 47—the kicker finally pushes the kickoff returner out of bounds.

With a face like someone has insulted his manhood, Lucky looks to Cindy, "See what you made me do—made me miss the damn kick-off. All I got to see was Washington running all over us. Always nagging me—see what it gets me?"

Chester leans in close, "It's a long game, Lucky. Lots of time for things to change. Trust me."

A few grumpy moments later, Washington connects with a pass on the premiere offensive play for a first down in the initial three seconds of the game. Lucky is so beside himself he won't look at any of them or anything else but the screen on which he gazes with a hot, furrowed brow and a gnarled mouth.

Janet and Chester exchange nervous smiles in an attempt to freshen the scent of the rotting tension.

The next play is a handoff to the running back for a gain of nine. The second offensive play of the game is one yard away from being the second first down, and there has been no pressure on the quarterback at all.

However, the pressure throbs at the base of Lucky's neck. Chester feels no tension about the game, but he's concerned that his betting partner might lose his temper before the contest improves. The bottle in Lucky's strained right hand looks as though it could burst from his squeezing.

The third play, the quarterback jogs back a few steps and hands the ball off again. Washington's running back takes three steps and is confronted by a lineman who has broken through their defense. While running toward the sidelines looking for an opening, the running back turns away from his meaty adversary, keeping the ball away from his outstretched hands. The running back doesn't see the other lineman coming at him from the opposite direction. The ball is stripped from him by two giant paws, and the home team's lineman takes off toward the end zone, running in the same fashion as an excited three-year-old.

Choppy, uneven movements propel him down the open field, invading Washington territory, nothing between him and six points but an open sea of green and a voice in his head saying that he's too slow and someone will catch him. He sees his team's colors on both sides just behind him.

He can hear a collision on his right. His heart races faster; his feet smack the ground harder. His vision begins to bounce as his breaths come harder and less recuperative. He can see it like a seaman can see the shore after crossing a tempestuous ocean. The end zone even looks to be softer than all the turf that he's traversed so far.

He hears one more collision, which is his other teammate falling down from exhaustion beside him.

He's all alone.

His chest betrays him as it convulses, straining for air and commanding an end to his unusual run. He falls forward; he can see the goal. He outstretches his heavy arms as he crashes to the ground. His forearms hit the grass followed by his knees, and the ball is completely across the white end zone line.

As soon as he can breathe, he smiles inside his helmet. He soon feels hands slapping his back with enough force to sting, but he cares not. With their unsolicited help, he gets to his feet, does a strange dance involving swiveling knees, and the crowd cheers. He throws the ball into the screaming mass of people, attempts a cartwheel, and falls over halfway through. He'll be fined for throwing the ball, but he doesn't care. He knows well that this may never happen again, especially not against the best team in the league.

As the player's teammates yank him up from his crashed cartwheel on the television screen, Chester's attention is diverted by Lucky hugging him sideways, with the time traveler's shoulder pressed into the man's beefy but soft chest.

"Woo-hoo! Hooo-ooo!" Lucky screams, his beer bottle toppled sideways and gushing out sudsy celebration onto the bar.

He jumps around giving his sister-in-law a high five and a hug, and his wife a firm kiss on the lips and a pat on her buttocks. Part of Cindy wants to scold him for the pat, but she can't bring herself to ruin the moment of happiness or the enjoyment of his public kiss. However, she does return the gesture a little harder than she received it.

Janet holds her hand up to Chester. He gives her a five, and she slides her fingers between his and squeezes, holding it for a moment before letting go.

Lucky leans in toward Chester, "You're right, Chaz; this one's a long way from being over! I believe you."

"So, if you dislike Shrew so much, why haven't you changed your last name back to your maiden name?" asks Chester before taking a sip of his soft drink, talking about something that holds his interest for the first time since he was with Rhonda at the party.

"My maiden name is Glasscock."

Gushing and burning its way up the back of Chester's nose is the cola that he has just sipped.

The petite brunette laughs and smacks his shoulder, "You making fun of my daddy's name?"

He shakes his head in negation, the nasal fizzing still a bit too distracting to allow talking.

Smacking his shoulder again, "Just messin' witchya, Chaz! My maiden name's Morton."

Chester laughs.

"Shrew should have been a sign to all women everywhere to never marry that man. I never changed it because I want to remember how much I hate it and make sure I don't end up with another dummy. I ain't changing it till I get married again; this time for good."

"Sounds like a good plan."

"Think so?" she poses, starting to blush.

A little confused at the rising of blood to her cheeks, he says unevenly, "Yeah, sure."

Janet leans in close to Cindy's ear and whispers something. They head off to the restroom which is to the right of the bar.

"Told you they'd be in there for most of the day," says Lucky with an unintentional snort.

"Yep," says Chester, not particularly thrilled with the prospect of conversing with Lucky, who has consumed four more beers during the first two quarters, alone for the duration of half time.

"I'm gonna pay you, but I'm gonna pay you for the spread—not that side bet that you were talking about," Manny explains.

"No, it's the side bet that we agreed upon," words flying out of Chester faster than he's used to.

"Well, it's too weird—too crazy to have worked out like that. That's why I don't like taking those kinda bets," spouts Manny.

"But you did take this one—already happened. A little late to back out now."

A voice inside Chester screams for him to take the spread money and to not worry about making two to one since regular payout would cover his bills for another week or so, but there's something new inside of him that keeps the voice quiet and allows him to breathe nearly normally while cruising into the red zone.

Lucky's rough voice booms, "I lost more'n five

thousand bucks to ya last playoffs. Remember that?" stepping his voice up louder with each subsequent word, "I think you're gonna pay me and my friend all the money ya owe us."

Pool sticks hang in the air or serve as leaning staffs to everyone in the room. The ceasing of clacking balls wails trouble more powerfully than a blaring alarm.

Lucky feels the tension and its power over the room, and he continues, more boisterous than before, "Unless you're gonna back out on your bet. We got our stubs right here."

The tiny betting stubs with Manny's childlike scribbling on them are clenched in and sticking out of the top of Lucky's fist, a pair of daring accusations of dishonor, writs of distrust, declarations that their issuer renders a sham business; one stub horribly crumpled and one as straight as a torn stub can be.

Manny looks around the room, and people don't take their gazes away from him as they usually do. Their eyes pulse as do their chests as they think of their own little folded-over rectangles in their pockets. For a moment, the eyes of the tall man dart from one spot in the room to another, and his mouth snarls up in one corner, drops back down to a frown, and finally lurches into a forced smile that has little verisimilitude.

Long, thin lips break, "'Course I'm gonna cover ya bets, but I don't take these crazy deals no more," he pauses waiting for the room to respond, which remains silent, "Never."

Lucky smiles, "You're a good man, Manny; that's what I thought. Knew you'd stick to your word."

Most of the breathing in the room regains a natural rhythm, and as they see Manny reaching for his back left pocket they slowly return their attention to table-top geometry, chalky felt, and bottled spirits. Had he reached underneath his shirt at the small of his back, they all would have dived to the floor.

Chester, who has no knowledge of the tall man's habits, watches the emaciated, giant hand intently. Its five bony digits remind him of Charon, the ferryman of Hades, and he waits to see if he'll be granted permission to cross Acheron or drown in its current trying to traverse it.

Nearly five minutes later, following a final restroom stop of the two ladies, they are outside, and Chester feels the wad of money in his pocket. It feels all the better knowing it's the full amount he bargained for. Getting what was just from a challenging person is not something that he's used to. The feeling is but a thousandth of what he felt when Rhonda first smiled at him at the party, but it is something more than what he's experienced in the past few weeks and for most of his life before traveling back here.

"See ya next week, Chaz?" Lucky asks.

"Well, I don't know about Manny. Do you know any other bars to bet at?"

Smiling the smile of one who's greatest talent has been stumbled upon by another, "With a name like Lucky? I know all of them."

"Your name is Lester. If you were lucky, we'd have gone to Hawaii last year," shoots his wife.

"And we—if you—if you'd stop nag—nagging me, I'd still have all my hair."

One pair of female eyes rolls and quivers, but the other pair twinkles as their owner coos, "Bye, Chaz!" while waiving her arm as if painting the air.

If his love were not already molded in the shape of a redhead who has told him not to follow her, he might be tempted to see if his affection could match the twinkling brunette's form, but he's still holding the shape of Rhonda in his heart.

He smiles, nods his head, and makes his way toward the rear of the parking lot and his car.

As he walks he thinks over the exchange between Lucky and Cindy when he told her that he had indeed bet on the game and won one hundred and fifty dollars. Although

Chester knew that Lucky had technically only profited one hundred dollars since he had put up fifty for the bet, he kept his mouth quiet and his senses alert to their interaction.

Cindy's eyes welled up as though she would cry, and she raised her hand to smack his shoulder. But she ended up shaking her head and saying, "Damn it, Lucky. When's it going to be enough for you?"

He said, "Baby, we won. A hundred and fifty bucks! Chaz here told me it was a sure thing, and, damn it, he was dead on."

That was a cue for Janet to grab Chester's arm tightly and press her face against his shoulder. This made Cindy's face lighten.

Chester was expecting more of a scene. He had actually expected Lucky to concoct a plan worthy of Fred Flintstone to collect the money without the girls noticing at all. He certainly wasn't expecting Cindy to get over it so quickly. Chester reasons that her reluctant acceptance of Lucky's vices is why they are still married.

Before his jaunt through time, he would never have parked his Chevelle amidst the vehicles in a crowded bar parking lot, especially during a sporting event. Today he hasn't thought about any possible damage to the car. He doesn't even make his habitual walk completely around the vehicle before getting in and backing out of the space.

A half smile surfaces when he realizes he has money to get his pillows and a mattress cover.

He turns left on the street out of the parking lot and navigates toward the mall. The trip to the shopping center is a familiar series of turns that requires little of his attention, and his thoughts roam along the events at the bar.

At least once a minute, his mind steers him off course to focus on green luminance flickering beneath waves of flowing red. He derails his serotonin surge from her image and aims it back at his hours in the sports bar and the lump of cash in his pocket. He'd still rather think of her, but he has to make it through his mall shopping in order to sleep easier tonight.

There'll be ample sleepless time to think of her then.

He comes to a stop at the last light before the entrance to the mall. He sees an odd-looking dog on the end of a multi-pointed leash walking up the sidewalk in his passenger mirror. The owner's pants shift on the skinny legs beneath as he walks behind the tethered animal.

A memory comes into focus.

The leash.

It's not a dog at all.

It's a cat. His cat.

He knows he should look away immediately, speed through the red light, and uphold the safety of mankind, but he can't look away.

He has to see.

A cat it is for sure; its features clear now—its walk unmistakable. He's watching the ill-fated cat leash adventure that he embarked upon two decades prior. Scratches, hisses, rah-ow-ooos, unplanned stops, obscure obstacles, and cat limbs adamantly wrapped around the blue straps of the leash are all that his efforts had warranted him. A memory rushes through his mind of the cat hugging the right side of the sidewalk and cowering as each car passed.

Chester sees his past self staring at the blue Chevelle. He hates the idea of what he's about to do, but he doesn't see another alternative.

As the man and the feline approach his side mirror, Chester revs his engine. The furry one lunges to the far side of the sidewalk, and the owner grasps the leash tightly. The kitten rolls onto her back off the sidewalk and onto the grass, fastening her limbs around the leash.

Chester glances at the light—still red. Cars from the left side of the intersection start turning. He knows his side of the traffic signal should be next, hoping the disturbance with the cat will distract his counterpart long enough for him to escape without being seen.

With irritation that can only come from an hour-long failed training endeavor with a pet in early autumn heat, his past self ignores the feline knotting itself up in its leash and looks to the loud car that has scared the animal. His eyes lust over the vehicle, an exact embodiment of the one in his dreams, and he slowly drags his gaze over it to the rude engine-revver in the driver's seat of the classic car.

Eyes lock.

Chester can't pry his vision away from his past self, completely fixed on him. It's as if he's watching his own mirror reflection move independently of himself, disobedient, sentient, beyond reason, and peering into him.

Chester stares at the look that he's only seen from the inside his whole life. He is as mesmerized and shocked as someone first hearing a recording of one's own voice. It's the look that comes over him when he feels the most alone, the most hopeless. It's the look that consumed him when he was institutionalized, and it now consumes his counterpart. Light turns green, and while he pulls away, he watches his side mirror as raised and curved astonishment on his past self's face slide into an angry downward brow.

CHAPTER 12

E lise leans close to the wall but not touching it. In fact, she'd prefer to not be touching the floor beneath her feet either if it were possible.

The less her surroundings touch her skin, the less trapped she feels. Her arms folded tightly and twitching across her chest are all that she wants to embrace her.

She looks out the window and over the parking lot at the darkened canal that runs behind the assisted care facility. The water is dark, poorly reflecting distant streetlights and the parking lot illumination. It looks to be as dense as syrup, but its meager current reminds her of escape.

Her ears have been glued to the news all day, hoping to hear words that she doesn't think will come. The recapture of this escaped criminal is not likely to happen at all; she's convinced herself that it certainly won't come in time to save her.

She's reminded herself all day that she is in the safest place she can be with the guard downstairs. Now she worries that picking up the double shift might not have been the great idea that it appeared to be earlier.

Elise has moved since she's seen him last, but he knows she was working at the assisted care home and that she's likely to still be here.

More importantly, he knows how to get at her inside the work building.

Her eyebrows tense and tremble in regular pulses as she focuses on a car that has just pulled into the parking lot. Is it him already? Is he going to be stomping down her corridor, breaking into the patientless room in which she is holed up, and slamming his large hands at the back of her neck?

Lame is her breathing, staring at the moving headlights waiting to see if they've come for her.

The window before her is sealed and immovable; easily opened exits are dangerous in an assisted living home, especially on the second floor. As the roots of her black hair feel as electric as her frightened blue eyes, she wonders about the veracity of the shatterproof claims on the window, a two-story drop seeming more inviting than facing him cornered in this room.

Her mind goes wild, staring at the car as it makes its turn around the u-shaped parking lot. The empty spaces are plentiful in the lot, not a visitor in the complex at 11:43 p.m. As the car passes up the available spots closest to the entrance, she is unsure if she should feel relieved or further panicked.

The vehicle has a thin layer of tint on the front windows and the parking lot lights make the windshield bright and full of glare. Despite her frantic struggle, she can't make out the driver through the hindrances. As the car passes directly in front of the second floor window that she peers out, all she can see is the driver is alone in the car and that the driver is likely to be a man.

A large man.

She watches as the car passes below the room she is holed up inside, approaching the last available parking spots, which happen to be close to the rear exit. The squeal of brakes whines, echoing her strained emotions.

The nose of the car sticks its way into the street but

halts abruptly. Suddenly it jerks forward, turns right and goes back the way it came.

The physical panic fades, but her thoughts remain frenzied. Was it him scoping out the facility? Was he looking for her car? Did he pass through just to see if there was still a night guard? Or was it just someone who needed to turn around?

She has no resolution to any of the above, but she spins the questions around anyway, wearing her mind thin while gaining nothing. Aware that she's growing weaker and that he's gaining on her, comfort is something that she is paid to dispense but is foreign to herself.

Having calmed herself down a tiny level from intensely frenzied over immediate fatal danger back to terrified over likely death in the near future, her black hair is as unwarmed and cold as space. Her light eyes burn like a blue nebula into the darkness, like the Seven Sisters of Pleiades shining their luminance into black space, except unlike the sisters, she burns alone.

CHAPTER 13

H e's tried to come to terms with how dangerous he has become.

He has been working his brain tirelessly trying to think of every possible thought in the head of his past self. What could his past self have been thinking when he saw an exact replica of himself, except for a slightly more stylish haircut, sitting in his dream car mere feet away from him?

The whole event was bizarre enough for Chester even with the knowledge of how the unnatural meeting came to be. He can't imagine how it must have felt to be his past self experiencing it without any information explaining the situation, without an answer to quench a dehydrated mind sprinting nonstop to seek an answer that might make the world make sense again.

Chester knows his past self's reaction was a telling one with him standing on the sidewalk, leash in hand, the anxiety and curiosity controlling his absorbing stare. Unfortunately, the last phase of the facial expression had been one of fearful anger in the passenger side mirror as the blue Chevelle pulled away.

He knows that his past self is not stupid, that he'd never try to report the incident to anyone. He'd know how crazy it would sound and the negative repercussions that it would cause.

Chester's pondered the possibilities for hours. The sun glows around the edges of his window shade, reminding him how long he has been spinning his wheels. At least the time's been spent lying on his new mattress cover and pillows.

Throughout his entire life, he's loved puzzles and paradoxes—examining theory for faults, searching for unification of others. Without his questioning hours, he would never have discovered how to beat time. But this time, while he may be right, he's come up with nothing useful. The one thought, the conclusion that he can't prove wrong, is what frustrates him.

During the long hours of staring at the ceiling, the dots have spelled out his thoughts in pictographs and the shapes of letters, seeming to move and reform their alignment with the movement of his mind. Negative connect-the-dots pictures embodying the negative thoughts. A morphing Rorschach to bring his fears to life.

He knows his past self got a good look at him. The severely harsh expressions on his past self's face gave away the emotions that would have only been stirred up by seeing himself.

He knows his past self will think about how it would be possible over and over again, not being able to let it go. He no doubt will consider that he's gone insane. That would be a plausible solution. He's just started a fantastic new job in a new city with a great deal of anxiety, but the lack of any other symptoms will disprove that theory, as pat as it would have been in explaining the event.

His past self will think about how time and space could be manipulated to produce two of him. He'll consider that his counterpart must have come from the future.

Then, he'll wonder why his future self didn't look any older than himself. He'll throw in the factor that he doesn't know from how far in the future his time traveling self came from or what technology his society had prior to leaving. He'll know the only possibility will be that the person he saw is indeed himself and from the future.

His past self will realize how dangerous one from the future could prove to be, even himself from the future. He'll think of the power that can come from abusing the knowledge of all that will happen—how one could manipulate everyone around them by always being one step ahead. If power corrupts, what would the power over time do to someone?

The obligation will set in. Society will have to be protected.

The fabric of time will have to be held secure.

No one can come back without changing the environment one has come back to.

His past self will know that the temptation for one to abuse the knowledge of things to come could make one a dictator, be it political, social, or economic. One could usurp everything around them by knowing when to strike and where innovation and victory can be found at every turn. All of the great ideas of mankind can be claimed by one interloper, assuming a power beyond any man in history. His past self will decide that he needs to protect the world, and especially Rhonda, from his time traveling counterpart.

The past Chester will decide he has to kill his future self. Chester's sure of it, yet he has no idea how to stop himself.

CHAPTER 14

C hester had no intention of going to the premiere the first time around, but tonight it sounds too much more inviting than staring at his stained ceiling to pass up the event.

Dangerous? Sure. But, he knows his past self won't show up.

He remembers how he spent this night all too well: fleshing out a script to add another minute and fifteen seconds of airtime and punching it up, desperately second-guessing his own jokes that garnered laughs in the writer's room just two weeks before when he first pitched the story.

It was his first script for the show, and he spent many caffeine-filled hours in a coffee shop booth pouring over his writing, clenching his jaw which produced a migraine headache, and sweating in his tight dress shoes. Several years later when he started to become more seclusive, he had a coffee shop booth installed in his kitchen so he could work from there.

He's certain his past self is so anxious over the script that he won't be a factor this evening.

The only trick will be remembering how to behave with other members of the cast as they are meeting up at Omar's house and going to the premiere in a limo. He'll have to emulate his past level of social discomfort with his new colleagues nearly perfectly, or he'll cause more problems for his past self on Monday at work.

He'll have to recall exactly how he felt around each individual coworker and the group as a whole. Omar J. is going to be there, but he's the easiest one for him to behave the same around. Chester never got over his awe of him before leaving the show and pursuing a career in technical writing. All he'll have to do around the head honcho is act a little nervous and mostly quiet.

He'll have to remember conversations and events that have not yet happened and keep himself from mentioning them. Reese's wife is still alive; he can ask about her. But, he can't ask about Mirkwood's little girl, Savannah, because she hasn't been born yet. Omar J.'s new show can be asked about as it's still in production and won't be cancelled until next fall. And, he can't ask about David's wife, because he hasn't met her yet.

Stressful and challenging it will be, but a little danger is better than another night of lonely television and stained ceiling bumps.

Attire for the event is easily obtained. The network uses the same formal attire vendor for its staff whenever they are up for an award or are going to a network sponsored event. The store is on Westwood Boulevard, and the charges will be sent to the network. He's already on the list of approved employees with his network ID and lot pass still in his wallet.

They were surprised to see him.

Chester had watched the other staff writers stare at his

face trying to figure out what looked different, but men are rarely aware of a slight hairstyle change of one of their own. After a few minutes of Chester bantering carefully with them, they left the house of Omar J. and headed to the premiere in their shiny, yet overcrowded limo. Five of the seven staff writers going to the premiere brought dates, which was more than was planned for.

Omar sat at the back of the limo in the center seat, flanked by the two senior-most writers. With the limo packed with excited comedy writers, the ride was filled with off-the-cuff joke riffing, many being a pile-on of others taking another person's joke one step further and then in turn being followed by someone else. In this joke harvesting, Omar spoke the most prominently, others granting him silence while he did so, which was not difficult given how funny he is.

Chester threw in a few jokes of his own. He's always been quite timid around Omar, but tonight he hasn't felt as inhibited. After stirring up some of his own laughs, he decided to reign in his contributions to the conversation, not wanting to stray too far from the past Chester's behavior that they have become accustomed.

Now, as the limo pulls in front of the grand theater, he can see the flashes of cameras, the poking of microphones over the press barricade, and the movement of all the people. Something about it reminds him of Mardi Gras back home.

He's been to these events before, but those events that he's been to haven't happened yet. The past Chester has yet to attend one. He's not worried about pretending for this to be his first time because the glamorous, over-produced clamor of a premiere is something that piques one's interest and senses every time.

The Hollywood premiere is the epitome of hyperbole, following the belief that the way to make someone believe your hype is by convincing the person that everyone else believes the hype is true. Once one thinks everyone else loves an item, it takes a strong will to not concede along with them.

Fashion often follows the same guidelines of nonobjectively following the flow of perceived greatness, but it usually takes a bit longer for the individual to declare the trend was bad. It produces the never-ending phenomena of *I can't believe I used to dress like that*. For Chester, he's never experienced it as he has stayed away from flashy clothing, keeping to simple styles that are not conspicuous. He's also been lonely.

At a premiere, a large portion of the masses in attendance are those who have a personal vestment in whether the movie is wonderful or not—the actors and actresses, the director, studio execs, producers, their families, and obsequious entourages. Their response is protectively over-positive—their acclaim has been decided before the first scene plays. It usually takes a few hours or days to realize that the film wasn't that great after viewing it at a gala premiere.

Omar opens the door. As he steps out, there is a silent murmuring. A few people call out his name, and he grants them a smile and a wave.

As the first writer steps out following Omar, there is murmuring but no one calls out.

As the next few writers step out of the limo, the murmuring grows quieter.

By the time Chester exits the vehicle, the murmuring has stopped.

The lane in front of Chester is red carpeted with a press barricade on the left and a wall of promotional materials on the right. The wall of promotion includes framed versions of the official movie posters—one as big as a billboard, stills from the movie, and various props.

Omar talks with a handful of older reporters near the barricade a few yards down the red carpeted lane. The rest of the reporters look past their limo to one that has not opened its doors yet, waiting to take the place of the writers' limo.

As Chester makes his way to where Omar stands, the conversation with the reporters ends with a, "Great to see you guys."

Omar's hand lands on Chester's shoulder. Chester's not

sure if it is a polite way to end the conversation with the older reporters or if it is a friendly gesture.

Omar leans in and says, "You're a funny guy, Chaz. Glad to have you on the staff."

"Thank you, sir."

"Never saw you relax like that in the limo. You've got good presence."

Chester smiles.

"How's that script you're working on? Figured you'd be punching it up this weekend."

"It's good. I mean…it's where I want it to be. Can't wait to hear what the room thinks of it on Monday."

"Great, Chaz, great. You know most new writers are a nervous wreck."

"Yeah, actually I've been one too."

"Glad to see you relaxing toni—"

Omar's last word is cut off by a loud voice near the press barricade to their left, "What do you mean I'm not important enough for a picture? What gives you the right to be so damn rude? You stopped me and asked who I was—I didn't ask you to take my picture!"

A shrugging shoulder is the only response from a man with a microphone in his hand and two cameramen beside him.

The irate man standing on the red carpet continues, "I may not be a movie star, but every word that you love that comes out of the actors' mouths was written by me."

"No offense, but I'd love to watch Simona read the dictionary as long as she's wearin' one of those skimpy outfits from the movie," snickering from behind the barricade.

Omar steps beside the angry writer and waves his hand in front of the reporter's laughing face. He leans in and talks to the man; his laughter stops. The reporter nods his head listening to Omar. Then the newsman smiles and nods his head again, saying something to Omar that Chester can't hear.

Grabbing the upset writer by the shoulder, Omar says, "Oh, I've been waiting to see you; come with me. It's very important that you meet someone."

The writer looks confused but follows on Omar's left. Chester keeps in step on his right.

"Thought you could use a save there. You can't let these vultures get to you. They just want the shots that'll make them money. Don't take it personally; they can't make any money off us."

"You're Omar J. Sobelsk, aren't you?"

"Yes, I am. Forgive me for not knowing your name yet."

"It's Gary. Gary Leemer."

"Congratulations on your movie, Gary. It's a big accomplishment."

"Thanks."

"Look, Gary, I've been in this business a long time— movies, TV. Can I give you some advice?"

"Sure," says Gary with a bit of hesitation.

"Don't give those guys a quote or a clip of you losing your temper. They've never cared about taking my pictures either; they probably never will. And, they are rude. You've got a right to be upset with a comment like that. You worked just as hard as anyone else on this film. It's your idea—your creativity that got it started in the first place. We're just not the draw that the cast are."

Gary nods, and Omar continues, "Best to smile when they're rude and curse them out on the inside."

Gary smiles.

"That jerk won't be quoting you; I took care of that. So, shake it off and have a great evening. I've heard good things about your movie. That's why we took the whole staff with us tonight."

"Thank you, sir. That's an honor coming from you."

The director, who is talking to a small group of reporters near the barricade, calls Gary over to him.

Omar pats him on the shoulder and says, "Best of luck, son."

Gary nods in his direction and walks over to the director.

Omar and Chester keep walking.

"That was very nice of you."

"Every once in awhile I try to do something nice," smirks Omar, "You know, throw everyone a curveball."

"How did you take care of that reporter?"

"Easy. I look at the logo on their equipment and mention that I know their boss. Usually I do; sometimes I only know their boss's name. Then, I'll invite them to my next party. I'll take a guess at how old the reporter is. If they're forty or older, I mention Rosalee Gretan will be there. If they're under forty, I'll mention Christina Branson. If they're under thirty, I'll mention Jennie Harris will be there. If the reporter's a woman, I just offer to get her a casting appointment in my next project. A lot of movies need a reporter in them—it's best to use a real one for authenticity anyway."

"Do you give them what you say?"

"Sure. Those actresses are at every one of my parties looking to score more work, and every boy from their generation had a crush on them when they were on TV. I just make sure the actress that I mentioned is escorted and protected at the party. No cameras are allowed anyway. And just because I get a girl a casting appointment, it doesn't mean she'll get the part. If she's good, she's got a shot; if she's terrible, she shouldn't have it anyway. I just get their foot in the door to get a chance at it. It's all really not that hard."

"If you say so, Omar," Chester responds as a slew of blinding flashes go off to his right.

"But, it's a lot harder to write a good script, huh, Chaz?"

Chester nods his head, and then asks pointing to the place where the incident between the writer and the reporter happened, "Is it always this way?"

"What? What happened with the writer? Yeah, it's always that way. The public perception is that the actors make the movie; the writers are not important. They think the movie could be made without us altogether, or that anyone could do it as good as we can. It's the same reason why people don't tip at a fast food restaurant."

"What?" poses Chester with a quiet laugh.

"We don't tip at fast food restaurants because they're not glamorous, but they take our order, fix our drinks, cook the food, package the food and serve it to us. It's everything that we get at a fancy restaurant. There are tables for us to eat at a fast food place too. If you leave a mess, someone will have to come clean it up. And, the fast food employee serves a lot more customers in one hour than a regular waiter handles in a whole shift. It's definitely just as hard of a job, if not a harder job altogether. If it weren't harder, people would rather work at a fast food joint than another restaurant. They don't work there because it's harder, and we have this image that working at another restaurant is higher class. We tip the one that we deem higher class. There's really no difference. Just our collective pretense. Just like the actors are the stars, and we're nothing."

"Omar! Omar!" shouts a former teen star with crow's feet scratching their way through his temples, "How's that new show coming along?"

"*Cold Streak*? It's looking good despite the hack writer."

"Looking for guest stars? I'm looking for work."

Chester's eyes rotate away from the conversation, sliding over people walking down the red carpet lane into the theater, some movie posters, and finally landing upon a large display. It is a scene set up in the same fashion as the movie poster. A cut-out standee of the hero is placed next to the real-life car used in the movie, *Midnight Bandit*. Leaning on the hood and trunk of the car are two live models in bikinis who smile and wave at the people entering the theater.

Behind the models is a giant screen looping an extended trailer for the movie with high action scenes cut rapidly together. Against the wall of the theater to the left of all of this is a giant twelve-foot-high mirror that runs the length of the display, making the garish exhibit appear far vaster than it is.

Most people smile at the models or are taken in by the flash of the gargantuan screen. Either way, they pass quickly, eager to get inside the air conditioning and get to their seats.

But, Chester stops and stands in front of the display. He sneers at the lifeless standee of the lead actor, complete with racing gloves, a leather jacket and matching pants, a gun in one hand, and the obligatory hip sunglasses blocking out his eyes.

The lead actor's stage name is Max Stone, and later this week he'll make headline news. Not for the success of tonight's premiere movie or a great opening weekend, but he'll be known for slamming his Ferrari into a hot dog stand during the same week that he starred as the world's greatest race car driver in *Midnight Bandit*.

To further warrant public ridicule when Chester watched it happen the first time around was the lawsuit involving minor injuries to the seventeen-year-old passenger, who happened to be the daughter of a studio executive. The rumor was Stone was leaning over to steal a kiss when his exotic Italian sports car invaded Walt's Weiner World splattering his hood and windshield with hot dogs, relish, and mustard, leaving one broken and dangling frankfurter hanging off the rear spoiler.

Although Chester's sure people walking past will either think he's mad and snickering at nothing or a pervert and leering at the girls posturing in their thongs around the car, he doesn't care.

The humor is irresistible in being at such an ornate movie premiere gala, saturated in hype from every angle, for a racing film whose lead actor will crash his car and his career in a few days while trying to coax a kiss from an underage girl. It's almost enough to make his snicker a smile, but he thinks of the woman who still holds his heart and that makes a genuine and warm smile impossible.

"Oh, Mr. Fuze," coos a voice as soft as a slow current over dangling bare feet.

The last time he heard this voice, his heart turned to wax and melted all over his soul, running liquidy fingers burning their paths across his tender-most being, scalding him in a grip of heartache and then cooling into a layer of melancholy that has insulated him from the warm touch of hope. A crack has just formed the moment he heard the female voice. Before he even turns around, red winds dig into the layer of congealed heart matter, and green warmth radiates through the openings made by the ruby colored breeze.

When his eyes take in the image of her, the wax melts into its liquid lava state. He can feel the pain and tenderness working through it, kneading itself into her shape. The muck of his destroyed emotions breathes with life for the first time since he saw her last. Its lumbering, excruciating journey to numbness is reversing itself; tingles pulse through that which has mimicked the dead, water through roots shriveled by drought.

Unsure if it's joy, panic, or both, he realizes that the gun of action is being cocked before him, and he has little say as to whether it will slay him with happiness or resurrect his emotions only to restart their tedious process of melting, burning, and a slow freezing death.

Despite his fears and the gripping emothermal war in his chest, his lips form a fragile smile, his eyes shine with excess fluid, and his mouth opens to speak before his mind can form a word.

"Mr. Fuze, I am in your debt."

"Wh-what?" smiling.

"How did you know about, Dane?"

His smile gains strength against gravity and habit, "Just observant, I guess," eyes growing troubled as his voice grows more serious, "Are you okay, Rhonda? Did anything happen?"

Now, her smile is the one turning awkward, "Yes, horrible damage. Terribly regrettable."

"Oh, no," he says as he reaches out to touch her forearm, but stops very close.

"My poor garbage can will never be the same," holding

her face serious.

"Your garbage can?"

"Yes, the angry fool kicked it into the street and stomped it into a lumpy potato shape when I refused to kiss him goodnight."

"Really?"

"Yeah, a kiss on the cheek for the ride home wasn't enough for him apparently. So, he knocked the trash over. He got really mad when he realized I had gone inside and locked the door while he was in the middle of his trash-can kicking tirade. I did watch through the blinds in my kitchen window. One of his kicks missed the can he had knocked over and smashed into the trash that had spilled out on the ground—got garbage all over his pants. But, he was gone before the police showed up."

Chester exhales loudly, and his smile grows wider.

"And that," she says pointing to his chest that has just sighed, "is why I owe you an apology. You weren't trying to harm me, Mr. Fuze, and I'm sorry that I ever thought so. First, I noticed how right you were about Dane. To tell the truth, I might've ended up with him if I wasn't looking to see if you were right. Took me awhile to realize that you weren't trying to take me home. It was that you begged me to take a cab— away from Dane, but away from you too. Am I wrong, Chester, or were you just worried about me?"

His jaw makes a few false starts before pushing out, "Ya-yes, Rhonda. I was scared you were going to be hurt, and," pausing, "I'm sorry that I didn't follow you anyway. Hope that doesn't freak you out. I just felt guilty that I didn't make sure you got home safe."

"And, what if I would've asked him inside, Mr. Fuze? What would you have done then?"

"Cry. Alone."

Her lips push together starting a fire of warmth. It loosens his tongue.

"Just wanted to be there in case you wanted him to leave and he wouldn't."

"Sweetie, are you mad at me if I say that still scares me a little bit?"

"Of course not. You need to be careful."

His eyes drop to his shoes. A hand followed by red streams cups his chin and cheek. Her face welcomes in a way that makes him ache and relax. Green eyes take possession of his own, staring into his brown counterparts, both pairs firing and consuming each other. The green is eclipsed by soft flesh as she pushes her warm lips against his.

His eyes gloss over with emotion as his lids close too. Passion and compassion entwine through him in a double helix, one that could rival the recipe for life itself. The wax inside of him feels lighter, more molten but as free as air. The skin over his entire body feels as though it's never been touched before. Every ounce of him screams as everything that he's wanted has flown to him, landed on his lips, and filled him.

His left hand goes to her face, and his right lands at her waist. Her left hand is still on his cheek, and she places her right at his neck. As she pulls herself closer to him, he can feel her breathing, and it feels like the rhythm of life, awakening every part of him, a gift meant to birth truth and all that is good.

He doesn't remember when his mouth opened—it all has been so fluid, so beyond anything that he physically thought himself capable.

The kiss eventually subsides into stares and smiles. Chester's face twitches from a smile to a countenance braced for an assault.

"What's wrong, buster, don'tchya like me anymore?"

"No, no!" her face warms at his enthusiasm, "These things just never happen to me. Usually more careful and boring."

"Never?"

"Never in my life."

"Well, Chester, today is a new day."

"Indeed it is."

"You know, careful is good in the right place. In the

wrong, it can lead to a lonely life."

"And lots of regret."

She smiles fiendishly, her eyes adding a sparkle, "So, you're regretting kissing me, Chester?"

"No, but every moment I've spent when I wasn't kissing you."

She kisses him on the lips in a quick but firm motion. Staring at him she says, "You know every girl wants to hear that. We just get scared when it happens out loud. Makes us realize life is for us to make it the way we want. Sometimes it's easier to pretend love isn't real and just head straight for the jerk so we'll never be reminded of how things could be if we weren't so scared to hold out for it."

"Holding out can be scary."

"But, it's also the sweetest thing. As long as you come talk to me at a crowded party, being different than anyone else there. It's only scary if you never let me know."

"So, what made you change your mind about me?"

"It was the stuff I told you before. You were right about Dane; you weren't trying to take me home—you said you wanted to take me out. A date is different. A date is talking to someone, not trying to take them home. You said you wanted to ask me out, which means for another time, not that night. That's different for Hollywood. That's different for most places."

He nods.

"You were happy to take me out for coffee or a movie, and you weren't getting drunk either. You didn't say dirty things to me. You said you thought I was wonderful. And beautiful. Just 'cause I was scared doesn't mean I didn't like what you had to say."

"Uh huh, what else?"

Looking sheepishly, "I-uh, had Harvey check into some things for me too."

"Oh, so you're calling him Harvey now?"

"Well, not to his face, but I'm working up to it. Been thinking about what you had to say about him."

"Yeah?"

"Maybe, he isn't such a nice guy, but he is a good agent. Doesn't mean there aren't other good agents though."

Chester smiles.

"See, you only said things that were good for me, and all of them were true. Just didn't know it at the time."

"Was a lot to digest, I guess."

"Yeah, it was a lot at once," pauses as she stares at his face that looks troubled, "but not bad."

"So, what kind of things did you have Harvey look into?"

"Umm, just some stuff about you."

"Like what?" he asks smiling, leaning in closer to her face that is growing with embarrassment.

"Oh, come on, Chester," she says smacking his shoulder playfully, turning red, and looking away from him.

"Hey, Rhonda, you thought I was a weirdo, remember? You can tell me whatever it is; it'll be alright."

Despite how embarrassed she's become, she loves the last three words and the tone behind them too much to deny his request.

"I had Harvey call a few people and ask about you. That's how I knew you'd be here."

"Well, I almost didn't come. But, that's not so bad that you had Harvey ask about me."

"Just not so bad?" she asks with a raised eyebrow.

"Best kiss of my life."

She turns even more flushed.

"Rhonda, I'm sorry. I'm not very good at being cool."

"Cool's not where I want to be right now," she says grabbing his hand and pulling him in a little closer, "Chester, there's something else."

"What is it?"

"I had Harvey call in a favor and get your police records. I didn't ask for it, but he got your school transcripts, medical records, pics from your school yearbooks. Guess the guy really owed Harvey. I just wanted the police info, which there wasn't any of anyway."

Chester's face grows worried.

"Chester, I'm so sorry. I just had to know about you before I could feel safe. Things with that crazy man in my bushes had me so scared I was afraid to think of dating anyone—you're my first kiss since all this started about a year ago. None of the guys I've known have acted like you. All of the people who knew that creepy man said he was a nice, quiet guy. Made me afraid of nice…"

"No, no, that's not what's bothering me, Rhonda," he interrupts.

"Then, what?"

"I'm…nothing special. You know that, right? I didn't have many friends. Don't have a lot of money. I've lived a boring life before coming out to L.A., and I haven't done much since being here. I don't know why you would…"

"Hey! Hey, hey, hey! Don't you talk like that," she says lifting his chin off his chest, and peering closely into his face, "You talked to one girl who thinks you're pretty great. That's something, right? Isn't it?"

"Yes. Yes, it is," squeezing her hand.

The movie has been inconsequential, an action flick without much of a plot or acting. But, the *Most Hipness* writers have been all smiles. The film has been giving them a lot to lampoon in quiet whispers and nervous snickers, an elbow to the ribs in the next seat to point out a particularly bad line. Despite all of the professional critiquing, the redhead sitting next to one of their own has proven to be far more interesting.

Rhonda's hand has remained in his with her shoulder held snugly against him. At a dark part in the middle, she placed her head on his shoulder, an action which the other writers had to make sure was noticed by all of their ranks. No jokes have been made about her being with him, just smiles and surprise.

The music swells, and the screen fades to credits.

The crowd concedes ostentatious applause while giving each other dissatisfied or comedic looks. The people in the front nearest the director, writer, producers, and cast decide to stand while clapping, making an obsequious wall around the movie makers. The rest of the theater does not follow.

Chester wonders if the thin wall of ovation surrounds them closely enough to provide the illusion that the gushing wall is universal throughout the theater and maybe even the world. He also wonders if they care that they're being fooled or if they are simply enjoying the acclaim. Surely, the inevitable two and three star reviews will start pouring in tomorrow, and their remembrances of the ovation will turn from warm and hearty to transparent and thin.

Rhonda's hand squeezes his, and as she says his name, he cares not for tomorrow but for the wonder of the present.

"Chester?"

He looks to her and sees that her face is flushed and her lips look nervous. His response comes immediately.

"Rhonda, would you like to do something tonight?"

"Yes," with a smile, relief, and cheeks returning to their normal color. Her eyes still dart bashfully, but not foolishly.

Fourteen minutes later inside the limo, Rhonda sits next to Chester near the rear passenger door. The seats to their left at the immediate back of the limo are filled by Omar and the two show runners. The rest of the seats are taken by the writing staff. She is the only lady in the vehicle to which they pay any attention.

Omar has been leaning forward talking to Rhonda since the limo pulled away from the curb. She has been cordial like a princess, but she has squeezed Chester's hand while answering any question and not letting go until a positive response has been made.

Another writer, Josh Oakley, leans forward and asks, "So, you guys met at the show party a few weeks ago?"

"Sort of," answers Chester before she has a chance to

respond.

"What kind of answer is 'sort of'?"

"The kind of mysterious answer that a talented TV writer would conjure up purely for your amusement," extending his arm bent at the elbow before him and bowing his head and shoulders.

Omar laughs along with the other writers.

"Miss Romero, what projects are you working on now? More TV, or are you looking to make more movies?"

"I've been considering both. I'd rather start making more movies, although I enjoyed TV too. Right now I'm looking for different kinds of roles. I want something different than what I played on *The Arcade Life*. So far the roles that I want I haven't gotten, and the ones they're begging me for I don't want. Just seems like I need to pick the right roles now if I'm going to make it past the TV show and do other things."

Omar says, "I can't believe you've been turned down for roles. Were you auditioning for male leads or parts that required homely women? It seems you could land about anything else that you'd want."

Laughs and says, "No, just leads in movies with good scripts. They're usually trying to cast the same six or seven actresses for those roles. They're not very willing to take a chance on anyone else. Comedies—they're offering me comedies left and right along with the role of the girlfriend in a ton of movies with lousy scripts and trashy jokes."

Grinning, Omar replies, "Come on now; I've made a career out of lousy scripts and trashy jokes."

Rhonda's face becomes flushed, and she tries to explain over the laughter, "No, I didn't mean scripts like your shows."

Chester tugs gently on her hand, and her breathing slows. She looks at him, and he leans close to her.

"Omar knows; he just loves a good joke, especially when it's at himself."

She looks to Omar who is still laughing but quieter now, "It would be an honor to be on one of your TV shows or movies. Good scripts are what I'm really looking for. The comedies they've been sending me are just disgusting."

A little more serious in tone, Omar says, "Yeah, it's getting harder to make a comedy without naked girls bouncing around and some kind of weird sex joke. Not that I'm above all that, but I can see why you're holding out for something else."

She responds, "Well, I did just finish up shooting a movie called *The Ever After*. It's a psychological horror about a guy trying to reach his own version of heaven through the power of his mind. He creates his perfect place inside his head and lives there. Then things start to go wrong."

"It's great," supports Chester.

"How would you know, Chaz?" asks Omar.

"Yeah, how would you know?" poses Rhonda.

All eyes looking upon him, his insides far more nervous than his skin shows, "I've heard things. You know this town. Heard there might be some Oscar nods in this one."

"Really?" asks Rhonda.

Omar adds, "Yeah, I've heard some good buzz too. Heard it might be up for director and screenplay."

"Yeah, it was a crazy script. Good though. A fun one to work on—something different," she explains.

Chester's heart races at the close call, and he fidgets with his fingers for the rest of the ride to Omar's home.

His car glistens in the night, parked underneath a tall streetlight in front of Omar's neighbor's house. The night hides the thin layer of dirt that he's allowed to build on it. It may not be that much, but it's more than he's ever allowed. He hasn't paid much attention to it, but he wishes it were cleaner now for Rhonda to ride inside.

The limo parks in Omar's long driveway, and Omar gets out first, being the closest to the door, followed by Chester who has moved around Rhonda in order to hold her hand as she exits.

Breaking his attention from her hand in his, something is moving along the far side of his car. He can see it peaking just slightly into the passenger windows as it slinks along.

"Rhonda," he says pulling her to her feet and grasping her hand firmly, "you need to get inside Omar's house with the others now."

"Wha—"

"Someone's by my car. Go inside now, and I'm going to check this out."

"No, you can't—"

"Too dangerous for you. Please, go now."

As soon as he sees her heading toward the house following Omar who is opening the front door, he runs toward his car.

His eyes focus on the dark spot near the passenger window that he saw move a few moments ago. He approaches the car from the street side, hoping to trap the mysterious trespasser between the street and the houses.

As he nears, the spot turns away and runs.

Chester can see it's a man about his size, wearing black with a matching baseball cap. Chester sprints after him, having trouble catching up with the man in black. He stares at his target and notices something odd about his movements. They're familiar, but he can't quite place them.

Chester shouts, "Hey, stop! What the hell were you doing by my car?"

The man makes no effort to do so or to divert his attention to the face that is yelling at him.

He runs toward the driveway of one of Omar's neighbors. Two cars sit in the driveway. A dark blue split-window Stingray Corvette and a new Jaguar. The man slows his pace slightly and lifts his arms as he steps between the two cars. Chester sees the unnecessary movement to avoid damaging the automobiles, and he knows exactly who the would-be saboteur is. Chester makes his way between the cars, but he bumps them slightly with a knee and an elbow.

The man runs down the side of Omar's neighbor's house and grabs the top of the six-foot wooden fence.

Chester can see the man's awkwardness in pulling himself over the fence, and he stops pursuing him, knowing this would not be the place to confront him. Too many people around, including Rhonda. Especially Rhonda.

He walks back out of the side of the neighbor's house and between the two shiny cars. Rhonda sees him immediately, and the sadness on her face lightens some. She runs toward him.

"Chester, are you alright?"

"Yeah, everything except my ego. Got outrun pretty good."

"I was so worried that you were gonna get hurt. Looked like you were going to catch him on side of the house."

"He jumped the fence, and I couldn't get myself up there fast enough."

"Good! I'm glad that you're safe. He could've hurt you. Could've had a gun."

He kisses her on the forehead, "Rhonda, I need to check out the car. Will you wait with the other writers? I'll walk you back over there."

She nods her head and follows closely beside him.

As they approach the bewildered writers on the lawn, Omar calls out, "Chaz, are you alright? What the hell was all of that?"

"Just some punk trying to break into my car. I'm going to check it out and see if there's any damage."

"Who knew our new writer was a superhero?" says Omar as Chester walks away.

Laughs.

Mirkwood, one of the staff writers says, "Naw, it's a buddy of his that he paid to pretend to break into the car so he could chase him off and look tough in front of Rhonda."

They all laugh except Rhonda who watches him approach the car.

A pair of snips lies on the ground near the front passenger tire. The black rubber grips with the thin green stripe stir a memory in his brain. They're from the first set of tools that he bought after arriving in L.A. Later, he'd use and break most of them working on the same car they were meant to damage this evening.

He leans over and looks under the front passenger tire. Seeing nothing out of the ordinary, he moves to the gas filler cap, removes it, and looks for traces of anything that shouldn't be there. It smells solely of gasoline, and there are no traces around the filler tube or cap to indicate any unwanted additives.

He thinks he must have arrived and scared the man just in time. He picks up the snips, not wanting to leave anything with fingerprints on it that might lead back to his past self, revealing the dual existence of Chester Fuze.

He decides he'll start the car while Rhonda's still a safe distance away in front of Omar's house. He can see her talking to the other writers while keeping her eyes on him; her face is still panicked.

Chester smiles, waves, and hopes he'll still be grinning after turning the key in the ignition.

CHAPTER 15

W hen he crawled out of the river, he was certain he was going to die.

Skin shriveled and pruned, the inside of his mouth gritty from the murky water that had seeped in, and his lungs pounding roughly, his body produced a sickly wheezing with a spattering rattle of thick saliva battering about his mouth and throat. A chunk of the fluid landed on the corner of his mouth, saggy and lifeless along with a handful of other little spatters about his chin, lips, and nose.

His left leg wound was an angry red and throbbed at a faster rate than the rhythm of his breathing.

He felt that his exhaustion and injuries were consuming more and more of his depleted energy. The pace of the insatiable aching in his pounding chest, the throbbing in his calf, the rattling in his throat, and the worn pain over every piece of muscle and skin, it all seemed to keep speeding up.

Once Edmund had stopped swimming, drifting, and getting knocked around in the current, his physical needs not only caught up with him, but ran him over, forcing his body to pump blood, breathe, and hurt faster and faster until he could not keep up. Having what little vigor he had left to keep alive sucked out of him at an escalating pace, he closed his eyes accepting the fact that it would be all for him. The relief of sleep would be the last thing that he would know before his body ceased to be alive.

Death scared him, but deep down he hoped it would be a clean slate, a chance to start over. He believed all of his problems in life were because he was dealt a bad hand, not attributing any of his terrible decisions or behaviors to himself but to bad luck.

He was certain things would have been better if he was born into someone else's life. Getting a new hand would be another chance. As in most else in his life, he knew he was wrong, that there'd be a penalty for all he'd done, no clean slate, nothing left to gamble; and knowing he was wrong has always given birth to an anger inordinately larger than the seriousness of the subject.

His thoughts were hostile and dark, and his only glowing gem in the darkness was that they didn't catch him. He made it. He would die free of any man having any authority over him.

He beat them.

Even if it cost him death, he beat them, glowing in hatred the whole way.

That was sixteen hours ago. He had crawled into the patch of rozo cane knowing nothing about his surroundings except he was out of the river whose endurance had long outlasted his own and showed no sign of relenting. With vision as lame as a newborn, he felt that he had pulled himself out of one world and into another.

He couldn't have found a better hiding place in the immediate area even if he had been fully aware to choose one. The tall rozo stalks at the river bank provided him secrecy and held enough solid mud together to keep him from sliding back into the water or being seen by the passing boats. There he slept the heaviest sleep he's ever known, his right shoulder sinking nearly four inches into the mire during its course.

Now, his eyes flutter, little flecks of river and shore sticking to his lashes. The long, skinny shape of the rozos, the color of the mud, the stickiness all over his skin, the subtle warmth of the overcast setting sun, and the stale scent of the stagnant water trapped in the mud of the bank creeping up his nose and seasoning his thoughts: all of it enters his head, making it a cluttered, unsorted, and untraversable chamber, the only prevailing thought being *Where am I?*

River grime covers the inside of his ears, but filthy fingers are not able to dig out the grit, only capable of adding to it.

His hand dives into the slop of embankment, diving just past his wrist before gaining enough leverage to lift himself up. Looking around the area, he knows it's the Mississippi. Looking for any type of a landmark, he tries to figure out where his body has crawled ashore in the river's two thousand plus long vein down widely varying temperatures, altitudes, and cultures.

Surely, he knows he's down current from the prison, somewhere between his escape and the mouth of the river where it meets the Gulf of Mexico. But, that stretch covers a long area. The further he's made it away from the penitentiary, the less intense the search will be for him where he has landed.

New Orleans is in the path. Being the most populated area in the rest of the river's course, it would be a poor destination for him, despite having grown up in Riverview, a suburb just outside of the city, living most of his life one block off Planeline Highway.

It's also the place where he committed his crimes, and more importantly the place where the police arrested him for each of his offenses, the few that they've discovered anyway. It would be logical that the local law enforcement would be keeping an eye out for him to return to the area.

Being on foot, half his body caked in river mud, his hair dirty and unbrushed, and with two obvious wounds on his calves underneath his torn and stained pants legs, he'd blend in as well as a female streaker in a monastery.

The first feeling to strike him besides his general soreness and the tender wounds on his calves is the acute stabbing pains in his stomach.

Prison food did little to satisfy, and he never fed himself good food before being incarcerated. Cooking is something he's despised. Usually a girlfriend or a female hanging around to share the drugs would take care of the meals. When they were scarce or incapacitated, he'd order pizza or hit up a drive-through. Through all of that, he's never felt any hunger like this. His food choices may have been poor, but he always made sure he grabbed it in large quantities. Intense hunger is something new to him.

It's been two days since he's eaten. He broke out of the prison before breakfast, having not eaten since dinner the night before, slept none, ran all day, swam for much of the night until exhausted, passed out in the rozos all morning and nearly all of the daylight hours.

All of his energy being completely spent plus the long hours without eating have left him primally famished. It swells so much that he hates the rozos for not being edible, the river for not being drinkable, and the air for not smelling like anything appetizing or anything other than revolting, stagnant, marshy shore.

Hatred and hunger push him to move. Standing, he sees the faint outline of a bridge named after a crooked politician and knows he's not far from the place where he was born, maybe fifteen miles, nor is he far from uniformed men with guns who are looking for him.

His sour-tasting mouth utters, "Cursed."

The hunger grows.

CHAPTER 16

C lassy Cue is the name on the sign above the doorway they are entering. It's been Chester's experience that any business with the word classy in its name never is.

As he swings open the tinted glass door to the tavern that is located in the corner section of an L-shaped strip mall, he is sure that his theory about its name is correct, and feeling her fingernails tap gently on his forearm before she steps through the opened door that he holds for her, it's certainly not an establishment to which he's thrilled to bring Rhonda.

She's stayed by his side since Friday's premiere with few exceptions. Early into the morning on Saturday after leaving Omar's house, following a drive to the beach, coffee, and microwavable pizza snacks at Rhonda's condo, Chester announced he was going home. She had waited for him to ask her to join him, but he didn't.

When he had hugged and kissed her and had begun making his way to the door, she told him he didn't need to leave, to which he smiled and said that he did. He kissed her again at the door and felt the uneasiness streaming inside her.

He told her, touching her chin with his hand, "I'd love to see you tomorrow if you're not busy."

Her smile bent beauty on her face with an outline of awkward relief.

"I'll call you tomorrow," he said.

Much to her surprise, he really left. It made her feel both a little empty and very cherished.

Yesterday involved a trip to the zoo, a museum, dinner, a movie, and a nightcap that was much the same as the previous night, except that she was much more able to appreciate it when he left her to go home and sleep at his own apartment.

When he called her this morning, he didn't want to bring her to a place like this, but the activities of the last two days had left him with only $8.32 atop the amount he set aside to bet on today's game. Being that he had to go or find another way to come up with a lot of money before tomorrow morning's rent deadline, he was happy that she was just as interested in being with him today as he was in being with her, regardless of where he was going.

Now as they step into the darkened room, the dim sights are very similar to the bar from the weekend before. The clack of pool balls breaks the air, and a familiar face smiles with specks of salt and a bit of popcorn. He takes a sip of his drink and hops off his stool to walk toward them.

After a brief introduction, Lucky squints and releases his eyes several times at Rhonda before he asks the question that she knows is coming.

"Hey, are you that girl from that show?"

"Yes, I was on *The Arcade Life* for three seasons."

"Yeah, I watched it a few times. Wasn't one of my favorites. I'm more of a comedy or sports fan."

"She was really wonderful in it. Definitely the best part of the show," inserts Chester.

"Yeah," says Lucky with a nervous voice and eyes that suddenly grow wider, "yeah, you were good. Definitely the best one on it."

"Thank you," offers Rhonda quickly looking away from Lucky to the surrounding TVs and then to Chester.

"Been holding you guys's seats all morning, well noon—whatever the hell it is. You guys should sit down."

"Alright. Thanks, Lucky," says Chester as he stands in front of the stool closest to Lucky and pulls the one to the left of it away from the bar so Rhonda can have room to sit on it before he pushes it and her snugly to the bar. Chester wipes his hand across her stool's cushion to make sure it's clean. Before he can finish the motion, she sits atop his hand, not knowing it is there.

Chester pulls it away quickly, and she glances at him while he laughs and turns red.

"Chester!" she says, "You dirty boy!"

He laughs, takes her hand, and kisses it, "Excuse me, madam, I'm a bit of a cad. My lascivious nature even comes through in my accidents."

She smiles, taking a moment to absorb his words.

Lucky interjects, "I don't know what the heck you two are talking about, but the pregame show just started. Chaz, who are we taking today? We should bet on more than one game."

Rhonda's face has changed to disillusioned at the word bet.

"Chester, you're betting on the games? You're gambling?"

He throws Lucky a dirty look, who cowers away from it, and then he answers Rhonda, "Yeah, we like to bet on the games."

Unchanging, she stares at him.

Chester continues, "We just started last week, but we won big, and it's a lot of fun."

"Chester, I don't like gambling. Brings out the worst in people."

Lucky seems intent on flagging down the bartender, but his ears ache to hear the back and forth between his betting partner and the starlet.

"Rhonda, I promise I'll be as happy as a clam if we lose or if we win."

Turning away from the bar, Lucky adds, "Hey, Chaz, you told me this was a sure thing. Are you not so sure anymore?"

"Relax, Lucky, we're going to win. I promise you," turning away from his betting partner, "Rhonda, I promise it'll be nothing but fun today. I'm not one of those people that takes this too seriously. It's just like a Vegas vacation to me. It's just for fun—no big deal. I swear."

The tone in the last two words pulls at her resolve, "Don't you let me down, Mr. Chester Fuze. I was really starting to think the world of you."

"I won't let you down, Rhonda. I promise."

"Okay. But I'm not too sure how happy a clam really is anyway."

Her lips don't return to a full smile, but she keeps them from frowning and takes hold of his hand.

Halftime.

The good guys, as far as their bet is concerned, are down by three.

Before the game started, Chester thought it best to have Lucky place the bet, that it would be easier having Lucky talk the new bookie into better odds on the long shot, since the bar's usual residents know Lucky and how inappropriate his name is. Based on the briefness of the conversation before the money changed hands, Lucky's reputation is infamous.

Rhonda is nowhere to be seen.

"Lucky, what would you do if a guy walked up to Cindy and grabbed her breast?"

He huffs some beer particles out of his mouth and says, "Some guy walks up and grabs her boob? I'd beat his freakin' head in. Why you asking 'bout that? Was somebody messing wit' Cindy last week?"

"No, no, I just wanted to explain that saying things like 'This team's got its nuts cut off' when Rhonda is around is to me like someone grabbing Cindy to you."

"Come on, Chaz, I never touched her. I didn't even hug her hello."

"I know, Lucky, I know. It's just that talking like that makes me feel like she's being violated, like someone's trampling on something special to me."

"Well, shuh, I don't—I always talk like this, Chaz. You's with me last week—ya know that. I's always talked like that. Don't mean nuttin' by it."

"I know. I remember last week. That's why I'm asking you as a friend to not say things like that around Rhonda. I can't allow her to be around that."

"Well, hell, there's lotta other places to sit in here. Don't need to be up here in my business."

"You're right. We can sit somewhere else. Just thought you'd rather us be here."

Chester takes a few steps away and looks around the bar for another place to sit. Rhonda has not reappeared from the bathroom.

He sees a small table with one chair on the outer edge of the pool tables. A TV is not too far from it.

"Chaz. Chaz!"

He turns and sees Lucky nodding his head.

"Come back over here. It's alright."

Chester walks over and places a leg up on one of the lower bars of the stool he has just vacated.

"Man, I'm sorry. I get bent out of shape pretty easy, even sometimes when people aren't messing wit' me. Little touchy I guess. Sorry bout the language. Cindy don't like it neither—she just puts up wit' it. You guys can stay here— shouldn't be no more trash talk."

"Alright, thanks, Lucky."

Lucky's left hand clumsily pats Chester's shoulder as

he takes a swig of his beer at the same time.

The game resumes, and the good guys drive down field.

Slender red-tipped explorers slide a path around his waist, meeting in the center and clasping each other. Chester grins bashfully, that area being highly sensitive and mostly untouched.

The crowd erupts as a fourth-down quarterback sneak with a missed defensive tackle results in a touchdown.

Two stools over from Lucky, a voice shouts, "Bout time they played like they had a pair!"

"Hey, pal," Lucky shouts back, "watch your language! Can't you see that my buddy's lady's right here?"

At Rhonda's condo nearly three hours later.

Rhonda says, "I don't know if I can be around a man whose life is all up to chance—someone who might lose the rent money if Chicago wins on Sunday."

"But I never lose; it's a lock."

"Someday you will, Chester. Everybody loses sometime, or they're not human."

"Not me."

"My daddy always swore the same thing, and he'd be angry and yelling and breaking things every time he lost— swearing he'd been cheated: stupid ref, lousy quarterback, idiot coach. There was always a reason why he lost that had nothing to do with him."

Pause. She holds onto the handle straps of her large purse that sits before her atop her kitchen table. Her fingers say take out her keys, ask him to leave, and lock the door behind him, but her eyes plead wait.

Chester doesn't know what to say. The truth not only could drive her away forever, but it could be dangerous to the entire world. Light breaks the fog.

"Look, Rhonda, what if I tell you the names of every

winner in baseball, football, horse races, and any other event you can find in the paper?"

She puckers and unpuckers her lips nervously.

"What if I don't miss one? Would you believe me? You know I've been with you all day, and we left before the other games were over. You know I haven't seen any scores since we left. What do you think?"

Releasing her tightly puckered lips, "I don't like it, Chester, but it would be something. Should be nearly impossible to get them all right."

Seven minutes later sitting at her kitchen table.

"Chester, it's just not natural."

"No, for most people it's not, but for me it is."

"For everybody it is. I went to dozens of fortune tellers when I was trying to find my way, and none of them could've done this. None of them told me anything that was going to happen and then had it come true. If any of them could do this, they wouldn't be living in rundown houses by the airport and with no one ever knowing who they were and what amazing things they could do."

"They're not me."

"I know, Chester. I just don't...are you really a writer, or do you study sports all day long—memorizing stats? Is that it? Is that what you do all day? If that's the case, wouldn't it be easier just to work for someone else or start your own business?"

"No, it only takes me about fifteen minutes."

Pause.

She asks, "What else do you know?"

"What?" responds Chester.

"What else do you know about me?"

"That I love you."

Her face holds still as if she were trying to feel the

magnitude of a slap—if it will sting through her flesh or fade away quickly. Her eyes remain wide in its wake; a little flicker gives birth to warmth in her chest.

He tries to think of something to say, fails, and exhales loudly in the gasp of one who has incriminated oneself in a dire matter.

"Che-Chester, I-I don't know what to say."

His lips move to speak but produce nothing.

"How can you love me? You've only known me for a few days."

He stares with full eyes, but no motion and no plan.

"It's sweet, and I liked hearing it. But, you can't say that without meaning it, and you can't mean that yet…Can you?"

"Yes," comes from his mouth without his permission.

"Chester, that just can't be, baby. Love takes time, and we haven't spent enough of it yet."

Long pause.

Rhonda's eyes start to water over with the sadness of a new hope being crushed. He's afraid she's going to leave him.

Chester says, "You're never going to believe me until I tell you the truth."

"Of course I won't believe you until you tell me the truth. You want me to believe a lie?"

"No, it's not like that. You'd understand if I tell you everything," a voice in his head berates him for having said this much and pleads with him to stop before making it worse.

"If you don't tell me the truth, none of this has been real. This wonderful weekend will all be fake. If it's not based on truth, it's not real."

"More real than anything for me." *Shut up, you idiot. She's going to run if you tell the truth. Think you're insane. Knows where you live. She'll call the police, an asylum, maybe even Harvey and then the show.*

"Then tell me, and we'll test it," she says.

Don't. Don't do it. A lie—tell her you're divorced or something. Lie. Make a joke. Anything but the truth.

"If I tell you, you'll think I'm insane."

"We're all a little insane, Chester, but some of us can be honest. Some of us can trust a person."

"I trust you. It's just…it's just a lot to believe."

Grabbing his hand, "There's nothing left to do but to do it. Tell me."

"I can say I love you because I've known you for a lot longer than two days."

A tingle of panic spreads in her eyes.

"I mean I've only seen you in person or talked to you for this weekend and at the party. I've never spied on you or followed you or any of that crazy stuff."

The panic subsides but doesn't disappear.

"I've watched you on TV and in films for more than twenty years."

Her eyes and mouth scream the question that she doesn't speak.

"I'm from the future, Rhonda."

"Oh, my God, Chester," she says with a voice that has begun to sob, "Honey, you are insane."

Her hand still holds his, and so holds his confidence.

"No, Rhonda, it's true. That's how I know who's going to win in sports. That's how I never lose. That's why I said it wasn't gambling with me. There's no chance I can miss; I already know how it's going to happen."

"You're talking crazy; I'm sorry, but this is nuts."

She pulls her hand away, but he grabs hers before it gets too far. She doesn't squeeze back, but she doesn't fight his touch.

She continues before he can, "You need help. I can't help you with this. Anything else, maybe. But, I-I just don't know what to do here. Are you playing with me? Are—are you joking? 'Cause I don't like this at all."

"No," sighs, "no, it's true."

She shakes her head making red swirls put a whirling wall of color between them.

"Wait, wait. Please, wait."

Head still shakes. The red blur becomes blurrier in her eyes, and her sob is as sad as a child's.

"Rhonda, I can prove it. I can prove it!"

He lets go of her hand, and the power in his last sentence scares her.

She stops shaking, and her glossy eyes see his back heading toward the bedroom. A voice in her head screams for her to leave, a voice that came to her often in childhood, and every time she's ignored it in the past, it has lead to unpleasant memories.

She surges out of the chair and onto her bare feet. The grooves of the tile floor entice her to run like the edges of grass blades beneath the paws of a cheetah. Bounding toward the door, each step patters the ground. Her hand reaches out to flip the deadbolt latch open, and she hears the sound that she knew would come.

"Rhonda, wait! I can—" calls from the opened doorway to the bedroom.

She keeps her eyes focused, yanks the handle open, and darts onto the balcony toward the stairs, all of it soaked and darkened in the night's drizzle. The light from the parking lot post is a dim beam exposing the thin sheet of rain, making the evening air appear to be crying.

She looks to her car below and realizes she didn't grab her keys before running out, her large purse still sitting on the kitchen table. Scanning the parking lot she scours for anyone who can keep her safe.

Movement catches her attention as she hits the top of the stairs. It is a man pulling himself from under the back of Chester's Chevelle. She can hear the recoiling of a tape measure whose metal casing shines in the night. The man looks up at her on the stairs, and she freezes. It's a face she's thought of constantly over the past few days, her heart's sunshine, but it has no warmth as it stares back at her.

Chester plows through the opened front door and onto the balcony. He sees the red hair, mildly damp from the weak rain, stopped at the edge of the stairs, no longer running from him. Following the angle of her head down into the parking lot, he sees his past self staring at her. His past self moves his stare from Rhonda, growing angrier in its expression until it lands on Chester.

From behind her Chester shouts, "Rhonda, he's dangerous—get back inside! Please!"

He darts toward her but not in a sprint, afraid to approach her too quickly and have her fall down the stairs. His past self runs toward the street. After three steps he drops a notebook and a pencil.

Chester's hands reach Rhonda's shoulders, and they pull her back a step before placing himself between her and the ill-willed version of himself below.

Scrambling around, his past self grabs the notebook that is now speckled with wet parking lot debris and run over with watermarks that resemble rivers on an old world map. The pencil has rolled beneath the nearest vehicle, and he runs with full force toward the street and his car parked on it two buildings down. His shoes stomp into puddles splashing his legs with water and grime that used to be part of useful objects but are now crushed and ground into useless and tainting particles, more of them clinging to him with every step of his path.

On the balcony, with one hand on the rail and the other holding her trembling palm behind his back, the breeze pricks over his skin, still pulsing with the summoned energy to confront his past self. Chester turns to her.

The words blow from her lips on the winds of astonishment, "It was yo—"

Putting his hand over her mouth, "Shhh! Can't talk out here. Inside."

Keeping his hand over her lips that seem to be controlled from two inches higher by her mystified irises, he walks her back into her apartment.

Releasing her mouth as he shuts the door, he pleads, "Rhonda, I'm sorr—"

"It's you!"

"Sorry I had to put my hand ove—"

"It's you! Oh, my God, it's you with a bad haircut."

"I know. I know. Just keep your voice down, please. We don't want anyone to hear you."

She nods her head, but her mouth remains open.

Chester says, "If you want me to tell you everything, maybe you should go lie down. It's a lot to take in."

"You were telling the truth? Chester, is it true?"

"I think you better lie down, and I'll tell you everything."

"I've wanted this more than anything in my life. I mean not the sex, but loving you—having you love me back and being together. But, maybe we should wait. Take it slow. Do it all right."

"You're waiting till marriage, Chester?"

"No, I'm not a virgin. Well, I guess most of the women I've been with have never been with me now that I've gone back in time, but I still have the memory. I wish I didn't, and it'll fade. It'll all fade next to you."

"Well, then why not now? It feels right to me."

"You feel right to me too. But, I've already waited a lifetime, Rhonda. All this time for you. I don't want to mess it up now. Every other relationship starts this way—well, nearly all of them do. Most of them fail. Let's make this special; I don't want us to fail. I want to be with you forever."

She puckers and unpuckers her lips.

"I know that scares you; I can't blame you. There's no way for you to feel everything that I do so quickly."

"It's not that it feels wrong—just feels scary."

"I'm thrilled that it doesn't feel wrong—I love that I feel right to you. That's enough. That's more than enough for now. That could've taken much longer. I've never felt that way about anyone before you."

She smiles and tucks her head into his shoulder.

"That's why I think we should wait. I want you to have time to feel things out, for us to grow."

She nods her head into his flesh.

With a tone that sounds more like a little girl than he's ever heard from her, "Never had a guy turn me down before."

"I'd believe that. My body's pretty furious with me right now," he says with a quiet chuckle.

"Oh, yeah?" she says with a laugh, tempted to make a bawdy joke, but letting the urge pass.

"Yeah, I promise. If all I get to do later in life is to be with you, I'll be the luckiest guy on Earth. Way luckier than I deserve."

"So, why did you come back?"

"For you."

"Why didn't you just come after me then—in the future?" poking his ribs, "Am I not a pretty older lady?"

"No, of course not, you're gorgeous then too."

"Gorgeous, huh?"

"As long as you're you, yes, you're gorgeous."

She smiles; he can feel her eyelashes on his chest. Eyelash fluttering halts, and the smile drops back to normal.

"What aren't you telling me, Chester? Why didn't you go after me then?"

Sigh, "Are you sure you want to know?"

"I want to know everything that's important about us."

"First time around I never went to that party. I never went to the premiere either. I actually didn't know that you went. Maybe you didn't do the premiere the first time around either. But, you met Dane at the *Most Hipness* party, started dating, and got married."

"Eww!" she pauses, taking it in, "Eww, I couldn't have been happy. Was I happy?"

"No. If you were, I would've left you alone."

Propping herself on an elbow to look in his eyes, "You would've, wouldn't you?

"I'd be a monster not to."

"No, you'd be someone other than Chester not to." Putting her arms around him, she asks, "Children?"

"Yes. A boy."

"What was his name?"

"Tristan."

She sits up suddenly, ruffling sheets and knocking a pillow to the floor.

"Chester, what about him? Tristan? What about him now that you're back here? Is he never going to exist?"

"I don't know, Rhonda," he says as he sits up to join her.

"How could you come back here without thinking of the consequences? I'm glad you're here for me, but what about the rest? Is he dead now?"

Seeing his face is somber and that he's waiting for her to come down from her rush of emotion, she breathes deeply.

"What is it?" she asks.

"He committed suicide. I'm sorry to have to tell you this."

"Oh, God, that's terrible. Oh, my God."

"Yes. It was the only time I ever contacted you. I sent a letter to say how sorry I was about it, but I didn't put my name on it."

"Why? Why did he do it? Was I a terrible mom?"

"No, of course not. Dane was a terrible dad. Abusive alcoholic. He made the divorce long and ugly. It was in the papers. He told Tristan a lot of things that weren't true. Your mother took his side in the divorce. Thought you should stay in the marriage anyway and make it work even though he was hitting you and your son."

"Good ole, mom," she says putting her hands over her face and crying.

He pulls her to him and says, "They said you were moody and mean at that time. I never believed it, Rhonda. Your doctor had been giving you pills to deal with the stress of the separation to calm you down. Turns out it was a prescription that makes some people angry and moody."

Her head shakes, still covering her eyes with her hands.

"I never believed you could've been that bad, even with the stupid pills. I still can't imagine it. But, the doctor was a friend of Dane's before you started going to him. Could've been done on purpose. Dane was fighting you for custody."

"Did he win?"

"No. His police record outweighed any reported moodiness on your part. But, the whole country was watching your case. The news gets nastier by then. Much nastier. The judge felt like he had to make an example out of you two for the rest of the country. He made you take public parenting classes—classes for delinquent parents. The reporters loved showing pictures of you going in and out of that building. That made me so angry; you were crying beneath sunglasses in most of them."

"When...when did it happen?"

"About six months later. You took a half year off work. You actually turned down a role in a thriller that wound up being the biggest movie of the year. It made a no-name actress a star. I felt so sorry for you. After the six months were up, you left him with your mom to film a guest spot on a TV show. The courts ordered Dane to have a court appointed supervisor or he couldn't see Tristan anymore. However, they did let him call whenever he wanted. He called late while you were gone—knew you were gone and that Tristan was at grandma's. No one knows what he said, but after he got off the phone, Tristan hung himself in the garage. He didn't leave a note."

She sobs for about five minutes. He caresses her, keeping her hair out of her face, and rubbing her forehead.

"I'm sorry for having to tell you all of this. It's not right to hear years of trouble in a few minutes. It's not natural; we're not built to withstand this."

Lifting her head, "But, in a way, you prevented all this," sniffling, "Dane will never hurt me now or a son. Not my child anyway. I won't have to go through that nightmare...How long were we married?"

"Thirteen years. Tristan was born about a year before

you married."

"My God, he was fourteen? Fourteen when he died?"

"Yes."

Her brow is burdened, but no more tears flow.

"Thank God that that horrible death will be prevented."

A few minutes of silence.

"Chester, do you...do you think that if I had a child it might end up to be the same child as Tristan? Like a second chance?"

"His DNA will have to be different, but I always got the impression that he was a lot like you and nothing like his father."

"Keeping Dane's DNA out of any child sounds like a miraculous improvement...I shouldn't be so hateful; the things he did haven't happened now, right? Can you hate someone for something they would have done but didn't get the chance?"

"I don't know. I guess you'd have to hate me too for not taking the chance the first time around, for not coming after you then and telling you how I felt."

"You're raising questions that I don't think we were meant to think about. But, it seems like it's all working out," pauses, "Were you afraid that it wouldn't work out?"

"Of course. Afraid I'd end up somewhere else: the wrong place or the wrong time. Afraid of causing the world a lot of damage; giving information to someone who could hurt people with it. If someone found my device, they could gain so much power, hurt so many people whether they meant to or not."

"So, that's why you gamble?"

"Yeah. How can I get a job writing, even under a fake name, when I already know what is going to be popular for the next two decades? I have every good idea and know every misstep to avoid. It's not fair."

"So, what made you decide to come back? What was the final straw?"

He lets go of her and scoots back against the headboard,

"You don't want to know this one."

"Maybe so, but have to."

"No, you really don't have to; you really don't want to. Please, trust me on this one."

"Is it really that bad?"

"Worse."

Pressing and unpressing her lips while fidgeting with her shiny nails, she says, "But if it's not going to happen now, because I'm never going to be with Dane or live that same life, then it's just a story. It's made-up. It won't ever be the truth."

"I guess, but it's not pretty."

"Well, you have to hear a sad story to appreciate a happy one."

"I don't know about that, but I'll tell you since it's not going to be now."

She maneuvers herself directly in front of him and looks into his face as he begins to speak.

"Dane kept you from taking roles with popular leading men. If they were attractive, he was threatened, and he told you that you couldn't do the movie. I don't know how or what he did at home, but it couldn't have been nice and it worked. You turned down a lot of roles after you had already been cast because of who they named as your costar. The movies that you did act in lacked a popular costar, so they usually weren't very good. Eventually you stopped getting cast. You were a wonderful actress, but you were always a great spot in a lousy production. Before long people associated you as the common factor in a lot of bad movies. But, you were always great; I promise you."

"That isn't as bad as I thought."

"Not finished."

"Oh."

"Your money ran out. Divorce was expensive. Dane had racked up an amazing amount of debt. He never worked after his two years of being the host of that stupid show on the music channel. You had to sell your house. You moved out of L.A. and went back home to live with your mother."

"That is depressing."

"Things got so bad that you did something sad."

"Not me too!" she exclaims.

Realizing she's thinking of Tristan, he continues, "No, no, not suicide. You were alive when I left, but you weren't exactly you anymore. They developed a procedure to help burn victims and other people who have been through an accident or birth defect that deformed their face. It was wonderful. Faces would be donated from organ donors, and it would help someone put their life back to where it was before."

"I had an accident?"

"No, you didn't. The surgery became something that doctors finally grew comfortable with. In the beginning it was a marathon procedure that no one took lightly, even the best surgeons. But, the surgery started happening more often once a few successful attempts had been made. The procedure started involving several surgeons to combat the fatigue, and it eventually was a good option with healthy results for many people."

"What does this have to do with me if I'm not dead and didn't have an accident?"

"Someone else wanted to look like you, and you needed the money. I don't think you needed it that badly, but maybe you did. The buyer had facial implants put in—cheekbones and a chin reshaping, so it would fit her head."

"What? What! I sold my face?" her arms shaking as she sits in front of him.

"Yes."

"I sold my face!" her hands rushing to touch her cheeks.

"It was the first time that it had been done this way. People wanted to do it for cosmetic reasons for awhile, but they could never justify the organ donation just to make someone look prettier. There were too many people in need of the repair to get back to an average lifestyle. Yours was the first."

"I sold my face," she says in a whisper, "What happened to me then? What did I look like?"

"You got the woman's face when she got yours."

"I-I can't take this in."

"I know. I didn't want to tell you, but it won't happen now. Even if I'm not around, it won't happen."

"You'll be around. You need to keep me together...literally."

"I'll be here as long as you want me, and as long as I'm alive."

"Don't worry about that. I'm looking out for you now. We'll keep an eye on your past self," she says as she lifts his arm, lies back on his chest, drapes his arm across her, and continues, "He's not you, you know?"

"What are you talking about?"

"He—your past self. He's not you anymore. You'd never try to hurt someone unless you had to do it to protect someone else. You'd never be like that. He's not you."

"Well, I pushed him to it. He never would've been that way had I not come back in time. Seeing me has warped him. I've interfered in his life three times now. I went to the party, and he had to deal with people having thought they'd seen him there striking out with you publicly. I saw him by the mall walking my crazy cat—his crazy cat. I went to the premiere, and worst of all for him, I've ended up with you. I've caused him trouble, stolen his identity in a way, interacted with the people he works with, and I've taken the one thing he wants and has dreamed about but never believed he could actually have. Sounds like I gave him a reason to go nuts."

"Well, Dane gave you a reason at the party, and you didn't start a fight. You would've fought to protect me, but not because you were angry. You didn't do anything to harm Dane; you left the choice up to me. Your past self is trying to kill you. He's not giving things a chance to work out."

"He can't call the police and tell them his future self is here stealing his identity and his dream woman. If they were to find out there's two of us, if he could even get them to believe him, his freedom'd be gone too. He'd be studied and tested and confined like a prisoner. I've given him no choice. I'm cutting in on his space—his freedom, and no one else can help him. Actions have been made by me that are being attributed to him. It's not right. People at work are going to be asking him about you and me, if they haven't already called him over the weekend to get the scoop. It's an essential right in life to be yourself and not have someone else steal your life. It is a reason for war. In this case, a war on just me. I'm a plague to him. And just by being here—existing—I always will be."

"But, that's not right anymore, Chester. It involves me now. If he hurts you, he's tampering with *my* life, my freedom, my happiness," tapping his chest as she says each of the three items, "No one has the right to do that. I have just as much a right to my life and freedom as he does to his. Besides, you're already here. You're not a part of the future anymore. You can't go back home and have it be the same because you've already changed it. Your home doesn't exist anymore like it did when you left it. You're a part of this time—right now, right here," raising her arms outward, "This time is your home—you do belong now. He doesn't have the right to remove you like you don't belong. You do. You do belong."

He smiles and for the moment is not concerned at all with the threat on his life, "But, he thinks it's bigger than that. He knows I'm from the future, and he knows that's dangerous. I could become powerful with the knowledge that I have. I could be almost unstoppable. A tyrant."

She smiles, "Living in the place that you live? Gambling just to get by?"

Smiling, "Yeah, I guess I'm the tyrant ruler of my crummy apartment, the roaches, and those damn sugar ants."

"You're not so bad, Chester, not even the tiniest bit bad. And if he cared to look, he'd see it too."

"Maybe."

"But, he's not looking that way. He's looking for a chance to kill you."

CHAPTER 17

E lise knows she shouldn't have dated him for three good reasons and one frivolity:

1) he was a coworker
2) he was 15 years younger than her
3) he reminded her of her three past boyfriends, all with whom she wished she were never paired
4) Elise and Eddie would never work—too silly like Jack & Jill, Tim & Tammy, or Brandy & Brendan

She doesn't take the last reason seriously, but it is one more observation to throw on the pile of warning signs—a pile she likes to keep as a gargantuan blazing bonfire in her mind, perpetually burning scaldingly hot and intensely bright to keep her from looking fondly on the past or taking in a new version of a recurring mistake.

Exhausted is how she feels sometimes fighting the old

thought patterns in her mind, holding back pulses from firing down their easy, worn, familiar paths. Despite how hard it still remains for her, it gets a little easier with every passing day. Too bad she has little hope that she'll have many of them left.

She knows he's coming for her.

Edmund is neither ignorant nor incapable, but so blinded by the urge to take what he wants now and the fury that he does not already have it, stupid decisions have been commonplace in his life. One rushed decision, even one with a heinous result, pushes on the next decision to be made even faster, like a canine chasing after something rushing past, not out of decision but instinct. The more objects that fly past, the more frenzied the day becomes.

The last time she saw him, his build was massive although not defined. Being a former steroid user who never worked out much rendered him built more to tear a wall down than to scale it.

When he doesn't like what he sees in the mirror, he turns from it angrily. Usually he'll squint his eyes at his reflection that dares not coincide with his self image. Then he'll throw his intimidating look at the mirror—it's the look that he puts on before he throws a right cross at someone. Following the stare, he'll grunt and turn away in a strut-stomp. Many times he'll actually throw the punch at the mirror. While he was incarcerated, other prisoners witnessed the exchange, often hearing him mumble at his reflection, "Beat your freakin' head in," before turning away.

Turning her mind from memories, Elise thinks of the roll of cash underneath Mr. Titor's mattress—thick, tight, and fragrant with the peculiar air of worn currency. It was just yesterday that he asked her to get it out for him so he could count it and make sure the night caretaker hadn't thinned its girth. It's a common concern among the elderly in care, but especially so since Edmund was caught stealing from nearly all of the residents while working there. Mr. Titor had her count the bills three times in the morning and once in the early evening—she knows the number well. It's over four times her monthly pay.

Ghosts from her past taunt her that the money could get her out of town, away from the danger that is creeping closer, slinking to her side every second of the night. She shakes her head and thinks these words so hard that they spill out her mouth, "I don't want that life anymore. I'm not like that anymore; I'm a new person."

Besides all that, she knows he'd find her wherever she could run.

CHAPTER 18

"**W**e need a plan," she says with her red hair shimmering, casting a bit of magic on her words. A large white tiger paces behind her.

The light hitting the glass shines in a similar fashion as it does on her hair, except the glass doesn't shimmer. Contrary to the seriousness of the conversation, she hasn't stopped smiling since they entered this foreign environment, but the zoo has always made her relax.

Her favorite animals are the tigers. Their grace despite their size and their unbroken will that survives even in captivity is what draws her to them.

Chester says, "I don't know what there is for us to plan."

Leaning in close to him, although the zoo is pretty devoid of people at 5:30 p.m. on a Sunday, she says, "We can't just sit around waiting for him to try to kill you again."

"It's a little hard to blame him."

"Well, then you don't blame him, but you let me blame him. He's trying to take you away from me, and I haven't done a thing to him."

Nods his head.

"Plus, I'm with you all the time, Chester. It would be hard for him to kill you without killing me too. Doesn't that make you blame him? If he had finished cutting your brakes or whatever he was trying to do at Omar's house for the premiere, I would've been in that car with you too. Would've been just as hurt as you."

"Of course. I think about that all the time, but he didn't know you were going to be with me. Hell, I didn't know you were going to be with me."

"Maybe, but what's to stop him when he's done with you? What's to keep him from removing anyone who takes something that he deems to be his?"

"A man has a right to fight for his freedom, for his name. If he wouldn't stop with me, then he'd be taking other people's freedoms from them, and he'd need to be stopped."

"You are a person too, Chester. Your life would be just as easy if he wasn't around. It's your name too. In fact, you've had it a lot longer than he has. What right does he have to remove you?"

"I don't know."

"Exactly. It's not right. He doesn't have an excuse. Two Chester Fuzes exist now. You're not trying to kill him. He just needs to accept it."

"Why does it sound so much easier when you say it than when I think about it?"

"Because you love me," she says as she kisses the tip of his nose.

He smiles, glances at the tiger pacing its domain, and poses, "Okay, so we have the right to stop him. How?"

"That's what I've been thinking about, but you're not going to like it."

He scans his mind for what action she could be so sure that he would be against. It fires.

"No!"

"Yes, Chester, it's the only way."

"No, it's too dangerous. I won't let you."

"You have to."

"Rhonda, you can't go near him. He's dangerous!"

"I'm the only one who can talk to him. *You* certainly can't go near him. That's for sure."

"Maybe I can."

Determined, narrow, red eyebrows press down toward her eyes.

He continues before the eyebrows can influence her speech, "I've never been good at confrontations. Well, not back then anyway. I don't think he'd be so brave if I went after him. He ran away when I saw him the other night at your apartment, and he ran away at Omar's too."

"Maybe he wasn't running from you at the premiere. Maybe he was running from the chance of getting caught or arrested. Especially in front of everyone he works with. He couldn't explain to them how there were two of you anymore than you could."

"Twins. He'd think of long lost twins. It's a bad TV plot cliché. He'd think of it, and grind his teeth while he used it," smiling at the certainty of his past self's hatred of hackneyed sitcom plots.

"But you don't have a twin. There's no evidence to back it up. Somehow, people would figure it out."

"Exactly. That would've just been an emergency excuse if he was caught at Omar's. That's why he's resolved to kill me. Wait a minute…"

"What? What is it?"

"The body. My body. If he just kills me, there will be proof that there were two of us. Two sets of prints. DNA evidence."

"Oh."

"He'll come up with something better."

She frowns.

The pacing tiger settles down on a smooth, flat rock

that is higher than the others.

"He's too smart not to. He'll find a way to get rid of the body. Or..."

"What?"

"He'll make sure none of the remains are identifiable."

Shivers vibrate her frame, "Let's not talk about that."

Grabbing her hand, "Sorry. But if we know how he plans on doing it, it might make it easier to avoid."

"It sounds like a better plan to stop him before he tries."

Exhales roughly, "Rhonda, I don't want you going to talk to him. He's lost it. He was desperate enough to try to cut my brakes one house down from his boss's house, and who knows what he was up to at your apartment. You can't—"

"But, would he hurt *me*, Chester?"

He stares at her in pain, and she already knows the answer.

"You know he wouldn't hurt me."

He looks to his shoes.

"Honestly, would you ever have hurt me? Even in your darkest moments? Ever?"

"No," he says so softly that he hopes she can't hear.

"I knew it. That's why I'm the only way. I'm the only answer."

"Rhonda, I don't—"

"You can't expect me to sit around and wait for him to do something to you, not when I might be able to stop it all, not when I might be able to protect you."

"But, he's not exactly me—not exactly the old me. He's facing something his mind can't entirely comprehend. I never had to go through this. Never had someone drop out of nowhere who looks like me, goes to work parties and everyone thinks he's me, and you. It was bad enough watching you end up with a jerk, but I don't know if I could have taken it being some imposter pretending to be me."

"Maybe so. But, what else have we got? Can't go to the police. I can't tell them it was Chester Fuze who works at *Most Hipness* who was trying to sabotage a car that has a phony registration and is owned by my boyfriend who happens to also be named Chester B. Fuze. Everyone at the party saw you, thinking you were the same guy that they work with. It would be impossible to prove it was him when everyone thought he was you standing right in front of them."

Chester nods, "You're right; there's nothing to be done about it with the police. Besides all that, I happen to have the same exact fingerprints; that's going to be a hard one to explain."

He kicks his right foot at the ground.

Rhonda says, "He has to want to know what's going on anyway. Don't you think he's figured some of this out? Do you really think he'd be upset with me going to talk to him?"

The kicking stops, and he looks back at her face, "He wouldn't hurt you, but he'd try to protect you. He has to think I'm something evil, something dangerous. He wouldn't want you around me. He might try to kidnap you or something to keep you away from me."

"Well, you'll just have to follow me," she says smiling, "I know you'll keep me safe, even from your past self."

"I don't like this."

"C'mon, Chester. You fought time and got back here to me. You did what no one else has ever done. Don't you think we can deal with one person that you know everything about?"

"Desperation can bring about unexpected things. Crazy things. Remember he is desperate. Remember when you're looking at him that that's not me, even though he looks like me."

"I could tell you apart from a thousand clones, Chester."

"I'm still uncomfortable with the idea of just one."

She wraps her arm around his back, and she offers quietly, "There is another possibility, but I didn't want to ask."

"What?"

"Is it possible for us to go somewhere else in time? To get away from all of this—both of us together?"

"I thought about that too."

"And?"

"It was hard enough for me to get here. Honestly, it's on a miracle level that I arrived in the right time at all, despite all my years of figuring. I knew the time travel would work—just wasn't sure if I could make it send me to exactly when I wanted to arrive. I don't know if I got lucky, or if it would always work. It's only been done once; it could go horribly wrong the next time."

"But, it worked once."

"Yeah, we could also jog across the interstate blindfolded and have it work once. The next time—splat! I don't want to risk anything with you."

"We're risking every moment now with your past self after you."

"Yeah, but we're not blindfolded," he snickers.

She pinches his back lightly.

"Rhonda, it takes a lot. I have an ID, my birth certificate is still valid, I have credit cards although I don't use them, I look like the person I claim to be—it's not that easy to jump to another place and have a story that doesn't get you thrown in jail, interrogated by a government, or killed. If anyone knew where I'm from, I'd be tortured, questioned, maybe even dissected. I'd be a threat to national security, and the secret to the ultimate weapon. If anyone knew what I've done, I wouldn't be here with you, not while there is still anyone with the power to take the secret from me. And it's not just the government—anyone who desperately wants to undo one bad event, to make a different choice, to live a better life—that's just about everybody. Even a good person could go crazy if they knew that kind of power was within their grasp."

"What if we went far enough back where there were no records—no IDs, no birth certificates, no fingerprints on file?"

"Life was hard back then."

"I'm okay with hard."

"No penicillin, no cure for most things, our immune system is not used to what was around then. Life expectancy is only thirty-some years, and that's not a guarantee. I want more than ten years with you."

Her face was troubled while he was speaking, but her cheeks strain with a bursting smile, "Okay, okay. I already figured that if it was a good option, you'd have already asked me to go to another time with you. I just wanted to ask."

"It's not that I wouldn't want to, Rhonda; it's just a huge risk. No one has ever done this before. Well, no one that we know of. There were rumors of The Philadelphia Experiment, but no one has any evidence."

"The Philadelphia Experiment?"

"Government thing. Tesla and Einstein were supposedly both a part of it. Both are rumored to have resigned. Lots of speculation; little proof. Pushed into the same category as Moon Landing Hoaxers and Bigfoot sightings."

"Yeah, but you made it. Maybe the government did too."

"Not too likely, not the way the next twenty years turned out. There would've been some key mistakes that would have been avoided. They'd have covered their tracks better on some other things. Some embarrassing moments would have been done over again. But, yeah, the bizarre can be true sometimes."

Roaring like an explosion thrashes through their eardrums.

One of the white tigers shows its flesh-ripping teeth jutting out pink and black gums. Its lips are sucked back fully, exposing its pointy weapons as it eyes another tiger approaching its perch on the smooth, topmost rock in their habitat.

The approaching tiger crouches low, growling but not roaring, looking for a way to take what the other has.

Turning her head from the commotion, Rhonda asks, "And what about the gambling? Did you see the bookie's face today while he was paying you guys? I thought for sure there'd be a fight. So, have you really come all this way to get stabbed in a bar brawl over a few hundred dollars?"

"It was actually a few grand today."

"Chester!"

"Sorry," chuckling.

"Aren't you afraid you'll have come all this way— found me—have me with you now only for you to die over a bet?"

"What else can I do?"

"Anything."

"Can't get any official job where they'll need my social security number. I was only good at writing stories. What else can I do?"

"What if it were me, Chester? Would you let me gamble like you are?"

"Never. Not for a second," his face serious at the thought.

"Then, why don't you just stay with me?"

"And have you pay for everything—be a leech?"

"No, be safe, with me."

"I can't. If I lived with you, he'd come after me there; it'd bring him too close to you. He's already tried once— imagine if I'm there all the time. The bars are safer than him."

The patter of tiny tennis shoes on the concrete approaches them. The child smacks Rhonda's rear with an echoing sound and runs away.

Rhonda's lips purse into an appalled "O".

"Did that just happen, or did I leave a chunk of my brain in the space-time foam?"

Grasping her derriere with both hands she says, "I can tell you the stinging through my butt is happening right now."

Only halfway sure his response is appropriate, "We could kill him."

Her lips only break from the "O" circle to an oval.

"No, really. We could casually be walking along and nudge him over the rail into the tiger den. Then, later, if we felt guilty about it, we could go back in time and push him into the bears."

As she starts to smile, the flap and stomp of the untied shoes closes in on them again. The small hand cocks back with all the gusto of a victoriously celebrating athlete. The hand, covered in grime and cotton candy residue, flings forward toward the unprotected space between Rhonda's two hands. The little wrist is grasped quickly by Chester, producing a crisp sound.

Unphased, the other small arm swings at Rhonda. Chester catches the counterpart. Now the youthful face turns toward Chester.

"Lemme go, dammit—you ain't my daddy."

"Hey, you can't go around slapping ladies. What do you think you're doing?"

"Just playin' wit' her. I didn't hurt her none. Now let me go!"

"That's right: you didn't hurt her none—which means you hurt her some, and that's what makes it something you can't do."

"Let me go!"

Booming from a bench under a tree about thirty yards away, "Oh, h-e-l-l no! You best let go of my child right nah."

"Ma'am, he slapped my girlfriend on the butt, and I caught him trying to do it again."

Coming closer, "Don't matter nuttin' what he was doing. He's just a child and you a man."

"Lady, I'm only holding his wrists to keep him from slapping her again."

"O-o-o, yeah, she looks real hurt."

"Screw you, lady," says Rhonda as the shy dam can no longer hold back reason from flooding the valley of absurdity.

"Oh, it's gonna get ugly now."

Letting go of the child's hands and stepping between the angry and the innocent, he says, "No, you're going to take away your little boy and keep him away from my girlfriend."

"I see—now you're gonna tell me what to do."

"Where do you get the audacity to yell at us when your unwatched child is sexually harassing women right in front of you?"

"I've got plenty of audacity with you putting your

hands on my boy."

"I couldn't have said it better," smirks Chester.

Janet walks up to them screaming at Chester, "Chaz, you idiot, what are you doing to this woman?"

"Uh…"

"Always quick with the response, huh, Chaz? I'm tired of all your screwing up. You're fired."

Chester looks to Rhonda who returns his befuddled expression.

The angry woman asks Janet, "You trying to tell me that you're this one's boss?"

"I was; he's fired now 'cause of this."

"What ya'll doing in the zoo then?"

"Company picnic."

"Mmm-hmmm. Well, that ain't good enough. If he was working for you then while he was doing this, then I'm suing your company."

"What?" Chester wheezes.

Janet says, "Shut up, Chaz. I'm handling this," turning to the woman, "That's fine. The company is Aardvark Shipping, and my name is Miss Glasscock. We're the second one in the phonebook; right past Triple A."

"Na-uh, no, that ain't good enough, lady. Ain't you got a card?"

"Sure," fumbling in her purse and handing the card to the woman, "Call first thing in the morning."

"Call whenever I damn well please. I'm gonna own that damn company," continuing to talk out loud while walking away, waving her finger in the air with a three inch, glossy-polished glue-on nail, looking straight ahead at her bench, while her child throws pinecones down at the bears in their habitat.

"Janet, why on earth did you do that?" asks Chester as they start to walk to the zoo food court where Lucky is still finishing his third burger and Cindy waits patiently.

With a deep resolve, "Trying to reason with a crazy person is about as good as putting on makeup to impress a blind man. Logic is no good with an illogical person. When someone's as unreasonable as that, you only have two choices: beat them to the punch or just agree with'em. Anything else is a waste of your time, so I just agreed with this one to shut her up."

"I just have one question then: whose card did you give her?"

"Miss Glasscock is the name of my ex-husband's secretary with whom he got awfully snuggly during the last year of our marriage. Still had the card 'cause I had to call her during the divorce proceedings—she's still his secretary. She can deal with the screaming *happy* woman early tomorrow morning."

Chester grins, "Even tragedy has its funny side."

A bear roars vociferously.

CHAPTER 19

I t's an odd thing to stare at the most gorgeous woman you've ever seen and know you're going to do a terrible thing to her. That thought ruminates in his head as she begins to speak.

"So, why are you trying to kill my man?"

"Funny. Your man looks a lot like me."

A small fluff of curiosity creeps into the edge of Rhonda's periphery, peeking around the corner of the recliner in which she sits. The left set of whiskers are pointed at her, but the giant black pupils in the yellow-green oval eyes are watching Chester sitting on an adjacent couch. All the while its paws step uncertainly forward and then comfortably backward and then repeat.

"You used to act like him too, but you're different now."

"Proudly so. Like to think I never shared the same thought with that lunatic imposter."

"Watch it now," seeing the rigidity of his face, she eases her tone, "He has beautiful thoughts all the time. What happened to you?"

"Little things. Little things that change your outlook. Showing up for work the first day at my dream job and finding out that everyone thinks I was at a party that I wasn't and that I hit on you in front of everyone and you left with some drunk. And on top of that, they think I walked away from my new boss when he was trying to talk to me—completely blew him off after I was supposedly blown off. I was only halfway to L.A. while that party was going on—nearly a thousand miles away. Couldn't tell if they thought I was cool or if they were making fun of me, but I could tell for sure that it wasn't some elaborate joke—they all believed it—they weren't making it up. Then I see the guy—looks exactly like me, driving my dream car that I don't even have myself."

He leans forward quickly, sending the feline retreating behind the recliner, and asks, "Do you have any idea how it feels to know that either everyone around you is playing a horrible trick on you or that you've gone insane? Or…"

"Or what?"

"Or some psychopath is messing with your life…Little cracks running through what was my life, spreading a little more each day. Then, he goes to the premiere pretending to be me. I'd had never known he was trying anything like that until it was all over if the tux rental store hadn't called to tell me my tux was ready. So, I went to Omar's to watch—to see what he'd do and try to figure out why the hell someone would want to be me. I stayed in my car out of sight, watching everyone arrive, and then the limo pulled up to take them to the premiere. As he was getting in the limo with the rest, I saw the scar on his hand—it's just like mine. That plus the car—never told anyone about wanting that year and model—knew he wasn't a conman, but me. Somehow he was me."

She looks away from the intensity of his face and down at her knees. The cat mounts a new offensive, lightly stepping between them, dancing around the coffee table and looking at Chester on the sofa while nuzzling the side of its face against the corner of the squat glass tabletop.

"He *is* me, right? Somehow?"

She watches the stalking tail sail above the edge of the table like a shark's fin.

"For the love of God, tell me! He's interfering in all of my life—he's taken my dreams away from me," looking in her eyes as she finally brings her stare back to him, "even the ones I haven't had a chance at yet."

"Yes. He's you."

"From where?"

"You wouldn't believe me if I told you."

"Then, why are you here?"

"For love."

The Chester on the sofa sputters in a choppy exhale, and she continues, "To ask you to leave the man I love alone."

Shaking his head, "I've gone my whole life without hurting anybody, certainly never on purpose. But, I think his big, unbelievable secret that you're having trouble telling me makes him too dangerous to be left alone."

"Alone or alive?" she says with a squeak in her throat on the third word.

"Don't know how to answer you without knowing all the facts, but I think I already know enough to say both—it's neither safe to leave him alone or alive."

She looks to the cat which lunges onto the opposite side of the couch as Chester and then, taking a moment to gain his bearings, timidly approaches him.

Chester says, "You might as well just spit it out. It's all bizarre to start with—the explanation has to be bizarre too. Strange offspring sprout out of strange circumstances. So, where is he from?"

"The future. Twenty years in the future."

His face is stunned, but not quite enough for the revelation.

"Knew it. It doesn't make sense, but neither does anyone looking exactly like me and knowing my desires that I've never told anyone…and the scar—my scar."

"And you've been trying to kill him?"

"Con man, clone, time traveler—it didn't really matter, did it? All three are dangerous; whatever it was, it was already taking my life away. But, it was too perfect—knew it had to be from the future. If it looks that much like me, can't go to the police about it. If it has my scar, my memories, my dreams, it might have my fingerprints and DNA too."

"*He*. Not an *it*."

"Nothing but an it to me. Can't be me; I'm me. It's only some future copy of me. It's not real—not human."

A damp pink nose sniffs at his forearm, whiskers tickling him, the cat finding much more warmth in the man than she can see.

Rhonda responds, "He's a wonderful man—the best I've ever known, and he doesn't want to hurt you at all. And, I know you've had feelings for me since my show first went on the air years ago."

From beneath the brim of his hat blocking out his forehead and covering his fashionable haircut, he looks to the cat snuggled against his thigh. As he scratches its head, the feline squints its eyes and flattens its ears. The cat puts its paws in front of him, setting his head atop them in a regal pose. Everyone likes to be king of their own domain, their own space, even if it's just the sofa.

The tag that dangles from the end of its collar reads "Mouse" in big letters, followed by smaller writing that Rhonda can't make out. It is indeed a cat but named Mouse, at heart being something different than what its name claims to be.

"Chester, listen to me. I know you must still have some kind of feelings for me."

She waits for him to look up, but he doesn't.

"I'm happy with him, Chester. I've never been happy before—didn't even know what it was until I met him. Scared me at first. My whole life that happened before he came back here was miserable. Everything that was going to happen to me between now and then turned out to be a disaster. He did all of this to undo all that damage—to save me from it. He didn't come back here to hurt anybody; it was all for me. He could've come back anytime he wanted to, but he only did it when my life hit a really ugly spot. He didn't come back for power or to mess with your life; it's all for me. Can't you leave him alone for me?"

A smile forms and fades as he starts, "Sorry, Rhonda, I can't do that. The information that he has is just too powerful. If anyone figures out what he's done—what he knows, it's the ultimate advantage. Being able to undo anything that's been done, to reshape history with the knowledge of the future. Horrifying to think about. Any government with that kind of knowledge could take over the world. Any person with that kind of power could bring the world to its knees. Everyone would want to know what is going to happen next, which disaster to avoid, will a cure be found in time. It's endless."

A little furry belly twitches with rapid breaths, eyes barely open.

"And wait a minute! Why doesn't he look older than me?"

"He doesn't know—hasn't figured it out."

"It's impossible—an abomination—it's not natural. And, he knows. He knows, Miss Romero—he did all this himself—he has to know how it happened. He just doesn't want to tell you."

"He has no idea—I swear it. He told me that himself. He said people were experimenting with sine waves to reverse effects of aging, but they hadn't figured it out yet when he left."

"Phhhh. Sounds like he's lying to you. Guy figures out how to travel to his past and can't figure out what happened to his own body."

"Chester would never lie to me."

"You might be surprised."

Leaning forward with her hands clasped and held at the top of her closed knees, "Chester, would you lie to me? He told me how you feel about me—could you lie to me?"

"Might be surprised."

The fact that he didn't look away while delivering the line makes her believe it and worry about what she's gotten herself into.

His words couldn't be any more resolute than if they were written by an apt judge and decreed by a quickened preacher. His body looks identical to her Chester's in every way despite the baseball cap on his head that she's never seen her Chester wear. Even to her, the faint scar on his hand looks the same as the one she frequently slides her fingers over, not being able to see the difference between her boyfriend and the one who wants to kill him sitting a foot and a half from her. Her only clues to the differences between the man she knows and the facsimile before her are in the tone of the words he's let out and the expression on his face.

The cat jumps to the floor and walks down the hallway behind Rhonda's chair toward the front door.

And then there are his eyes. Irises are seas full of angry despair with small islands of calm pupils. She wonders if the pupils are little paradises straining to survive amid the corrosive salt water waves, signaling there may still be hope alive in this lost, rightful Chester of this time. But, she's also aware that the sparkling hope embedded deep within the dense aggressive water might be nothing more than the afterglow of a past sunset, the glimmer of a star's last gasp of luminance flashing in our sky thousands of years after it's burned out, a light whose source no longer exists, a remnant of the past reaching us in the present, unable to ever burn again.

Keys grind into a lock down the hallway at the door. Chester's eyes drain of their angry look and are pumped full of panic. He flings off the sofa into a standing position.

"Oh, are you living with someone?" Rhonda asks.

"Not exactly. Get behind me."

"What?"

"Just trust me—get behind me!"

As he pulls her by her arm out of the chair, the sound of the door opening reaches their ears. When he plops her down on the sofa, the door shuts.

Desperately trying to see what she is being protected from, she leans into the open area of the sofa to see around the side of Chester.

The form of a man leaves her anxious. As it starts to come into focus, she begins to smile. His purple shirt beams familiarity, but his face is twisted in anger and staring at his doppelganger before her.

"Leave her alone. I'm the one that you want. Let her get out of here, and then we can talk," says the man directly in front of her and closest to her.

From the edge of the hallway, "Looks to me like I want both of you, being that you're both sitting in my living room while I'm supposed to be at work."

"What?" Rhonda asks.

The Chester, whom she's been talking with and who stands between her and the angry one that just walked in, turns his head where he can still keep an eye on his counterpart and catch her within the edge of his periphery and says, "Rhonda, it's true. This is his apartment. I couldn't let you come here and talk with him."

"What?" shouts his purple-shirted counterpart.

Chester counters, "Why are you here? Why aren't you at work?"

As he begins to speak, still standing at the edge of the hallway and the living room, the word choice sounds like her Chester, but the tone and the heavy pacing are nothing like the man she knows. Even when her Chester was talking to her earlier, imitating what he thought his past self would be like, it was but a cartoonish impression of the man who talks at them now. "A little odd that you're asking that, being that you've broken into my apartment. Don't you know why I'm not at work? You seem to know everything else."

Hard stares.

"I came home from work to take Mouse to the vet. Has a urinary tract infection. Don't you remember that?"

"That never happened the first time around."

Looking toward Rhonda, "Yeah, apparently a lot of

things were different the first time around."

"Why are you trying to kill me?"

"Are you serious?"

"I asked."

"You're dangerous."

"We all can be dangerous."

"Well, no one else is pretending to be me, interfering in my life, and…" he stops short, looking to Rhonda who is still poking her head around the side of Chester.

Speaking to his past self, her Chester says, "I know. I know. I've felt everything you've felt for her plus another twenty years. If it weren't for how you feel, I'd never have figured out how to get back here—it was all for her."

"Says the man who has broken into my apartment and lied to his girlfriend."

"It's true."

"Doesn't matter if it's true. No one should know what you know. No one should be able to go back and tamper with other people's lives. I'm alive outside of you! I'm not some past shadow whose life is a tool for you to use to carve out your own."

"You're right. I can't pretend to be you ever again— that was only for her."

"Was it? Or was it for you? Tell me it wasn't a dream come true for you."

"The first night it wasn't. The show party was awful."

"What about the premiere? Do you know what it's like to have coworkers pat your back and make admiring jokes about a dream you'll never have? What it's like to find out someone pretending to be you has met the girl of your dreams and taken her away from you?"

"I am you."

"Not from where I stand."

His purple shirt is brighter than the one she's seen her Chester wear frequently, and his eyes seem darker to her.

His hand.

His hand seems to have no scar at all. She stares closer

at it, focusing on it.

No scar.

Maybe it's the light of the living room casting a shadow over his eyes in the dim hallway, but his ocular cavities seem to be smothered by the darkness of a heavy brow, sucking in, crushing, and imprisoning light where her Chester would exude it.

The harsher voice, "Tell me, Chaz, in twenty years, provided no one else tampers with our timeline, I'll be the age you are now, and you'll still be you separate from me, right?"

"Yeah, that's right."

"Doesn't sound like you're me at all. Sounds like we're about as separate as we could be—as separate as any two people on earth. You could be in another part of the world with Rhonda, and I could still be right here in L.A."

"Sounds like a good plan to me—for Rhonda and me to go away. There's no need for us to be at odds, or for you to keep trying to kill me."

A crooked smile forms under his darkened brow, "See, that's where you're wrong, Chaz. You messed up my life something painful already. You had no more right to do that to me than you did to anyone else. Can't let you walk away with that kind of power."

"Why not?"

"Because you're dangerous wherever you go. Someday you'll have an accident and go to the hospital. Someday one of us is going to die, and there'll be a coroner's report. But, the other one of us will still be alive. They'll figure out there's two of us, and they'll know you came from the future or they'll think one of us was a clone or something nuts. They'll eventually figure it out, and that's too dangerous for everybody else in the world."

"Then, why not settle this right now? I'm right here."

"In front of a witness in my apartment? I think not."

Rhonda says, "I'll be a witness anyway; I'm with him all the time."

"If there's not much left of him, you won't be a witness

to much. No one's gonna believe that there was two of me and I killed the other one. Without any remains, no one's going to believe a crazy story like that."

"Monster," she says.

"Am I?" pointing to the Chester directly in front of her, "Or is the monster this abomination here? The one who has stolen my life and lied to you? Do you really think it's me?"

"He's not trying to kill anyone."

"Most heroes throughout history have had to kill someone—someone who was doing something they shouldn't have, someone whom the world would be a safer place without them in it."

"Stop talking to her, you psychopath. I can't believe you came from the same origins as me and turned out like this."

"Really? How would you feel if someone took Rhonda away from you?"

"Miserable. And, I've had to deal with it twice."

"Ever lose her to someone who could wipe away everything man has ever accomplished? Someone who could do horrible things to anyone he wants and then travel back before he did them and get away with all of it? It's a criminal's dream—no one would remember their crime, not even the victim."

"No, of course not, but I've lost her and learned to live with it. I was miserable, but I took it. I didn't come back here to take what I wanted. I came back to save her from the terrible life that she made for herself."

Roughly, "It was her life to wreck."

From around Chester's side, she says, "It still is. I'm where I want to be."

"Well, Miss Romero, it might be safer if you find some different company."

Rushing toward his somber counterpart at the edge of the hallway, "Alright, that's enough. You want me—I'm right here right now, tough guy. You threaten her again, and I'll beat your head in."

Glancing toward Rhonda with a voice that shakes subtly, "You still think he's harmless, Miss Romero? Seems a bit off-balanced if you ask me."

"You're a coward. You've been coming after me when I'm not looking, and now that I'm standing right in front of you, you've got no guts at all."

"Guts—I may not have so much, but stupidity I've got even less. Explaining how a dead man ended up in my apartment who looks exactly like me, fingerprints and all, is not something that will end up well for me. Think I'd end up being interrogated by the government on how you came to be—incarcerated and disposed of when I'm deemed to be no longer useful. No, I plan on taking my life back when you're gone, not taking the penalty you should get for toying with time."

Chester's fist yearns to punch his past self, but he knows the logic of his doppelganger is sound. There won't be any way to assume his past life if there is any evidence that there were two of him. Even a loud argument could bring the police, which would expose their secret.

"Come on, Rhonda, let's go."

Past Chester says, "Thought you might see it my way after your hormones cooled down."

"Try not to think about me, and maybe we'll both live longer."

"Don't worry about me, time bandit; I don't plan on living a short life."

Rhonda approaches behind, and Chester pushes his past self by the shoulder to clear the entrance to the hallway. His counterpart doesn't resist and steps to the side.

As she passes, his past self says, "Miss Romero, you're always welcome here. You don't need him to break in for you to stop by. You can come here any time of *night*," pauses, "or day."

She doesn't turn around but keeps walking to the door.

Just as he turns his attention back to the Chester from the future, a fist smashes directly on the brim of his nose.

"Don't you ever talk to her like that again. Don't you ever come near her again. If you ever try to harm either one of us, I'll kill you myself, and Rhonda and I will run off to another country where no one'll ever know about the two Chester Fuzes; all they'll know about is one dead one who was too stupid to try to enjoy the rest of his life instead of wasting it trying to kill me. Don't think you're the only one who can act differently. And by the way, it's not breaking and entering—I have a key."

Holding his bleeding nose in his hand, his past self nods his head. The cat has wandered between them, curiosity outweighing the fear of the noisy exchange.

Chester stares at his bleeding past self, and at about knee level the tail twitches.

Less than three minutes later they are in her car. Having taken a cab there to not involve his conspicuous vehicle which would have ruined his ability to trick Rhonda into believing he was the past Chester with whom she wanted to talk, he rides in her passenger seat. Neither talks much having so much to comprehend and digest. It isn't until they step foot into her condo that she asks what has been on her mind.

"How long, Chester?"

"I guess he's been after me ever since he saw me driving that day. Don't think he'll ever stop now that I've been in his apartment."

"No, how long have you been planning all those lies to say to me?"

"At the zoo. The second I knew you were going to try to talk to him."

"Why didn't you just tell me it was you when I got there? Why not tell me and take me home?"

"Would you have listened? Would you have given up on talking to him, or would you have tried to go there again?"

"Chester, would you have listened to me if things were reversed? Could I have talked you out of trying to protect me from someone who was trying to kill me?"

"No, nothing you could've said would've stopped me," he pauses holding her arms at her elbows, "That's why I had to do it. I knew you wouldn't stop until you at least gave it a shot—I knew that's what I would do too. But, I couldn't let you be alone with him. You saw how he was for just a few minutes. All this hate for me is making him nasty."

She drops her head to the side, her chin hitting the top of her chest, her eyes taking in a glossy crooked view of her shoulder, upper arm, and the ground past it.

"Rhonda, I'm so sorry. I hated every second of it. Please forgive me."

"I'm not mad at you, Chester. I'm just sad that it didn't work."

CHAPTER 20

Turning a corner into a familiar Riverview subdivision, he wishes he needn't do what he is about to. He's gone over it in his head nonstop—now time is running out, and there's nothing left to do but to do it, bracing himself for horror as he begins.

With one hand he knocks on the door; experience has taught him to use force or risk having to do it again.

The noise from the TV is loud even as it works its way to his ears in the night air just outside the locked door. The noise is the one thing he feels thankful for. It might create just enough distraction for him to do his dreaded deed and escape unnoticed.

With the trepidation building up inside him, one might conclude this is his first time, despite having done this hundreds of times before. While he's never been comfortable intruding into people's homes, he knows there's no way out of it now. It's not the act that makes him anxious, or the fear of the hot, primal work, but the recipient.

The names of those on his list have never held much interest to him as long as the money was good. But, this name sparks the image of a high school princess, and the heat, which he hasn't felt this intensely since his first job a little over two years ago, seeps into his fingertips, nearly scorching them and threatening to make them useless, possibly botching the job and leaving him vulnerable.

Besides the burning in his digits, he feels the image of her burning in his head.

The flame of his memory materializes in two brown eyes as the door jerks open before him. Her eyes flash a moment of panic, and her ponytail bounces as she quickly looks away.

Just as in his memory, she's still in her red and black cheerleader uniform.

"Four large pizzas and a diet two liter?"

"Yeah," she says extending her hands to take the boxes.

"Careful, they're hot," he warns trying to sound no different than on any of his other jobs or any other delivery person that's been on her doorstep.

"Okay, thanks," she pauses, "Hey, you go to school with me, don't you?"

"Yeah," he says looking at his feet while she takes the two liter from him and sits it just inside her opened door.

"Brian, right?" her voice cracking slightly.

"Brendan."

"Brandon?" she asks.

"Sure. Why not?"

"Did you go to the game tonight?"

"No," pointing to the logo on the left breast of his shirt, "Been working all night."

"O-h-h," she says in the pitch that makes him tingle, "It was fantastic. We were down by thirteen before the fourth quarter, and we won. Can you believe it?"

"That's great, Brandy. I'm glad you guys won."

"We won; the school won."

"Yeah."

They both start to fidget with their feet.

"Look, I'd ask you in to tell everyone hi and hang out, but it's girls' night tonight, and some of them are already in their sleepy clothes."

"S'okay, I gotta get to my next job anyway."

"'Kay," she says handing him a thin wad of bills folded over twice, "Well, see ya 'round school."

"Yeah, see ya. Thanks."

The door closes behind him, and the laughter that he expects to come bellowing through it doesn't. The sounds of action movie bombardment continue to pump out the speakers.

As soon as that order came through thirty-two minutes ago, he knew it was going to be trouble. A large order on a game night with the last name of Melancon: he knew he wasn't lucky enough for it not to be her, and worse, he knew it was a party.

Pondering his fate pacing around the oven, he wasn't sure if he would prefer it to be an all-girl sleepover where he'd definitely be seen by at least one of the girls from school or if he'd rather it be a sans supervision co-ed bash. At least then, it might have been a guy from school to answer the door, and if Brendan was very lucky, it might have been someone with no interest in embarrassing him.

His father owns the store, which is part of a franchise, and is constantly scolding him for being ashamed of delivering pizzas, reminding him that delivering pizzas is what has provided his car and will take care of his college expenses.

"It's no different than being a sales clerk in one of the fancy stores in the mall," his father would say, "They wait on a customer, get what they want, and take their money. You do the same. They want the pizza; you deliver the pizza—you get the money. You're not out there trying to hawk pizza to people who don't want it."

He'd respond, "But, dad, I go to school with these people."

"So what? We saw that cute girl from your class waiting on us at the Italian restaurant a few weeks ago. And, didn't you say she was a cheerleader?"

"That's different, dad. She's not pulling up to our house in a silly uniform."

"It's honest work—no different than a waitress—or a waiter. People order the food, and you bring it. You get tips just like them. The world's a sad place when you have to be ashamed of your work; you should only be ashamed if you can work and don't."

He can still hear his father's words as he turns on the ignition. He agrees with his father on one thing though; the tips are good. As if to prove it to himself, he turns up the sound system in his car that he's recently purchased. And, it is an enticing prospect to not have burdensome student loans like his older brother who refused to work in the pizza shop. He just wishes the logo shirt and khaki pants that he hates wearing would come with a mask when he had to knock on the door of his classmates.

Pulling up to the curb in front of his next delivery, he smiles a little when he thinks that it didn't go as badly as he had anticipated at Brandy's house, and nothing like a few incidents with other classmates who made sure everyone else at school the next week heard about him being a delivery boy, including elaborate descriptions of his uniform and impressions of him walking up the sidewalk and knocking on the front door.

"Boy" is the part of the title that he can't stand. Delivery person would make him feel so much better. The titles of pizza technician or delivery engineer would be running the gamut; he knows that. Nevertheless, as he steps out the door to get the pizzas out the backseat, he thinks that being called a boy at eighteen makes him feel like a—but his thoughts are interrupted by a hand grabbing his throat and slamming him against the car.

His body makes a thud similar to when his father backs into the dumpster in the pizza shop parking lot. His shoulders and upper back feel as though they're crumbling.

The large man choking and pinning him against his car

has a clump of mud stuck to his right earlobe. As Brendan looks over the lumbering attacker, straining to find a way out of this predicament, he sees another small glop of mud stuck to the right side of his shaved head, and the man is damp, clothes clinging to his body and seeping muddy water from his sloshy shoes.

As the pizza delivery engineer tries in vain to scream, he notices his attacker is not even looking at him, but into the backseat.

Pulling the young man's face close to his, Edmund says, "The pizza and the money right now," releasing his throat and tossing him back against the car with the last spoken word.

"Pizza first," demands Edmund, grabbing the boy's shoulder and turning him toward the backseat.

The heat shield container that holds the boxes is blurry, and Brendan's vision bounces back and forth as he raises his stinging shoulders to get the pizzas. Feeling like he's moving in slow motion, he straightens himself up and hands the boxes to Edmund.

"The other ones too," he orders.

As two larges and an order of cheesy bread are apparently not enough, he leans into the backseat to grab his next delivery. Bringing them out of the car, they are quickly grabbed by one giant paw of a hand with the thumb at the bottom and the four sausage-link fingers on top of the three boxes. The other hand drops the previous order on top of the new one, leaving the smaller cheesy bread box on top.

Sticking out his free hand, Edmund says, "Now the money."

Reaching into his pocket, Brendan pulls out the money that just recently came from Brandy's gentle hand. Something in his head screams for him not to let the attacker take that money from him. The pizza he doesn't care about, but the money from Brandy awakens a fighting spirit.

Edmund slaps him across the face, "Faster—let's go; let's go."

Bringing his hand out, Edmund takes the money from

him, and feeling how thin it feels between his thumb and finger, he gives the delivery person an annoyed look.

"Only had one stop before this one," offers a scared voice.

Hard stare.

"I swear it."

Headlights flicker in their direction as a car turns from an all-way stop three blocks down.

"Get in your car and drive off. No cops, or I'll come back for you."

Those words sting through the driver's face, but he says nothing outside of defiant but defeated eyes.

Edmund grumbles, "I swear it; don't be stupid," as he turns and walks quickly down the sidewalk away from the headlights that are slowly coming down the street.

A house door opens, and a voice asks, "Hey, what the hell is taking so long to get our pizza to the door?"

No response.

It comes again, "Hey, I said, 'What is going on out there?'"

"Uh, got the wrong order; I'll have to go ba..."

The voices trail off as Edmund's feet move faster, turning the corner onto a side street, and his eyes scope out a place where he could eat the food in secrecy.

A clubhouse roof sticks out over a wooden fence. He's found his place; thinking of sharp teeth and his wounded calves, he hopes the yard is vacant of canine resistance.

Fourteen ravenous minutes later, Edmund kneels down, drinking from a hose on the side of a standard suburban one-story house, uncaptured water running down his chin and neck.

It took him seven tries before he found a house with a hose between it and its neighbor. The goal was a hose and not just a spout, out of the way on the side of a house, but not in a backyard where he could be cornered easier.

A large gulp goes down his throat, and then he turns the stream of water to his head, arms, and clothing. He's been following this same pattern for nearly two minutes now. A tremendous amount of poorly chewed pizza demands a lot of water from his already dehydrated body.

Earlier this evening, he tried to rinse himself off in a park bathroom before obtaining his pizza. The park backs up to the river and has bathrooms opened all night long. It was the first restroom he could find, but the wall had no mirror, only the broken brackets that used to press the mirror against the wall.

Surprisingly, it didn't occur to him to try the women's side next door. Had he thought of it, he would've enjoyed trespassing into the taboo region.

He splashed water all over his body, scrubbing at the dried mud spots that he could see and frantically rubbing everywhere that he couldn't view. Swallowing a few deep gulps in the process, he helped relieve his water deficiency somewhat, but his hunger demanded action before fully satisfying the former.

The whole time a clock was ticking in his mind, counting down the seconds until someone would find him. Although his calves burned with pain, he didn't lift his pants legs to look at them, deciding there was nothing he could do about their injuries right then anyway and that he's better off not knowing how bad of shape he's in until he has the time to deal with it.

A similar theory with his finances left him with an overdrawn bank account and turned off utilities in the only apartment he's ever had on his own. The bills sat unopened until he felt like he had the time and resources to deal with them. When one would become urgent enough to interfere with his television and video games, he'd write a check from a book with no records.

Perhaps it's that apartment and the dingy ones he lived in during his years of bouncing foster care that leave him full of awe and hatred for the warmth of the suburbs, the freshly cut lawns instead of a trash-laden parking lot, the flowering gardens in place of decaying dreams, and the backyard clubhouses instead of corners of closets where one could hide during a violent episode involving this month's caregivers.

In the shadow of the alleyway where the streetlight is blocked out at a sharp angle by the rooftop, a familiar deep sound rakes over his brain, triggering a slew of uncomfortable impulses.

"Uhruff! Raoo! Roo!" bellows from behind a wooden gate that meets the side of the house just a few feet from where he crouches with the running hose.

"I can't f..." his sentence is cut short as the creature slams its head into the gate, ripping the screws that hold the latch in place out of the wood.

The gate juts open a few inches, and a furry, pointy-eared head can be seen in its gap. With another cranial slam into the gate, the latch falls atop the ramming beast as the gate flings open.

Snarl and blur are upon him before he can get from his squat to his feet.

The dog rages at him. Without thought, Edmund's hand clasps the dog's throat just as his paw smacks Edmund's left eye. Clasping his wounded eye closed and bringing his other hand to the dog's throat, he gets a strong grip, and rising to his feet, he holds the dog at arm's length from his body and level with his head, fur wrapping around the edges of his hands as he squeezes.

A creak and a slam break through the night alley air.

"Mister, don't kill my dog!" shouts a small voice.

With a face contorted with the irritation of restraint, Edmund looks down at the small body, "Where are your parents, kid?"

"Out. That's why Kirsten's outside," pointing at the dog dangling in the air, "and Toby's inside."

For the first time, Edmund hears a muffled dog bark coming from behind the side garage door to the alley which the boy has shut behind him.

"Please, mister, let her go."

Gritting teeth and groaning, "An animal like this needs to be chained up. Never let him loose."

The boy looks to the fence at the opened gate and the mangled latch on the ground. The dog's body flies through the air into the fence. The dog whimpers, but jumps back to her feet, lunging at the convict again. The boy grabs the dog in a hug, wrapping his arms tightly around her torso, and looks up past the dog's barking snout, but the man is gone.

Running, the convict throws curses over his shoulder though he knows he desperately needs to be silent, "...cursed. Freakin' dogs everywhere I go. Rotten luck my whole life."

CHAPTER 21

C alamity is the bizarre offspring of coincidence and pushing your luck one time too many. We assume it's a tragic and unlikely event, but really it's just a matter of probability. Plan enough outdoor charity fundraisers and one will eventually be rained out, leaving the needy without food, shelter, or medicine until the next event. The organizer might like to imagine some evil force spoiling the event, but the weather is merely indifferent. Walk through a crime-riddled neighborhood enough times, and one will be mugged. Leave a child unsupervised long enough, and something bad will happen.

Calamity is not fate or chance, but ignoring a dangerous possibility until it comes to life.

One's participation in creating calamity, failing to prepare for an unfortunate outcome before it happens, is often the answer to *Why me?*, but many times one would prefer for it to remain rhetorical and an illogical, unanswered mystery, since a random occurrence is no one's fault with no responsibility in it. A cruel twist of fate is beyond the control of the victim, and it generates sympathy from others, possibly even making it something valuable. But, something bad that could have been prevented is a different matter altogether, emitting the embarrassment of neglect.

The perfect rows of sparkling paint, fins, antiques as well preserved as their brand new counterparts, chrome adornments polished to a mirror-shine, all flawlessly cleaned, vacuumed, and wiped—if not for the crowds of people, it would be an obsessive-compulsive dream, far from a likely womb to incubate misfortune.

However, calamity indeed reflects off the neatly-trimmed goateed face smiling at Chester, beaming in the sunlight bouncing off its thin-framed prescription sunglasses. It's David, a clever member of the *Most Hipness* writing staff, and he briskly walks toward Chester, Rhonda, Lucky, Cindy, and Janet, who all have just met up in front of the entrance to the sports bar of the week, Beefy O'Bristol's. Despite the bar's Irish theme, Lucky swears it's owned by a short Italian guy named Tariano.

The bar is on the far end of a giant C-shaped strip mall. The back row of stores spans nine blocks in length. The two ends, the top and bottom curves of the C, are smaller rows of stores connecting the long back row across the three block deep parking lot to the street. Sprinkled in the giant parking lot close to the street are islands of chain restaurants.

In the vast space of the C, half the parking lot is roped off for today's event, inside which the car show glistens and bustles. The show is not supposed to start for forty-eight minutes, but anticipation typically brings out both participants and crowd long before the advertised beginning.

"Chester! Hey, Chester!" shouts David.

The shouting writer can make anyone smile in any situation that Chester's witnessed, and now as David approaches, unwittingly pulling on a loose thread in Chester's fabric of existence, Chester can't help but surrender a smile despite the swirling panic inside him.

The sunglasses-sporting face asks, "Chester, what brings you to *Nerds on Wheels 3: What Coolness Can't Provide Money Can Buy?*"

Group laughs.

David continues, "We were also considering the alternative subtitles: *Geeks Hiding Behind 3500 Pounds of Metal* and *Who's got all the chicks now, jock boy?*"

Smaller laughter.

"Seriously, Chester, none of us thought you'd come out here today."

Suddenly hit with memories of the writing staff spending exorbitant amounts of cash on vintage cars during his first year on the show, Chester pieces together how his coworker whom he knew in a past present has come to be in the same place as his gambling crew of the current present time that he has usurped and the girl who is his burning love which has survived traversing through the lost past, the future that's gone, and into the present. Having all these lines intersect in the same place is overwhelming.

David says, "Give a bunch o' nerds a lot of money and watch what they do with it. Someone should be following us around with TV cameras and a snarky host to comment on us; it'd be the hit of the year."

Chuckling from everyone except Lucky who is staring at his watch.

"Hell, throw in a few shows with a tacked-on environmental agenda, and it'll be an award-winning show of the season."

That line pulls a laugh through Chester's wall of panic.

David adds, "Of course, none of Chester's *Most Hipness* scripts have used that tactic."

Cindy pokes Chester in the shoulder, "I thought you said you were a technical writer—you never said anything about writing for some TV show."

Voice cracking at the start, "Well, I don't like to talk about it too much, but that's how I met Rhonda."

David adds, "So, he's dating a movie star, working on a

hit show, and modest too? Chester, my man, there's something new about you every day."

"You don't know the half of it," Chester mumbles inaudibly.

Janet takes a step away from Lucky and Cindy, getting closer to David as she asks, "So, do you have a car in this show?"

"No, I've been spending my money on trilobites. I'm trying to stay in the deep end of the nerd pool, not like these shallow-end socialites," nodding his head in the general direction of the other staff writers in the mass of cars behind him, "Who needs adoration from crowds and a glistening, powerful machine when you can have the remains of dead marine arthropods?"

Only Chester smiles.

Janet continues, "You're very funny."

"That's what my paycheck says, but don't tell anyone that you think so or they'll expect me to work harder on the show."

"Well, Mr. Funny Man, what does it say on the 'Pay To' line of the check?"

"David Kreller, math-nerd telling jokes. What's your name?"

"Janet Shrew, charming divorced lady needing a drink and a few laughs."

"Well, let's take care of the drink first, and all that can't be bought will be free."

Lucky opens and steps through the door pulling Cindy by her arm behind him. In mid-pull, Cindy looks back at the group with an embarrassed expression.

Janet and David follow. Bumping her shoulder into him as they walk toward the front door of the bar, Janet says, "Well, of course, all that can't be bought will be free. Why would you try to buy something that's free?"

"See, every time I try to use a fancy line, it falls flat. They're always telling me to keep it simple."

As the others disappear into the bar, Rhonda moves

directly in front of Chester who has not taken a step since David walked up to them.

"What's going on, Chester? Are you okay, baby?"

"I...I guess he's joining us for the game...never thought there'd be a car show near the bar Lucky was talking about—never thought the guys from work could possibly be near a sports bar like this, not their kind of place...never put it together that they could be here."

"Do we need to leave? What do we do? One of them's gonna come out and check on us in a second."

"I dunno. I don't know what to do. Never thought of this...Made it through the premiere alright—maybe we could get through today alright too. But I had nothing to lose then. Now I've got you."

"Is it going to be suspicious if we just get out of here right now?"

"Yeah, it will. David's gonna mention seeing us here at work on Monday for sure—no way of getting around it now. And if we leave them here, it'll be an even bigger deal—David'd have a thousand jokes before my past self even walked into the studio on Monday morning.

"The past me is going to know about all this; me interfering in his life again. What in the world would he think about hearing all this at work? Hearing about him being here over the weekend, and knowing it wasn't him at all? How did he respond after the premiere? They had to make a big deal about you and me at work—they thought he hooked up with a movie star. And before that, how they had to have made fun of him after you left with Dane at the show party.

"I don't know if he's denying he was there, and they think it's all a joke. Maybe he's been going along with it, trying to find out from them what I've been up to. And you with me—it's like I'm taunting him. They've got to ask him about you all the time. What can he say? You're all I ever dreamed about. How can he deal with pretending? And David being around Janet and Lucky and Cindy—I'm leaving him a trail back to me...and you."

Rhonda says, "I've been hoping that after he saw us in his apartment that he'd change his mind, that seeing that we're human would make it click in his head how wrong it would be to hurt you—that you're not some monster here to mess up his life and that you're a living, breathing human being just like him."

"Yeah, me too. Was even hoping that the punch in the nose would knock some sense into him—at least make him think he might not be able to pull it off without getting caught or hurt. Don't think it's very likely. And after this gets back to him—one more time that I've thrust myself into his life—it'll probably get him all fired up again."

"I don't know, Chester. But, what do we do right now? Do we just go in and play along like you're the past-you working on the show with David?"

"I don't see a better way...Maybe if it gets too bad, I'll fake like I'm sick, and we can get out of here. David might still joke about that at work, but it could be an emergency out if we need it."

"You could try to find out some info on your past self. Get some feedback on how he's been acting since our little visit. Might help us..."

Door swings open, Lucky steps halfway out, "Chaz, you gotta get in here; we only got two minutes to take care of business before they lock the bets down."

Cindy's hand smacks Lucky's shoulder, and a faint "shhh" can be heard coming out of her mouth.

"Well, what do you want me to do, Cindy; let the game start without him in here? We might as well have stayed the hell home."

Cindy's voice cuts louder this time, "Shut up, you big idiot! You're gonna get us all in..."

Door closes as Lucky steps back inside.

A breeze blows through, blanketing Rhonda's bangs across her face.

She asks, "What's it gonna be? Sit this one out, or go inside?"

"You're with me either way, aren't you?"

Green swells beneath red, and she presses her lips against his.

Chester's never pretended harder to be engrossed in a game.

Rhonda's busied herself talking to Cindy. Between the drinking, buying more drinks, shouting at the TV screen, and the in-between vigil of the movement of the football, conversation with Lucky is haphazard to nonexistent, leaving Chester with nothing other than staring at the game to divert himself from dangerous conversation with David.

Fortunately, Janet and David are keeping each other occupied in an ongoing get-to-know-you conversation including talking about Janet's job, classic arcade games, her divorce, and dodecahedrons. Once David drew one and explained what they look like, Janet smiled and said that she always thought twelve-sided dice were cool too.

However, every few minutes David taps Chester on the shoulder to include him in their conversation, as if it were a repeated validation that David has a reason to be here because he's Chester's friend. David's laughter is frequent and like a nervous panting sprinkled with a rhythmless stutter.

Besides the worries of slipping up with David, Chester's been eying the bookie at the bar. Lucky placed the bet as usual, and in typical fashion the bookmaker accepted Lucky's money with a knowing grin. Chester thinks the new bookkeeper looks too young to be in the bar at all, much less a bookie. He also doesn't have the demeanor of any of the other betting bosses they've dealt with in the past few weeks.

After asking Lucky on three different points in the first quarter, Chester has finally found out that the bookie's name is Sammy.

Sammy has stared at them with an arrogant smile since

Lucky placed their bet. Chester has even seen the bookie pointing to them and grinning while talking to other people. None of the other bookies wanted anyone to know that they took a bizarre bet; this guy can't stop bragging about the money he's going to take from them and mocking their stupidity in placing such a wager.

A lack of business etiquette usually marks a novice, one who could be easily manipulated, but it makes Chester feel anything but comfortable as he anxiously waits for the game to be over, every play seemingly stretched out and slow, each one a separate battle on his nerves. Besides the differences in behavior, there is the difference in name. Last week's bookie was named Cisco and the week before was Lucien. Manny is a perfectly normal name; it's just not that common. Sammy is definitely the most familiar of the bunch. Odd that the bookie with the most normal name behaves in the strangest ways.

The rest of the first two quarters passes the same way. It's not until five minutes into the third quarter that Sammy stops laughing and starts looking enraged. Some of the people, to whom Sammy was bragging about the bet with Lucky, start coming around and poking him with jokes. His face turns angrier.

It's the kind of game that makes the indifferent become football fans.

The veteran quarterback is having the best game he's had in eight years, possibly the best of his career. It's likely to be his last season; the playoff spot for his team is unlikely, but if they lose this game it will be impossible. They have to win to keep their postseason hopes alive, and they're well on their way to the upset victory.

Adding to the drama, the quarterback was let go during spring training earlier this year from the team with whom he spent his entire career and wasn't picked up by his current team until halfway through the season when their star quarterback tore his rotator cuff. This is the kind of game that makes a sportscaster's job easy.

Everyone in the bar is excited except for Chester and

Sammy.

The third quarter ends with the bet looking more and more probable to be a huge loss for Sammy, and Chester sees him making a phone call. At the end of the call, Sammy still seems angry, but nods his head knowingly as if the call has given him some assurance.

Staring at the screen but thinking of other things, Chester remembers the rumors that were circulating about David when he first came to the show, so they're rumors that must be passing through the show staff right now. The gossip was that Omar was grooming David to start running the show. The stories gained strength when David and Omar were often seen having private meetings in Omar's office. As the meetings grew longer, so did the extent of the rumors. An even more interesting rumor, spoken in hushed secrecy, was that Omar and David were meeting to brainstorm ideas for pitching a new show of their own to the network.

Of course Chester knows how it all turned out. David wrote for *Most Hipness* for one more year, and then they created a hit comedic show about a man who travels one thousand years into the future. Omar helped with the character development, but the idea for the show came out of David's background in science.

But, David was single then, not marrying for another five years. Sadly, three years after they were married, his wife left him for a movie producer and died of an overdose. Being single at the time of the show's creation might have been crucial in David choosing the escapist time travel setting.

Oddly, Chester wonders if his real-life time travel to the past will erase the show's fictional time travel to the future.

Fourth quarter, the veteran quarterback has driven his team down to their own forty-yard line. They've played a great game but are still down by two field goals with seven seconds left on the clock. Casting gloom on the remaining few seconds of the game, the last play was a dead duck of a short throw that was nearly intercepted—the worst throw of the game for the seasoned quarterback, leaving some to say he's run out of steam. The defense celebrated excessively, elevating their confidence to stratospheric levels and increasing their intimidation factor.

The ball is hiked. Veteran QB fakes a handoff, scrambles away from a rushing defender, runs toward the line of scrimmage, and sees a receiver breaking across field at the other team's thirty-seven yard line.

The ball leaves his fingers spiraling and slicing the air. It soars over the large hands of a jumping lineman, traversing over the grassy yards to its target. The hands of the receiver grasp the ball with a crisp slapping sound. He tucks the ball to his ribs and sprints. He had the man covering him beaten by three steps before he caught the ball, and he still maintains a two step lead as he races toward the end zone.

Open field is all that blurs around in his vision as he flings his legs ahead of him as fast as he can. As he crosses the line into the end zone, he can't slow himself down to a stop. His body keeps moving until he passes the back out of bounds marker and the field goal post, and lightly crashes into the padded wall by the crowd. Hands drape down to pat his helmet, and one spectator falls completely over, landing on his back right next to the receiver. While on the ground, the spectator continues to pat the receiver's shoe and calf.

As security picks the man up and escorts him off the field, Sammy holds perfectly still watching the screen.

The extra point kick that comes quickly after the touchdown pass is replayed several times. The kick is good, almost perfectly placed between the uprights, but the offense is called for holding.

After the ball has been placed further away, the extra point is attempted again. It is a wobbly kick that hits the left upright and then falls inside and through the uprights to score the winning point.

The bar goes wild.

Most people are on their feet shouting to someone who is also shouting, neither able to hear what the other is saying.

The wildness stays wild but tapers in volume as the

minutes pass. The team still might not make the playoffs, but by fighting to keep their hopes alive, everyone in the bar would swear they're the best in the league.

Chester looks around for Sammy, but doesn't see him anywhere.

"Lucky," says Chester.

No response from Lucky who is staring at the back of a young bartender trying to get her attention to order more drinks.

"Lucky!"

"What? Whatchyou need, Chester, a drink?"

"No, Sammy's nowhere to be seen, man."

Lucky glances around the bar, "Don't worry bout it, Chaz, he ain't skipping out. Too many people want their money, and a lot of us know where he lives too—including me. Don't worry 'bout it; we'll get ours. I promise ya that; we'll get ours. Bartender!"

Several minutes have passed, and Sammy has indeed reappeared inside the bar. Everyone's been paid except for Lucky and Chester. Sammy swears the money's coming and that he's waiting on his partner to bring it to him—but not to worry since they can sit here and wait till his partner arrives and make sure he doesn't skip out on them.

Something about it worries Chester, and he wants to get out of here, so much so that he's tempted to leave without the money.

David says, "Come on, Chester, you've got to at least come see the other guys' cars before you leave. They'll die if they knew you were here with Rhonda and didn't stop by to say hi. Even Mirkwood's ex-wife and Meyer's mom were hanging around when I ditched them for you guys."

Before Chester can respond, Janet asks David, "How'd you run into us anyway?"

"Well, I was going to get a burger from the tent when I passed near the bar and saw Chester walking with you guys up to the door."

"Oh," she says quietly.

"But, then I was taken in by a captivating newly-divorced woman whom I decided I just had to meet."

"Much better answer, David," stepping closer to him, "and I'm glad you ditched your friends for us. Oh, but you must be starving by now—talking to me all this time."

"I've been hoping you wouldn't hear my stomach growling."

Janet continues, "Well, we'll have to get this boy some food," turning to Chester, "I'd like to go with David to see their cars and get a burger. Don't you guys want to come too?"

"Uh, I don't know. I'm not feeling that great. Thinking of settling up and getting on out of here."

She counters, "Come on, Chester, it'll be fun; don't tell me you're not interested in checking it out and seeing your friends. Even Mirkwood's ex-wife is here."

David adds, "Well, if you'd ever met Mirkwood's ex-wife, you might want to settle up and go home too."

Chester fights a smile as Janet gives him a pleading expression. Looking to Rhonda, she gives him a twitch of a smile and a squeeze on his hand.

"Well, I guess we can…"

A loud explosion pulses through the air inside the bar, cutting Chester's words short.

The large wooden entrance doors shake. Confused looks are exchanged between all of them, except Lucky who turns his attention back to the TV screen replaying the day's football highlights.

Chester is the first of them to rush toward the doors. As he nears them, he can see the door to the left is warped as if it were struck by a battering ram.

The only other person to beat them out the door is the bookie.

Outside the bar, one minute and forty-five seconds earlier.

A tall, skinny man walks with his shoulders and legs moving in an exaggerated fashion, slowed down by dragging pretension hanging at his knees and ostentation wrapped around his shoulders. The quirky movements follow a rhythm that no one else can hear, but he marches on as if his theme song were being blast to everyone in his line of vision. Far more social than functional, his walk depicts his life. Tattoos scream from the pale skin on arms that dangle out of his wife-beater t-shirt.

Following three steps behind is a younger girl who keeps her head down and whose eroding teeth suggest her boyfriend deals in more than games of chance. She walks with her arms crossed, sliding her fingers over each side of her tiny belly. She's been doing it whenever she's nervous, and she has worn the skin raw lately.

His eyes are on the front doors. He hasn't been back here since he was arrested a year and a half ago for pulling his gun on a man over what was reported as a billiards dispute. The uneasiness over returning to the scene from which he's been banned adds to the animosity and the thrill of defiance that's been proliferating inside him since the call came a short while ago. As it's grown, the girl has retreated further into herself.

The rumble of a thin metal container bending in and popping out under uncertain fingers catches Manny's attention, breaking through his internal theme song. Looking to his right, he sees a man crouching down in front of an open gas filler tube. Manny's eyebrows become steep, pointed slopes and his smile grows narrow and sharp. He stops short and his girlfriend, keeping her head aimed sharply downward, walks into his back full stride.

Giving her a quick annoyed look, he returns his stare to

the man with the nervous fingers wrapped around a canister that has just been drained of inflammatory fluid.

"Running a little low, lucky boy?"

"U-h-h, yeah. Top-topping it off," he responds with nervousness and confusion, barely giving the speaker a glance as he places the canister on the ground and fumbles as he picks up his next tool.

"L.A.'s a big town, but not big enough that I wouldn't find you again. Didn'tchya think I'd come looking for you after what you two idiots pulled?"

Chester stares back consumed with confusion.

Manny continues, "Know all aboutchoo, Chaz. Been askin' 'round 'boutchoo. Know you and Lucky been makin' da rounds. Know all about your TV star girlfriend. Run a business 'round here. Can't have two smartasses running bar to bar ripping me off."

The tool fumbles in Chester's hand; his face is pained while his mind scrambles to make a connection to anything the man has said to him.

"Whatchyou doing wit dat tire iron in yo' hand, son? You thinkin' a-hitting me wit' it?"

"What? W-wait. Wait! The guy you want is inside the bar. I swear."

Reaching around to the small of his back, he says, "No, the guy I want is right here," unleashing the shining barrel into the newly birthed night illuminated by the overhead parking lot light.

"No, don't shoot—you'll kill us both! The car's—"

"You're half right."

The gun fires.

Fireball like a cloud. Draws out sweat before the heat can register in his mind. Ravaging. Cars to the right and left get pushed into the cars next to them. Tire slams into the bar door.

Glass sparkles and flies like raindrops and slices like reality. The heat hits Manny's girlfriend's face, reminding her of standing too close to a crawfish boiler. She throws a hand over the side of her face and the other over her stomach.

The shape of the man that was just a few inches from the explosion is a black silhouette inside swirling orange and red flames, flickering and consuming as it explodes into the expanding fire.

The door is shoved open, and all are drawn to the flame. After staring at the fiery wreckage beneath the first light post, watching the debris of a dream of metal disintegrate, and seeing a wave of red hair blowing in the fall breeze between him and the flickering flames of the carnage, Chester's chest flares up, determined to not let the destruction spread to more important things. He is the only one to pull himself away from the destruction and see Sammy running to the far corner of the outside of the bar.

Leaning in close to Rhonda's ear, "Stay here."

"Wher—"

"Please, trust me this time."

"But, Chester…"

Whispering directly in her ear, "Rhonda, see that burning shoe in the middle of the parking lot? It used to be mine—was on our host's foot the other day at the apartment."

"Oh, my God!"

"Shh. You have to act like you don't know anything. No one knows that's my car besides us."

As soon as her head starts to nod, he turns away from her. The crowd watches the flame, as mesmerized as cavemen were at its first appearance, but Chester starts after the bookie.

Locating Sammy took just one glance to the far corner of the bar's facade. Standing next to today's bookie, a tall, skinny man leans over a woman who is on her knees with her hands over her face. The two men have their backs to Chester as he approaches, and their words become audible.

"…you alright?" asks the tall one.

"Yeah, we're okay," answers a small voice from behind the hands covering her face.

"What did you say?"

"We're okay—uh, you and me."

"You sure?" he asks in a tone far too harsh for following an injury.

Sammy says, "Damn, Manny, give 'er a break—her face."

Raising his hand, "Shut up, Sammy. Chantelle, answer me."

"Yeah. Just meant you an' me. I'm sure."

"Better be."

Something about her accent is familiar to Chester, but he can't focus enough to place it.

"Manny, you blew up my car?" Chester asks in a powerful tone.

As the tall man twists his torso around to look at the person speaking, Chester can see the woman who is also trying to catch a glimpse of who dared speak to her man so forcefully. Her face is red and sweaty with one deep cut running along her cheek and several miniscule bits of glass embedded into her skin, but she has no burn marks. Manny has some scrapes on his right forearm, but she took the worst of the explosion.

Horror creeps over Manny's face, "That's impossible, man. I watched you burn. I watched you burn."

"Time to let this one go, Manny; you've done enough damage here."

He nods in agreement feeling the truth of the comment, but quickly remembering who he is, he says, "No way, man. This won't make any sense 'till it's over."

"It'll never make sense. Don't come near me again, Manny."

Reaching around to the small of his back and then grimacing as he looks at the growing crowd staring at the burning car a mere dozen yards away from them, "Some kind of a freak—a monster. Can't have nobody running 'round cheating the odds, especially not something like you."

"Let it go before you can't."

"Too late, Ch—"

Sirens cut through the smoky air, which is pungent with eradication, and invade their ears.

Manny grabs Chantelle by her arm, yanking her to her feet and into a brisk stride toward Chester. They walk so closely past him that they nearly touch, but they keep a straight line to walk through the crowd in front of the bar and into the mass of people at the car show.

"Melted remains of car alarm control box stuck to rear wheel well, shock sensor inside the tailpipe, charred remains of a spark plug mounted in front of the gas filler tube. Haven't found any other remains of the body besides the bit of foot in the scorched shoe."

With his arms folded, the one policeman in a suit nods his head as he listens to the report coming from his detective standing in front of him.

"The way this car blew up and burned—might have been an explosive placed near the gas tank too. There's residue of some type of homemade napalm, probably Styrofoam and gasoline mix, which is most likely why there hasn't been any more of the body found. It'd also account for some of the smell. We found the filler cap blown toward the back of the parking lot. None of the threads are stripped—was off the car when it exploded. No eyewitnesses. Several people swear they heard a gunshot go off before the big explosion."

"What was all of this supposed to do? Besides destroying the guy trying to set it up, that is. How was it supposed to work?"

"Shock sensor in the exhaust would set off the alarm as soon as the engine fired, the alarm would turn on power to the spark plug he rigged in the gas filler tube, which would ignite the accelerant-saturated rag that runs down the tube into the gas tank itself. Once that car started or maybe even the car door slammed hard enough, this vehicle was going to turn into a fireball. Napalm suggests he wanted to make sure there wasn't anything left of the bodies. Apparently it went off while he was still trying to set it up."

"Seems like a lot to set up in a busy parking lot."

"Not really. Not if you wire it before you come out here. Then all you'd have to do is stick the alarm box to the wheel well with duct tape, wire the alarm up to the battery, stick the shock sensor into the exhaust pipe, shove the presoaked rag down the gas filler tube, and place the spark plug close to the rag. If you've got the wires that run to the battery already wired to clips, which they were, it'd take you just a few seconds to hook it up to the battery terminals, especially on an old car like this—there's not much in your way under the hood. With some duct tape, mounting tape, or that magnetic tape to mount everything, you could set this whole thing up in less than five minutes. If someone's practiced, less than three. Hardest thing would be shoving the rag down the filler tube. We found a warped and melted tire iron not too far from the car—could've used that to shove the rag down the tube if it was skinny enough."

"Seems like someone would have seen him."

"Yeah, you'd think so, but with that game going on today—*can you believe that? Never thought they would've won*—and the car show, people were preoccupied. Besides that, seeing someone tinkering on an old car at one of these shows is pretty commonplace, nothing out of the ordinary."

"Good work, detective, but I've got to disagree with you there."

"On what?" asks the detective surprised by the challenge.

"I wouldn't say the hardest part was shoving the rag down the filler tube. I'd say the hardest thing about it was getting away before a noise tripped the sensor and it went boom."

"Did it just like he said. No evidence; they'll never

know there were two of us. Car's not registered to anybody, not legally anyway—it'll be a mystery too. Even if they can find a VIN number in that mess and find out there's two cars with the same number, it'll be no big deal. They'll assume the one involved in the fire was a fake. Stolen cars with fake numbers attract trouble. Just didn't want to leave any evidence; needed to burn me so bad—right through my teeth. I was thinking he'd cut my brakes, shoot me, something—not this."

"What about his teeth? Dental evidence?"

"Didn't see much of him left to find any teeth. Never had a cavity. Still haven't. No metal in my mouth—they'd have to compare teeth and jawbone."

"Really? No cavities your whole life?"

"When your social calendar is pretty bare, you have time to floss."

When Chester sees it's too soon for him to unburden her worry by making her smile, he continues, "They'd have to know to look for me in the first place though. The crime's a mystery; no motive, no witnesses. They'd never know to get my records to compare to the corpse to start with. In cases like this, they request the records for everyone they think could be the victim. When they don't have clues, they've got no one's record to request. There's no central database to compare dental records—they have to come from the specific dentist. If you don't have any idea who the victim is, you have nothing to go on—usually they'll take a look into missing people in the area if there are no other clues to the ID."

"How on earth do you know all that?"

"Research for writing is where I learned stuff like that. Get it wrong in your story and someone who knows will call you on it…I guess even before they can attempt any type of ID that they'd have to find some remains of the corpse."

"Oh, God. So awful…"

"He knew all of this. That's what did him in. He made sure there would've been nothing left of me to make an I.D. Wanted to make sure he could live his life after this without anyone harassing him about how I was there—how there were two of him. If he hadn't been so thorough, they could identify him, and I'd be busted right now."

"How could he turn out this crazy? His life was the same as yours until you got here. You'd never do this."

"Didn't have you anymore—I took that dream away from him, so he filled his life with hating me. Just seeing me the first time had to drive him insane. How do you make sense of that? Killing me was the new obsession, not dreaming about you. Thought he was doing something good—solving a mystery, protecting people from the bad things time travel could cause. He filled himself with thinking about it until he had to do it. Empty people will always try to fill themselves with something. That's why we have to be careful not to feed them anything poisonous."

She hugs him with an urgency that telegraphs a question she's waiting to ask.

"What is it, Rhonda?"

"You—you seem…Are you surprised that you didn't disappear when your past self died—that somehow it'd wipe away your existence too? I know you said it couldn't affect you, but…"

"Yeah. It was scary. Scared I was going to lose you. Scared to see myself die."

"He stopped being you as soon as he saw you for the first time driving that car. Remember that."

"It's one thing to believe the theory, and it's another to watch yourself burn."

CHAPTER 22

It's been eighteen months since she's seen him last, but she can still feel his fingers pressed into her throat. Every time she takes her stare away from the window, she can feel them at her neck, pulling her to keep a vigil awaiting his arrival.

He'd be after her even if she hadn't testified against him. She'd be a piece of his property that he'd snatch back from the authorities that put him away. It'd be more symbolic than sentimental. Grabbing her away from the rest of society would be his way of hording what he deemed to be his property. Of that she's sure.

Having been close enough to be hit with beer and blood, she witnessed Edmund split a man's head open with a half-empty glass bottle from which the stranger had erroneously taken a sip. Edmund may not have treated her much better, but she knows she ranks higher than a sip of beer. And more than that, bottled up anger bubbling in hot intensity is already flying toward her head.

She can feel him getting closer.

When she was approached to testify, her eye was still discolored from their last altercation, and she still hadn't scrounged up enough money to move out of their apartment. The remaining food was spoiling in the refrigerator; her makeup was gone, having been thrown into the toilet when he was feeling suspicious days before his arrest; and the electricity was going to be turned off in three days.

All of her money was tied up in the gun, car, and bulletproof vest he purchased without her knowledge for the armed bank robbery. He had told her he loaned the cash to a friend and they'd get paid back triple the amount in two weeks time. Within a week, he was arrested, and she was waiting on her next paycheck to sustain herself, which wouldn't be coming for a few weeks.

Disgusted and hopeless, she didn't care what happened to her; it was good enough that someone was taking a shot at Edmund—consequences don't seem real when eviction could come faster than payday. So, she wasn't worried about Edmund's vengeance when she agreed to testify. Without anything enticing on her horizon, she wasn't worried about what would happen to her at all.

Eleven months of therapy later, now she does care what happens to her.

She can hear him coming for her with every squirm in her stomach. Feet trudging through a swamp. Beer swirling in a bottle. Blood hitting face.

Fear sounds like sloshing.

CHAPTER 23

"**T**he claim that the future has not yet been written holds perfectly true relative to any point at which you find yourself.

"If you go back in time, the future that you came from is no longer there. It could be written over again in a way so similar that you wouldn't notice anything has changed at all, except that there'd be another version of yourself wandering around, but it could also be something that has zero connection to anything that you remember. It's a slate that's been wiped out, and it can be rewritten in an infinite number of ways.

"It's a directional hazard in time travel to the past. What you considered to be your past is now the present, and where you came from no longer exists. In a way, it's no different than everyday life. You find yourself existing today, and the world's slightly different for you being here. What you did yesterday is behind you, and the world will never be the same again. No matter what you do, you could never recreate yesterday today. The weather will never be exactly the same; someone will have died; someone will be born; someone's chemical balance will be different, altering their moods and thoughts along with countless other changes. The innumerable variables that make up our existence will never be exactly the same again. It's the same for traveling to the past. The future can never be exactly the same because your added existence to the past has already made things different.

"The future that you came from is built on years of building blocks that are made up of an incalculable number of events going on around you, but none of them included you going back in time. Even if you just sat there in the past and breathed, things would be slightly different; you would consume food, throw off heat, and create carbon-dioxide, changing the environmental conditions that were there the first time around. Anyone that you talk to will be different from having interacted with you—if nothing else, the time that it takes for them to listen to you will change their daily schedule. Imagine if you met your wife standing behind her in line at the grocery. Now, imagine the time traveler standing in line between the two of you on the same day and you never meet because of it. No marriage, no kids, no grandkids. The existence of the time traveler in the timeline can make even the smallest action, like buying groceries, result in huge changes to what would have been.

"Your timeline as a time traveler—the track of your life goes on uninterrupted. Everything is consistent in relation to you. The world around you is your environment, and it's pliable. Your relative timeline is entirely independent of the type of environment, or specifically the time of your environment, as long as it is one that can sustain your life. For example, if you went back to the Ice Age, you'll likely freeze or starve to death. The Middle Ages or the Wild West would be much more suitable for sustaining your life.

"The irony of time travel is that you have the capability of redoing everyone else's life path, removing and replacing their experiences, but you can't do it to your own. The time traveler carries all of his life experiences and their consequences around inside of him. Going back in time means going back with all of the bad memories and experiences, all of your unwanted baggage, while you have the ability to take away the bad experiences of others by preventing them from ever happening."

Watching Chester take in a deep breath following his lengthy explanation, Omar asks, "You think that people are going to be able to understand all this in a half hour TV show?"

"Yes, I think so."

"How are we going to get this information to the viewer? It won't fit in a theme song," followed by awkward laughter.

David interrupts, "I don't think we need to have it said; the situation of the show will reveal to the audience how the rules of our time travel universe will work. But, the issue that's bugging me is most theoretical physicists don't seem to agree with your rules."

Chester responds, "Well, the quantum space-time foam is proven, and most agree with being able to find a wormhole in there. I think our rules are logical, and if they're logical they'll stand, at least for a work of fiction. Not many scientists agreed with H. G. Wells that time travel was possible when he wrote *The Time Machine* back in the 1890s, but time has proven him to be more right than them. We don't need to be that brilliant or fortunate; just logical."

"Okay, okay," concedes Omar, stroking his thickly-bearded chin, "How is the actual time travel going to work?"

David looks to Chester anxiously waiting for his answer.

"It'll happen through a handheld electrical device that is barely small enough to fit inside a large pants' pocket."

David looks worried.

Continuing, "It'll have the functions of a full-sized computer that will allow our main character to bring a library of information back with him, but its main purpose will be as a control unit for the time travel."

"How will it work?" asks David less excited than a moment before.

"We can describe it as being able to open, stretch, and stabilize a wormhole in the space-time foam from a collision in a particle accelerator."

Omar's eyes scrunch, and David's enthusiasm starts to return with the acknowledgment of some theories known to him and discussed at MIT. Time travel is an obsession among nearly all involved in science, but for an unknown reason, it is an absolute fixation among every computer science student David's ever known. David has theorized it to be the result of numerous computer science students having spent too many hours behind a computer screen and longing to reuse them.

Looking to Omar, Chester continues, "But I think it best to leave the device's inner functions to the imagination or at least to be vague. Newer discoveries could prove it to not be able to work in the way that we describe. We need some headroom to account for discoveries that might happen in the near future."

Laughing, Omar says, "Well, we'll have to get it past its first year on the air for any of that to matter anyway. Who's our lead, and why do we care about them?"

"I was thinking we could have a former TV comedy writer who spends his later years working as a technical writer for theoretical physicists. In the course of his years of technical writing, he discovers a method for making time travel possible, which sends him back after a lost love. When he gets there, he resumes his work as a TV writer, which would let us throw in a lot of meta jokes about writing a show while we're writing the show—kind of make the audience aware that it's writers making jokes about writing a show. And, it could be a little bit of behind the scenes satire of working in television."

David can no longer hold back his grin.

"Who is the girl?" asks Omar.

"Should she be a movie star?" poses David smiling broadly.

Panic floods over Chester, but he says casually, "Well, it is L.A."

"Not everybody in L.A. is as lucky as you, you closet

geek-stud," David says smacking Chester on the shoulder, "but maybe our hero could be. Makes a good story: nerd with the movie star."

Chester glances over his body.

David adds, "Oh, no offense, Chaz. I'm easily the nerd you are to the third power; I just think the unlikely meager writer character would be a great person to pair with the movie star."

Omar interrupts with words flying at speed, "Imagine him at a premiere! Surrounded by her and the beautiful cast. Security could constantly be trying to escort him away. He could make a joke that no one else gets but him and the audience, or at least some of our audience—you know, David, the kind of joke that you pitch and only Kenny and Chaz laugh at it."

David snickers.

Omar continues, "And we could make the stars behave like actors we've worked with. Tantrums, working while sick, ridiculous contract demands, not getting along with other stars, supporting charity, coffee breath and kissing scenes, taking a socially awkward role to push prejudices—we could mix it all together, the good and the bad, but laughing at the phony and the funny in all of them."

Chester smiles as he can see the thoughts spinning in their eyes. The chance to make fun of asinine executives, inconsistent censors, and the daily eccentricities of Hollywood has hooked them.

The science has double hooked David, and Chester knows he needs David to help him run the show. Where else is he going to find a hilarious comedy writer with a master's in science and nearly a doctorate in computer science?

Omar will have to sell the show to the network. Neither David nor himself has the clout to sell a time travel satire to a network, but Omar could sell them a three-hour-long game show involving a clumsy kangaroo, blind-folded three-year-olds riding chimpanzees, a man reading the dictionary backwards aloud, a gassy nanny, and a mime with

Tourette's—as long as Omar J. Sobelsk's name is on it, they would buy it. Three decades of hit television will do that for someone, and thankfully for Chester, it will allow Omar to sell his show, providing a chance to make an honest living using his own new idea and avoiding the abuse of his knowledge of every popular entertainment work for the next twenty years.

It would be easy to pitch every hit show before the original creators had their chance, but stealing their ideas, even before they've developed them, is something Chester can't stomach.

Despite his relief and ease of conscience in not having to gamble anymore, Chester feels panic wiggling in his chest. David stares at him with admiration for having pitched a show that he is thrilled to run, but there is something else in the stare. Chester sees a glimmer of discovery, and he hopes for all the happiness he's found that David hasn't figured out the pitch is more than fantasy.

CHAPTER 24

A straining hand holds her compressed throat pinned to the edge of her car's roof. She swings an opened palm at his face. It stops mid-air, her wrist caught in his other hand that aches to strangle her too.

"Get in the car," he says in a tone that drags a memory to her consciousness of walking across an aunt's rock driveway and the grating sound of the crushing and grinding beneath her feet.

The memory snaps as fast as it had appeared. Her eyes widen and pulse with only the lingering remembered taste of broken rock-dust surviving.

Two vehicles have passed since he lunged down upon her while she peered into her purse for her keys. It's growing dark, but the streetlights have not turned on yet. It's already been the longest eighteen seconds of her life.

Dusk coats her in its fading glow, kissing her with thoughts of the night that has just begun to roughly embrace her.

His hand squeezes her throat tighter, pushing the inner walls closer together, peeling her lids further back from her exposed eyes. Quickly, the hand pulls her body forward and slams her back to the car. As her head bobbles, she feels like she might black out.

With more urgency than he's exhibited in the one line he's delivered to her, he says quickly, "I need your car. *Now.* Things'll be better for you if you do what I tell you to."

She begins to nod her head as a loud exhaust rumbles past them from right to left.

His eyes follow the sound and the red blur. He's sure he hears the RPMs drop followed by a downshift.

Fear pumps the neurons at the front of her brain, each firing at a different rate, but all of them pulsing in an awareness-heightened panic. With her mind's stopwatch racing, the outside world appears slow and unreal.

She's sure he's the one that's been blasted on the local news all day. Repeating in her head, she can hear Judy from work laughing and saying just before she left for the day, "Now, don't pick up that escaped convict on the way home."

Hearing her coworker's warning on an endless loop in her mind is bizarre now that he's squeezing her in a chokehold. The surrealness of it all equals her terror. The two mix together and make it impossible for her to decipher the words he is spouting from his lips brushing over her earlobe.

Now, the tightening on her throat increases and cuts off her oxygen, strangling the surrealness out of her, leaving only her fear.

Her complete attention awakened, she can feel every square inch of her skin, the tips of her toes, and the follicles of every hair.

"Get in the car; get out your keys."

The words come in clear, each only slightly louder than a whisper but booming with the weight of malice.

He spent a large majority of the night before searching for an inconspicuous location. Somewhere around two in the morning he found the Riverview Family Therapy Center. Its parking lot was what cinched it for him. The brick building has no windows on its front. Each side of the parking lot has a brick wall mostly covered in vines. The front side that meets the street is also nearly completely closed in with a brick fence, barely leaving enough space for one car to exit and another to enter at the same time. Its business name is attached to the outside of the fence in unassuming metal letters.

These measures taken to protect their clients' privacy are exactly what have made the woman, who is being choked against her car, susceptible to his attack.

Realizing he needed a place to sleep out of sight and not wanting to miss an opportunity to seize a car, he climbed the brick fence close to where it joined the side of the building. Standing atop the fence, he grabbed hold of the roof, and with some struggling, he pulled his fatigued body onto it.

Lying behind an industrial air conditioning compressor, sleep fell over him quickly until the heat of late morning started to bake his skin touching the black roof. Since he didn't want to stand, out of fear of being seen, he had to alternate which part of his body touched the blistering roof for the rest of the day, every minute of it dense with sweating and cursing.

The heat did nothing to relieve the pressure of the mass of pepperoni and cheese in his bloated stomach, but it did add another flavor to the fury boiling in his head. By the time the parking lot had dwindled down to the last three cars, he kept catching himself muttering sharp words aloud.

Two of the cars had been there all day, except when one of them left around lunchtime only to return seventeen minutes later with bags discolored and seeping with fast food grease. The third car is what he had assumed to be the last patient.

Apparently, late Friday appointments are unpopular for both the givers and receivers of therapy, as only one of each and an office manager had remained.

The last patient's vehicle was perfect: the most commonly sold econo-box car in the country in silver. As long as he could lunge on her and take off before the staff closed up, it was a dream for the deviant.

Now, all the hours of preparation and the urgency to quickly escape are lost on him as he stares through the opening in the brick fence at the street, trying to feel every bit of his ears as they strain to hear another sound from the rumbling, red car that has just passed.

Her knee burns.

His eyes watch the street, and hers watch his.

She flings the hot knee at him. Underestimating how tall he is, she only glances her target, but it's enough to make him gasp.

His hold on her neck becomes loose.

Twisting her torso left and right, his fingers slip off her throat. She turns and takes one step away. The rush of this one step of freedom tantalizes her, and she'd trade all that she owns for just a few more feet of it.

Lifting her leg for the next step, strong fingers sink into the back of her arm and yank her entire body in reverse. She slams into what feels like a wall, the rear of her head whipping into his chest. Before she gains any balance, he thrusts her forward into the car. Getting her hands in front of her before crashing into the vehicle, her palms take most of the force, pain stinging into her wrists and up her arms.

"Keys now."

The stinging in her hands is what makes her dare not do anything but obey and dig into the side pocket of her purse. With numb fingers, she pulls out the key ring.

"Open it and get in."

As she unlocks her door, the faint sound comes to her ears of another car door slamming from a distance. She doesn't trust her senses or her mind. The sting in her hands has rendered both of them unreliable to her.

Lifting the door handle and pulling the door open, she sees the vacant front seats and starts to cry at the vision of her being a prisoner in the passenger side.

His hand lands on her back, shoving her forcefully into the cockpit, her knees on the driver's seat, the shifter jabbing her midsection, and her stinging hands on the passenger cushion. Although it wouldn't have granted her much better treatment, she wishes she hadn't backed into the spot so that she now would be entering the passenger side instead of being pushed roughly across the center console and impaled by her shifter.

"Climb across," he says starting to put his body into the car behind her.

Dragging her knees across her center console, smashing window and sunroof buttons, she hears a rumbling sound. She looks up to see the loud car pull up to the edge of the parking lot.

The heavy lobe of the rumble rattles deeply inside Edmund's mind. The passenger door opens. A short man with broad shoulders steps out.

"Danny, don't do this," pleads a brunette from the driver's seat.

"I love you," he says as he shuts the door and points down the street to the right of the parking lot.

The female driver watches him take two steps away, and before she can pull off, the tears run down her face.

His face is a well-defined landscape of a stern chin, defiant cheekbones, and a stare that is earnest and devoid of fear.

Edmund thinks it must be easy to be so heroic stepping out of a thundering chariot that resembles a crimson panther, wearing unstained clothes, and not carrying the biting scent of a piece of driftwood that's been bounced in the current for hours. The young man looks to be in his early twenties and the latest edition in a long lineage of guys who drive fast cars and date beautiful women.

Edmund loathes him.

She sees the determination in his eyes, the soft look of his lips, and most importantly that he's walking directly toward them, and she couldn't love anyone any more at first sight.

He shouts from a distance, "Let her go, and you won't

get hurt."

Shaking his head, still behind the opened driver's door, his body only halfway in the car, "You've gotta be kidding me, boy scout. Get outta here while you still can."

"Don't think so. The lady doesn't seem to want to be with you. Doesn't seem like she likes being choked either."

"Maybe I should try it out on you."

"Might be a little different with me, big man."

Edmund looks across the seat to his captive, pulling the stolen police pistol from under his shirt and out the top of his pants, "Don't try anything stupid. This won't take long."

Keeping the gun hidden behind the opened door, Edmund steps completely out of the car, the smaller man now only a few yards away from the hood. Ignoring a faint click coming from the other side of the vehicle, he sees his challenger is standing on his toes with his arms loose at his sides and confidence on his face. Recognizing the traits of a grappler, Edmund pulls out his gun and fires.

Blood bursts out the man's shoulder, and he falls to the ground.

Grinning, Edmund takes a step closer to survey the damage. Blood continues to pour out the shoulder coursing over the fingers that are pressed against it. He hears an engine running from somewhere down the street, and the urgency of the getaway floods over him.

"Damn it!" he shouts as he turns from the wounded to his way out.

Shoving the key in the ignition, he turns it roughly, and the meager engine starts a muffled hum. Throwing the car into gear, he slams the gas pedal down. The wounded on the ground begins to roll, trying in vain to get out of the way of the launching car.

Edmund's anxiety of escape turns to a hideous smile as the car takes off.

"No!" screams out as two female hands lunge for the wheel pulling it harshly in her direction. The front driver's tire squeals just centimeters past the head of the man on the ground only rolling over his hair.

A fast hand shoves her with force sending her crashing back to her side of the car, her hands coming immediately off the wheel. Her right shoulder lands against the door that she had opened a crack as soon as he stepped out with the gun earlier. The door swings open dumping her shoulders first onto the parking lot, her legs flinging out behind her. The opened door swings wildly.

"Go—" he starts to curse but is cut off as a horn blares from the entrance to the parking lot.

The rumbling red sports car is entering the lot just ahead of him.

Jerking the wheel with all his might, Edmund's front bumper just grazes the corner of the approaching car's front fascia. Having to turn so harshly, his passenger side rubs the edge of the brick fence.

Unknown to him but moving in his rearview mirror are two women running out of the therapy center, one screaming, the other pulling out a phone.

The car continues its chaotic exit, barreling across the intersection. An approaching pickup truck slams on its brakes to avoid broadsiding Edmund's smaller, stolen vehicle. Screeching his tires into a hard ninety degree left turn, Edmund is finally in a lane going in the right direction.

"Unff—" pause just long enough for the emotion to simmer, "believable!"

Looking in his rearview mirror, he sees nothing but ordinary traffic waiting at the light several blocks down. The pickup truck has resumed its original course in the opposite direction of him.

"People carjack cars every frickin' day with no fight. No hero, no damn Houdini girl escaping. Phfff...witnesses. Why's everything so hard for me? Frickin' cursed."

He switches on the air condition, but no air blows out of the vents.

"Un-ff-believable!" smacking the dashboard, "Social worker said dad would'a spent his whole life in jail if he hadn't got shot—maybe I'm gonna end up back there too. Cursed. Frickin' cursed."

CHAPTER 25

"I t was a stupid move."

"Chester, you've got to stop beating yourself up over it. You were just trying to make sure it was all over. It's not your fault."

"It is my fault. If I had just grabbed your hand and got us the hell away from there before Manny saw us, he'd think I was dead and this would be over. Now he knows I'm still alive and is going to come after me. How is all this not my fault?"

"Yeah, it might've worked for a little while—until he sees a pic of you and me together at one of my events on TV or in some magazine. If I'm ever in the limelight again, there'll be tabloids and paparazzi following us, another crazed fan in my bushes—already had one. Eventually it would have happened—there'd be a pic of us together. Then, it would've started all over again. He'd have come after you—would've found you through me. Either Manny would have had to die, or we would have had to disappear—I'd have had to quit acting."

"You would've done it though, right? If we finally had a chance to be free…and safe?"

Looking sad and serious, "Of course, I would've, but I would've hated it. Happy to be safe with you, but hated having to give it up."

"Thank you."

Quiet for a moment then saying, "Well, Chester, you're doing the opposite for me now, right? That's almost as hard, isn't it?"

"I just feel weird taking over his life."

"It's not his life. He never had the idea for your new show, and neither did anyone else. This is *your new* life, and it's an honest one."

"But, they think I'm him, and he was burned to death."

"Chester B. Fuze is your name too. You have every right to use it just as much as he did before he died."

"I don't know about that. I'm not like anyone else."

"Of course not, you're wonderful, and you're mine. But, what are you talking about?"

"I'm the only person on earth who has no direct connection to his existence in this world."

"What are you talking about?"

"I'm the only one who has no chronological or logical right to be here. At least no reason that anyone can see but me."

"Sweety, you're over my head again. Sometimes I think you forget how smart you are compared to the rest of us. You've got to explain better than that if you want me to get it."

"Alrighty…let me think…If I go back in time leaving my timeline in I-don't-know-let's-say 2010 traveling back to the year 2002, my knowledge contains my entire experience, but my experience, those eight years that I knew, may never turn out the same way now that I've gone back. The present is nothing more than the result of all the actions leading up to it—the sum total of an innumerable amount of actions happening every second. Me going back in time automatically changes that sum total; all of my actions are being added to it, and they weren't there the first time around. It can never be exactly the same once I go back."

"Starting to make sense but need some examples."

"What if I accidentally kill my future wife in a car accident? Or, what if I find a way to start a world war? My original 2002-2010 experience would still be inside me in my memory but would have been completely undone from existence and undone to the rest of the universe's reality except what else I may have brought back with me."

"Wow, that makes my head hurt."

Eyes glossed over, staring at thin air, "It broke mine for awhile."

Chester feels a hand on his shoulder which seems to pull out the next line that he has been struggling to keep pinned inside, "It gets worse."

Hand squeezes his shoulder, and he continues, "When I came back, it reset all the years that I traveled through; none of the events are guaranteed to unfold the same way again or even at all."

"Well, what's so bad about that? I'm much better off."

"It could be all undone again. We'll be here together perhaps for the rest of our lives, but it could all end in a moment and what we are now would never have been."

"How? What are you talking about?"

"If someone else were to come back in time just one second before I did, it would reset all of the time they have traversed. For most people, their lives are likely to run the same course or at least a very similar one—it's at least a possibility for them, if not probable. It could be happening right now, and no one would notice even if things were being changed. They'd know nothing different than the reset reality—the new series of events would be all they would have experienced, all that they grew up with.

"Just like you right now—you only know the reality since I reset things. If I wouldn't have told you about the way things were the first time around, you'd never know anything had been reset at all. You would've never known about being married to Dane, or what happened to Tristan, or about you…"

"Losing my face? Yeah, I wouldn't have thought of that in a thousand years."

"Yeah."

"Well, keep going."

"Okay. If things were reset again, other people's lives could remain very similar to their past experience. For example, a farmer in Kansas is not likely to be effected at all by my interference so far in Riverview and out here in L.A. But for you and me, if things get reset, I'm gone. There is no way that I could end up here from events that happened even one second before I arrived. One second before I arrived, there was only my past self—the lonely writer who ended up burned alive this time around and in an assisted care facility far away from you the first time."

"Now wait a minute; I thought you were safe here with me no matter what changes were made in the future. Right?"

"That's right. My timeline up to the present can't be changed by future events. But, it can be if someone resets my past. Just like for anyone else, if things are reset, the only bits of my life that would still exist would be what happened before things were reset—before the time traveler arrived in the past. If someone reset things just one second *after* I arrived, I'd still be here because I existed here before they came back, even if for only a second. But, if they come back even a fraction of a second *before* I arrived here, me coming back here has been erased. Remember that where I came from no longer exists exactly the same as when I left because I'm an added element here. So, if someone goes back a second before I arrived, they would wipe out everything that came after. I wouldn't appear one second after they do or at all, because the place that I came from doesn't exist anymore—my launching pad is gone. All of the events that have happened a second before I arrived don't include me. I won't show up here. I'm an anomaly."

"That doesn't make sense to me," Rhonda says rubbing her right temple.

"Okay. If someone comes back in time two days ago, what we're saying and doing right now may or may not happen. If the time traveler's existence here makes little to no interference in our lives or the lives of anyone around us, then maybe it will be exactly the same for us. You existed here before he came back and so did I, so it could turn out the same way for us—saying the same words right now in this room.

"But if the time traveler comes back to even a fraction of a second before I arrived here, I'm gone. I didn't exist here before I arrived—you did, and you'd exist here without me, so would everyone else on earth for that matter. But, I didn't exist here then, so I'd be wiped out. One second before I got here, I existed in my future. That future doesn't exist the same way anymore, so I'm completely erased."

She slides her arms under his and around his torso and kisses his cheek.

"If things are reset, other people have the chance of their lives following the same basic course—marrying the same person, having the same children, achieving the same accomplishments, but we have no chance of that. Granted, it would all be painless, and we'd never know any different. It's just a sad thought that I am the only freak whose line of existence is outside of everyone else's timeline."

"What would happen if someone reset all of this?"

"The only me that would exist would be the original me of this time without the results of my interference—the timid TV show writer that is likely to pine away over you for years, later working as a technical writer, and ending up half crazy in a home."

She presses her lips into his shoulder then says, "It had to be so hard for you."

Nods, "It wouldn't be me going through it all again; it would be my past self living his life for the first time, or at least what he thought was the first time."

Her body goes stiff, "And what about me, Chester? Are all those terrible things that you said going to happen? I mean if someone resets all this? That poor boy—my son!"

"Those things aren't certain, just very likely. That they've already happened once proves that there is a strong possibility they could happen again. My past self was trying to kill me—he was obsessed with it. His actions and life were changed dramatically. I never tried to hurt anyone the first time around. Granted, there wasn't some future version of me interfering in my life, but for there to be a reset at all, things will be altered. It could be so small of a change that nothing noticeable would differ in your life. Or, it could be barely noticeable like the added body of the time traveler standing ahead of you in line at the grocery, which could make you just a few minutes later doing the rest of your day's activities. But, those few minutes, or even seconds, could put you in a different place in traffic, getting you involved in an accident that you missed the first time around. Those few seconds could kill you, whereas the first time around you lived for decades longer. Even the slightest alteration of events can cause huge changes to the future that the time traveler knew."

"Woah."

"And that's only if the time traveler is benign. If he or she wants to, coming from an advanced society and knowledge, mass destruction is possible. Knowing exactly when and where disaster will or could happen and then making it worse."

Silence. He turns to face her and hugs her to him.

She asks, "Will there be a flash or some sign if it happens?"

"I don't know; I can't imagine there would be anything, but no one knows."

She makes a muffled sound between a squeal and a sigh.

"Hey! Don't worry, Rhonda. None of this can affect us yet: we get to live our lives without any interruption."

"What! What about all you've just said?"

"I was talking about things being reset and having never existed for everyone except the new time traveler. I was talking about things turning out the same way if someone resets our timeline—what would happen to us if my coming back here was wiped out by someone resetting things before I got here. That's all about us not being together the second time around. Well, I guess it would actually be the third time around now. But, none of that can affect us until someone goes back."

"But you came back and reset all of this. Why can't someone else?"

"Because I was the first to figure it out, that we know of anyway, and it took me twenty years from now to make it work. I had to live those twenty years, as did the rest of the world with me, for my trip to be possible. During those twenty years, everyone's lives were real, and nothing could affect that until the day that I reset things and wiped it all out. Even if someone else figures it out on the same day that I did, we still have twenty years until someone can develop the technology to reset things and bring this timeline to an end. And, who knows how long it will take for someone else to figure it out?

"Time has to run its natural course for a time traveler to have a runway to take off. There has to be one uninterrupted passing of time for someone to develop the idea and technology of time travel before anyone can come back in the first place. You have to invent the invention before you can use it, and that takes time. This is why we haven't seen any signs of successful time travel even though it is obviously possible and will happen one day. Well, excluding evidence of my trip of course. Any evidence at all of time travel means that everything we're doing and everything we're going to do up to the moment that the time traveler left his present to go back in time, his point of origin, has already happened once and has been reset. Just like right now. This is the second time that this day has happened. The first time we weren't together, and now we are."

"So if we can detect any signs of time travel, it means we're doing things all over again?"

"Yeah, although it will be done over again at least slightly differently."

Her eyebrows stretch upward, thin red rainbows, and she poses, "Is that what déjà vu is? Us doing something over again and remembering before it was reset? Like when the new experience is the same as what happened the first time around? Could we feel that somehow?"

Thinks for a moment, "That's interesting, Rhonda, and I guess no one really knows. But, I don't see how it's possible to remember anything that's been reset except for the time traveler," noticing she looks mildly wounded, "But it's a wonderful thought. I surely don't know everything, and there's no way to tell just how lucky I was in having the conditions right to get back here—variables may exist to the traveling that I don't even know about. So, I could easily be wrong. I'd sure love it if you could remember me if things were reset."

His smile breaks through the intellectual overload, and her body relaxes. A slow smile of her own emerges on her face and doesn't stop widening until it can grow no further. She rubs the tip of her nose over his shoulder, and he knows something has tickled her heart.

"What is it?" asks Chester. "I can see it on your face."

"You trust me; you really trust me."

"Of course I do."

"No, I mean with all of this. All of this dangerous information that you're hiding from the whole world—you're just giving it to me."

"Well, without wanting to get back here to you, I don't think I ever would have put it together or had the guts to try it out."

She buries her face into him, "And, you didn't dumb it down; you talked to me like an equal. Never had a man talk to me like that about something so hard to understand, especially 'bout all of that crazy resetting stuff. Made my head hurt—and I don't get every piece of it, but I think I got the big picture. Don't know how a computer works either, but I know how to use one."

"Well, to keep anyone from resetting things earlier than in the next twenty years, we can't let anyone get their hands on this device," patting his pocket, "much less make any slip-up on our part."

"See! That's something that no one else should know, and out of all the people in the world, you're only trusting it with me."

He tenses up, and she looks at his vexed face.

"Chester, what is it?"

"Don't be upset, but there might be another."

CHAPTER 26

S he's been expecting tragedy all day. Her imagination has been running wild with images of new horrors around every corner. She had no idea something bizarrely old would be terrifying her.

As her fingers unfold the paper freshly removed from the envelope delivered only moments ago to her by courier but dated nine years earlier, she braces herself for bad news. At the sixteenth word, fear shoots through her.

"You don't know me, but you were my only friend in a time that's been erased from the world, although it will always have existed within me. Before you deem me insane, consider the following: I know you love no one more than your late grandfather, your favorite fruit is an avocado, and your high school boyfriend died in a car accident and the last words he said to you were, 'I think we should see other people when I go off to college.' When you confided the latter to me, you said that I was the only one you've ever told that to. If you've never said that to anyone now that you've never known me, then you have proof that I'm telling the truth.

"While the future is always subject to be changed, you died on September 25th. That should be tomorrow if this letter has arrived on time. Your ex-boyfriend, Edmund, who used to work at the home with you, broke out of prison and strangled you. It had already been a traumatic week for me before losing you. I'm sure we were only friends because I paid to be a resident at the assisted living home at which you worked—after all, I never saw you when you were off on Sundays—but, besides just doing your job, you were kind to me. You gave me a card on my birthday and bought me a stocking filled with candy for Christmas. None of the other caregivers were like you.

"When you were gone and my last dream had been crushed, I lost my fears of what might go wrong and finally tried to go back in time as I had planned years ago. It worked, and, Elise, I got her—the one I pined over my whole life; the one you listened to me talk about every day. She's with me now as I write this. I have all that I ever wanted, and I'll never end up in a sad little room, crushed and afraid. I couldn't bear the thought of leaving you to die.

"If the things I've mentioned are wrong— namely no convict ex-boyfriend, the world's changed enough through my interference that you're safe. If what I've said is true, if you have an ex-boyfriend named Edmund who has been in jail, then please protect yourself. I don't know everything the future holds; I may not be alive at the time you're reading this. So, this letter was written nine years before it's been scheduled to be delivered to make sure it got to you even if I couldn't. If I'm alive; I'll be there looking after you on that day. But, be aware that you could very well be alone.

Take excellent care,
C."

CHAPTER 27

F our eyes follow the shiny pistol barrel.

It's just behind the glass doors that lead from the back of the lobby to the parking garage in which they sit. It all started about an hour ago when David heard Chester's hotel room door open and close. Being awake for his own reasons, David decided to come out into the hallway and accompany Chester on his trip to get some fresh air.

The last few minutes of conversation have happened like this:

"I just feel like I've already blown it," David wheezed.

"What makes you think that?" laughed Chester for the first time since they came down to the parking garage and sat down on the trunk of David's car.

"We went out, had dinner, caught a movie, got gelato after, and nothing happened."

"Didn't you have a good time?"

"Sure, Janet's amazingly cool. She even catches my *Star Wars* references. It's just I was too chicken to do anything, and if she wanted something to happen, maybe it would've. So, maybe she didn't want anything to happen."

Chester laughed.

"Man, you're really going to laugh at me—right here to my face?"

"No, David, that's not it. It's just you don't even know."

"Don't know what? What're you talking about?"

"I'm not supposed to say, but I promise you haven't blown it; call the girl."

"Well, what're you talking about? You have to tell me now. You can't say something like that and not tell me."

"Oh, man, I don't know; I promised."

"Come on, I'm out here with you in the ever-fragrant parking garage at three in the morning. That deserves some inside information. We have a parking garage confidentiality clause—isn't this where all crooks plan their crimes?"

"On TV it is."

David said quietly staring off into nothing, "And they all seem to get caught on TV too. Guess that doesn't help my case any."

"No, no, it doesn't. But, we're not criminal masterminds, so I'm going to tell you anyway."

David's stare returned from the nothingness to Chester saying, "Janet tried to call you one day this week. She was so nervous that she threw up before she could get up the courage to dial your number."

"What?"

"I swear it's true. She really liked you too and is worried that she's going to mess it up with you."

"Really? She seems so confident."

"She is, except in her love life. Bad divorce'll do that to you."

"So, she really was nervous trying to call me?"

"Yeah, in fact Cindy made Lucky call me to find out if you were interested in Janet. Lucky wasn't too happy about it, but Cindy kept telling him what to ask me over the phone. That's when he told me Janet was so nervous that she threw up—I think he spilled the beans just to irritate Cindy as payback for making him call me about it in the first place."

"A girl that cool is nervous about calling me. Wow. Now, I'm really nervous."

"What?"

"Now, there's more pressure to not mess it up. If I've actually got a shot with a girl like her, the pressure's harder. If I don't have a chance at all, then I have nothing to lose and can just try to enjoy the ride."

"Look, Dave, the only way you can mess this up is to not call her. She was calling you to ask you to go to some wedding—Cindy and Janet's niece or something, I think. If you don't call her soon she's going to end up going with some jerk she doesn't even want to be with. You've got to make your move."

"Alright, I'll give her a call."

"Good, and don't be nervous. Rhonda and I went with all of them to the zoo, and she was asking about you the— "

That's when Chester's eyes grew focused and intense, forcing David to follow their direction to the cause.

Four eyes follow a shiny pistol barrel. It's just behind the glass doors that lead from the back of the lobby to the parking garage. It's in the hand of someone who has just stepped out of the elevator which is at a ninety-degree angle to the glass doors, just out of sight for Chester and David.

David's hand goes to his goatee, stroking the thinly trimmed layer of brown hair beneath chewed fingernails.

The body slowly steps into their view. The casual and relaxed manner of walk are more nerve-racking than the depth of night in which it's happening or the shining metal hand cannon coming their way.

A man with a thick, wild, black beard steps forward and pushes the glass door open with his free hand.

"Oh, Omar, it's you. You can't sleep either?" Chester asks.

"No, I was sleeping so well that I thought I'd try it out in the garage amidst the exhaust fumes."

Through years of TV writing, his words have been broadcast in many living rooms more often than the voices of the families that live in them. His personality has made an imprint on the culture of the country and much of the world, yet he has no problem awkwardly stepping on the bumper and taking a seat next to David and Chester on the trunk of the car, pressing his plaid pajamas against the car's dusty body.

Leaning forward to look around Chester to Omar, David asks, "Not to be second-guessing you, Mr. Executive Producer, sir, but do you think it was such a great idea to walk out the elevator door with the gun first—glistening in the hallway light? Our man Chester here is a bit jumpy with a deranged killer after him."

"Was it really that bad, Chaz?" chuckles Omar.

Chester responds, "Could've been worse. You know, if you walked in wearing a hockey mask, a gray wig made to resemble your mother's hair, a gleaming machete covered in entrails in one hand and a chainsaw in the other—yeah, it might've been a little worse than the gun."

"You've been watching too many weird movies."

"Where do you think I get the fodder for our critically-acclaimed satirical commentary? Weird entertainment is an ironic goldmine."

David laughs into his turn at the verbal jousting, "A-h-h-h, satirical, ironic, and fodder all used in the same response. Does it get any better than that? That's why I dropped out of my doctorate in computer science," altering his voice to a more sophisticated tone, "Inside any happy man, aestheticism and the allure of an apt appellation are more appealing than avarice and ambition."

Chuckling starts and Chester says loudly, "Not to mention ostentatious alliteration."

Laughter escalates for eleven seconds and then ebbs for seven.

"God, are we pathetic or what? Out here in the middle of the night, giggling like schoolgirls, sitting on a car, and completely enthralled with our own playing with words. If we were any more full of ourselves we'd be cannibals," offers Omar.

David answers, "No dork possesses more self-absorbed geekery than the writer-nerd," pausing for the line's absorption before pointing out, "By the way, he prefers Chester. He hates Chaz."

"Is that right, Chester?"

"Well, yeah, but it wasn't a big deal."

Omar explains, "No, someone's name is always a big deal. Know the name of everyone on your set—the name they like to be called. Every episode will turn out better that way; trust me. Have the same celebration for the crew on their birthdays as you do for the stars. It's the only way to have a team. And for the love of God, you better get the same size cake for everyone. You wouldn't believe how many times I've had to hear someone complain about that. Heaven forbid Jane's cheesecake was a little bigger than John's carrot cake. It can bring a whole production to a halt faster than an L.A. earthquake."

"That's mighty nice of you to do things that way," David says.

"Well, nice or not, it's the most practical way to run a creative ship—you'll end up with better quality shows when everyone's happy. It's the best strategy for the opportunist whether they're a great person or just interested in the bottom line productivity. It's Machiavellian and saccharine at the same time."

"Mach-a-Saccharine?" David asks.

"Something like that," concedes Omar.

Chester smiles and says, "We should trademark Mach-a-Saccharine as a new business leadership model. It'll be the new idiot buzzword, the next *multimedia*, *proactive*, *paradigm*, *sustainability* or *facilitate*. We could put out books and double-talking overpriced seminars."

"Yeah, we could probably talk Mirkwood into giving the seminars for free. Can't you see him spouting out some inanity to a group of people just to see who buys it? It'd be like an amusement park for him. Remember when he swore to all the women on staff that he read chocolate helps speed up the metabolism and aids in losing weight? He kept it up until nearly all of them were adding candy bars to their lunch. Hell, by the second week of him swearing to it, I almost believed him too," says David piling on.

Chester adds, "A joke's never over for Mirkwood until he gets to say the word 'suckers.'"

"Sounds like a good policy for life to me," Omar says.

Throughout Omar's career, he's enacted some highly successful policies and habits of his own. To the bewilderment of every writer on *Most Hipness* and any other show Omar's produced, whenever the writers have been stuck on a plot point or a line, Omar's immediate response has always been right and usually became the most memorable line in the entire episode. The most intimidating aspect of this strength is that it takes Omar no time at all to come to a solution—as soon as the dilemma is explained to him, the answer is shooting out of him. And, he's never asked for detailed help until after the entire writing staff has been stalemated for hours on the issue. His instant solution is mind-boggling.

This uncanny skill is loved and hated simultaneously just like Murphy's Law. Loved because it happens on cue a statistically improbable number of times. Anything that defies logic is a deviant and innate curiosity to man. Maybe it gives us hope that we can overcome the probability of the world around us, most notably Ben Franklin's first certainty of life, but maybe to lesser extents, too, such as overcoming the low odds of recovery from a nasty illness, marrying at a late age, or winning a lottery. Hated because its unnatural accuracy seems more powerful than any performance we could muster to challenge it.

It's not much different than the love-hate relationship of the public to a celebrity. The celebrity is loved when viewed vicariously as one displaying the charisma that we might possess ourselves, a trailblazer who proves it's possible for the rest of us to achieve the same fame. But, the famous one is hated when viewed as competition to our own abilities, usually happening when the celeb has stayed popular long enough to make us realize they have something we'd like to have but we're making no progress toward obtaining. It's what makes many applaud the rise of the famous yet still gloat at their fall: loving someone for reminding us of what we're capable, but then hating the same person for obtaining it, jealously wishing they'd lose it. Deplorable. Hypocritical. Inexcusable. Enslaver of all the discontented. Defeated only by the humble.

"Omar, do you think the other guys are okay with me insisting Rhonda be here even though none of them could bring anyone with them?"

"No, I told them there was some nut following her around and it wasn't safe to leave her alone. They're all fine with it."

"Good."

"Family's important, Chester; I wouldn't have gotten very far without my own. Show business is nuts, and if you don't have a normal life to go home to after sixteen hours of rewriting a script that just won't play, you'll go crazy.

"Back in the early days I embraced nepotism like she was the lone beautiful woman in homely town, and one with beer-flavored lips to boot. Took a lot of heat for that, but Hollywood's a weird place and you have to surround yourself with people who are more than just honest but actually care if you make it. So why not start with your own family? At least you have years of experience in telling when they're lying to you," perfectly timed pause, "Seriously though, having the support is priceless. But, that doesn't mean that things didn't get crazy every now and then. I cast my brother as a C-level character in my first series; nothing special, just a classmate of one of the kids—a desk-filler and sometimes a reaction shot, but he was getting a regular paycheck, which was more than he had had for awhile.

"So, one day my brother says to me, 'Mar, when am I gonna get my check?'

"'Every Friday just like everybody else.'

"'I ain't been paid in two weeks.'

"So, I look into it. I'm thinking accounting's got their wires crossed, lost a social security number—something like that. Studio swears all the checks had been given to my mother who I hired to work for me in payroll—she served as the bad cop when people needed to be told no or fired or whatever else, which she was good at, and it let me work with my actors without them holding a grudge against me. You know, she could really play the bad guy when it was necessary and didn't mind doing it.

"Anyway, I go down and ask her about the payroll. She tells me she's got both of his checks, and she's not gonna give them to him until he apologizes for getting flip with her in front of the whole cast in the commissary. We were number two in the ratings at that point, fighting it out for the top spot in all of television, and I had to spend half a day getting my brother to tell my mom he was sorry.

"So while it was good most of the time, it was a real sitcom behind the scenes of the TV sitcom. At least it could give you material for an episode of the show sometimes. Dysfunction is the clown-shoed mother of comedy. And your real mother will always let you know you're still just her kid no matter how big of a star you've become."

David asks, "Is that why you got that pistol? To settle family disputes?"

Sighs, "No, we actually had a little problem with a disgruntled young actor who we cast in a spot and he just didn't work out. We let him go, and he started making a lot of threatening phone calls. When he slashed some tires in the parking lot, I decided I needed something to protect myself. Just in case."

Silence is given birth as their minds all drift to the current threat on Chester's life. Chester told Omar and David that he had been making bets with Lucky and that one of the bookies has gone nuts over a loss and has been threatening to kill him. Since David has already met Lucky and witnessed the betting first hand, it was a believable story. Omar told the rest of the staff the excuse of Rhonda having a stalker just so no one would gripe about the rules being bent. He also didn't see any benefit in informing the staff that the show's chief creator is being hunted down for his exotic gambling activities.

"Say, David?" Omar starts.

"Yes."

"I heard a little rumor that you had a star going psycho on you a few weeks back."

"Whatever do you mean?"

"Something about a *Most Hipness* rehearsal."

"Err, yeah, uh, we had a little incident."

Omar says, "Well, a sleepless night in a parking garage is the most appropriate place to discuss little incidents."

"Well, there was a car accident that sent a pickup crashing into a fire hydrant and water gushed toward a transformer directly above it, shooting out all power to the neighborhood including our studio…"

Chester's mind drifts from the conversation to the trouble he's facing. Bits of the story come in and out his attention.

"…she starts screaming, 'Get me out of here! Get me out of here, you morons!'…I had no idea she was locked in a dark closet when she was a kid…she didn't apologize, but the next weekend she threw an incredible party for the whole cast."

So lost in his wondering where Manny is and what he's up to, he hasn't noticed Omar has launched into a show business diatribe.

"…still trying to get those snobs to accept me as a filmmaker—don't want to let me out of my cheap, flashy, discount store packaging on the TV aisle to be in their fancier venue. My movies all make money—people seem to like them, but all the critics hate 'em. They're comfortable with me where they've labeled me, and they become enraged and snarky at the thought of having to reassign me to a new category in their minds. Guess they have me shoved between two hard posts that are labeled pliable but are solid and cold—there's not much worse than someone who thinks he's open-minded and creative but is really closed-minded and chained to conventions.

"Conventions are like a life jacket; sticking to them will keep you afloat long enough to fool most people into believing you know what you're talking about, but they'll slow you down if you ever try to race—you'll never win pulling their weight," pausing for a moment, "See—that was one heck of a little rant there. Every time a critic complains about one of my scripts saying that people don't talk like that in real life; I do it all the time—just need a subject that I have a mouthful to say about. Dontcha think so, Cha—I mean Chester?"

"Huh?"

Laughing, "I guess that's a good answer to all that flew outta my mouth. That's my wife's favorite answer when I go off on a tangent."

"Sorry, Omar, I zoned out, daydreaming—thinking about the lunatic that's after me."

Omar says, "It's alright. Daydreaming's a big part of our job. Years ago I was arguing with a studio exec about the budget of a show we were shooting on location. I kept arguing that we needed to use a real streetcar for a shot, and he wouldn't see it my way. He was getting pretty mad at me and told me that my head must either be in the clouds or up a nefarious place in my body, and my response was, 'I get equal ideas out of both.'"

Laughing, David says, "Hope this morning's meeting goes as well as yesterday did. We got some great story ideas pitched out yesterday."

Omar says, "Still need a few more to flesh out the rest of the first season. Speaking of which, we oughtta try and get some sleep so we're somewhat useful during tomorrow morning's session, that is if the parking garage pajama party is over."

"Yeah, I think it's time we turn in," David agrees.

They hop off the trunk, one more gingerly than the others, and begin walking to the elevator.

They walk past a stack of morning papers, bundled together and sitting on the ground a few feet from the glass doors to the rear of the lobby and the elevators. Omar fishes one of them out between their confining twine. A picture of Rhonda is on the bottom half of the front page in her bathing suit by the pool. Her picture is next to a photo of the towering façade of the hotel. The headline reads, "L.A. Landmark turns 75." The article is on the hotel's seventy-fifth anniversary, and the picture was taken the day before while they were hashing out episode ideas.

Omar says, "Good day for Rhonda with the hotel full of us writer nerds. She was the only star they could get a shot of."

"My God, what is it gonna take to be free of this?" Chester asks painfully.

"What? The article doesn't seem so bad, and her bathing suit looks fine. What's the problem?"

"It's not that; Manny-the-bookie's looking for me. If he's figured out Rhonda's seeing me, he'll know where we are *right now*."

"Look, we told hotel security to be on their toes that there's some nut following someone here on the retreat around. And, I'll make sure I'm with you guys the whole time. I don't go anywhere without this," tapping his gun on his thigh as he says the end.

"So, are you a good shot, Omar?" David asks.

"At the range twice a week. You know me; compulsive personality. Besides, it's good stress relief."

"If you say so."

"Works for me. Usually a lot more careful with it than this. Just couldn't see wearing a holster strap with the pj's— not a good fashion choice. And with all that's been going on with Chester, didn't want to come down without it."

The air seems to get heavy with worry.

"Well, we still better get to bed. Morning'll be here soon, and we're supposed to be leading everybody else tomorrow. It'll kill the room if we're sleepy and uninterested in their ideas."

Letting Omar lead the way to the elevator, David asks quietly, "Hey, Chester, are you sure, man?"

"About what?"

David's uncomfortable look and a nod in Omar's direction answer Chester's question.

"Oh, yeah, positive. It's a done deal; just do it."

Without looking in their direction, Omar pushes the button for their floor and asks, "Do what? What are you two doing at four in the morning? Rhonda's gonna be waiting for Chaz—I mean Chester—with a rolling pin in her hand. "

The internal cringing inside David can almost be heard in the cramped metal box whose doors are closing and sealing him inside.

Since David seems to be without response, Chester says, "Nothing tonight—just something for tomorrow after the writer's retreat is over."

"Really, what're you guys up to? Anything interesting?"

"Not really. Just something to do."

"So, let me get this straight. David's asking you quietly *if you're sure* about something at four in the morning when we should all be sleeping on the writer's retreat planning out the first season of both of you's biggest career project so far, all the while there's some nut out there trying to kill you over a bet, and you're trying to tell me it's nothing interesting? That hound won't hunt, Monsignor. Spill it."

They both laugh as they step out of the elevator onto their floor, David doing so choppily and in the fashion of an engine that won't turn over.

When his uneven laughter subsides, David concedes, "Like every good secret, it's about a girl."

"O-h-h," coos Omar, suddenly with wider eyes and more energy in his demeanor, "It's about a girl, is it? Well, who is she?"

"She's a girl that Chester introduced me too. We went out once. It's no big deal."

"Well, all that may be true, but it definitely's a big deal

if you were asking in secret."

"Well, yeah, but not of cosmic importance."

"Don't kid yourself, Dave; it is. I wouldn't have done half the things I've been able to do without my wife keeping me sane and going the extra mile taking care of the family while I was in neck-deep trying to save some episode. The right girl makes all the difference. So, do you like her? You must."

"Sure, she's really cool."

"Does she feel the same?"

"I, err, I guess I don't know. S'why I was asking Chester what he tho—"

"Yeah, she definitely likes him," Chester interrupts.

"Definitely?" asks Omar.

"Absolutely."

"Then, why's David so unsure about it? What do you know that he doesn't?"

They come to a stop in front of Omar's door which is the closest to the elevator. Chester looks to David who gives him a troubled look.

Omar prods, "Come on, guys. You know I'm gonna be on you like a hawk, an annoying old hawk picking at you until you tell me what's going on."

"Her name's Janet, she's the sister-in-law of a friend of mine, and she likes David so much that she threw up while trying to get up the nerve to call him."

Omar says, "Well, love's a strange, nauseous ride."

Chester, "There are stranger."

"Like what?" both Omar and David ask simultaneously.

"Being in love in Hollywood."

Frozen night fears have thawed with the brightness of day and the friction of activity.

The morning started without a gunman waiting at

Chester's doorstep, and the meeting went quite well with exciting ideas from the staff of hired writers, many of whom have been pilfered from the ranks of *Most Hipness*. But most notably, no one got shot.

David has called Janet, and she's meeting him at the hotel any minute now for them to go out with Rhonda and Chester. Currently, Chester, Rhonda, David, and Omar are checking out at the lobby desk.

The desk clerk asks Omar, "So, was everything satisfactory with your stay, Mr. Sobelsk?"

Omar's face looks as though he's pondering deeply over his answer, "Mostly everything was alright," looking to David at his left, "but I felt awfully queasy after eating the complimentary breakfast this morning. I dunno, maybe it was just love."

David puts his head in his hands and shakes the lot of it.

The clerk responds, "I'm terribly sorry that you didn't enjoy the meal, sir. I'll be sure to discount your room for the inconvenience."

Omar reaches over the desk and lightly taps the clerk's arm, and as soon as a quick and quiet chuckle passes, he says, "No, no, it's fine. I'm sorry. I was just making a bad joke."

"Oh, alright. Very well, sir."

David uncovers his face and says, "You know you're killing me, right? As if I'm not nervous enough already."

"Of course, just trying to make you relax before she gets here."

After the bill is signed and having exited through the front doors, David sees her, her brown hair looking like gold in the sunlight. Leaving his rolling suitcase standing on its own, he walks toward her. His hand goes halfway out, and his other arm raises a little and to the side, unsure if a handshake or a hug is appropriate. She grabs his hand and throws her other arm around his neck, giving him a quick, tight hug.

"Great to see you, Janet."

"I'm glad that you called me."

"I'm glad that you came."

Hearing feet treading the ground close to them, David turns skittishly.

"Oh, Janet, you know Rhonda and Chester, of course. And this," pointing to his bearded boss, "is Omar J. Sobelsk. He's a friend of ours and the executive producer of our new show. Omar, this is Janet Shrew."

Heads nod.

Omar asks, "So where are you four heading this afternoon?"

"Thought we could head down to the zoo," answers Chester.

Janet says, "Back to the zoo? Alright, if you guys want to go again."

Chester says, "It's our favorite place; the zoo and romance go together."

"Regurgitation and romance go together too," Omar says.

Smacking Chester in the arm, Janet whines, "O-h-h-h-h, you told them."

"Sorry," is all Chester can muster as her face swells with embarrassment.

David grabs her forearm and offers, "Hey, I felt the same way about calling you."

Omar says while taking the tips of her fingers in his hand, "Very nice to meet you, Miss Shrew. I'm sorry about my little joke—I don't mean any harm—just never been able to help myself. I sweat punch lines, mostly bad ones—drives my wife nuts. But, I swear that's my last joke on the topic."

"Well, okay," she says regaining her smile.

Omar continues, "Good. And, I must say that you're far prettier than David has told me."

As Janet looks to David for an explanation, Chester offers, "Don't listen to Omar for a second; David's said nothing but great things about you."

A car pulls up to the curb, its brakes squeaking as it stops.

Omar asks, "So, wait a minute; I'm confused, David. I

often feel nauseous around you too. Does that make me a woman, or does it just mean that you're in love with me?"

The giggling overtakes Janet, cracking through her feelings of awkwardness, which turns Omar's smile from devious to warm.

Janet says, "Hey, now, you promised no more jokes, Grizzly Adams. With that beard you look like the lost member of ZZ Top, the West Coast Wookiee."

They all laugh, but Omar laughs the loudest.

"So, I'm a liar and a swearer, no wonder this is my third decade in television." As soon as the words leave Omar's mouth, he sees a tall man in a mask step out of the car parked at the curb. Tuning out the conversation in front of him, he follows the shape that looks like an elongated stick figure. With his wife beater, jeans, and mask—all black, he looks like a starving shadow creeping toward them. He walks steadily closer, his eyes fixed on Mr. Fuze.

Holding his pistol pointed at Chester, his long arm fully extended, he barks, "Hey, lucky boy, loo—"

Bullet breaks through the air, digs into the thin flesh of the chest. Two more shots fire out in quick succession—one landing in the lower ribs and the other tearing into the abdomen. Legs buckle, and the long skinny body falls. A mouthful of crimson puffs out of the lips and spatters the black cloth mask. Before the body hits the ground, the gun slides out of the hand. The body thuds and the gun clanks on the concrete entranceway. Omar stands with a hot pistol in his hands, watching the slain writhe on the ground.

In most fiction, people can be knocked out with one punch and bad guys who are shot drop to the ground and die with leaving only a neat, controlled puddle of blood. In reality, it just doesn't happen that way. In many cases it's easier to kill someone than to knock them unconscious with a blow. Wounds pump and squirt in anything but neat shapes, and most gunshots don't result in instant death. Watching someone die is more often an ugly, lingering scene, and there's nothing satisfying about it.

The car peels out of the horseshoe loading area in front of the hotel. Manny lies on his side, coughing and sputtering blood. Omar walks up still clutching his gun. Placing one foot atop the masked man's pistol, he slides it away from them.

David grabs both of the girls and walks them quickly inside the hotel, where the clerk is already on the phone with the police.

The next few minutes are a blur of movement and emotion.

Directly over the bleeding torso is Chester who constantly repeats, "Help is on the way; hold on. They're coming."

Manny's garbled response is the same every time, "Where's Chantelle? Have to ask."

Chester doesn't need to pull the mask off to know who it is; he knew the voice as soon as he heard it. The long pale arms, thin harvesters of ink designs, are all that he needed to see to confirm the voice.

"Ch-Chant—," cough taking over the last word.

Omar now stands about ten feet away, his gun still in his hand and Manny's gun beneath his foot. David is just returning to the scene after escorting the girls inside, and he stands a few feet behind Chester with his hand over his goatee.

"Chantelle, where's she?"

The same car that peeled out of the parking lot returns and pulls up to the circular curb just in front of Chester and Manny. Her eyes that are as scared as they are pained take in the scene as she runs up to them.

Looking to Chester, she asks, "Is he? Is he?"

"Not yet."

Chester stands and backs up quickly as she approaches closer.

"Manny, Manny, are you alive? Can you hear me?" she asks rubbing at his face.

He coughs a bloody cough.

Gently she grabs the mask at its bottom and peels it over his head. Her fingers become red and wet.

Chester finally places her accent, and he can't believe it.
"Manny?" she asks.

His dull eyes roll and then focus on her.

"Don't leave us, Manny. You hear me? You have a son!"

Coughs, "The abortion?"

"No."

"Bitch," wheezes, spits blood, eyes and chest go perfectly still.

She wails the wail of one who has gotten something she's asked for but hates the taste of it and herself now that she has it. Chester tries to console her as she vacillates between punching and sobbing on his shoulder—punches, squeezes in comfort, and punches the shoulder again.

As the trauma exhausts her adrenaline, she says, "Two of you. Lucky ain't won nothing in 'is life. Something ain't right here—you winning that crazy bet. You knew. Wasn't no guess—luck never tells nobody number odds. Cheaters win—ain't no use in trying to do right. What a world I'm bringing Edmund into," the end trails off with her blubbering into Chester's shoulder, leaning her weight on him while rubbing her belly with both hands like Aladdin running his coaxing fingers over a gold lamp.

She says, "Guess I'll go back to New Orleans."

CHAPTER 28

"**O**h, my God, you're C! You're the nutjob that wrote me the letter."

"My friends call me Chester. You used to call me Chester too."

"Is that so?" her voice fluctuating in the space between hysteria and despair, panicked from the strange man walking in and asking if she's gotten any interesting letters lately.

"Everyone else here called me Chaz. Especially old man Titor across the hall; he knew I preferred Chester, so he loved calling me Chaz. Old grump. Only person he ever liked was you and his grandson Rory."

"How? How in the hell do you know all this?"

"I know those marks on your bottom lip are from your teeth. You always tucked your bottom lip underneath your teeth when you were nervous."

She releases her trembling lip of which she's just been made self conscious, "Sick. Are you some kind of sick stalker?"

"You know, that's not the first time I've gotten that response," snickers Chester, shaking his head. Seeing the humor of the comment is unknown to her, he continues, "Would you ever have told a stalker about your grandfather and living by the lake? The day that you two pulled up a twenty-three pound catfish on the catfish line? Your pet turtle named Baxter? Your grandpa's shirts smelling like baby powder and coffee? Would you ever tell these things to someone you didn't trust?"

Putting the palms of her hands at her temples, "Don't know what to think of this."

"I get that a lot too, but I haven't had to convince anyone in a long time. So you'll have to excuse me if I'm not doing too good of a job."

"Well, you're not doing that great a job, and if you're telling the truth I don't have much time to figure it out. And if you're lying, I need to get the hell away from you anyway."

"I thought of that, actually."

"You did?"

"Yeah, you can do both. You can get far away from me and this crazy boyfriend, Edmund, who is trying to kill you."

"How do I know you're not trying to send me exactly where Eddie wants me to be? He's always got some kind of power over people around him, and he uses them to do things for him. Maybe he decided he can't get in here easy, but he could send somebody in here to get me to come out to him."

"Well, you could call the cops right now. Of course, I'd have to deny everything I told you about coming back in time. But, you'd be safe."

"Might could get a restraining order on you. If you ain't family or friend, and if you didn't sign in, you're trespassing here."

"Signed in with Marvin downstairs as a friend of old man Titor's. He's got severe Alzheimer's; won't matter none if he don't remember me when they ask him. Why don't you call the police? I'll be just fine, and you'll be safe. Just get out of here now—far away."

"Where? Where would I go? Edmund knows I don't have a car. How can I get away from you without knowing you're following me or signaling someone else to follow me? And how do you know about Titor's Alzheimer's?"

"My story is true; that's how I know—only way I could know all this. I know Titor remembers what happened this week alright, but he doesn't remember anything that happened a decade ago. But, here's what you do whether you believe me or not: tell the cops I harassed you. When I'm in cuffs talking to them, you slip away. It'd be impossible for me to do anything in their custody with my hands behind my back being asked a lot of questions. When you're gone, there'll be no evidence and no witness—charges will be dropped anyway."

"If your story's real, where's the girl you were talking about?"

His chin drops to his chest, and his shoulders slouch forward. She can hear him sniffling.

"Rhonda didn't make it. Car accident on our way down here two years ago. Were going to see my parents. Took her car—thought it'd be more reliable. Mine would've been safer."

He raises his left hand to wipe his eyes, and she sees he still wears his ring.

Asking softly, "Shouldn't you have known it was going to happen?"

"Didn't happen first time around. Weren't even together then."

Sniffling.

"Don't know what to think of all this. You know how insane this sounds?"

Shaking his head trying to clear his emotions, he says, "Whether you believe me or not, he's after you, and it's not safe for you here."

"It's the safest place for me."

"No, it's not."

"Yes, it is. Marvin's downstairs with a gun—don't have that kinda protection anywhere else."

"This is where he killed you."

Silence.

He continues, "Besides, I'm here right now. Right in front of you. Couldn't he find a way to get to you here too? After all, he worked here."

"But, I don't have anywhere else to go."

Trapped between crazy and violent, her mind is a scale weighing which she fears most. She can feel the fingers at her neck again, pulling her to the window. Their pressure is so intense and so familiar that she feels like they've never released her.

Chester says, "I have a lot of history here."

Elise doesn't look away from the window.

"Used to go to the old school that was here. This building's on the field where I had some of the best moments of my old life. It's one of the reasons I picked this place when I needed people to take care of me."

Still stares at the parking lot.

"At some point, you've got to stop staring at the same old view and make a new one for yourself. I got stuck staring out that same window myself. Took a long time to believe I could change what goes on outside of it."

It's 6:15 p.m. Elise watches Mrs. Johnson sneak out for her mid-game-show cigarette, propping the auto-closing and auto-locking back door open with her fuzzy pink slipper that has developed a brownish, aged tint. She makes her way to a wrought iron table and chair set that is used for outdoor lunches on nice days.

Most residents are not allowed to smoke; many have struggling lungs still recovering from smoking damage. Mrs. Johnson is eighty-six years old and insists on having a cigarette halfway through the second segment of her favorite game show. When the staff tried to prevent these tobacco burning getaways, she became verbally nasty and as violent as her emaciated arms could be in grabbing and squeezing whoever was standing in her way. After three miserable weeks, the staff pretended to not see her mid-game-show cigarette. This has been going on for the past two and a half years now.

It wasn't decided at a staff meeting or even spoken aloud, but each caretaker came to the same conclusion.

Before her first exhale can rise toward the top of the building, a dented silver car pulls into the parking lot. Its distance from the second floor window only allows Elise to make out that the driver is a large person, most likely a man. The mangled car passes empty spaces close to the front door along with a beautiful blue classic car that has been recently washed and parks near the rear of the building where Mrs. Johnson sits and smokes.

A shaven head is the first thing she can see coming out of the car. Her heart relaxes. As his entire body steps into view, she panics again, the body shape being familiar, but the scowl is an unmistakable part of her nightmares.

She strains to scream, "It's him!" but all that emerges is a breathless squeal.

Edmund walks up to the table and chairs, pulling something out of his pocket.

Elise flings her hands in the air, trying to sound some type of warning to Mrs. Johnson, which does nothing but bring Chester to her side.

Edmund hands the woman a pack of cigarettes. She just nods her head, the most common reaction to confusion among the residents here, and he walks toward the door propped open with her discolored slipper.

Chester shouts, "Come on, get with it; he's coming after us!"

"Doesn't matter; he'll find me. It's over."

"Hey! Snap out of it. You're killing me. You're killing me before he can come up here and kill us, and I can only take dying once in a day."

Glaze coming off her eyes, "You're joking? You're making jokes while this maniac is coming up here to get me? If he finds you with me, you're as good as dead too. Are you nuts?"

"Used to be. About eighty-five percent sane now. Seventy-five's the magic number between boring and insane.

Maybe I could use a bump on the head from Edmund, make me a little more interesting."

"And you're my protector?" starts crying.

"Hey, I'm sorry. Look, we've gotta get you outta here now; I was just trying to make you snap out of it. You can still get out of here."

Pulling her up to her feet, he says, "He came in the back entrance, we've got to run to the front steps and get away without him seeing us. Hopefully he'll be busy looking on the first floor until we're at the front with Marvin."

Holding onto her wrist, he leads the way out the room. Their feet smack the tiled floor sending an echo down the corridor. Running to the front stairwell, she feels unbalanced but tries to pump her legs faster.

"Hey!" calls out from behind them.

Chester stops and turns himself around while swinging Elise behind him, sheltering her from the voice calling after them.

Sooty coughing beckons them two feet above a cherry stained cane with a worn handle, "Where're you runnin' with Miss Elise?"

Elise shouts, "Stay in your room, Mr. Titor! I've gotta get outta here."

"From what, darl—"

The squealing of the decrepit hinges on the opening door to the back stairwell interrupts Titor's question.

Stepping into the hallway is the man who is built like a wall, physically as broad, emotionally as dull, and complexion as pale, except for the areas of his face that peak in anger.

"Been a long time, sweetheart," looking to the man still holding her wrist, "Looks like a real long time for you—forgot all about me."

She can feel all the progress seeping out of her that she's made since he's been gone. His cold words infiltrate the warmth she's fought so hard to gather. It's been months since she's shaken in uncertainty or trembled in intimidation, but it all started again with his escape. The icy aura of one towering malcontent summons her warm comfort out of her, melting the mortar keeping her emotions separated and from colliding into each other. She boils with fear on the inside, evaporating her heated strength into the air where his chill can consume it. Through every clench of her jaw and every dart of her eyes, her security singes, and he inhales the sizzle.

Breathing in deeply, she says, "Not coming with you, Edmund. Never again."

"You are coming with me, Elise," then pointing to Chester, "He's not."

Edmund lifts his shirt and reaches for the gun.

Chester runs toward an opened door to a supply room. It's a door that he never saw left ajar during his stay here, but he spent most of his time in his room. It's only open today because Elise has been preoccupied with impending death.

"In here!" she shouts slamming into Chester's back, shoving him into the room, "Shut it! Shut it! It's already locked."

"I was just going to—"

The door shuts.

Shaking his head, Edmund mutters, "In the supply room? Don't believe this. Stupid. Ain't nobody scared of a gun no mo—"

Stepping slowly into the hallway and pointing a finger up at Edmund's face, Titor says, "I remember you, you no-good bum. Stealing people's money, gone to jail. You're gonna go back there too, because you're still too stupid coming back here. Too stupid to stay a—"

Pointing the gun close to the bridge of the wrinkled nose, "Out of my way, old man, and shut yer mouth."

Titor steps back and raises his one free hand, his other trembling on the cane's handle. Keeping his head down until Edmund is one step past him, he raises his cane off the ground, grabbing it at its bottom, and he flings the handle at Edmund's ankle, snagging it in the hook.

The crash onto the floor is thunderous in its echo, both the gunman and the cane smacking the tiled ground.

Titor hobbles into his room, closing the door, flipping the lock, and grabbing the lamp with the yellowed shade off his nightstand. He stands against the wall by his door waiting and shaking for it to open.

"Son of a—" shouts Edmund as the stinging registers through his body. His knuckles are raw and busted on his right hand from getting smashed between the gun and the floor.

His thoughts are already upon kicking in the door and pumping a round into Titor, but they're interrupted by the same repeated dings that signify most of the floor's resident's have called for assistance. The calls go to Elise's station, which is unmanned, but eventually someone downstairs is going to notice all of the unanswered attendant lights and come investigate what is going on.

Edmund knows his time is limited before things get much more complicated.

"Friggin' old people," he mutters getting to his feet and looking at the windowless locked door to the supply room.

Inside the long, narrow supply room several moments before, just after Elise made Chester close the door, he says "—grab a broom."

"Come on, come on! Supply room's got a door to the entertainment room. We can try to hide in there. What're ya doing with that broom?"

Grasping it near the bristles and holding it like a baseball bat, "He's a little bigger'n me if you haven't noticed. Plus, there's the whole gun thing."

"We're not fighting—we're running," she says as she runs toward the other door at the back right of the supply room.

Just as a loud crash echoes from the outer hallway, Chester says, "We'll never make it away from him."

Pleading with him, eyes filled with panic as she shoves a key into the lock on the door to the entertainment room, "We've got to try."

Titor's door slams out in the hallway, and its lock

clicks.

Chester says, "You can get away if I stall him."

"He'll kill you!"

A loud thud booms from the door to the supply room.

"Come on! In here," she shouts turning the handle to the door to the entertainment room, "Shut the door behind you; it'll lock."

They sprint across the large room filled with a giant video screen, three sofas, two recliners, numerous randomly scattered chairs, small tables with Scrabble boards, puzzles, decks of cards, and a bookshelf along the back wall that is stocked with many haggard boxes that are labeled Bingo.

Chester runs with the broom still in his hand, looking over his shoulder to make sure Edmund has not broken through the first door and caught up to them yet.

Elise keeps her head ducked as she runs, the sound of bullets firing repeating in the imaginary world of her mind and pulsing through the real world of her nerves.

Her shoulder bumps the closet door on the other side of the room as she comes to a stop. Fumbling with her key ring, she opens it.

The light exposes worn Bingo boxes from decades past stretching from the bottommost shelf to the ceiling. Some lids are torn and sticking out at them, others are mended with yellowed and cracking tape. Pulling Chester inside with her, she closes the door.

The closet is cramped. Chester's back is pressed against the door, and his chin pushes into Elise's forehead. Elise is sandwiched between him and cardboard Bingo containers that give and bend.

"This is like a little bomb shelter stocked full of Bingo. What kind of emergency are you guys planning for? A mob of bored ninety-year-olds hellbent on destruction?"

"Shh! He'll be in that room any second."

Another loud thud travels from the supply room door.

Changing to a grave tone, Chester whispers, "I know. He'll figure out we're in here and break that door down soon."

"Whatdowedo?" she squeals in a slur, "This is all I could think of with him in the hallway."

Chester opens the closet door, and grabbing her arm he pulls her out into the entertainment room.

"*What're you doing?*" she squeals, yearning to get back inside the thin security of the closet and out of the nakedness of the vast room.

"Take this," he says pulling the device out of his pocket and shoving it in her hand, "This is what took me back in time. Use it to get away."

A deeper thud along with the sound of cracking wood.

Shaking her head, "No!"

Chester bends down below the first shelf and throws a picnic basket from out of the closet into the entertainment room. Several Bingo games that were atop and around the basket fall into its former space at the bottom of the closet. As he flings them out of his way, their lids fly off, markers and sheets scattering across the room.

Chester cocks back and kicks with all his might into the cleared wall space at the bottom of the closet. His foot cracks through the sheet rock on the closet side and exposes the remaining sheetrock that is the outer layer to the stairwell.

Elise flips open the picnic basket and pulls something out.

Kicking again, his foot breaks through the outer sheetrock into the stairwell. With a few quick blows, he clears an opening to the stairs.

Looking back to Elise, he sees her holding an odd-looking gun at him.

"Take it. Flare gun; brought it along on picnics."

Taking it from her and looking over its unfinished fat barrel and primitive-looking wooden handle, he asks, "Did this come over on the Santa Maria? Sure it works?"

"No."

"Excellent."

"Don't have nothing else but the broom."

"Well, alright then. I'll keep him busy—you get out of

here," handing her his keys to a car that took years to modify as an exact replacement for the one that turned into a fireball, "It's a 1969 Chevelle Super Sport. It's in the first row. You can't miss it."

"No."

A heavy thump reverberates followed by a stream of unintelligible profanity. The lock is broken, and the door into the supply room opens.

"You don't have a choice here. I lived my life; I got a second chance at it. I don't have anything else to lose. You need a second chance at yours. It's the only way."

Words flying like debris in a hurricane, "How long were you trying before this worked?"

"Eleven years."

"When did it work the first time?"

"Today, but twenty years ago."

A flurry of vulgar words cuts through the air and startles them.

"He just found out the back supply door's locked too. Only got a minute to get out of here."

"What was different then? What made it work that time?"

"She lost her face. Had to help her. Urgency's what did it."

Voice cracking and shaking her head, "Well, how many times have you used this thing?" she asks holding it up in her quivering hand.

"Just once."

"Did it work right? Safe?"

"'Course it did, or I wouldn't be here."

She tucks her bottom lip beneath her top front teeth.

A pounding comes at the door from the supply room to the entertainment room, and a split rips the wood in its center.

"Running out of options."

She nods her head.

He pushes her back into the closet, closing the door behind them. The light from the hole in the wall makes the closet dimly visible.

"Don't look back once you get through that hole. While I'm fighting this gorilla; you're running. Got it?"

"Yes."

The door to the entertainment room rips deeper down its center, its lock breaking loose and flinging open. Loud stomping of his feet follows, momentum pushing him through the jagged hole in the door and making him stumble into the room.

"Once you're away from him, unlock the keypad, and put in the password. It's Dr. Moses. D-R-Moses, no spaces, no periods. Go. Go!"

"I don't know—"

"Do it! Now."

Butting his head against the outside of the door, a cold, deep voice speaks, "Elise, I'd rather you come back with me alive, but you ain't getting away after whatchyou did to me. Giving you to the count o' five to decide to come out, or I'm gonna shoot up that closet and everything in it."

Chester pushes her down toward the opening. She doesn't resist.

"One."

Sticking her feet into the stairwell, they touch nothing but air.

"Two."

Sliding her body down with the shelf digging into her back and scraping her knees over the uneven hole in the sheetrock, she still touches no ground in the stairwell.

"Three."

Holding her at her wrists, Chester eases her down, her right hand still clutching the device.

"Four."

He lets her go. Dropping the remaining few inches, her ankles buckle to catch her weight on the turnaround platform at the middle point of the stairs.

"Five."

The handle turns.

"Hold on there, caveman. I'm coming out."

The door swings open, and Chester steps toward Edmund.

"Where's Elise?"

"She's gone, but let me ask you something. How long did you work here? Six months? A year? And you didn't remember the supply room has another door?"

"Shut up!"

"You know if you weren't so stupid you could've killed both of us by now."

"Entertainment room's locked too, genius. Woulda had to break it down too."

"Maybe so, but that'd only be one door to break down instead of two, and you're still stupid."

"Maybe so, but you're still dead," he says stepping forward and punching Chester in his left temple with the tip of the pistol barrel.

Chester falls to the ground.

Edmund kicks him square in the forehead.

Sparks and colors are all Chester sees as he digs under his shirt to pull the flare gun out of his pants. The next kick hits the tip of his chin, flinging his head backward, pain shooting through his neck, his hand still under his shirt.

Vision comes clear.

Edmund's gun is pointed at his head.

"Where is she? One chance."

Blood running out of Chester's mouth, his hand moving under his shirt, "Gone. Before you were born."

He pulls the trigger on the flare gun. Bright yellow bursts onto Edmund's chest. The searing color spreads across his torso, blindingly luminous.

Edmund's finger pulls on the trigger, firing a bullet at Chester.

Breathing like an attacking animal, she runs past Marvin's desk, screaming, "Police! Police!"

Marvin jumps to his feet, "What-tha hell is happening up th—"

Her flats slap the ground loudly as she steps through the automatic doors and down the ramp to the parking lot. She sees the car immediately, shiny and definitely the only classic in the lot. Running between the car and the one next to it, she accidentally scrapes the key on the metallic blue quarter panel.

"Bang!"

The gunshot pulses from the second floor of the building, stopping her in her tracks. She thinks of Chester. She thinks of Titor. She thinks of Chester's last words to her.

The rear exit flings open, and Edmund stumbles out, his shirt tattered and bloody. The skin on his neck and chin is charred as he raises his head staring directly at her eyes. His body wavers.

She shoves the key in the lock, frantically opens the door, jumps in, tosses the device on the passenger seat, and starts the car.

Chirping the tires in reverse, she nearly hits Edmund who has just stepped into the parking lot. Peeling out of the lot, the car fishtails, tearing into the rubber of the rear tires. Leaving smoke of exhaust and rubber, she pulls onto the four-lane street as he stumbles toward the gray wreck of a car.

The gunshot rings through her head, and she cries. Looking in her rearview mirror, she sees nothing but open street. Grabbing the device, she unlocks the keypad and types in the password.

A box lights up on the screen:

```
ERROR. INCORRECT PASSWORD.
2 MORE ATTEMPTS BEFORE LOCKOUT.
```

"Damn it, no spaces."

She begins typing it again, with one hand on the wheel, one holding the device and punching on its keyboard. As she types in the M, she wonders if she's going mad as a high-pitched whining pierces her eardrums.

Metal crashes into metal, roughly jerking the car forward. The device flies out of her hand and lands on the floor between her legs. Tugging on the wheel to straighten the car, she looks in the rearview mirror.

The gray dented mess is behind her. As soon as she sees it, it rams her again, sending her head bouncing off the steering wheel.

She reaches down to grab the device. Her fingers slide over its edge. Another crash smashes the side of her face into the wheel.

Straightening herself up, she slams the accelerator down, and the engine roars fiercely. Her torso and head are knocked back flat against the seat. The scenery begins to get blurry, pistons pumping faster and faster as the engine races closer to the redline. She flies through an intersection just after the traffic light turns red. The gray car is small in her mirror.

Slowing down, she picks up the device and begins where she left off in typing Dr. Moses. After completing the o-s-e-s, she presses ENTER.

ERROR. INCORRECT PASSWORD.
1 MORE ATTEMPT BEFORE LOCKOUT.

"Oh, my God. Oh, my God!"

Her fingers type the fictional name over again, praying that every asterisk on the password line of the screen is masking the correct letter. Holding her breath and all her dwindling hope, she presses ENTER.

Pounding into the rear bumper again is the gray car, whipping her neck forward. Before she can look up, the gray vehicle is on side of her, now leaking radiator fluid all over the road and sliding toward the passenger side of her car. She swerves into oncoming traffic, the device leaves her hands again, smacking the center console and landing wedged in the space between the console and the seat.

Just as a luxury sedan is about to plow into her, she returns to the right side of the road and looks out the window to see Edmund's intense eyes, flooded with malevolence, his neck horribly singed.

A van pulls out in front of Edmund, and he slams on his brakes. His car bumps the curb—one of the hubcaps shoots off, the other wobbling wildly.

Stomping on the gas again, the Chevelle's tires chirp, pinning her back against her seat. A car in each lane blocks her path. Dodging them, she swerves into oncoming traffic again.

Pulling in front of the two slower vehicles, while her thoughts usurp her speech, "Get away. Then try device again. God, hope not locked out."

The speedometer needle dives into triple digits. Her eyes watch the rearview mirror. She can see the gray mess pulling in front of the two slow cars, but it grows smaller in her sight with every desperate breath.

Returning her eyes to the road in front of her, she sees a red light that is far too close for her to slow down for. She had no idea she was so close to the intersection or the danger beyond it. It's a street she's been down hundreds of times but usually as a passenger, and now she's vaulting through it three times faster than she's ever been.

Closing her eyes, the Chevelle is a metallic blue blur screaming through the intersection. Brakes scream and horns shout, but there is no collision. Opening her eyes, she sees no relief as the huge turn is ahead of her. Planeline Highway follows the river, and both the Mississippi and the street make a nasty, near ninety-degree turn just ahead of her.

Smashing the brake pedal, the car bucks from one side to the other and slides out of control. The performance brake rotors that Chester installed turn bright red. As the car invades oncoming lanes, it heads straight for an imposing brick building, a bowling alley. The tires squeal dragging across the pavement, but she also hears another noise. A whirring.

As her mind pleads to a higher power, some things become blue and stretched out, and others turn red and squashed. The tires slide, maintaining no traction, and the brick wall stands resolute, growing bigger and bigger in her windshield, inches from colliding with the rampaging metal behemoth from a bygone era.

CHAPTER 29

"**Y**ou saved my life, but in a future that no longer exists, which came from a friendship that neither of us remembers."

"Excuse me?" asks Chester, holding Rhonda's trembling hand.

The dark-haired, blue-eyed girl throws her arms around him and presses the side of her face against his neck. He still hangs onto Rhonda's hand. The girl looks to be no older than sixteen, and Chester looks no less than helpless.

Gazing at Rhonda with pleading eyes, "I swear I've never seen this girl in my life."

Taking her arms from around him, "You really don't remember me?"

"No."

"I'm Elise. You don't even remember my name after all you did for me?"

"No, I'm sorry I don't. Are you sure you've found the right guy?"

Leaning forward to his right ear and whispering quietly enough so Rhonda will not hear her, "How many other time travelers can there be?"

Chester's eyes soak in her facial expressions as he squeezes Rhonda's hand tighter, feeling that all he's put together might instantly unwind, fearing he'll be pulled away from her.

Elise says, "It all makes sense. I knew you wouldn't remember me, but somehow it's weird to look at you and watch it happen."

In little more than a mumble, he says, "I think I know that feeling."

"It's just amazing that you don't remember me. When I first met you, you were trying to convince me of the same thing—that we were once friends although I'd never remember it."

"How?"

Elise points to Rhonda but looks at Chester and asks, "Can we talk in front of her?"

"She knows everything about me."

"*Everything?*"

"Absolutely."

Nodding to the nervous woman at his side who has clenched her left fist over the course of the last minute, "And, are you Rhonda?"

"Yes," raising a red eyebrow that glistens in the afternoon sun.

"Thank God."

Lowering her brow, she asks, "Why do you say that?"

Feeling that since she's already said too much she might as well explain, "No reason—he just talks about you like your love is more certain than time. Besides trying to save me and convincing me that he was a friend, all he'd talk about was you. I was afraid that somehow me coming back here would mess things up for you."

As Chester can feel the tenderness of Rhonda's hand interweaved in his own, he repeats his unanswered question,

"How? How can this be?"

Hesitating and exchanging glances and counter-glances, she starts, "As far as I can tell, you reset the timeline that you knew me when you came back for her. Twenty years after that you came to save me but I didn't know who you were—you sent me back in time. My ex-boyfriend," a pause and a whisper, "strangled me to death the first time around."

"Oh, my God," escapes from Rhonda's thoughts and out her mouth.

"You saved me, Chester. And you wrote me this letter."

Out of her back pocket, she pulls the letter folded in six partitions and holds it out at Chester. He stares at it. The shape of the letters that can be seen bleeding through the back of the folded page is familiar to him.

He tries to grasp the thought of a note, worn and discolored with age, written by him in a year that hasn't happened yet, made of wood from a tree that has probably not been cut down. And, whether the tree is never cut down, whether it burns to the earth, or if it is discarded as inferior paper stock, this letter will exist without an origin or dependency in this timeline. The world has no logical explanation for it because it hasn't traveled with the paper. Without the knowledge of the trip, the paper is beyond logic, a truly alien form, an unaccounted addition to the mass of the universe. It's an anomaly, just like him. But if left alone, it'll survive longer than his lifetime.

"Take it," demands Elise, "Take it. Quick."

His mind still spins over the prospect of a note he's written traveling through places that no longer exist, written when his hands were older and in a different time that will never happen, now just a future past that is only remembered by either a blue-eyed being of unique experience or a fantasy of a madwoman.

Rhonda grasps the letter and places it against his chest. Feeling her pressing fingernails awakening his flesh through his purple shirt, he raises his hand and takes the paper from her.

Elise says, "Came a long way to bring that to you. Do

you know what a bus ride from Riverview to L.A.'s like? Weirdoes all around—perverts, lunatics, compulsive liars. And all of them want to sit right next to you and tell you their story. The normal people are the only ones who keep quiet; the crazy ones want to talk to you. And, the worst part is that my story is the craziest of them all, but I can't share it, not even with nuts on the bus." Seeing he still hasn't unfolded the note, "Aren't you gonna read it now?"

"No, I don't know if I want to. Some things maybe I shouldn't know," he says sliding the note into his pocket.

"Ever wonder how your car was there waiting for you?"

Patting his right hand on the air between them as if he were trying to squish it down, "Don't talk anymore here. Let's go up there," pointing to the top of a nearby hill that is part of a children's play area. On one side of the hill, there is a giant rope net made in the shape of a spider's web. It connects the hill to a Swiss Family Robinson style tree house.

Halfway up the hill, he turns to Rhonda, "On top of a grassy knoll—what an appropriate spot for a secret parley."

Her tension doesn't ease.

Squeezing her hand, he whispers in her ear, "Between a child slapping your butt, a rude parent yelling at the both of us, the shooting outside the hotel, and a teenage girl I've never seen before swearing she knows me—someone just doesn't want us to go to the zoo anymore."

She doesn't smile, but she squeezes back and kisses him. She asks, "So, she's the other one you told me about? The one that might exist?"

"The car and the shirt on the seat never made any sense without there being another traveler."

Turning to Elise, he asks, "So, you're the one who scratched my car?"

"Uhh, sorry, was kinda in a hurry."

"And the dings in my bumper?"

"I was the victim on those—they weren't my fault."

"Just giving you a hard time. It's okay; it's all gone now anyway."

"Huh?"

"Exploded."

"Wow."

"Yeah, that's what I thought too."

Elise's face lights up, "Hey! You'll get another car like that one. You have to if you had one later to give to me. That right?"

"Yeah, maybe, I guess so," pauses thinking of the possibilities, "Actually, I could go buy my original Chevelle for the first time from its owner. Can't believe I didn't think of that before."

Rhonda, "Well, you were a bit busy trying not to be killed until a few days ago."

Elise's face harvests confusion, "Wait, someone was trying to kill you too? You never mentioned that in your log at all. All you talked about was time travel and being with Rhonda. Don't you think someone trying to kill you is important to your story?"

Chester looking serious and troubled, "Actually, it was two people trying to kill me, but it doesn't matter. Now, why was your ex-boyfriend trying to strangle you? What exactly did I save you from?"

"Ex-boyfriend escaped from jail, and he was coming to kidnap me or kill me if I wouldn't go quietly."

Rhonda says, "Honey, you're too young to have ex-boyfriends in jail."

"Was thirty-five then. Look younger than I really am just like this one does," she says pointing to Chester, "You never told me I'd come out looking like a teenager either. Was a bit of a shock."

"What happened? Why did I send you back, and why'd you take the car anyway? I wasn't sure that it'd be possible to bring back something that big."

"You didn't explain any of that to me. You gave me this black electronic gizmo, told me the password, told me to run away while you fought off my ex. I was nearly to your car and heard a gunshot. I guess he killed you…I'm so sorry."

Silence.

Chester says, "S'okay. Doesn't affect me now, I guess. What happened then?"

"Eddie, my ex, came running out the back door of the home. So, I—"

"Wait a minute. 'The home'—what home? Not the Riverview Assisted Care Facility?"

"Yeah, that's where you knew me from. That's why you helped me. I worked there, and we were friends. That's what your whole letter to me said—just trying to prove to me that we were friends, even though I didn't remember any of it."

Chester's mind spins for a moment before asking, "Hey, if you're telling the truth, how did you know where to find me now? How would you know where we were going to be?"

She unzips her purse that has taken the shape of the device wedged tightly inside, and she pries it out.

"I'm sorry, but I read all of your journal entries on here. Had to know how all this happened to me. That's the only way I understand this resetting stuff, well at least some of it anyway. You wrote about being here today; that it was kind of your special place. You wrote logs about everything you and Rhonda did together. Very sweet actually."

His eyes stare at it. His hands pat at his pants pocket, feeling over the same shape that he sees in her young hands. Every contour consumed his thoughts for years, wearing his sanity. Now, it resides in her hands as well as his pocket.

"What about the car? What does it say about how I got the car when I came back the first time—the time before you brought one to me?"

"Didn't say. Guess you bought your first one from the original owner like you were just thinking about doing. I swear all you talked about was Rhonda and time," holding the device out to him, "You can read it for yourself."

Shaking his head, "What happened when you came back—when you first got here?"

"It was the craziest thing. I was about to slam into the

brick wall of a bowling alley trying to get away from my ex chasing after me—car was out of control. Then, I could see the field appearing on the bricks like a warped reflection, but just before the crash the car drove onto the field—the wall disappeared, like I passed through it or something."

"Then what?"

"I had just gotten the device out of the side of the seat and stepped out the car and closed the door—then you appeared out of nothing. I got scared, dropped the keys, and ran. Didn't know who it was that appeared there. Just knew something completely weird had happened to me—my ex was chasing me—went through a brick wall. Had to get away. Didn't know if he was going to be coming through behind me. Didn't know if I was in trouble or going nuts. Either way wanted to go and hide. Didn't know for sure that it was you until I read your log on the device later on. Said you arrived in a field but didn't mention anything about the car."

"Wait a second—wait a second. If you got there before me, how am I still here? Thought you must've shown up right after me, not before."

"I don't know—you popped up about a minute after I got there."

Rubbing his brow, "What'd it look like?"

"Like I was going crazy. There was nothing—just this field. Then, you were there with your back to me. It was instant. Wasn't even like lightning. Like magic. Not real. A trick."

"That's it!" says Chester.

"What's it?"

Chester steps closer to Elise, pulling Rhonda with him, "Any sign of time travel means things are happening over again—a reset. When you came back, at first I didn't come back. There was no way for me to get back. It was just my original past self running through his regular life, ending up in a home and eventually, twenty years later, coming back in time to get to you, Rhonda. That's me. That's the only history that I remember. I don't remember Elise and I being friends—I remember being alone in the home. But when I came back for you, I came back one minute or so after she got here. All she remembers is me popping up right after her, but she lived a whole life for twenty years just like you did, Rhonda. She doesn't remember any of it because it all got reset the moment that I came back."

"Woah," Elise says, "So this is my third—no fourth time doing today? My first was when we later became friends at the home, my second was the reset when you came and saved Rhonda and then me, the third was when I came back, and the fourth is now—when you reset things *after* I came back?"

"Yep."

Rubbing her temples, "Too weird. Makes my head hurt."

"Yeah, it does that. Don't think about it too much; it drove me nuts once. But…"

"But what?"

"We do know one thing about your time back here before the reset."

"What's that?"

"You didn't end up at the home with your ex-boyfriend coming after you, or I would remember it now. I remember all of my life from before the last reset, because I'm the one who came back and reset it. And I know neither you or your past self ended up there—I didn't have any friends at the home. But, maybe both of you had a much better life."

She smiles. After a moment, she asks, "Rhonda, what's it like being in love with the smartest man in the world?"

"Pretty unbelievable, but that's not what I love most about him."

"Grandpa's pretty smart too, but different. Sometimes there's naturally smart—smart about life and people. My Grandpa didn't know anything about how I got there or how there could be two of me, but he knew it was me. Knew I was family. Believed me."

"Two of you? You're both living with Grandpa? Your

past self knows too?"

"Sure, she lives with Grandpa."

"So, a fifteen-year-old knows her future self has gone back in time? Teens are famous for their secret-keeping abilities. Why didn't you just run out and tell the F.B.I.?"

"What did you want me to do? I came out looking like I did when I was eighteen, which is a lot like a fifteen-year-old, with nowhere to go and thirty-two dollars in my wallet. Hell, my past self might even look a little older than me. Of course, I went home. Long walk too, let me tell you. Fifty miles down the shoulder of the interstate is no picnic."

After a pause, she continues, "Besides, without this," holding up the device, "there's no proof. She won't say a word, but even if she does, no one will believe her."

Letting go of Rhonda's hand and grabbing Elise's hand gently, he lifts it to her eye level and says, "Except for this. You have the same fingerprints. She could prove it."

"She won't."

"How do you know?" he asks letting her hand free.

"Because I'm the answer to her prayers. I knew back then that Grandpa wouldn't be around forever. I had no idea how soon he'd go though. Every night I prayed for my mother to come back and live with us. Guess it's better that she never did, but I wanted it more than anything else at the time. Now, I'm filling that spot for her. I'll make sure she keeps it secret. We've been becoming friends since I've been back. Great friends. She seems more like my sister than myself. Weird we look so alike but are so different inside—I've lived more than twice the life she has. Gonna make sure she doesn't make any of the mistakes that I did."

"And Grandpa?"

"He's been eating healthier since I've been there; I'm seeing to that. It's hard to argue with future facts—he's already been to the doctor, and on top o' that, he's promised to go back every month. We're gonna prevent that heart attack from ever happening."

"That's wonderful, but I meant: *will he talk?*"

"Of course not. He doesn't understand—hell, I barely even understand it, and I've watched it all happen—been through it firsthand. He's not gonna tell anybody about what makes no sense to him. Never runs his mouth about things he don't know. More important than that, he knows it'd hurt me, and he'd never let anything hurt me. He'd die before he'd say anything to harm me."

Chester sighs, "I don't know."

Rhonda pulls on his hand and says softly, "Chester, you told me your secret when you came back."

"Rhonda's right. You told her everything. You and me are the only two people who've traveled through time, but you told her about it," Elise says.

"Had to. I tell her everything."

"Me too. Grandpa's it for me. Never had anybody else to tell. And my past self, well, she's me. Can't do nothing else with that."

His face grows troubled.

Elise says, "You trusted me with your secret when you sent me back here in the first place; you must've had a good reason. If you trusted me that much then, isn't that enough to make you trust me now?"

"Yeah, I guess so…just so scary to think other people know…I'm sorry—I guess you didn't ask for any of this anyway. Sounds like I dumped it on you."

"You still saved me. I'd be dead without your help, and to be able to come back here, see Grandpa again, be the friend I never had…"

As she starts to cry, Rhonda steps forward and hugs her, patting the back of her black hair, she says, "I know, I know. He saved me too, Elise. He saved me too."

Smiling, Elise wipes away her tears and says, "Thank you, Chester. Thank you." Looking back to Rhonda, her face crumbles into worry, "Oh. Oh, no."

"What? What is it?" asks Rhonda.

"Chester came for me by himself. Said you didn't make it, got in a car accident driving to Riverview to visit Chester's parents. He said it didn't happen the first time around."

"When?" asks Chester, "When did it happen?"

"A few years before you saved me, I think."

Anguish infects Chester's face, and Elise says, "I'm sorry; it was just a story when I heard it, and I wasn't sure if you were insane or not. Never thought Rhonda'd be real. Much less ever meeting her. I'd've paid more attention if I knew."

"It's okay. It's enough."

Rhonda looks to Chester with stirred up eyes, and he hugs her and kisses the top of her head saying, "We'll never drive to Riverview during the next twenty years. Hell, we'll never drive there ever. There are trains and planes. Better yet, we'll fly my parents out here to visit us."

She looks up at him, still worried.

"Rhonda, it didn't happen the first time around. It doesn't have to happen at all. We know enough; we can avoid it. I'll take care of you; I promise."

Her expression begins to relax.

"Because of Elise coming back here, we can stop it now. We'll be together for many more years. Knowing this isn't something to be sad about; it's a gift, a blessing. My God, a web through time is an incestuous one."

Elise says, "Chester, I have a question for you about there being two of me here."

"Yeah. What is it?"

"So, the note, your car, that shirt, you, and me—all of this is here but made from nothing that is here now. The material used to make that shirt still exists here in the world and the shirt does too?"

"Yeah. The whole untouched cow and the steak taken from it exist at the same time. The tree that was used to make the paper for the note you brought with you has probably not been cut down yet, and even if it's never cut down, this note will still exist. It won't fade away because our history has changed—its history will stay the same no matter what happens to the tree it came from."

"Chester, you know, if people only knew what you've

done, you'd be the most famous person on earth."

"No one can ever know. It's too dangerous. Don't know if the world'll ever be able to handle it," he pauses looking at the electronic marvel that she holds, and reaching out his hand, he continues, "In fact, we have to fix all of this. Give me your device."

"What're you going to do with it?"

"Give it to me, and I'll show you."

She raises her hand to him as if the weight she holds has suddenly grown much lighter.

He takes it from Elise. Looking to Rhonda he says, "Sweetheart, I'm going to need your purse."

She hands him her oversized purse, which he quickly unzips and dumps its contents on the grass at their feet. He drops Elise's device inside, and digging his own out of his pocket, he puts it next to hers and zips up the handbag.

Walking briskly down the hill to the nearest tree, he grasps the purse body like a ball. Violently, he smashes the bag against the trunk. His hand pulls back and continues the crushing motion eleven more times, breaking and cracking the contents inside.

Walking back up the hill to the girls, he says, "We'll burn what's left when we get back home."

Elise asks, "So, no one will have any way to travel again?"

"I could build another one. All those years of work are still too fresh in my mind. Won't do it unless the world gets itself into such a mess that it's the only way out. Won't do it for any other reason."

"You won't, will you? Even though you could be the most famous man who ever lived?"

"Of course I won't," turning to look into Rhonda's face beaming warmth into him, green shimmering beneath red hair blowing in the fall breeze, "I have everything I've ever wanted. All the rest can fade away."

LEWIS ALEMAN is the author of the dark literary thriller, Cold Streak, an Amazon Bestseller, a Kindle Bestseller, and #1 in Myspace Books. He graduated from Louisiana State University with a degree in Creative Writing. He grew up and still resides just outside of New Orleans. Currently, he is fast at work on the first book in a realistic fantasy series, entitled *A BROTHER, A DRUNKARD, AND SOMETHING ODD*.

All upcoming works, events, and news are updated on the website listed below. Also on the site are excerpts from other works, press/reviews, and free stuff.

He can be contacted through his website
WWW.LEWISALEMAN.COM.

MYSPACE: myspace.com/LewisAleman
FACEBOOK: facebook.com/LewisAleman

CPSIA information can be obtained at www.ICGtesting.com
Printed in the USA
LVOW130315250512

283117LV00006B/127/P